Michelle Smart's love affair with books started when she was a baby and would cuddle them in her cot. A voracious reader of all genres, she found her love of romance established when she stumbled across her first Mills & Boon book at the age of twelve. She's been reading them—and writing them—ever since. Michelle lives in Northamptonshire, England, with her husband and two young Smarties.

Canadian **Dani Collins** knew in high school that she wanted to write romance for a living. Twenty-five years later, after marrying her high school sweetheart, having two kids with him, working at several generic office jobs and submitting countless manuscripts, she got The Call. Her first Mills & Boon novel won the Reviewers' Choice Award for Best First in Series from *RT Book Reviews*. She now works in her own office, writing romance.

STRANDED WITH HER GREEK HUSBAND

MICHELLE SMART

ONE SNOWBOUND NEW YEAR'S NIGHT

DANI COLLINS

MILLS & BOON

First Published in Great Britain 2021
by Mills & Boon, an imprint of HarperCollins*Publishers* Ltd,
1 London Bridge Street, London, SE1 9GF

www.harpercollins.co.uk

HarperCollins*Publishers*
1st Floor, Watermarque Building,
Ringsend Road, Dublin 4, Ireland

Stranded with Her Greek Husband © 2021 Michelle Smart

One Snowbound New Year's Night © 2021 Dani Collins

ISBN: 978-0-263-28275-7

12/21

MIX
Paper from
responsible sources
FSC™ C007454

This book is produced from independently certified FSC™ paper
to ensure responsible forest management.
For more information visit www.harpercollins.co.uk/green.

Printed and Bound in Spain using 100% Renewable Electricity
at CPI Black Print, Barcelona

STRANDED WITH HER GREEK HUSBAND

MICHELLE SMART

MILLS & BOON

To my always fabulous editor, Nicola Caws.
Thank you for all your faith and encouragement. xxx

CHAPTER ONE

THE CALM AEGEAN WATERS that Keren Burridge was sailing her thirty-four-foot cutter *The Sophia* through were in complete contrast to the tempest happening beneath her skin. The storm inside her had been growing since the island of Agon appeared on the horizon.

Habit had her release the tiller to grab her sunscreen and smear her face and as much of her body with it as she could reach. She'd suffered sunburn in Bermuda, a painful enough experience for her to ensure she always had a month's supply of sunscreen on board. In this respect, Keren was a quick learner. She only needed to suffer pain once for her to do anything to stop it afflicting her a second time.

Pain was coming her way today though. It was unavoidable.

A breeze swirled around her and caught the sails. *The Sophia* responded by increasing its speed. The beats of Keren's heart increased with it.

Familiar landmarks came into clearer focus. There was Agon's royal palace. There were the ruins of a once majestic temple dating back three millenia. Landmarks she'd once visited and explored at a time when she'd believed this island would be her home for ever.

The imposing crisp white villa set back in the cove she was steering towards came into clearer focus too. The rising sun danced over it, making it gleam enticingly. Fraudulently.

There was nothing enticing about it. If she could spend the rest of her life never setting eyes on that villa again then she would spend her life content, but choices made in grief were choices you lived with for the rest of your life.

The left side of the cove, a sheer circular wall of rock, had a small, seemingly natural jetty. She recognised the yacht already moored there. It was slightly larger than her cutter and used purely for the purpose of transporting its owner to his superyacht moored in Agon's main marina.

Once she'd sailed into her mooring space and secured her boat, Keren clipped her mini grab-bag around her waist then carefully snipped the base of the pink lilies she'd been lovingly growing in pots.

Holding the lilies, she stepped barefoot onto the jetty. It was time.

The jetty merged onto a pristine white beach as beautiful as any beach her fifteen months as a sea-wanderer had taken her. Fine, warm sand sank between her toes as she treaded through it to the gently inclining pebbled steps that led up to the villa. The closer she got to the steps, the heavier the weight of her legs and the heavier the weight in her chest.

At the top of the steps was a wide metal gate connecting a high wall designed to keep intruders out.

The gate opened automatically for her, just as she knew it would. Every move she'd made since sailing into the cove had been watched by an army of security cameras. The faceless people watching them knew to admit her at any time without question or intrusion. Yannis had kept his word on that score, if nothing else.

The villa's grounds were vast and immaculately maintained. She followed the path that snaked the swimming pool and entertaining space, refusing to let memories pierce her or slow her pace.

The peach tree was in a secluded part of the grounds, the only area not under surveillance. It had grown a lot in the almost two years since they'd planted it and was now old enough to bear fruit. The masses of fruit on it were beginning to ripen. Close to the foot of its trunk sat a granite headstone carved in the shape of an angel. The words *Sophia Filipidis* were engraved into it in English and Greek. It was to the side of this headstone that Keren sank to her knees.

Fresh flowers had recently been placed in the headstone's vase. She added the lilies to it then bowed her head and whispered a prayer for her daughter's soul. And then she talked to her. Told her the places she'd been. The people she'd met. The flowers she'd sniffed. The new foods she'd tried. Talking to her here came so naturally even though Sophia experienced everything with her from the wide space in Keren's heart she occupied.

When she'd finished talking, she looked again at the peach tree. They'd chosen it together. In Chinese culture, the peach tree is considered the tree of life, the peaches a symbol of immortality. Their daughter had never taken a breath of her own but in this tree her memory would live on.

'I knew you would come today.'

Her bruised heart thumped and she closed her eyes. Keren hadn't seen her estranged husband in eighteen months. Their only communications came via their lawyers.

If he'd approached her on any of her other visits here, she would have reminded him of their agreement, reminded him of his promise to let her come here whenever she wanted to mourn in peace and solitude.

Taking a long, deep breath, she got to her feet then turned her face to him.

'Hello, Yannis.'

Startlingly blue eyes met hers. Her heart thumped again. Expanded and rose up her throat.

His broad shoulders rose and fell heavily, a gesture that lanced her chest, and then he stepped forward to stand beside her.

They stood in silence until she felt a flash of warm pressure on her hand, and she stretched her fingers so he could lace his through them and, for that brief moment, unify their grief.

It was the first touch they'd shared since they'd first stood at this spot and said goodbye to their child. If Sophia had survived her birth, today would have been her second birthday.

Returning the squeeze of Yannis's fingers, she then gently tugged her hand from his and hugged her arms around herself. 'How have you been?'

His head rocked forward. 'Good. You?'

'Good.'

'Good.'

More silence passed.

Conversation had once flowed so easily between them. But that had been a long time ago.

She took a step back. 'I should get back to my boat.'

'Stay for a drink?'

Her fingers tightened on her biceps. 'I don't think that's a good idea.'

'There are things I want to talk to you about.'

'Do it through our lawyers.' Like they had done since she'd left him.

'Not everything can go through them.' He rammed his hands into his trousers and rolled his shoulders. 'Stay for a drink. Share lunch with me. Let us talk. And then I'll sign the papers.'

She turned her face sharply back to him. Keren had been waiting for three months for Yannis to sign the papers that would finalise their divorce and cast in iron the financial settlement.

'You have them here?' she asked.

'Locked in my safe.'

Could it really be that easy? One conversation and then they would finally be officially over?

Either the solemnity of the day had softened him or he'd got bored with toying with her.

In the eighteen months since she'd left him, all the magnanimous generosity Yannis had initially declared he wanted to lavish her with had been stripped away to the bare bones.

She'd accepted his initial settlement offer without countering it only for him to change his mind and halve it. And then halve it again. And again.

The chateau in Provence and the town house in Milan, the Aston Martin, the Maserati...all had been dangled before her then snatched away.

Now all that was left was a fraction of his initial settlement offer and she wouldn't care if he revoked that too.

She hadn't fought back. Not on any of it. Not even

when her lawyer had begged, telling her she was settling for a fraction of what she was entitled to by law.

Keren didn't want to fight. She didn't care if Yannis got the satisfaction of believing he'd won. She didn't care what the law said. They'd been married only fourteen months. She wanted nothing from Yannis but the right to visit their daughter's grave.

'Okay. We can talk.' She gazed at their daughter's headstone. 'But not today,' she added softly. She would not fight on a day of mourning. Today was Sophia's day.

Yannis either felt the same way or understood for he bowed his head and said, 'Stay in the cove for the night and we'll meet for breakfast on the poolside terrace.'

'Okay.'

'Do you have food on your boat or shall I have lunch and dinner brought to you?'

'I have provisions. But thank you.' Maybe he really had softened towards her. Maybe the conversation he wanted to have was a peace offering. Maybe he wanted to apologise...

A sad smile curved her lips. Yannis had never apologised for anything in his life.

He bowed his head again. 'I'll see you in the morning.'

Keren waited until he'd disappeared from view before returning to the cove.

Keren was on the deck at the stern of *The Sophia*, draining the water of her makeshift washing machine, when a figure on the beach caught her eye.

He couldn't be coming to see her, she reasoned. They'd agreed to meet in the morning.

But this was Yannis, she reminded herself. A man who'd proved his word was as stable as a chocolate teapot.

He waded into the water. She did her best to ignore his presence.

Screwing the base tap of the barrel back in place, she lifted her wet clothes out and placed them in a clean plastic basket.

Although he was a good distance from her, she felt exposed. Since she'd returned to her boat, she'd changed from the simple summer dress she'd been wearing into a yellow bikini and tiny blue sarong that she'd tied around her waist and which hardly skimmed her bottom.

Stubbornness fisted in her. She'd changed her 'that's not very suitable for where we're going, *glyko mou*' clothing too many times for Yannis in the fourteen months of their marriage.

'What are you doing?'

Why his voice made her jump when she'd been pretending not to watch him swim to within a few meters of her, she didn't know.

'Hanging my washing.'

'You have a washing machine?'

She tapped her repurposed barrel.

'That's your washing machine?'

'Yep. There's rocks in the bottom of it. Add clothes, washing powder and water and set sail. The motion of the waves makes it all act as a washing machine and my clothes come out all clean and fresh.' She didn't mean to babble. Nerves and a need to prove his second unexpected appearance that day didn't bother her in the slightest had loosened her tongue.

How could he make that puzzled look when treading water? It was a look she'd become far too familiar with and usually came about when she did something he wouldn't do or didn't understand.

'Wouldn't a washing machine be easier?'

'Doubt it. Takes too much room and uses too much electricity. Plus there's not many washing machine repairers out at sea if it breaks down.'

He didn't look convinced.

'Can I come on board?' he asked.

She took a deep breath to keep hold of her temper. 'We agreed to talk tomorrow.'

'I know but I'm curious to see how you live. I won't stay long.'

She supposed she could always push him overboard if he outstayed his unwelcome.

Smiling tightly, she threw the nearest rope ladder overboard.

He heaved himself up with supreme ease and stood on the deck, salt water dripping off him, rivulets forming over the scattering of dark hair across his hard, bronzed chest and snaking down the plane of his ripped abdomen to the band of his black swim-shorts.

Keren turned away and snatched up a T-shirt to wring overboard, doing everything she could to blot out the sight of Yannis's almost naked body. That he had a fantastic body was nothing new. She'd been married to him, for heaven's sake, had shared a bed with him almost every night from the day they'd met...

She wasn't quick enough to blot those memories before a pulse of heat zinged in her pelvis. She reflexively grabbed the railing she was leaning against.

His deep voice rang out close to her ear. Too close. 'Can I help?'

She sidestepped away. 'No. Thank you.' Jerking her head at the open hatch, she added, 'Go and explore.'

Explore and go.

'Don't you want me to dry off first?'

'It's a boat. It gets wet. Just don't sit on anything.'

He shrugged. 'It's your home.'

He disappeared inside.

Her chest loosened. Taking a moment to breathe and compose herself, she then got on with the job of hanging the wrung clothes on the line she'd fashioned.

Yannis's head appeared. 'You have an oven.'

'I do.'

He pulled an impressed face and vanished again.

His absence didn't last long. 'You have a fridge too.'

'Wow. I'd never spotted that before.'

He flashed his teeth at her and ducked down again.

Amongst the clothes that needed drying was her underwear. The thought of Yannis seeing them on a washing line shouldn't make her skin feel all prickly and her insides all squirmy. It was underwear, that was all. Everyone—well, almost everyone—wore it. It was nothing to be ashamed of.

A deeper, squirming pulse right in her core rent through her to remember all the times he'd stripped her underwear from her. Sometimes with his teeth.

It was the knowledge that Yannis would take one look at these particular items and consider them ugly and unsexy that spurred her into hanging them instead of hiding them.

Who cared what he thought? Not her. Not any more.

By the time she'd finished hanging her clothes, Yannis was still exploring. There was no good reason it was taking him so long.

'Are you done yet?' she called down through the hatch. There was no way she was going down there with Yannis sucking all the oxygen out of what was already a limited space.

'Just making us a coffee,' he called back.

She gritted her teeth and breathed deeply. She would not allow herself to get angry today. 'You said you wouldn't stay long.'

If he heard that, he did an excellent job of ignoring it. Soon, his voice carried back up the steps. 'Is instant coffee pre-sweetened?'

'No.'

'I can't find any sugar.'

'I said you could explore, not ransack the place.'

'How can I find sugar if I don't look?' he said in a reasonable voice that made her want to set the fire extinguisher on him.

'It's in the cupboard next to the fridge in a blue and white packet with *sugar* written on it... Have you ever made coffee before?' Yannis came from a family who could trace their ancestry all the way back to Agon's founding, a family considered nobility, a family who counted the Kalliakis royal family as personal friends. Yannis himself had gone to the same English boarding school as the King and his two younger brothers, albeit a few years after them. Raised in unimaginable wealth he'd reached the age of thirty-four without having to do a single domestic chore.

'It can't be that difficult.'

If Keren gritted her teeth again she'd grind them to dust, so she busied herself with opening the canopy that provided shade over the small outside table and took a seat on one of the benches.

Horrified to find her legs were shaking, she clamped

her hands on her thighs and willed her fraught nerves to settle.

The rawness of Keren's grief at their daughter's grave-side and the knowledge that Yannis must be feeling his grief more strongly that day, too, had softened the impact of his unexpected appearance there. There was no soft-ening the impact of his visit to her boat. She'd thought she had a day to prepare herself for seeing him again but he'd caught her out and the impact his presence was having on her made her want to roll into a ball and shut the world out. She shouldn't feel like this. She shouldn't feel anything for him.

It's just the surprise of it all, she valiantly assured her-self. After eighteen months apart, seeing him again was bound to be a shock to her system.

Everything inside her contracted when he finally ap-peared out of the hatch, ducked his huge frame under the washing line and joined her at the table.

He pushed a mug of coffee to her and shook his head in bemusement. 'How do you cope living in such a cramped space?'

'It's ample for my needs.' Frightened of making eye contact, frightened at the well of disparate, painful emo-tions building in her stomach, she turned her face slightly and let her gaze settle on the calm, clear sea.

'My tender is bigger than this.' He meant the yacht moored next to *The Sophia*. Keren's tender was a kayak. She could anchor at sea, get into her kayak and row it straight up a beach, no faffing.

Her right leg started shaking again. She crossed her ankles together in an effort to calm it. 'I prefer substance over style.'

'Do I detect a dig?'

'Unfortunately, yes, so I think it best that you drink your coffee and leave. I don't want to argue with you today.' At least she had control of her voice. That was one small crumb of comfort.

'I do not wish to argue today either, *glyko mou*.'

'Then do me a favour and drink your coffee in silence.'

He leaned back and took a sip of it. His disgust was immediate. '*Theos*, that is awful.'

She clamped her trembling hand around her mug and took a sip. The coffee was a little stronger than she liked but passable. 'It's fine.'

'It's a sacrilege to coffee.' He had another sip to convince himself of its awfulness. 'I understand now why it's called instant coffee. It is instantly awful.'

'Then why don't you go home and get one of your staff to make you a proper one?'

'Soon. Your fridge and cupboards are almost empty. What are you going to eat for your dinner?'

'Food from the storage cubby.'

'Where is that?'

'What, you mean you didn't discover all my cramped boat's secrets?'

'Shall I look again?'

'Nope. There's a storage cubby behind the stairs at the bow. Now, if you're not going to finish that, you can leave. If you are going to finish it, you can drink it now and leave.'

'You want me to leave?'

'Yes. And if you come back before the morning, *I'm* going to leave.'

'And miss our talk?'

'You're the one who wants to talk, not me.'

'If you don't talk, I won't sign the papers.'

'Do you think I care?'

An edge came into his voice. 'I thought you couldn't wait for the divorce to be finalised.'

Somehow, she managed to keep control of her own voice. 'I would prefer sooner but if it has to be later then it has to be later.'

'I can refuse to sign it for ever.'

'You can,' she agreed with a coolness that totally belied the ragged heat of emotions bubbling beneath her skin. 'But if you don't sign it, I'll still get my divorce under Agon law.'

'In ten years.'

'Eight and a half,' she corrected. 'We've already been separated eighteen months.'

They'd married on the island of Agon and spent their short married life on it and so the dissolution of their marriage was bound under its laws. The law stipulated that if one spouse refused consent to divorce then the marriage could be dissolved without it after ten years of separation.

The thought of waiting that long to be fully free of him was unbearable. Surely he wouldn't hold out that long out of spite? Surely he had nothing left to torment her with?

'And how have you found those eighteen months?'

'Ask me that tomorrow.' She got to her feet and placed a palm on the table to support the weakness in her frame. 'Please, Yannis, just go. Your being here has made me angry and I don't want to be angry today. We both need to grieve and we can't do that together.' They'd never been able to.

His features tightened. His generous mouth pulled in. The startling blue eyes held hers.

Keren braced herself but the expected barb never came. Yannis inclined his head sharply and, with an,

'I'll see you in the morning,' rose from the bench and stepped off the boat and onto the jetty.

Only when he'd disappeared from sight did she sink back onto the bench and hug herself tightly.

CHAPTER TWO

KEREN WOKE WITH the birds. Their chirpy song did little to soothe the churning that set off in her belly before she even opened her eyes.

Yannis hadn't returned to the boat. He hadn't needed to. The peace she'd found in her little home had been shattered.

After eighteen months spent resolutely shoving him out of her mind whenever he tried to crash into it, he'd smashed those barriers down without any effort whatsoever. Now, he was all she could think about.

When they'd exchanged their vows, she hadn't had a doubt in her mind that they would be together for ever.

By the time she left she'd hated him with the same strength she'd once loved him. And he'd hated her too.

'Go on, then, you selfish cow, leave.'

That parting shot, delivered as he'd thrown her suitcases in the boot of the taxi she'd called to drive her away, haunted her.

It haunted her because his fury at her leaving had been so unexpected. The writing had been on the wall for months and Yannis could read fluently in four languages.

He'd punched a wall too. Blood had dripped from his

knuckles when he'd grabbed her suitcases and marched them outside.

She supposed his fury had been that she'd ended the marriage before he could.

Because Yannis *had* been planning to end it.

Suspicious of his growing closeness to his PA, the beautiful Marla, Keren had hacked his laptop—easy, when he used a combination of her middle name, Jane, and her date of birth for all his passwords—and gone through his search history. He'd been looking at divorce sites.

Three days later, Marla had accompanied him as his official guest to a palace function.

That had been the final straw for their marriage.

Agon's press had published a photo of Yannis and Marla together at that function. Keren had believed—*still* believed—his denials that anything had happened between them but she would never forgive him the humiliation or the way he'd tried to twist it to make it her fault for not accompanying him herself.

Nothing had happened between Yannis and Marla but he'd wanted it to.

He'd long stopped wanting Keren.

In the six months from Sophia's stillbirth to Keren leaving him, he'd made not a single move on her. Perversely, while he no longer desired her, his insistence about always needing to know of her whereabouts accelerated. He'd become resentful of her job. Resentful of anything that didn't involve him.

She'd set them both free. She'd escaped the gilded cage he'd suffocated her in and released him from his vows of fidelity. He could pursue Marla and anyone else who took his fancy.

How many women had he been with since she'd left? She couldn't guess. She never checked. She would not be one of those people who cyber-stalked their exes. She went online twice a week to update her blog and respond to questions from readers. Some were chattier than others. A couple in particular responded to every post and asked interesting, thoughtful questions about life at sea and the places she'd been to.

Keren also used that online time to catch up on emails with her parents and sister. That was the extent of her online presence.

She tried to make her emails to her family full of descriptive colour and always attached photos of the places she'd travelled to and the sites she'd visited, always hoping something would inject a spark of adventure in them. Keren's love of travelling baffled her family. Their responding emails detailed lives that had barely changed since she'd left England to explore the world four months after her eighteenth birthday. In the eight years since, her sister had had three promotions, married and bought a house in the same town as their family home.

Her family were like the zebra finches they'd kept all of Keren's life, content in their small world and frightened of what lay outside it. As a small child she'd felt sorry for the tiny finches, had been convinced they must hate their cage, large though it was. Once, when she'd been eight or nine, she'd opened the cage and living room window when no one was looking and encouraged them to fly free. One had perched on the windowsill but that was as far as any of them bothered to stretch their wings.

Keren had always felt like the human cuckoo in

the Burridge nest. Where the others were content and happy in their confinement, she was the bird who looked through the bars of the cage and yearned to explore, the bird who became depressed in captivity.

By the end of her marriage to Yannis, it had felt like she was living in captivity. They had both been trapped.

Her boat had only a small mirror above the sink in the tiny windowless bathroom in which to check her appearance. She rarely looked in it but that morning, after showering and dressing in a pair of denim shorts and a bright red chiffon top, she found herself examining her face. Yannis used to call her beautiful but Keren had always thought her jaw a little too square and her nose a little too small for her to be anything but pleasant looking. She liked her eyes though. They were dark brown, almost identical to the colour of her dark chestnut hair, which she'd tied into a loose knot at the top of her neck. Her mouth was boring, neither generous nor thin, wide nor narrow.

Yannis had a beautiful mouth, generous and naturally dark in colour. Everything about him was beautiful. His blue eyes. His high cheekbones. The devilish quirk of his dark eyebrows. His thick, dark brown hair which he styled into a quiff in the morning then would invariably flop over his forehead by lunch or stand up on end from him dragging his fingers through it. His strong neck. His tall frame that magically managed to be lean and broad at the same time. Yannis was a rarity, a man whose beauty enhanced his masculinity rather than lessened it. It was a beauty that had cast her in a spell.

Spells always broke.

It was time to face him one last time.

She slowly breathed in and out three times and stepped onto the jetty.

Yannis was already out on the terrace, sheltered from the rising sun by the huge pergola entwined and covered with vibrant flowers. Keren's nostrils twitched as their delicate scent reached her airwaves. It was a scent she loved.

Dressed in a pair of baggy tan shorts and a fitted black polo shirt, he rose when he noticed her approach.

Her heart was going like the clappers.

He indicated for her to sit.

She took the seat furthest from him. In the heady days of being in love, she'd always taken the seat closest. She'd sat further and further from him with each fracture in their marriage.

'What would you like to eat?' he asked politely. The table was laid with jugs of fruit juice and water and a *briki* of coffee.

'Whatever you're having.' Food was about the only thing they had in common. Their taste buds were remarkably similar...with the exception of instant coffee, she thought, suppressing her lips' unexpected attempts to curve into a smile at his disgust.

He beckoned a member of staff she didn't recognise over and spoke in rapid Greek to him. The staff member hurried around the side of the villa to the kitchen entrance.

Yannis poured a cup of the thick coffee from the *briki* and passed it to her. She waited until it was on the table before picking it up and taking a sip.

The first time she'd tasted Yannis's coffee had been on a morning just like this, after their first night together.

How shyly blissful she had felt that sunny morning. Shy because it was the first time she'd slept with a man and she'd become all tongue-tied. Blissful because it had been the most magical night of her life. She'd been too shy to ask for the sugar and milk she normally added to coffee but then she'd tasted its already sweetened perfection and developed an instant addiction to it.

'What did you want to talk about?' she asked, frightened at how easily that memory had slipped in.

She didn't want to remember the happy times. They hurt too much.

'Let us eat first. Tell me how you have been these last eighteen months.'

'I've been fine.'

He raised a mocking eyebrow. 'You make me wait until morning to ask that question and now you reply with that?'

'Life at sea suits me. That better?'

'You have seen much of the world?'

'Some.'

'You don't miss being on solid ground?'

'No.'

'You're not giving much away.'

'I agreed to discuss whatever it is you don't want to talk about through our lawyers. I didn't agree to small talk.'

'I think of it like learning to walk. Start with the small steps and build from there.'

'I already know how to walk so let's just get on with it because once breakfast is done, I'm walking back to my boat and sailing away.'

'So eager to be away from me. Does it unnerve you, being with me again?'

'Yes.'

'Why is that?'

'It just does.'

'Good. It means I still affect you.'

If he knew how deeply he still affected her his head would swell to the size of the moon.

She would never give him the satisfaction.

In less than an hour she would be gone. All she had to do was hold it together until then.

'I see your ego hasn't changed,' she observed.

'I'm still the same man you fell in love with, if that's what you mean?'

Her heart twisted painfully but she jutted her chin and pointedly said, 'And the same man I fell out of love with.'

His lips tightened almost imperceptibly but then he turned his head to the sound of approaching footsteps. Their breakfast had arrived.

Keren's stomach growled when the folded omelette was placed before her. She knew without cutting into it that it was made with cheese and olives. Her favourite. Yannis's favourite too.

How many other women had been served breakfast under this pergola since she'd left?

It was a thought that smothered the growling with nausea.

Using the side of her fork, she cut into it. She would force this omelette down her throat. Under no circumstances would she let Yannis think she'd lost her appetite because of him.

'How are your parents?' she asked. She imagined Nina and Aristidis Filipidis danced a refined jig of joy when she left. They'd treated her with their own particular type of kindness but they hadn't approved of the marriage.

An ordinary English girl raised in suburbia, descended from a long line of ordinary people and with a mind of her own was not the kind of person who usually married into the Filipidis family.

'They're doing well. They're flying to Athens this morning—they're hosting a fund-raiser tomorrow night for a specialist children's cancer hospital.'

'When will you join them?' Yannis's parents had turned their attention to philanthropy since passing the ancient family business to their two sons a decade ago. Keren gave them their due, they raised huge sums of money and awareness for the charities they favoured but it was a philanthropy that sat uncomfortably with her. The cultural divide between herself and the Filipidises had been as vast as the wealth and breeding divides.

She'd been as big a cuckoo in the Filipidis nest as she'd been in the Burridge one.

'I won't be.'

Surprised, she looked at him and found his stare already trained on her. Yannis and his brother always attended their parents' charitable dos. Always. Grandparents and other parts of the extended family attended too. It was what the Filipidises did.

He understood her expression and shrugged nonchalantly. 'They can do without my presence for one function. I have other plans.'

Her heart made a tiny rip. She put a forkful of fluffy omelette in her mouth and tried to chew the unexpected pain away.

Yannis must have plans to see a lover. Not just any lover, but one he was serious about. Serious enough that he would blow his parents off for her.

The only time he'd done that for Keren had been for

a function that had taken place a month after they'd lost Sophia.

There was another tear in her heart as she wondered if that's what he wanted to talk to her about. To tell her he was remarrying. It would be expected. Yannis needed an heir. Five months after losing Sophia he had sat on their marital bed with his back to her and asked when she thought she would be ready to try for another baby. She'd had to leave the room to stop herself from throwing a vase at his head with rage, furious and heartbroken that he could ask that of her when he slept with his back to her every night.

Did he want the satisfaction of seeing her expression when he told her she'd been permanently replaced or had he managed to dredge a bit of humanity into his soul and not want her to hear it from any other source? The way he'd behaved since she'd left made her think it must be the former.

He wanted to take delight in hurting her a little bit more first and then sign the divorce papers.

She would not let him see the hurt. There shouldn't even be any hurt. She'd left him and moved on. She'd spent three months learning how to sail and then she'd set off alone on the adventure of a lifetime and thrived.

He hated that she'd thrived. She knew that. He'd expected her to come crawling back. He'd shouted that at the taxi as the driver had accelerated off the estate. *'You'll be back.'*

The great Yannis Filipidis, one of the most eligible bachelors in the Mediterranean before Keren had come on the scene, a man with a life so charmed it should have been plated in gold, had to deal with the indignity of being deserted by the wife who should be grateful for being elevated to the lofty heights of a Filipidis. His ego must have taken one heck of a battering, and she'd long suspected that as being the root of his vindictive behaviour towards her throughout the divorce proceedings.

'And your family?' he enquired with the same politeness she'd asked after his, even though he'd only met them once, at their wedding. It was the first and only time her parents and sister had left the UK. Keren had hoped the trip might act as a spark for adventure in them but travelling abroad had terrified them. Her family liked the comfort of the familiar. When she'd been growing up, the Burridges' annual holiday had been to the same Dorset cottage year after year, the activities done the same as the year before and the year before that.

'They're all well,' she said. And they were. Her family were happy and well and plodding on with their lives.

'Good.'

She ate more of her omelette aware of the atmosphere developing between them. She could feel the tension encircling them, an invisible cloud of simmering anger and resentment. And pain. Pain of a love that had soured to hate and dreams that had turned to dust.

'Why did you change your name?' he asked suddenly, his tone so much tighter than the easy drawl he'd been speaking with up to that point that Keren's eyes darted back to his face before she could stop herself.

'What are you talking about?'

'Your blog.'

The piece of omelette she'd just popped in her mouth almost stuck in her throat.

Keren's travel blog was how they'd got together. When she'd left home she'd taken nothing but a rucksack full of clothes, her phone, all the cash she'd saved since the age of twelve and a laptop—a *bon voyage* present from her terrified parents. She'd created a blog in the first hostel in the first country she'd arrived at—Thailand—and began twice-weekly updates of her adventures, posting short videos and giving light-hearted reviews of the places she visited and the activities she undertook. To her surprise, she'd soon found herself with a following. Soon, she was garnering enough clicks to earn money from it. In time, she began receiving invitations from public relations people from all over the globe.

Yannis had hated that she still ran her blog after their marriage. Hated that there were occasions she couldn't accompany him to places and functions because she had other commitments.

'We're still legally married, Keren.'

'Not for much longer,' she whispered.

'Until I sign that document and a judge stamps it, you are still a Filipidis.'

'Actually, I can be anything I like, and if I'd been living an ordinary life I would have changed it back to Burridge, legally, the day I left you. It was only because I had better things to get on with that I didn't.'

'That didn't stop you changing it professionally.'

'I would have thought you'd be glad about that—didn't think you or your family would be happy to have the great Filipidis name sullied by a sea-wanderer.'

'Don't make it about me. Be honest, for once, and admit it was it your way of sticking two fingers up at me.'

Unable to stomach any more of the omelette and no longer caring what he would think about her rejection of food, she pushed her plate to one side and poured herself more coffee. God, her hand was shaking. Her insides were shaking too.

Her teeth were clenched so tightly together she could barely get the words out. 'I wanted to keep my professional name when we married but you emotionally blackmailed me into throwing away the four years I'd taken building my name and my blog and take *your* name. So, yes, I claimed my name back for myself but it was nothing to do with you—it was about reclaiming *me*.'

His face contorted. If he were an animal he would be snarling. 'You make it sound like I stole your name from you.'

'You stole everything from me. From the moment your ring was on my finger, you set about changing me.'

'I did no such thing.'

'Yes, you did! You disapproved—' Cutting herself off, Keren shoved her chair back and got to her feet without any real conscious thought and with such force the chair toppled over. 'Forget it. I'm not doing this again. Tell me what you want to talk about right now or I'm off.'

His throat moved. He closed his eyes and his shoulders rose and fell as he breathed in and out deeply. By the time his gaze landed back on her, only the steel in his eyes betrayed that he was feeling anything but nonchalant. 'I want us to try again.'

CHAPTER THREE

OPEN-MOUTHED, KEREN STARED at him with a violence of emotions building deep within her, bubbling and frothing, expanding and swelling, until they exploded in a gush of agonised fury.

'You cruel, vindictive *bastard*. You went to all these lengths just to toy with me and suck me into one of your sick games?'

And she'd fallen for it. She'd given him the benefit of the doubt and met with him when she should have known he just wanted to continue his torture of her a bit longer. He was like a cat with a mouse in its paws, clawing and clawing at it but never striking the deadly blow that would put it out of its misery.

'I'm not playing a game, *glyko mou*,' he said steadily. 'I want you back.'

'Oh…just *stop*! Do you really think I'm stupid enough to fall for that? And are you really so stupidly arrogant you think I want *you* back?'

Blue eyes locked on hers, Yannis rose slowly to his feet. 'Not arrogance. Hope.'

'Don't give me that. I know the way your pathetic mind works—you've imagined me secretly pining and regretting leaving you for all this time and thought you'd say the magic words and I'd fall at your feet in gratitude and relief, and then while I'm down there, give me a good kick and finally satisfy your pathetic ego by ending our marriage on *your* terms. Are you going to sign the damned papers or not?'

Jaw clenched tightly, knuckles on the table, he leaned forward. 'Not until you get off your soapbox and *talk*.'

'Then fine! Don't sign them. Stay married to a woman you hate and who hates you and stop yourself remarrying and producing the heir you're so desperate for out of spite.'

The deep burn behind her eyes blurring her sight, Keren spun around and stormed away before he could witness the tears fall. Angry tears. Furious tears. Pouring down her cheeks like a waterfall. Blinding her. But she didn't slow her pace, not even when she lost her footing and stumbled, corrected herself and walked as fast as she could to the steps that would lead her down to the beach and to her boat and freedom.

Holding tightly to the rail, she skipped down the pebbled steps, her pace turning to a run when her feet hit the sand. She was halfway to the jetty when she realised something was wrong. Wiping more tears away, she had to blink a number of times to clear her eyes enough to see.

And when she could see, her heart juddered to a stop.

The Sophia. It was gone.

Yannis had retaken his seat and donned his shades when Keren stormed back onto the terrace. His head was tilted back in the stance of someone taking a moment of peace and contemplation.

'What have you done to my boat?' she demanded to know.

'Borrowed it.'

Having expected him to deny any knowledge, his admission momentarily struck her dumb.

'What on earth for?' she finally managed to ask.

He removed the shades and set his piercing stare on her. 'Because I suspected from your attitude yesterday that you wouldn't have an adult discussion with me.'

'You mean you wanted a contingency plan in case I didn't fall for your little con trick.'

'It was no con, but you are correct in it being a contingency plan. I had hoped to talk to you yesterday about things but respected that with it being the day it was, you didn't want to.'

'Didn't respect it enough not to come on my boat and steal the engine keys.' The seas were too calm to set sail without using the engine. 'I assume that's why you took so long exploring?'

'I came to the boat to see you and to see how you lived and to make sure your boat is safe—'

'Make sure it's *safe*?' she interrupted, freshly furious. 'Still the same controlling sexist pig, making assumptions that I would—'

'There was nothing sexist about it,' he cut in, his own tone of voice rising. 'I have spent the last eighteen months worrying that you were sailing around on a floating coffin.'

'As if you've been worrying about me!'

'You're my *wife*!' His fist slammed down on the table making the coffee cups on it clatter in their saucers.

Keren's heart clattered in her chest with them. 'I wouldn't be if you'd stopped mucking me around and signed the blasted divorce papers!'

'I don't want a damned divorce! I want us to try again.

I want us to talk and see if there's a way we can make our marriage work—'

'But you *hate* me!'

A pulse throbbed at the side of his jaw below his ear. Breathing heavily, he looked her right in the eye. 'Only sometimes, *glyko mou*. Only sometimes.'

'Well, I hate you all the time.'

'You loved me once.'

It was the hoarseness in his voice that caused fresh tears to well behind her eyes. She turned her face away so he couldn't see, trying desperately to tamp down the wracking emotions inside her.

'Stealing your boat keys was a spur of the moment thing,' he said in a steadier tone. 'I didn't visit you with the intention of stealing them but when I saw them I saw an opportunity to force you to talk if force was needed and I took it.'

'I don't want to talk,' she whispered.

'I know. Since you left you have made it impossible to contact you.'

'Not for the people I wanted to remain in contact with.'

'I know that too. So I'm forcing it. You will get your boat back on Monday morning.'

'In three days? Are you mad? I'm not staying a single ruddy night here.'

'Yes, *glyko mou*, you are. Three days to talk and decide if it's worth trying again.'

'I've already decided! And you have too, so stop with this stupid game of pretence and give me back my boat!'

'No.'

'Fine, then I'm going to…' Her words trailed off as she patted her stomach and horror struck her to discover she wasn't wearing her grab-bag.

For the first time since she'd set off on the open seas alone, she'd left her boat without the nifty bit of kit she kept her passport, phone and emergency cash in.

'Going where?' Yannis asked silkily. 'The police? There is no theft between spouses in Agon. You have nothing on you but what you are wearing.' He folded his arms across his chest. The pulse in his jaw throbbed again before he visibly relaxed his stance. 'I will make a deal with you. I will sign the divorce papers right now but date them for Monday. You can keep hold of them. If by Monday you still think I'm playing games and you still want to divorce, then the signed papers will be right there in your hands to do with as you like.'

Keren followed Yannis through the bifold doors and into the villa's main entertaining room. She hadn't felt this sick since the day she'd discovered he'd been searching *divorce* on his laptop.

She was the mouse given a reprieve but who knew the final strike was close.

Yannis had wanted a divorce. Yannis had stopped making love to her. Yannis had taken his PA to a high-profile function he knew damn well the press would be in attendance at.

Yannis had dragged their divorce proceedings on in such a cruel manner that, according to her lawyer, his own lawyer had balked when he'd changed his mind and reduced the agreed financial settlement a fourth time.

Yannis had wanted her destitute. He'd wanted her to go begging to him. When that hadn't worked and she hadn't fallen into his trap—her revived blog, now titled *The Diary of a Sea-Wanderer*, had been even more successful than her first travel blog, earning her enough money to pay for her meagre needs and build a little nest for herself—his ego would have felt the blow of failure. It must have driven him mad that she'd earned enough to keep herself financially independent, that she hadn't sent a demand for him to pay her anything.

She didn't want anything from him.

And Yannis didn't want her back. He just wanted to hurt her. This was his last roll of the dice to get back at her for having the temerity to end their marriage before he could.

Keren hung back at the threshold of his study while he and the two household staff he'd rounded up to act as witnesses all signed the documents he'd retrieved from his safe.

When it was done and the staff dismissed, he handed the two identical pieces of paper to her.

Her eyes blurred to see her own signature already neatly written onto them. She'd signed them three months ago, when she'd last visited Sophia. She'd sailed to the other side of the island and anchored in the bay rather than the marina for the night, then in the morning rowed her kayak up the beach and visited her lawyer's office.

She blinked hard to focus and homed in on Yannis's signature. It was the same as she remembered. The date scrawled next to it was for the coming Monday.

In three days she would give these pieces of paper to her lawyer and then she would sail away knowing that a call would come at any time confirming a judge had rubber stamped them and that their divorce was final.

She would be free.

So why were her eyes burning again? And why were there such painful ripples in her heart?

'Shall I keep them in the safe for you?'

She swallowed and shook her head, blinking hard to keep the tears at bay. 'No.'

'The code hasn't changed. You can get them at any time.'

'And you can change the code at any time.'

'You don't trust me?'

'I'd trust the snake in the Garden of Eden more.'

The weight of his stare penetrated her skin sending tingles dancing through her.

'Then I must spend our days together rebuilding your trust,' he said slowly.

Keeping her gaze on the divorce papers, she folded them carefully then slid them into the back pocket of her shorts, kicking herself again for not clipping her grab-bag around her waist. As soon as she escaped Yannis, she would find somewhere safe to hide them. If she was lucky, she might find somewhere to hide herself for the next three days too.

She had no idea how she was going to cope for three days with him without either killing him or losing her mind. Or both.

'Ready for lunch?' he asked into the silence.

'I'm not hungry.'

'You hardly ate any of your breakfast.'

'I wonder why that was.'

He sighed and grabbed at his hair. 'Is it such a strain to be civil to me?'

'Actually, yes.'

'Would it help if I apologised?'

She couldn't stop her stare darting to him. 'I'm staying for three days not three weeks, Yannis.'

To her surprise, a grin spread over his face. It was a heartbreaker of a smile, all lopsided and…sexy.

She quickly looked away.

Keren didn't want to see his smile and remember how it had once been part of the Yannis Filipidis package that had seduced and charmed her from the moment she set eyes on him.

Their first meeting had been at the opening of a new contemporary art gallery at Agon's palace that Yannis and his brother had helped curate as a favour to the King. The palace had artwork and antiquities dating back millennia, but the modern King wanted to bring it more fully into the twenty-first century. Knowing their King wanted to attract a younger, hipper clientele, the PR people behind the launch reached out to Keren and invited her to attend and review. That she was no art critic and had only visited and reviewed two art galleries in all her travels—reviewing offbeat bars and restaurants and activities like elephant trekking were more her thing—didn't matter to them. It was her audience they wanted to connect with. They'd offered to pay for her flights and accommodation and promised no interference with what she published on her blog. As Agon had been on her wish list of countries to visit, she'd been thrilled to accept.

She remembered the funky feel of the gallery. The creative and delicious cocktails and canapés she'd been plied with by the eager PR team. The buzz that had permeated the air.

But mostly she remembered the incredibly tall, incredibly gorgeous man dressed in a dapper pinstriped suit propped against the wall with a bottle of lager in his hand, oblivious to the lusty stares being thrown his way because his entire focus had been on her.

Keren had come to Agon intending to stay for a long weekend. It had ended up being her home for two years.

The man whose attention she'd caught that night and married six months later was still grinning. 'But you *are* staying,' he pointed out smugly.

'Under duress. And only for three days.'

'Three days is long enough to convince you to stay.' Then the smile fell. He tilted his head. 'Would you believe any apology?'

'No.'

'Then I shall save my breath for when you do believe it.'

'Save it but don't hold it,' she advised.

The smile returned. 'You would give me the kiss of life, surely?'

Before she could respond, he swept past her, his arm brushing hers, and engulfed her in a cloud of the cologne she hadn't even realised she'd been avoiding inhaling until it was too late.

Grinding her toes into her sandals, Keren closed her eyes and tried her hardest to ride out the wave of longing ripping through her.

They were just echoes of the past. Memories.

Memories she'd locked away on her flight out of Agon.

'Where have you been hiding?'

Keren, bottle of water at her lips, ready for her first mouthful, hid the clatter of her heart at Yannis's appearance with an eye-roll.

When she'd left Yannis's study, she'd deliberately gone to the kitchen rather than follow him back out onto the poolside terrace as he'd assumed she would do.

The chef was the same from her days there and, after a wide-eyed greeting of disbelief followed by a tight embrace, had become all tense and awkward when Keren asked if there was anything prepared that she could take for her lunch. In the end, she'd rifled through the fridges until she'd found the evening's dessert—a huge bowl of chocolate mousse. Yannis was a chocaholic. He swam a hundred laps of the pool a day and said fifty of those were to work off his chocolate consumption.

If he could steal her boat she could steal his chocolate.

'As Yannis and I are still married, I'm still mistress of this villa,' she'd said to the anxious chef with a bright smile. 'Feel free to remind him of that if I forget to tell him first.'

She'd swiped a stray spoon on her way out, then carried the bowl all the way to the olive grove and demolished the lot of it in one sitting.

The chocolatey sweetness had soothed her frayed nerves and, breathing much easier than she had since waking, she'd meandered around searching for rocks, and built herself a little nest which she buried their divorce papers under, making sure to first wrap it in the plastic food bag she'd also helped herself to in the kitchen.

If she hadn't been so thirsty, she would still be in the olive grove happily avoiding him. She'd made it to the outside bar by the swimming pool less than a minute ago and already he'd found her. It had taken a fraction of that time for her heart to set off into overdrive.

He'd removed his polo shirt. His glorious chest was bare and, Keren being over a foot shorter than him, right in her line of sight.

Leaning her back against the bar, she went for the lesser of two evils and rested her eyes on his face. 'If I told you that, you'd know where to find me next time.'

He stepped closer to her, eyes glinting. 'Ah, so you're

planning to spend the time we've agreed to spend talking hiding.'

Her right leg was shaking again, and she ground her toes into her sandals as hard as she could and dropped her stare to the strong column of his throat thinking that would be a safe place to rest her gaze but staring at it evoked something in her and filled her mouth with the remembered musky taste of his skin.

'I didn't agree to talks but other than that, bingo,' she said, then drank her entire bottle of water in one go, hoping the cold liquid would kill the memory of his taste and douse the flickers of awareness building through her.

Yannis raised a quirky brow then his eyes narrowed as he clocked the empty bowl with only a few chocolate streaks to show what had originally been in it that she'd placed on the bar. His arm stretched and almost touched her as he picked it up. 'You ate all this?'

Her senses engulfed anew with his scent, Keren could only wipe the residue of water from her lips and nod.

'You didn't save me any?'

She shook her head, screaming at herself to pull herself together.

He put the bowl back and stared down at her with an adopted woebegone expression. But the glint in his eyes was stronger, filling her with memories of all the times she'd seen that glint before. 'You really do hate me.'

'Told you,' she croaked.

'That was for our dessert tonight.'

She swallowed before speaking this time, and her words came out clearer. Stronger. 'You'll have to take my word for it that it was delicious.'

The glint only deepened. 'And you'll have to make it up to me.'

'Or you could just order whoever you got to nick my boat to bring it back. All your desserts will be safe then.'

This time he raised both brows. 'You would sabotage food?'

She bit her cheeks to stop the giggle that wanted to fly out.

Yannis had a sense of humour. Like his sexy smile, gorgeous face and fabulous body it was part of the Yannis package that had reeled her in like a trusting kipper.

He'd had the power to make her laugh and orgasm in tandem, and suddenly she was slapped with the memory of a time she'd paraded around in a sheer sarong with nothing underneath and when he'd tried to grab her, she'd run off, laughing at him, goading him to catch her. This was the place he'd caught her. This was the bar he'd lifted her onto and buried himself deep inside her while laughter was still alive on her tongue.

She tried to push the memory away, but it was too late to stop the burn deep in her pelvis the memory evoked, and it was all she could do to stop herself from squirming and giving herself away.

'If you won't bring my boat back, maybe think about putting a padlock on the kitchen doors. Who knows what will take my fancy next?' she said, relieved she was able to keep her tone light and airy.

'Has anyone taken your fancy on your travels?' he asked.

All her relief and the amusement it had been entwined with were cut stone dead. 'That is none of your business.'

He leaned his face closer to hers and, without a hint of humour, said, 'It is, *glyko mou*. You're my wife.'

He was so close his warm breath whispered against her skin.

She had nowhere to step back to. By backing herself against the bar, she'd effectively trapped herself.

Eyeballing him, she summoned all the strength and rationality she had left. 'Only on paper. And being your wife does not make me your possession.'

'Not my possession, no, but you will always belong to me.'

'Does Marla know you think that?' The PA's name left her lips before she was aware she was even going to utter it.

He reared back.

'Are you still with her?' she asked, snatching at the chance to goad him into backing off some more even though the vocalisation of that woman's name…

Keren had forgotten the power that name had to hurt her, like a burning knife being slashed through her heart.

'Nothing happened between me and Marla,' he bit back. 'I already told you that.'

'I'm on about *after* I left,' she clarified, wagging a finger at him. She had to keep talking and goading. She had to. Emotions that had nothing to do with desire were swelling inside her again and she feared the moment she stopped, the tears would fall. 'I do hope you're not still with her or with anyone else for that matter. Obviously, I know stealing my boat and forcing me to stay here is all one big malicious jest for you but, personally, I would hate to think my lover was playing games with *his* estranged wife or—'

A flash of rage contorted his handsome features at the same moment his arm wrapped around her waist and pulled her off her feet and onto her tiptoes to crush her against the solidity of his hard chest, her words dissolving into the firm contours of Yannis's mouth.

CHAPTER FOUR

YANNIS'S KISS WAS HARD. Brutal. And Keren's response was equally savage. Her hand grabbed his shoulder and her lips parted as their mouths fused in a heated clash of angry passion that deepened and darkened until their arms were tightly wound around each other and their bodies were pressed so tightly nothing could prise them apart.

Maybe, if the recent lancing memory of their laughter-filled frantic coupling at this very spot wasn't so fresh in her mind, Keren would have remained lost in the headiness of a desire that had sprung from nothing to something in the blink of an eye, but when she was lifted entirely off her feet and sat on the bar, panic replaced the hunger and she wrenched her face away and pushed at his chest.

'Get off me!'

He released her immediately and stepped back. He stared at her, breathing heavily, jaw tight, not blinking.

Terrified that her words didn't match the heated feelings rampaging through her, she slid off the bar and, legs too jellified to run, staggered to the side of the pool and threw herself in.

Submerged, the effect of the chill of the water on her

sun-soaked skin was immediate. It doused the flames of Yannis's kisses and sharpened her mind.

She'd fallen for another of his traps. She'd kissed him back. She'd betrayed herself and handed him a weapon she knew he wouldn't hesitate to use again.

It had been so long since they'd been intimate that her poor body had reacted like a moth to a flame.

How many nights had she lain awake willing him to roll over and make love to her?

How many times had she pressed herself against his back and slipped an arm around his waist only for his hand to clamp onto hers and stop any roaming? Sometimes he would bring her hand to his mouth and kiss it but more often than not he would lace his fingers through hers and fall asleep without a word.

In the end, she'd stopped trying. A woman could only take rejection so many times before she protected herself from it.

The glue that had bound them together had dissolved.

And then they'd dissolved.

And now he had the nerve to kiss her like his desire for her had never died.

Or had it been so long that she'd become a novelty to him again?

The sharpening of her mind dulled at the edges the moment she broke the surface and found him at the water's edge looking down at her and another rush of longing ripped through her.

Turning from his stare, she kicked her legs and swam the length of the professional-size pool. When she reached the end, she climbed up the steps then stepped on the grass and laid with a flump on her back.

Eyes closed, her heart thumped so hard it was difficult

to breathe but she put all her focus on it, inhaling deeply, exhaling, in and out, in and out.

She had no idea how long it took for her heart to steady into a mere erratic shudder of beats.

She could still feel Yannis's mouth against hers.

A shadow fell over her.

Her heart careered back into a canter.

Keeping her eyes shut, she whispered, 'Go away.'

The movement of air around her told her Yannis was ignoring her order and had sat beside her.

'I really do affect you still,' he said.

Hating that she couldn't deny it without proving herself a liar, Keren clamped her lips together. She couldn't decide if his tone was smug, triumphant or relieved.

He gave a low rumble of laughter. 'You're not denying it.'

'You forced yourself on me,' she said with as much coldness as she could inject.

'Look at my shoulder and tell me who did the forcing.'

She opened her eyes to find Yannis's face hovering over hers.

He gave a knowing smile and pointed a finger to a bronzed shoulder with vivid red lines on it. Scratches. Made by her nails.

Mortified, she closed her eyes again. 'Sorry,' she muttered.

'I'm not. I've missed receiving your war wounds.'

She scrambled up and hugged her knees to her chest, bitterness filling her to hear such a lie, colour flaming over her cheeks to know his burst of passion towards her was a lie too. 'If you kiss me again, I'll bite your tongue.'

'Kinky.'

'This isn't a joke, Yannis. We're not together any more and you—'

'Yes, we are.'

'No, we're—'

'We're legally husband and wife.'

'Not for much longer.'

'But I still have time. I am prepared to do anything to convince you to destroy those papers and come home for good.'

She pulled her soggy sandals off. 'How many times do I have to tell you that I'm not coming home?'

'And how many times do I have to tell you that I'm going to change your mind? You loved me once, *glyko mou*. We were happy.'

'That happiness didn't last long.'

'But you admit we *were* happy once,' he said, pouncing on that admission. 'There is nothing to stop us being happy again, and I have already proved that I still affect you...' His eyes sparkled before he bowed his head and pressed a kiss to her bare knee.

Before she could react, Yannis jumped to his feet and grinned. 'I have all the tools I need and three days with you as my captive to make you see our marriage deserves a second chance.'

'So you admit I'm your captive?'

His grin widened. 'Trust me—I'm a very generous captor.'

'Where are you going?' she shouted as he bounded away.

He turned and, walking backwards, said, 'Missing me already?'

She scowled.

He laughed. 'Wait there. I will be back in five minutes. Don't try to hide from me again, *glyko mou*… Not unless you *want* to be caught…'

Yannis returned carrying a pitcher of fruit cocktail and two glasses and with a blanket slung over his shoulder.

Placing the drinks on the floor tiles by the pool, he then spread the blanket out on the grass, reached into the back pocket of his swim-shorts and pulled out a blue bottle. 'Catch,' he said cheerfully, and lobbed it over to her.

Keren caught it with one hand. It was a bottle of sunscreen.

Feeling strangely choked, she examined it, recognising it as the brand and factor she'd always used when she lived here. She'd never realised Yannis had noticed.

He must have gone out of his way to buy it for her… Okay, get a member of staff to buy it for her. But the idea would have come from him.

She should be angry that he'd been so certain he'd be able to trap her here, not touched that he'd thought of such a small thing for her.

'Thank you,' she whispered.

A gleam flashed in his eyes. 'Do you need help putting it on?'

'No.'

'Sure? I would be more than happy to help.'

She just fixed him with a stare then squirted some of the sunscreen in her hands and smeared it over her face.

'I remember when you liked for me to cover you in that stuff.'

'Don't go there,' she warned.

'Why? Scared it will make you hot?'

'No, scared it will make me vomit.'

He laughed. 'You are such a liar.' He patted the space

of the blanket next to him. 'This is more comfortable than lying on the grass.'

'My shorts are wet. I've got nothing to change into,' she added accusingly, only just realising. 'I'm going to be stuck in these things all weekend.'

'My wardrobe is at your disposal...just as it always was.'

She turned her face from him and wished she had her sunglasses. Yannis was too good at reading her. He was good at everything. But reading her, he was a pro. And she hated that. At least her sunglasses would give her a shield to hide behind and then he wouldn't be able to see the pain that lanced her whenever he casually referred to a time when they had been happy. Happy enough for Keren to steal his shirts and T-shirts to roam the villa and grounds in.

'If you don't want to wear my clothes then I suppose you'll just have to wear your own,' he said with a heavy, disappointed sigh.

'My own clothes are on my boat. You know, the boat you stole.'

'But the clothes you left behind are still here.'

She turned her stare sharply back to him. 'Seriously?'

His face was unreadable. 'In your dressing room exactly where you left them.'

'Why are they still there?'

'They've been waiting for you to return.'

'I don't believe you.'

He shrugged and poured them both a glass of the fruit cocktail. 'You will be able to see for yourself. For now, come and sit on the blanket before the bugs bite your skin.'

Damn him for knowing the exact thing to say, and it

was a measure of how affected she was at being here, with Yannis, in this situation, that Keren had laid herself on the grass and was still sat there with no thought of the pesky bugs she hated. But now she was thinking of them and plonked herself on the blanket but as far from him as she could get.

It wasn't far enough.

He passed a glass to her.

Taking care not to let their fingers touch, she took it from him and had a large drink.

'Wow, that's strong!' she gasped when her taste buds registered the unexpected hit of alcohol.

He grinned. 'I thought you needed something to loosen you up.'

'Returning my boat would do that far more effectively.'

The look in his eyes liquidised her bones. 'The next time you mention having your boat returned, I'm going to kiss you.'

'I've already told you—kiss me again and I'll bite your tongue.'

He stretched his huge form out and propped himself on an elbow facing her. 'I will. I will kiss you…' Eyes not leaving her face, he pressed his index finger against his lips then gently placed it to her mouth. '…like this.'

His touch was feather-light, but it was enough to send sensation dancing over her skin and turn her liquidised bones into lava.

'Yannis…' Her breath caught in her throat.

A glint came into his stare as he moved his finger from her mouth and kissed it back against his own lips.

Keren was helpless to stop the tremor that shot through her, and when his gaze drifted down to her breasts she was suddenly certain her breathy voice wasn't the only giveaway of the effect he was having on her.

His eyes flickered back to her face.

'Did you ever think how well our mouths fit together?' he murmured.

'No,' she lied.

'I did. Many times. And the next time they fit together you will be the one to start it.'

'Keep dreaming.'

'I never stopped dreaming of you, *glyko mou*, and now you are here, just like in my dreams.' His face moved an inch closer to her. 'You are here with me so stop fighting and relax.'

Impossible. 'I can't relax around you.'

'I can give you a massage if that would help?'

She swallowed the moisture that filled her mouth at the mere suggestion.

If Yannis touched her again she feared it would be more than just her bones liquidising.

How could her desire for him still exist? Not just exist but be so strong?

It should be dead. She'd thought it was dead. Thought all her feelings for him were dead.

'Oh...pack it in,' she muttered.

He grinned.

Keren found her lips curving in return and turned away. Seeing him smile, feeling her defences lower while the effects of his kiss and now the light touch of his finger still thrummed through her, and her skin and her lips still tingled...

She needed to escape him. But there was nowhere to go. He would take it as a challenge.

Not unless you want *to be caught...*

He'd remembered that time she'd enticed him into chasing her around the pool too. She was certain of it. And now she remembered all the other times she'd challenged and goaded him. How she'd quivered with excitement and desire when he'd stalked towards her like a panther ready to devour its prey.

There had been times, too, when she'd been the panther.

Hunter or prey, the end result had always been the same. Ecstasy.

'I don't suppose you've got any spare sunglasses, have you?' she asked abruptly, hugging her knees tightly to her chest, as if turning herself into a ball could compress the burning throbs deepening within her. If she couldn't escape for some space then she could engineer it for him to leave. And she did need sunglasses, so two birds, one stone. 'Only, mine are on my boat. You know, the one you stole.'

'What did I just say about your boat?'

'Nothing about me not being able to mention you stealing it.'

He leaned his face even closer to hers and gave another bone-liquidising stare. 'Next time you mention me stealing your boat...' His brow rose in sensuous promise.

Her pelvis pulsed so deeply she could barely speak through the delicious agony of it to say, 'Have you got any sunglasses or not?'

He held her stare a tantalising moment longer before jumping to his feet. 'Give me two minutes.'

Keren couldn't help herself from watching him stride back to the villa. Yannis had always been as sexy from behind as from the front and it pained her to feel the old swell in her chest at the rampant masculinity of his form.

And it pained her to see him being like this, like the Yannis she'd fallen in love with. A man with a buoyant energy and a ready gleam in his eye, a man who always, *always*, concerned himself with her needs. And her pleasure.

She had another large drink of the cocktail and closed her eyes as she swallowed.

When had she lost that man?

The fault lines in their marriage had been gradual. Keren had discovered she was pregnant a month after their honeymoon and the excitement of it all had papered over her disquiet at Yannis's growing possessiveness. It was a trait that exploded after they'd lost Sophia. He'd pulled away from her emotionally but his possessiveness had mushroomed. He'd wanted to control her.

For all that, she never would have believed the fun, charming man who'd swept her off her feet and sworn to love her for ever would turn into a merciless, vindictive bastard. And now he was being merciless in his pretence of wanting her back.

By the time he returned she'd finished her first glass of cocktail but any looseness she might have gained from the alcohol in it tightened again when he sat next to her and handed over the sunglasses.

They were her old ones.

Heart thumping, she looked from them to him.

Had he really kept her stuff here? She'd assumed he was making a joke at her expense and that when she finally looked in her old dressing room, she'd find shrouds or something in there.

She needed to look.

Clambering to her feet, she said, 'My stuff's still in my dressing room?'

'Yes.'

'I want to see.'

'This is your home, *glyko mou*. You don't need my permission to go in.'

Finding herself trapped in his stare, finding her heart swelling, she wrenched her gaze from him and set off to the beautiful villa that had started out as her home but morphed into a cage.

Keren's grip tightened on the banister when she reached the top of the stairs.

She took a deep breath and chided herself for being a big baby and letting a surge of memories make her hesitant.

Good memories. Bad memories. Heartbreaking memories.

Their bedroom was at the end of the wide corridor to the left of the stairs. To reach it, she had to pass the room they'd had decorated a muted yet vibrant yellow. Keren had spent three whole days hand-painting tropical flowers from countries she'd been excited to one day explore with their child onto the walls. Yannis had gone to an evaluation in Paris and surprised her by bringing back the most adorable newborn baby outfit and hanging it in the nursery wardrobe. Keren hadn't wanted to know the sex of their baby—she'd wanted it to be a surprise—but Yannis had known without having to ask. He'd been so certain they were having a little girl.

Placing her hand on the closed nursery door, she breathed slowly until the sharp pain in her chest lessened into an acute ache and the scream of the banshee in her head was muted.

'Do you think about her when you're at sea?' Yannis, who'd followed her up the stairs, asked quietly.

'All the time.' She took another long, slow inhalation, then continued to their bedroom and pushed the door open, not allowing hesitancy to grip her.

Nothing had changed.

The emperor bed with its hand-carved legs and matching hand-carved headboard had the same cream and mint-green bedsheets, the mint-green curtains tied back from the three sash windows were the same, as was the cream flooring. The artwork was the same. Everything the same. She could have climbed out of that bed that morning.

It was the same in the bathroom. The his-and-hers sinks. The huge double walk-in shower. The mammoth rolltop bath. Even the toiletries were the same, and she found her heart expanding as her eyes were drawn to the bottle of bubble bath.

They'd honeymooned in a private villa in the Maldives. Keren had fallen in love with the bubble bath and shower gel their bathroom had been supplied with. It smelled like pure fresh jasmine. When they'd returned home to Agon, Yannis had surprised her with a delivery of it. He'd gone out of his way to source it and import it, just for her. Every time she'd run low, he'd noticed and ordered more for her. She'd never had to ask.

A wave of sadness washed over her and she closed her eyes to ride through it before stepping into her dressing room.

The room had a wide central walkway splitting two walls of built-in floor-to-ceiling wardrobes. She slid the first door open.

When Keren had left, she'd packed two suitcases of

clothes and possessions to take with her. The rest, much of it never worn, she'd left.

The more she slid the wardrobe doors and pulled the drawers open, the more she realised it was exactly as she had left it. Exactly. Nothing had been moved.

Bewildered, she looked at Yannis, who was stood leant against a wardrobe by the door. 'Why have you kept all this?'

He folded his arms loosely around his chest. 'I told you, they've been waiting for your return.'

'I assumed you'd had a bonfire with them or something.'

A smile played on his lips. 'The thought did cross my mind on occasion.'

'So what stopped you? It's not as if you ever liked any of my clothes.'

'What are you talking about?'

'Yannis, you hated the way I dressed.'

A deep groove formed in his brow. The pulse on his jaw just below his earlobe throbbed. 'I loved the way you dressed. You always looked beautiful.'

'Every time we left the villa, you would check me over like I was some kind of prize pony about to enter its first dressage competition. You were always critical of what I wore.'

'I was never critical.'

'"*Do you not think that colour is a little gaudy for the palace, glyko mou?*"' she mimicked. 'If that's not a criticism then please, tell me what is.'

He stared at her for the longest time, breathing deeply. 'I was trying to help you.'

She laughed without mirth. 'Help me? Is that what you call it?'

The pulse in his jaw was going like the clappers. 'Don't you remember how upset you were when I introduced you to my parents, and my mother called your dress *interesting*?'

As if she was likely to forget that.

Keren had been incredibly nervous about meeting Yannis's parents. She'd met his brother, Andreas, and his husband, Pavlos, within days of her and Yannis getting together and they'd been friendly and welcoming, but his parents had been on a world cruise and she'd had to wait four months to meet them. By then, she and Yannis were engaged and their wedding preparations in full swing.

She'd chosen her dress for the occasion with great care. It had been vibrant red with Chinese flowers embroidered on it, a maxi-dress that actually suited her short frame.

Nina Filipidis, resplendently power-dressed from top to tail in designer fashion, had embraced her warmly enough then stepped back and, holding Keren's hands, looked her up and down. 'What an interesting dress,' she'd said in the tone of someone who'd just been presented with the most diabolical painting by a small child. Later, to add insult to injury, Nina had slipped her a business card with her personal shopper's details on it so that Keren, 'Could have some help refreshing your wardrobe.'

'You rightly interpreted that as her calling your dress horrible,' Yannis continued. 'She didn't say it to hurt you, that's just her way and it's what Agon high society as a whole is like, but you were hurt and I didn't want to see you upset like that again. That's why I occasionally commented on your choice of clothing if we were attending a high-profile function and I thought what you were wearing might raise eyebrows. I wanted you to feel comfortable in my world and that you belonged.'

'You mean you wanted me to conform in my clothing in the same way you expected me to conform with everything else in your world,' she disputed, doing her best to keep control of the emotions rising inside her.

'I never expected you to conform.' His face was so taut she could see the veins at his temples. 'I knew who I was marrying but it was my job as your husband to protect you and help you navigate my world.'

'No, it wasn't. Your job was to love and support me but you…' Something inside her snapped and she shoved the drawer she'd had her hand on the entire conversation shut. 'Oh, forget it. I'm not going to waste my breath on old arguments that never get resolved.'

This was too much. Emotions she'd believed dead were rising sickeningly fast. She needed to be away from Yannis. She needed air.

She hurried to the door, only just managing to stop before she collided into him when he stepped in front of her.

Taking a hasty step back, she gritted her teeth. 'Will you please let me pass.'

'No. Because we *are* going to have these arguments again, and this time we're going to resolve them.' To make his point, Yannis turned the key in the lock then put it in his back pocket, physically blocking her exit for good measure.

CHAPTER FIVE

KEREN SWALLOWED BACK the rising panic. 'Move away from the door, Yannis.'

'No.' He folded his arms around his chest. 'I'm not letting you run away again.'

'Let me out!'

'We're not going anywhere until we've thrashed this out.'

'You can't keep me prisoner!'

'If you want to leave, the key's in my pocket. Help yourself to it.'

'I will never touch you again,' she spat.

'Then sit down and talk to me.'

'This is ridiculous.'

'I agree. But we are still doing it. We're going to discuss all our grievances, like we should have done a long time ago.'

'If you have *grievances* against me then why in hell would you want me back? You're better off without me. You can't turn a macaw into a zebra finch. Your mother knew that from the moment she laid eyes on me. Go and get yourself a high-society Agonite bride and make everyone happy.'

'If I'd wanted an Agonite wife I would have married one and not an outsider.'

'Then why did you spend our marriage trying to change me into one?'

'I tried to help you adapt to my world. There is a big difference.'

She laughed grimly. 'Being an outsider is no big deal for me, Yannis. I've *always* been an outsider, you know that. My parents and sister have been baffled by me since I learned to talk but they still loved me and tried their best to understand me, but you just pretended to understand. You married me knowing I wouldn't be the kind of wife your family and Agon high society is used to. You told me you loved me exactly as I am but then as soon as your ring was on my finger, you tried to mould me into being an identikit high-society wife. I spent the first eighteen years of my life dreaming about the day I could break free from the straitjacket of my world and ended up with you trying to shoehorn me into a different kind of one.'

The pulse in his jaw set off again. 'Is that the excuse you tell yourself for running away from me?'

'It's not an excuse.'

'Yes, it is,' he disputed unwaveringly. 'And you know it too.'

'You are so ruddy arrogant, thinking you know my mind better than I do.'

'If it's arrogance then why are you crying?'

She'd hardly been aware of the hot tears splashing over her cheeks and, horrified to be crying in front of him, swiped them away violently. 'Because I'm *angry*.'

At least, that's what she thought it was frothing with such intensity inside her. Anger. But there was pain in there too. And fear. And the harder she tried to smother them, the harder they fought back and refused to be doused.

His chin jutted. 'Good.'

'My God, are you *trying* to make me angry?'

'I'm trying to make you open up and show some damn emotion. You bottle things up.'

'We spent the last few months of our marriage doing nothing but argue, so that was hardly bottling things up.'

'Arguing about everything but what really mattered to mask what we were really feeling. I was guilty of it too, but I'm not the one who ran away before we could resolve things.'

Fresh panic nibbled at her chest. 'You threw my suitcases in the back of the taxi! You called me a selfish cow!'

'Because I was angry, damn it!'

'Angry that I got there first, you mean. You wanted us to be over as much as I did.'

'Absolutely not. When I made our vows, I made them for life, not for fourteen months. I told you when we married, not one single Filipidis marriage has ended in divorce. Not ever.'

Sickened, remembering his search history, she shook her head in disbelief.

Yannis dragged his fingers over his face. 'You married into the Filipidis family, Keren. I didn't let you marry me blind. I did love you as you are, and I didn't want to change you, but you knew there would be expectations of you as my wife.'

Hearing his love for her in the past tense should not feel like a rip in her heart. It should not make her voice tremulous. 'Yes, to attend functions, host dinner parties, smile pleasantly and not say anything controversial.'

'Image is important to our business and to the family name,' he said, the steadiness of his tone belied by the pulse still throbbing madly on his jaw. 'You knew this. You knew this would be part of our marriage. You always knew the business would have to be a priority. It's been in the family since—'

'Time began,' she finished for him. Suddenly weary, Keren dragged her legs to the end of the room and sank onto her dressing table chair.

The Filipidises had traded in antiquities and fine art for so long the dates around the actual founding of the business were hazy. Best estimates were mid-sixteenth century, solid records established by the late sixteenth century. They had bought and sold items adorned by palaces and embassies the world over. Their monthly auctions regularly made international headlines.

'Whereas I just had a silly little blog.'

'I never called it that.'

'You thought it was insignificant.'

'In comparison, yes, and you admitted as much too but I always supported you with it.'

'Liar. You hated me running it.'

'No, *glyko mou*, I *did* support it in the beginning, as much as I could, because I knew how much it meant to you. You travelled with me on business, right from the time we got together, long before we married. You came on my overseas trips and went off exploring while I was in meetings…' He stopped mid-speech and inhaled deeply. 'But you lost interest in your blog long before you had to stop flying.'

'That's because we only ever travelled to boring cities. You promised we would see new places. I like travelling to new places, going off the beaten track, seeing things I've never seen before, new experiences...'

'We never had the chance to go to the new places I'd promised, but that wasn't why you lost interest in it,' he refuted calmly but tightly. 'You lost interest because we had something wonderful and amazing to look forward to but that something amazing and wonderful was taken from us...'

She wanted to cover her ears and scream to drown out his voice.

'...and when you started your blog up again, you did it without any consultation with me. You announced it over the dinner table, just casually mentioned you were flying to Morocco for a long weekend and then went mad when I objected.'

She swallowed hard and whispered, 'You had no right to object. You're not my lord and master. I didn't need your permission.'

'I never said you did but as your husband, I had every right to object.' He gritted his teeth and took an enormous breath. 'I never did anything without consulting you first—'

'Telling is not the same as consulting.'

'And you once consulted me over everything too,' he continued as if she hadn't just interrupted him. 'We discussed things. Like grown-ups.'

'You stopped treating me like a grown-up and started treating me like a possession. You criticised every little thing I did. You didn't want me doing anything. I *went mad* when you objected to me going to Morocco because I knew it was more than an objection. You didn't want me working.'

'You're right. I didn't.'

'I knew it! You wanted me to be a kept woman.'

'No, I wanted you home and safe.'

'Home and safe and under your thumb and under your control. Easier to watch over.'

'Yes.'

Unprepared for this admission, she stared at him. 'You *admit* it?'

His gaze didn't falter. 'Yes.'

Dumbfounded, her mind a sudden blank canvas, Keren stared at the man she'd once loved so much she'd been unable to envisage her life without him, and was scrambling for a coherent thought when the buzzer in their bedro Yannis grimaced and closed his eyes, and muttered something that sounded like a curse. 'I need to answer that.'

Still unable to speak, she nodded.

The buzzer that had rung out was part of a system installed in every room of the villa, used only in the event of an emergency if Yannis was uncontactable by any other means. It was the communications of last resort.

He pulled the key out of his back pocket and unlocked the door. 'This conversation isn't finished,' he warned.

And then he was gone.

Alone, Keren buried her head in her hands and fought back tears. Twice today she'd cried. They'd leaked out all by themselves and she didn't know why or where they'd come from. What frightened her the most was that she'd cried in front of Yannis. She'd cried with him the day they'd lost Sophia but then the tears had dried up, sucked away and swallowed into the giant crevice of pain in her heart. So many times she had caught him watching her.

It had felt almost that he was *willing* her to break down and cry. She'd been unable to.

She'd accused Yannis of wanting to police her every move many times and he'd always denied it. And now that he'd finally admitted it…

There was an irony that she'd spent the entire time Yannis had locked her in the dressing room wanting to do nothing but escape from him but now he'd left, she wanted nothing more than to drag him back and demand the answers her shattered brain had been unable to form.

She hadn't wanted any of this. She would have been happy to live the rest of her life without this conversation and without ever setting eyes on Yannis again. Why rake coals over the past and rip open old wounds just for the sake of it?

Raising her head, her eye was drawn to the beautiful frœ uitwood jewellery box that had pride of place on her dressing table. Yannis had bought it for her on their first wedding anniversary to home all the jewellery he'd lavished her with. Its lid was inlaid with a carving of their entwined wedding rings. On it, in the centre of the carving, were her real-life wedding and engagement rings. The last time she'd seen them had been when she'd left them on his dresser right before she'd walked out of their room for what she'd believed to be the last time.

She stared at the rings for an age before carefully picking them up and placing them in the palm of her trembling hand.

The wedding ring was a simple gold band with their initials and their wedding date delicately inscribed on the inside. Yannis had a matching one, and her heart lurched violently as she finally allowed herself to acknowledge that he still wore his, a fact she'd refused to let her mind travel to until now.

Had he kept it on for the entirety of their separation? Or had he put it back on today for effect?

Her engagement ring was an entirely different kettle of fish. It was a family heirloom, originally commissioned in the eighteenth century by Alexios Filipidis for his bride, the Agon Princess Theodora. The ring had been passed to Yannis on his paternal grandmother's death. When he'd slid the ring on Keren's finger she'd been overawed to think she was the possessor of a ring originally worn by a royal princess. She'd been overawed at the weight of history on her finger.

It had been the only moment prior to their marriage when doubt had reared its head over whether she was doing the right thing.

In that respect, Yannis was right. She *had* known what she was marrying into. An old and noble family. And she remembered, too, him telling her there had never been a Filipidis divorce.

There had never been a Burridge divorce that she was aware of either, but she'd always assumed that was because the rest of her clan were like her immediate family. Terrified of change. You married and you took the good with the bad and got on with it. But there was rarely good and bad in their lives because they thrived too much on the mundane. The same meal plan every week. Pork chops on Monday. Spag Bol—literally the most exotic meal on the menu—on Wednesdays. Sunday roast with alternating extending members of the family. One week the maternal grandparents, the next the paternal grandparents. Aunts, uncles and cousins often joined them too. It was the same pattern for Christmas. New Year's

Eve was always spent at the dining table playing cards for pennies, the New Year seen in with a small glass of champagne, a kiss on each other's cheek and then bed.

Keren had spent her first New Year away from her family in Australia on Bondi Beach with a group of girls she'd befriended. She'd had the time of her life. She'd video called her family soon after midnight, remembered their slightly bemused, dazed expressions when she'd flipped the camera of her phone so they could share the experience in some small way. She'd blown them kisses goodbye knowing perfectly well that when the UK came to see the New Year in some ten hours later, that they would be enacting the same routine they always enacted and probably wondering, again, whether their youngest daughter had been switched at birth. If she didn't have her kind father's jaw and colouring and her sweet mother's nose and height, they would probably have done a DNA test to check.

If she didn't fit in with the people who'd loved and raised her, the very people who'd created her, how could she have thought she'd be able to fit in with Yannis and his family?

She'd assumed love would be enough. She'd assumed that so long as she gave Yannis all the support he needed then he would support her too. She'd never dreamed he would try to clip her wings.

He had tried to clip her wings. He *had*. He'd wanted her to give up her freedom and submit to being nothing but a high-society Agonite wife while he lived his life as he pleased.

So why was there a voice in her head telling her it was more complicated than that?

It was being here, in her marital home, causing that

voice to pipe up. Being here and soaked in the memories of a marriage that had begun with such high hopes and disintegrated into nothing.

Yannis had fallen out of love with her. She'd known that even before he'd confirmed it when he'd described his love for her in the past tense.

But she was now certain that he did want her back. This wasn't an elaborate jest of revenge. He wanted her back for his pride. Yannis didn't want to go down in the annuls of history as the first Filipidis to divorce. The first Filipidis failure.

What she didn't understand was why this truth made her heart hurt so much.

Keren knocked lightly then pushed the study door open and poked her head around it. Yannis was in there talking on the phone.

His eyes locked onto hers. The strangest expression formed on his face before it fell back into its natural pose and he indicated for her to enter.

Curling onto the leather corner sofa, she waited for him to finish. Her Greek had never advanced enough for her to understand his language but she could tell by his body language that something bad had happened.

Whatever he was having to deal with, his stare didn't leave her face. And her stare didn't leave his. The beats of her heart drummed painfully in the growing expansion of her chest as she found herself flooded by memories of their lovemaking in this room. Yannis worked from home whenever he could but had always welcomed her interrupting him, would abandon whatever he was working on to pull her onto his lap and kiss her as if he hadn't seen her in months rather than a few hours.

But that had been in the days before he'd become secretive and had greeted her by immediately closing the lid of his laptop to hide whatever he was doing on it. The days before he'd lost interest in her as a woman and a lover. The days before he'd started seeing her only as his wife and possession.

Yet she remembered so vividly how it had felt in those wonderful intoxicating early days. The heat that had burned constantly through her veins. The sensitivity of her skin. The constant ache deep inside her. The incessant longing for him.

She was feeling it all in her now. The longer she looked at him, the greater her yearn to be pulled onto his lap and have his strong arms wrap around her and be crushed into the solid warmth of his body.

Was Yannis thinking of those earlier days too? Was he remembering how intoxicated they'd been with each other? Was he, at this moment, experiencing the same heavy ache of longing in his blood?

She wrapped her arms tighter around her chest and tried to will it all away. Tried to wrench her gaze away.

These feelings were supposed to be dead.

When Yannis's call was done with, he put his phone on his desk facedown and kneaded his forehead.

The urge to wrap her arms around him was almost unbearable, and she wrapped them even tighter around herself.

His stare entwined with hers again. His chest rose slowly.

She swallowed. 'What's happened?'

His lips curved into a faint smile before he gave a heavy sigh. 'Just a work problem.'

'Want to tell me about it?'

A groove appeared in his brow. 'Do you want to hear it?'

If he'd posed it as a challenge it might have been enough to cut through the weighty ache of the past and of awareness cloaking her. But there was just enough disbelief in his tone for it to not come across as challenging.

She nodded. 'Tell me.'

He leaned back in his chair and linked his fingers together. 'Have you heard of Phillipe Legarde?'

'No.'

'French billionaire? Founded the Legarde fashion house?'

'Oh, right, yes, I've heard of Legarde. Your mum wears a lot of their clothes, doesn't she?'

'Yes. Phillipe Legarde died a few years ago. His family are auctioning much of his art collection to pay for death duties.' His eyebrow quirked.

'They're cashing in on his death?' she guessed.

'They're selling what I would guess will bring in at least ten times what any death duties will be. There's a Rembrandt and two Rodins in the collection, along with nineteen other pieces. We're talking hundreds of millions. Probably more.'

Once, those kinds of numbers would have made her head explode.

'Let me guess, they're playing you off with Hoults?' Hoults was Filipidis Fine Art & Antiquities' biggest rivals.

He inclined his head. 'In one. I've been working on this for months. We've gone through the authentication process for all the pieces, valuations...you know how it goes.'

She hesitated before nodding. Usually Yannis insisted the contracts be signed before any of this was done.

Clearly reading her mind, he grimaced. 'There have been delays with the signing of the contract. I admit, I took my eye off the ball.'

'That's not like you.'

He shrugged but his handsome features were tight. 'Jeanie Legarde, Phillipe's sister and heir, has notified us that unless we lower our commission, she'll be going to Hoults.'

'What a cow.'

His full lips loosened and he gave a short laugh. 'Almost exactly what I was thinking.'

'You're not going to agree, are you?' Yannis and his brother had never, to her knowledge, compromised on their fees. Their expertise, vast wealth of knowledge and the Filipidis reputation dating back centuries more than justified them.

'No. But Jeanie Legarde is a problem for me to discuss with Andreas and to think over. Right now, I am more interested in knowing if you joined me here because you were missing me.'

His change of subject was so sudden and provocative that it caught Keren unawares and it took her a few moments to pull a retort together.

'You wish.' She could have slapped herself for the lameness and childishness of her riposte.

His blue eyes glittered. 'Indeed I do.'

She sank deeper into the sofa wishing she could disappear inside its richly textured confines. 'I was looking for you only because I wanted to finish our conversation.'

'A change of heart, *glyko mou*?'

'Only in the respect that I'm curious as to how you

can possibly think I'll ever come back to you when you openly admit that you want me under your thumb and under your control.'

The glimmer in his eyes deepened. 'You are thinking of coming back to me?'

She rolled her eyes. 'Get real.'

He leaned forward and put his elbows on the desk. 'What if I were to tell you that I never wanted you under my control—under my thumb, yes, because you certainly had me under yours. Under me…even better—but that I wanted you where I could keep an eye on you for reasons that were nothing to do with me being a control freak?'

The immediate slice of knives in her heart and the tight pull in her stomach stifled her vocal cords into a whisper. 'Then I would call you a liar.'

The glimmer had faded away. 'You wouldn't be curious what those reasons were?'

'The only vaguely reasonable excuse I can think of is a kidnap threat.'

'I would have increased our security and your bodyguard detail if that had happened.'

'That's why I called it only a vaguely reasonable excuse.'

'You know my reasons. You've always known. It's why you ran from me.'

'I left because I needed my freedom from the cage you put me in. There is no reason, no excuse in the world, to treat a fully grown woman as a rebellious child.'

The pulse on his tightened jaw was going again, the expression in his eyes slicing through her as much as his words had.

After it felt like an age had passed in thick, heavy silence, Yannis finally gave a sharp jerk of his head. 'You are right.'

She blinked. 'Sorry?'

'You are right. There is no excuse. But my reasons...' His shoulders rose. His strong throat moved.

Keren held her breath.

'I don't want to put you in a cage. I never wanted to. I just want you to come home. Where you belong.'

'I never belonged,' she refuted with a whisper.

His head tilted and he breathed heavily. 'You always belonged with me.' And then he smiled and rose gracefully to his feet. In a lighter tone, he said, 'And it is my promise to you that on Monday morning, you will believe that too.'

She closed her eyes. 'Yannis... Please... Don't. It's impossible.'

'Nothing is impossible, *glyko mou*. *You* taught me that.'

CHAPTER SIX

KEREN SAT WITH her feet in the swimming pool flicking her toes and watching the ripples they made. Yannis had needed to call his brother and tell him the news about the Legardes, so she'd grabbed the opportunity to escape him for a short while and left him to it.

All she'd done in that short while was think about him.

The sun was losing its brilliance. Afternoon was blurring with evening and her emotions were blurring with them. In one short day, the certainties she'd carried for so long had become muddled. Confused.

Footsteps sounded on the terrace. She didn't need to turn her head to know it was Yannis. The racing of her pulse told her. That was one certainty that wasn't muddled or blurred: her all-consuming awareness of him.

His shadow fell on her. 'I have run you a bath.'

She turned her face up to him. 'You have?'

That was another of the small things he'd liked to do for her before things had turned to dust between them. Run her evening bath.

His lips tugged at the corners and he extended a hand to her. 'I have to earn my gold stars where I can.'

Lifting her feet out of the pool she twisted round, then hesitated before raising her hand to his. The thuds of her heart were so strong the echoes vibrated through her bones.

When he wrapped his fingers around hers, warmth suffused her already sun-kissed skin, and then she was being gently helped to her feet.

Upright, she found herself trapped in a stare filled with so many emotions that, for the beat of a moment, a spasm of pain slashed through her at what she found in it.

And then he blinked and the moment was gone.

Mouth curving, Yannis bowed his head and kissed the back of her hand. The connection of his lips to her skin was fleeting but the heat that flooded her was as strong and as immediate as when he'd kissed her mouth.

And then he released her hand.

Keren fell into step with him and, unthinking, traced her fingers over the burning mark his lips had made. Huge butterflies were flapping their wings in her stomach and it was taking everything she had to move one foot in front of the other.

'How did it go with Andreas?' she asked as they walked into the villa.

'Better than it would have gone if he'd been the one to screw up.'

She smiled. Andreas had a much calmer nature than Yannis. Where Yannis was the fire in the business, Andreas was the soothing balm. Despite their differences, or maybe because of them, they were as close as brothers could be and both utterly dedicated to the business.

'Have you decided on an action plan?'

'Jeanie is attending our parents' function tomorrow night. Andreas is going to speak to her then.'

'And if that doesn't work?' Andreas took care of the art side of the business, was the one to arrange authenticity of their pieces and deal with valuations and catalogues. Yannis dealt with the clients and the pure business aspects: the contracts, shipping and finances. Dealing with a client in this kind of situation—although this specific situation was not one Keren had known of before—was something the brothers usually handled together with a combination of charm offensive and the arrogant certainty that their firm was undisputedly the best.

Yannis stopped walking. They'd reached the bottom of the stairs.

His smile was faint but his eyes gleamed as he traced a finger over the rim of her ear. 'We will cross that bridge if and when we come to it but I'm not going to give it any headspace until then. You are here and my only concern this weekend is doing everything I can to convince you that here is where you want to stay. Now come—your bath will be getting cold.'

Her ear tingling, Keren followed him up the stairs with a chest that felt like a balloon had inflated in it. More emotions filled it when she stepped into their bedroom and into the sweet scent of jasmine.

Helpless to stop her eyes from falling onto him, she had to tighten every sinew in her body to stop the balloon deflating and all the emotions pouring out.

She wanted him to touch her again. She wanted to touch him.

And then she remembered the long, long months of sleeping with his back turned to her. The pain of his rejection hadn't stopped her longing. Nothing had stopped her longing for him.

The longing for him was the one thing in their marriage that had never died. Even when she'd hated him, she'd never stopped wanting him. That want, that *need*, had been as essential to her as water. To no longer feel it reciprocated from him, to feel him slipping away from her, had tasted like poison. Because that need had, for a long time, been all Keren had been capable of feeling, and Yannis hadn't been able to return it because, for him, the desire had died. She'd stopped being his lover and confidante. Pillow talk no longer existed.

But she saw that old desire now. When he looked at her, she could feel him stripping her with his eyes, and it would be so easy to take the three steps to him and wind her arms around his neck, pull herself onto her toes and kiss him, and lose herself in the magic of his lovemaking.

It was the price she would have to pay for it that frightened her.

'I'm going to get a drink. Can I get you anything?' he asked.

She swallowed and raised her chin to smile. 'No, thank you.'

He waved a hand towards the bathroom door. 'Enjoy your bath.'

When he closed the bedroom door, her mouth opened and she only just stopped herself from calling him back. She didn't even know what she would have said to him.

Taking a deep breath in an attempt to pull herself together, Keren stepped into the bathroom. For the first time she noticed her robe hung on the back of the door. She pinched it with her fingers then dipped her nose into the silk and inhaled. It smelled of nothing. It smelled as if it had been hung on this door for eighteen months waiting for her to come home.

Stop it, she chided herself. Yannis's words had clearly rooted a little too deeply. Just because he said them did not make them true.

She stripped her clothes and popped them in the laundry chute. About to step into the bath, she suddenly found herself transfixed by her naked reflection in the walled mirror.

It was the first time she'd seen herself nude in eighteen months.

Dazed, she stepped closer, hardly able to comprehend the changes that had occurred. She'd always been petite but curvy. Her curves had reduced. Her stomach and thighs were toned in a way she'd never have imagined them capable of being. Eighteen months of sailing, fifteen of which had been single-handed, had toned her up and tanned her skin to a healthy golden hue. But her face was gaunter than the tiny mirror in her boat's tiny bathroom had let her believe, and as she registered this, tears pooled into her dark brown eyes.

She closed them shut and concentrated on breathing until the moment passed, then took one last look at her reflection and mustered a smile to acknowledge that at least her breasts hadn't changed.

Stepping into the deep bath, she slowly lowered herself into the frothy scented water and sighed with pleasure. Yannis had judged the water temperature perfectly.

Baths were one of the few things she'd missed from life on land. *The Sophia*'s shower trickled water out, which had never bothered her, just made her, on occasion, wistful.

The bathroom door opened and Yannis walked in carrying a glass of white wine.

'Oi!' she shouted. Well, tried to shout. It came out more like a squeak. 'You can't just barge in.' She automatically flung her arms across her breasts and a hand to her pubis even though the bath was almost as deep with bubbles as water.

He placed the glass on the drinks' ledge beside her and leaned over. Dazzling blue eyes rested barely inches from hers. 'Of course I can.' Then he flashed the most wicked of grins, so wicked it made her bones melt and her pelvis squirm, and straightened. 'Wine for my beautiful wife.'

'I'm not... What are you doing?'

Yannis was pulling his T-shirt up his chest. He winked before tugging it over his head. 'Taking a shower.'

'But...' All the breath had been knocked out of her. 'You can't.'

'Why not?'

'I'm having a bath.'

His brows quirked devilishly. 'You want me to join you?'

'No.'

'You're sure?'

'Very sure.' She had to force her voice to sound as certain as her words because memories were flooding her of all the times they'd shared this bath. Joyous, happy memories. 'Whatever happened to privacy?'

He put his hands to the waistband of his shorts. 'If you'd wanted privacy, you would have locked the door.'

Before she could come up with the outraged denial his comment deserved, Yannis yanked his shorts down and stepped out of them with a nonchalance that took her breath away almost as much as seeing him naked for the first time in two years did.

Then, with that same nonchalance, he crossed the bathroom to the huge walk-in shower.

Water drenched his gorgeous body and now Keren found herself flooded with memories of all the times they'd showered together. Those memories were a lot headier than the bath memories. The bath had always been a more fun, sensual experience—sharing a bottle of wine, teasing each other, flicking bubbles at each other, slyly groping each other. In the shower, they had been rampant and now, awash with memories and with the man she'd made those glorious memories with studiously ignoring her as he lathered himself, the burning ache intensified. Every inch of her skin tingled with the wish that the weight of water be replaced by the weight of Yannis.

And then he looked at her and caught her staring at him.

Her throat closed as mortified heat suffused her. A different kind of heat filled her when she wrenched her stare from his face and realised he was sporting a huge erection.

Her frustration reaching fever-pitch, she pinched her nose and slid her head and face under the water. Only when her lungs screamed at her did she come up for air.

Yannis was crouched beside the bath. A knowing smile played on his lips. 'For a moment there, I thought I was going to have to give you the kiss of life.'

Without thinking, Keren flicked bubbles and water at him.

Long fingers wrapped around her wrist. Blue eyes glittered as his face closed in on hers. 'You want to play, *glyko mou*?'

Trapped in the depths of his liquid blue eyes as much as his hold, time stretched, the ragged beats of her heart and shallow hitches of her breaths thudding dimly as the world condensed to only him.

His chest rose and fell rapidly, his eyes seeming to

drink her in, his breath as his mouth closed in on hers dancing over her skin.

Her eyes closed and her tingling lips parted, anticipation of Yannis's kiss flooding her mouth with moisture and heat flooding the rest of her, but before the connection could be made, the light pressure on her wrist disappeared and a swish of cool breezed over her face and she opened her eyes to find him rising to his feet.

Securing his towel around his waist, he strode to the door and turned his head back to her with a half-smile. 'When we play, it is for you to make the first move.' Then, as he disappeared into the bedroom, called out, 'Don't forget to drink your wine.'

It took Keren another twenty minutes before she felt her legs were strong enough to take her weight, and got out of the now-cold bath. The villa's rooms were so well sound-proofed that she had no way of knowing if Yannis was waiting in the bedroom. After drying, she cloaked herself in her old robe and summoned the courage to enter it.

He was on the bed, dressed in black chinos and a navy polo shirt, his back propped against the headboard, long legs stretched out, ankles hooked together, reading something on his phone.

One look was enough for her legs to weaken all over again. When he flashed his devilish grin at her, it seemed the rest of her body weakened too.

'Good timing,' he said. 'I was about to check you were still alive. Dinner will be served in thirty minutes on our terrace.'

Heart clenching at the mention of *our* terrace, Keren nodded tersely and dived into her dressing room. She made sure to lock the door behind her.

That was one of the things that had played on her mind while her skin had turned into a giant prune in the bath. The question of why she hadn't locked the bathroom door.

Had she subconsciously wanted him to join her in there?

Subconscious or not, her skin felt like it had come to life. There was a zing in her blood. Feelings, desires she hadn't felt for so long, hidden away like seeds buried deep in the earth waiting for spring to come and warm them to life.

Yannis had been spring, summer and autumn rolled into one glorious season. He'd brought the woman in her to life and bathed her world in colour and sunshine.

And then winter had come and all the flowers and colour had withered away, leaving only the thorns.

She sighed and slid one of her wardrobe doors open. It didn't matter how deeply her longing for Yannis rooted. She couldn't live through another winter again.

Earlier, when she'd looked through these wardrobes, she'd been too stunned to find her clothes still hanging where she'd left them and unnerved at Yannis's presence to look through them properly. There were many she'd never worn but an equal number that she had, and an ache twisted her heart to remember the good and bad memories she associated with them. There were some outfits she would think twice about donating to charity for fear of somehow cursing the wearer with them. But there were some—many—that made her heart sing.

Eventually she settled on a deep red boho skirt and paired it with a white Bardot top, the two together exposing an inch of her bare midriff. At her dressing table, she carefully brushed her damp hair, then opened the drawer that held her makeup. Again, nothing had been touched. Having not worn any cosmetics since she'd left Yannis, it felt strange to put the mascara wand to her lashes. The red lipgloss she'd always loved felt sticky on her lips.

She drew the line at changing her tiny diamond ear studs for anything more artful, mostly because her chest tightened too much when she put her hands on the jewellery box. Keren had always loved wearing earrings, big hooped ones being her favourite. She'd loved bracelets too. Yannis had loved to surprise her with them. In the almost two years they'd been together, she'd built a vast collection of earrings and bracelets. She'd left with only the studs she wore now, which had been an eighteenth birthday present from her parents.

She remembered opening that present knowing from the shape of it that it was jewellery and already readying herself to act as if they were just what she wanted. Her parents tried so hard to buy her gifts she would like but no matter how gently she tried to steer them in a particular direction, they always went for the gifts they thought she should like. The gifts she would like if she wasn't such a cuckoo in their nest. Gifts Diane, her sister, always gushed over.

Yannis had never needed steering. Yannis had always known exactly what she would like, right from the day they'd met. And, as she checked her reflection before leaving the dressing room, she conceded that, despite his criticisms of her outfits when they'd attended official functions, he'd never suggested that she change into something more appropriate.

Maybe, in his own clumsy way, he really had only been critical in an effort to protect her from his mother's disapproval and the pointed looks of the women who thrived in Agonite high society. Because that first meeting with his mother had upset her terribly. For four months she and Yannis had lived in a private bubble and then she'd been introduced to his parents, not as his new girlfriend but as his fiancée. He'd been honest with Keren and told her she wasn't the kind of woman his parents had wanted him to marry—she'd already guessed that anyway—and she'd been so desperate for them to approve of her that Nina's criticism had hit much harder than it would have otherwise done.

She'd held her hurt in until the drive back when she'd burst into tears in answer to Yannis's question about how she thought the evening had gone. He'd been furious, had wanted to drive straight back to his parents and confront them about it. Even though she'd calmed him down and managed to stop him doing that, looking back she thought he might have confronted them another time and without her knowledge because apart from the odd funny look, Nina never again commented on Keren's outfits.

Yannis had hated seeing her hurt.

She gritted her teeth and took a deep breath.

Not only was she softening towards him but now she was making excuses for him. Even if he'd only been critical about her clothes from a clumsy protective instinct, that didn't negate the rest of it. He'd still taken to viewing her as a personal asset rather than the flesh-and-blood woman he'd married. He'd still taken emotional solace with another.

Giving her hair one last run-through with her fingers, Keren braced herself before opening her dressing room door.

The bedroom was empty. The only sign of Yannis was the indentation of his body on their bed.

She stared at that indentation for the longest time, fighting the urge to press her hand to it and feel if it still held his warmth.

CHAPTER SEVEN

THE SCENT OF FRANGIPANI, which Keren loved almost as much as jasmine, was strong that warm summer evening as she dined with Yannis on the secluded side terrace. Unlike the poolside terrace, which was a real entertainment area of the villa, this terrace, backdropped with an abundance of scented shrubbery and with panoramic views of the Aegean, had strategically placed solar lighting and a much more intimate, romantic feel. It had been deliberately created that way. Keren and Yannis had designed it themselves in the months after they'd got together, before they'd married. An enclave only for them. No one else invited. No one else welcome.

She knew why Yannis had chosen to eat here tonight. He wanted the setting to remind her of happier, seductive times when they'd been greedy and selfish for each other.

She knew she had no right, but she fervently hoped he hadn't dined with any other women at this spot or sat with them on the double cocoon swing chair tucked away to the left of the table. Just to imagine it made her feel sick.

Doing her best to tune out the romantic music floating out from the discreetly placed speakers, she fought back the latest swell of memories the setting provoked and downed the shot of ouzo Yannis had poured her.

Starting an evening meal with a short aperitif of ouzo had been a Yannis tradition she'd enthusiastically embraced.

A meze of hot and cold food was brought out to them. Feta and tomato wedges. *Taramasalata* with pitta triangles. Stuffed peppers. Olives. Hot snacks of *keftedakia*—small meatballs—and fried potatoes drizzled with lemons. Savoury filo triangles. Stuffed vine leaves…

Every item placed before them was a firm favourite of hers. And a firm favourite of Yannis. They were the items they would feed to each other. The foods they would fight over to get the last bite. The food they would steal off each other's plates.

As with the setting, it had all been chosen deliberately by Yannis to remind her of the good times. And to seduce.

He was seducing her with every second that passed, with the blue eyes that hardly left her face, with the intimate tone of his voice, even with his clothes. She'd commented once how sexy the colour black was on him, and tonight he'd chosen a black shirt, unbuttoned at the throat, and a pair of snugly fitted black trousers that showcased his snake hips and the tight buttocks she had once so loved to squeeze.

She wished she could say his seduction wasn't working but every time she looked at him her veins heated to molten. It felt like her internal temperature had been set to a high simmer.

The only thing Yannis wasn't seducing her with was his touch. As close as they were sat at the wrought iron table designed for two, not an inch of his body made contact with hers, not so much as a brush of a finger. Instead of being thankful for this, she was having to forcibly stop her lower legs from inching forward to entwine with his like they used to do in the old days.

'Tell me how you learned to sail,' he said as he topped up their wine glasses.

It was the first stray into personal territory of their conversation that night. The first real question he'd asked about her life away from him.

'An American couple I got talking to in Barbados were kind enough to let me live on their clipper and learn the ropes.'

'Is Barbados where you went when you left?'

That there was no underlying sting in his tone gave her a semblance of confidence to nod and say, 'I was very lucky. I met Lola and Eddie my first week there. They've lived on the seas for ten years. They taught me everything I needed to know then when it was time for me to set off on my own helped me buy my boat—they made sure it was fully seaworthy, helped me get it insured and helped me find replacement parts for the things that weren't up to scratch.'

'Why didn't you go for a new boat?'

'I couldn't afford one and…'

His features tightened reflexively. Keren guessed what he was thinking. Yannis was thinking that he hadn't paid her a single cent in the eighteen months she'd been gone. He was experiencing a stab of guilt.

She supposed it was easy to be malicious to a person when they were thousands of miles away and you weren't in communication with them—less easy when the flesh-and-blood person your maliciousness had been directed at was right in front of you.

She should know. She was feeling the same. Being back with Yannis and flooded with the memories of how good things had once been between them, confronted with the flesh-and-blood man behind the monster she'd turned him into in her head...

She'd forgotten all the things she'd loved about him. All the little gestures that had proved his love more than any words could say.

God help her, she was weakening towards him in ways that had nothing to do with the desire coursing through her veins.

Her heart was softening.

Frightened at how quickly everything was turning on its head, terrified at the swelling of her softening heart, she had a quick drink of her wine and hastily added, 'In any case, I wouldn't have bought a new boat even if I'd had the money for one—older boats are better for long sea voyages. If a part breaks while I'm miles from anywhere, I need to be able to fix it myself. The old ones were built to last.'

He stared at her for the longest time as if weighing up whether she was telling him the truth. Yannis was from the school of thought that assumed the higher the price you paid for something, the higher the quality, and while that was certainly true for many things, it didn't apply to everything. It didn't apply to all boats.

His chest rose before he took a swig of his wine and his mouth relaxed into its usual sensuous form. 'So you are telling me that my wife is now an expert at boat maintenance?'

'I'm an expert at my own boat's maintenance if that counts?'

His glimmering eyes flickered down to her breasts and back up to her face. 'I would love to see you in a pair of blue overalls with a toolbox in your hands.'

'I'm impressed you know what a toolbox is,' she said, then immediately reproved herself for adopting such a teasing tone. Even her voice was softening towards him.

A quirky eyebrow rose. 'Every man takes pride in his toolbox, *glyko mou*. You are welcome to handle mine whenever you wish.'

Keren's throat ran dry at the innuendo. Crossing her legs tightly together and failing to come up with a non-smutty retort, she hastily forked a roasted red pepper into her mouth.

Smirking, Yannis helped himself to a *keftedakia* and, eyes smouldering, savagely bit into it.

Her skin completely overheating, she had a large drink of her crisp white wine to cool her insides.

'Are you feeling all right, *glyko mou*?' he asked with faux concern.

Finishing her wine, she nodded.

'Sure? You look a little warm from where I'm sitting.'

'It's a warm evening,' she managed to say.

He leaned forward. 'It does feel as if the heat has been turned up.' Then he grinned wickedly and plucked the stem of her empty wine glass.

'Do you always sail alone?' he asked as he pulled the wine bottle out of the ice bucket.

His ability to swerve the conversation into different directions without losing a beat was, she had to admit, impressive.

'Yes.'

'Is it not dangerous? I'm thinking of predatory men.'

'There's a whole community of sea-wanderers out there and we all look out for each other. In any case, I've been in more danger with predatory men on land than I ever could be at sea,' she retorted pointedly.

Amusement played on his mouth as he carefully placed her wine glass back down beside her plate and let his fingers linger on it. 'So you never get frightened out at sea?'

'I never said that.' His hand was so close to hers that she had to scramble her brain to make it coherent. 'Sometimes it can be terrifying—I've been caught in a couple of squalls—but so long as I keep a cool head and follow all my procedures correctly, I'm as safe as I can be. There are other things that scare me much more.'

'Like what?'

My feelings for you. 'Spiders.'

One side of Yannis's mouth curved making her certain he saw right through her lame answer. 'You must get lonely all alone out there.'

'There's too much to do for loneliness,' she answered. 'How about you? Have you managed to do much sailing?'

Keren wanted—needed—to get the subject away from her. She didn't want to have to talk about the nights anchored at sea when the weather was calm and there was nothing to distract her, when she would find herself unwittingly thinking of Yannis and then virtually crippled with the loneliness that came from missing him. Those moments had been few and far between but when they struck, the pain of everything she'd lost smacked her afresh.

His expression became suddenly inscrutable. 'Some.'

'Where?'

He shrugged. 'Nowhere you haven't been, I'm sure.' He chewed on a fried potato, swallowed, then added, 'Remember how we used to talk about sailing the world when we retired?'

A wave of sadness washed through her. 'We had a lot of pipe dreams then.'

'They were never pipe dreams,' he refuted.

She forced brightness into her voice. 'You're a Filipidis, Yannis.'

'And?'

'And you'll follow the same path as your parents and their parents before them.'

'My parents sailed the world,' he pointed out.

'They cruised the world on an ocean liner that had more staff than guests and with a full itinerary and always knowing the day they would return home. It's a wonderful way to see the world but not if you like adventure and want to take each day as it comes and go off the beaten track.'

'That can be done on *The Amphitrite*.'

She nearly laughed, and pinched a stuffed vine leaf with her fingers, remembering how awed she'd been the first time Yannis had taken her for a long weekend away on his yacht. She had guessed it would be magnificent but even that guess had been an understatement. A floating palace was the closest description she could come up with for it.

'Trust me, my love, your yacht is way too big and would cause way too much damage to get into the best places. It's not much smaller than the liner your parents sailed on and when you sail, you have dozens of crew. Everything is done for you. It's not the same.'

It was only when she bit into the stuffed vine that she noticed Yannis had stilled.

'What?' she said when she'd swallowed her food. 'Have I just offended you?'

There was a melancholic quality to his answering smile. 'No, *glyko mou*, you haven't offended me.'

It was his calling her by his pet endearment that made Keren realise that she'd just made an unconscious slip of the tongue and casually addressed him with her old pet endearment for him.

My love.

Oh, God, not only were her heart and thoughts and voice softening towards him, but now her words were too. This was horrendous. Terrifying.

Hugely aware of the heat enflaming her cheeks, she quickly popped the last of the stuffed vine leaf into her mouth and looked anywhere but at Yannis.

'I know what you mean,' he said.

Relieved he wasn't going to make anything more about her slip-up, she met his stare. What she found there filled the entirety of her chest.

'About me being a Filipidis.' He pulled a rueful face. 'I have always followed the same path as my parents. Andreas and I attended the same English boarding school as our father, then the same English university, then the same business shadowing programme our father followed with his father. We grew up knowing that when we had accumulated all the knowledge we needed for the business, our parents would retire and pass the mantle to us. There was never any question about doing anything else.'

'But I thought you said you'd never wanted to do anything else?' she reminded him, referring to one of their old mammoth conversations when they had been greedy to know every last thing about each other.

'I didn't, but I wonder if that's because that weight of five hundred years of history was always part of my thinking.'

'Okay, then think of it this way—if you woke up tomorrow and the business was gone, what would you do?'

'Would I still have all my money in this scenario?'

'Let's say no. You had nothing and had to start over again.'

He raised an eyebrow in mock alarm. 'I wouldn't even have a chef?'

'Nope.'

'Then I suppose the first thing I would have to do is learn to cook.'

She sniggered at the very thought of it. 'Then once you'd stopped yourself from starving, what would you do? Imagine you had the qualifications to do anything you wanted in the whole wide world.'

He sipped slowly at his wine, his brow narrowed in thought, then shook his head. 'I cannot think of anything.'

'Nothing?'

'Nothing. I am doing what I should be doing and what I want to be doing and the only thing missing in my life is having my wife at my side.'

Having just relaxed into the conversation for the first time since she'd joined him at the table, Keren sighed. 'Don't spoil things.'

'I'm not. I'm just pointing out that marrying you is the only path I've taken that diverges from the path set for me.'

'And even then you were following in Andreas's path,' she managed to tease lightly. Andreas had married Pavlos a year before Keren and Yannis met.

'At least he married an Agonite.'

'The goody two-shoes.'

Yannis's grin at this was infectious and Keren found her mouth pulling into a wide smile of its own.

She had missed this, she realised. Really missed it. The days when they could talk about anything, veering from serious conversation to the absurd in the breath of a sentence. She had once thought Yannis was the only person in the world tuned to the same wavelength as her. It made her heart ache to think he still might be.

'I know Andreas got there first but it must have been difficult for you to tell your parents you were marrying an outsider.' More difficult than he'd let her believe she now thought.

'I knew we were meant to be together.' Blue eyes boring into her, he leaned back in his chair. 'I wish I could make you understand what it was like for me meeting you.' He smiled but there was a tautness to it. 'My life was great. I'd grown up with all the riches in the world. I had the best education that money could buy and a loving family. I had a thriving business and a great social network. I wanted for nothing. I've never wanted for anything. And then I met you at the palace. You were the sexiest creature I had ever set eyes on, but it wasn't just your beauty that attracted me. I watched you circulate and...' He closed his eyes. 'You were like no one I had met before. The people in my world...everything is done consciously. You understand?'

Even though she had an idea of what he meant, Keren shook her head.

His eyes snapping back on her, Yannis rubbed the nape of his neck. 'Think of all the functions we attended together and the people we attended them with. The way those people behave in public, from the clothes they wear to the words they choose when in conversation, to the people they choose to have those conversations with. Everything is done with advancement in mind. People want to climb the hierarchy. Everyone wants to be first on a guest list. No one wants to be excluded from the in-crowd, and the result is that everyone behaves in the same conscious manner. I never noticed any of this until I met you.'

He leaned forward and rested his hand close to hers again. The seductive tone of his voice was becoming hypnotic.

'You were different, *glyko mou*, and it wasn't just because you dressed so much more brightly and more freely than anyone else. When you walked around that palace gallery there seemed no sense of purpose in your steps like there was with everyone else. You just wandered around studying whatever picture caught your attention, not whatever picture you thought you should be studying, and you didn't look the slightest bit awkward to be doing it with only yourself for company. You were so free, and so comfortable and happy in your skin in a way I had never seen before. I knew that to catch someone so vibrant and free would be hard and that to hold onto them would be next to impossible. I knew all that before we exchanged a single word or look. And then you looked at me and that was it for me—*you'd* caught *me*.'

Keren remembered how her flesh had prickled with the awareness that someone was watching her. Remembered turning her head and finding Yannis propped against a wall gazing at her. Remembered how their eyes had locked together and how the prickling of her flesh had intensified and spread through every part of her.

One look and that had been it for her too.

The difference was she had never stopped wanting him.

But her flesh was prickling now, tingling with a growing desperation for his touch.

If she moved her little finger an inch, it would brush against his.

Yannis wanted her to make the first move. He was waiting for it. She could no longer say with certainty that hell would have to freeze over first, not when hell burned so fiercely.

'Remember what you said earlier about me shoehorning you into a straitjacket?' he said, blue eyes ringing at her.

Spellbound, her throat too constricted to speak, she nodded.

'It was meeting you that made me see that *I* had been living in a straitjacket that had been wrapped around me since before I was born. I'd just never felt its constriction. You unlocked it for me.'

The temptation to brush her finger to his was so intense and the effects of his words on her so all-consuming that Keren had to fight with everything she had to stop herself from falling into the open trap he was laying for her.

This was what Yannis wanted. To seduce her back into his bed and back permanently into his life, seduce her with his words as well as the magnetism she'd always responded so strongly to. Make her feel special. Like she was the only woman in the world.

That had been true. Once. Before he'd stopped treating her as his lover and started treating her as his little wife and acting as her lord and master. Before he'd turned his back on her and sought emotional comfort, if not physical, from another.

But how badly she ached at the thought it could still be true and that his feelings for her were still true and that he wanted her back for *her* and not because his pride had decided he didn't want a divorce after all.

She had been so right in fleeing to Barbados when she'd left him. So right in refusing any communication other than through their lawyers. The affect Yannis had on her was as strong as the day they'd exchanged their wedding vows. It had been building inside her all day like a dormant volcano awakening.

She feared she was on the brink of it erupting.

CHAPTER EIGHT

PANIC RISING AT the tempest writhing inside her, Keren leaned over and pressed a trembling finger to the button connecting their private sanctuary to the kitchen.

Yannis's stare was shrewd and knowing. 'Feeling the need for a chapérone, *glyko mou*?'

Cheeks burning at his mind-reading abilities, she smiled tightly. 'Feeling the need for tea.'

He arched a brow. 'Tea?'

'The hot stuff we drink by the bucket in England.'

'The hot stuff you drink with a splash of milk and no sugar.'

Amazed, she shook her head. 'You have the memory of an elephant.'

He winked. 'And the trunk of one too.'

The flush that ran through her at this set her cheeks ablaze again but she never got the chance to think of a comeback for a member of staff appeared. It was another she didn't recognise.

Yannis spoke to him in their native language. The staff member's eyes flickered with alarm. Keren guessed he'd never been tasked with making a pot of tea before.

'Have you finished eating?' Yannis asked her.

'Yes, thank you.'

Their dishes and plates were cleared and then they were alone again.

Somehow, that brief interlude of company made the intimacy of the setting feel even more heightened, and Keren found herself tempted to grab the bottle of ouzo and pour herself a hefty measure to calm her nerves.

She'd had enough alcohol for one night. Any more and her inhibitions would loosen too much and she'd be vulnerable to doing something she would regret. She was close enough to the brink as it was. And Yannis knew it.

One day with him and she was coming undone.

How was she going to resist him for another two whole days?

She had to hold it together for a little while longer, that was all. She would drink her tea and then she would go to...

Bed.

Her brain turned to heated mush.

He wouldn't expect her to share his bed, would he?

Their bed.

'What happened to all the old staff?' she asked, desperate to make their remaining conversation neutral. 'There's hardly any of them left.'

His features set again in the inscrutable expression she was coming to think meant it was a subject *he* didn't want to talk about.

Why would that be the case with his staff? Yannis had always been a good boss. His household staff were devoted to him.

After a few beats too long, he said, 'They had to go.'

'Why?'

'Come back to me and I'll tell you.'

She tried to scowl. Her lips and cheeks refused to co-operate. 'Nice try.'

'I will try for ever.'

'Then you're going to be disappointed for ever.'

He put his elbow on the table and rested his chin in his palm. Her pelvis tightened at the playful, seductive gleam in his eyes. 'Who are you trying to convince of that? You or me?'

Two members of staff appeared, one carrying a tray with her tea and a coffee for Yannis, the other carrying their dessert. It was another batch of the chocolate mousse Keren had pilfered earlier.

How many hours ago had that been?

It felt like a day had passed for each hour spent with him.

Once everything was set before them and they were, again, alone, Yannis pulled the huge crystal bowl full of chocolate deliciousness in front of him and hugged an arm around it in protective fashion. 'What are you having?'

She held her dessert bowl out and nodded pointedly at the mousse.

'I have to share?' he queried.

'Yep.'

'*You* didn't share.'

'I would have done if you'd found me.'

'No, you wouldn't.'

'Well, you didn't find me, so we'll never know.'

He shook his head in mock disappointment and took her bowl. 'A pity. If I had found you, I could have fought you for it like we used to do.'

They'd fought over chocolate mousse many times. It had always ended with them having to shower the mess they hadn't licked off each other away.

They were happy memories. Pure. Untainted. And, God help her, the heat inside her pulsed even harder.

'Just fill the bowl,' she ordered.

Keren had never been much of a chocolate lover until she'd met Yannis. His addiction to it had proved contagious. The mousse they were currently sharing was from his school days. Yannis had made sure to take the recipe with him when he'd packed his school trunk the final time. The chefs he'd employed in his own homes since had had to prove themselves by making it before the job was offered to them. Muck it up and they could forget working for him.

'Can I not fill you instead?'

'Can you stop with the innuendoes?'

'Why? Are they turning you on too much for comfort?'

If he only knew how much... 'You wish.'

'To turn you on?' He passed the now-filled dessert bowl to her. 'Always, *glyko mou*.'

'Oh... Shut up.'

He smirked and dug his spoon into what was left in the crystal bowl.

'Are you planning to eat all that?' she asked, outraged. He had at least five times as much mousse as she did.

His eyes trained on her, the heaped spoon disappeared into his sensuous mouth.

'Seriously?'

He withdrew the spoon slowly. His eyes gleamed. 'You are welcome to fight me for it.'

Her attempt at a scowl was, this time, moderately more successful than her first attempt but too quickly turned into a smile that she hid by shoving her own spoon in her mouth.

He was irrepressible. Irresistible.

Dangerous.

Keren made quick work of the rest of her portion, drank her tea then pushed her chair back. 'I'm going to bed.'

The gleam in his eyes speared straight into her core. 'An excellent idea.'

'Alone,' she said pointedly.

A single eyebrow rose. A knowing silkiness threaded into his voice. 'You are planning to hide from me again?'

The clash of their gazes intensified. The beats of her heart intensified too, a loud tattoo drumming in her ears.

Keren knew exactly what Yannis was thinking because she was thinking the same thing. The liquid in his eyes told her he knew she was thinking it too.

They were both remembering the time she'd hidden from him as one of the many sensuous games they'd loved to play. He'd searched the villa for her, just as she'd known he would. She'd been waiting for him in his dressing room. Naked. Artfully splayed on his dressing table chair.

What had followed had been so erotic and so rampant that just to remember it was to feel the residue of the pleasure inside her.

By the time they'd finished, she'd been so weak and sated Yannis had had to carry her to their bed.

The charged silence connecting them stretched and tautened until his nostrils flared and his chest rose. 'The first move is yours to make, *glyko mou*.'

And then he dipped a finger in the bowl and slowly, provocatively, sucked the mousse off it.

Keren fled inside.

Yannis walked into their marital bedroom. He kept his hand on the door once he'd closed it and observed Keren burrowed under the duvet.

A slow smile spread over his gorgeous face. 'So you've decided to spend the night with me after all... Interesting.'

'No, I've decided to share our bed with you. I'm not going to play the games you want to play, Yannis.'

A knowing eyebrow rose. 'What games would they be?'

'You know exactly what I mean, and I mean it—I'm not playing them.'

'Whatever you say.'

'You stick to your side of the bed and I'll stick to mine.'

'Of course.' He pulled his shirt over his head.

'Can't you do that in your dressing room or the bathroom?'

'Why?'

'Because.'

He undid the button of his trousers. 'It's nothing you haven't seen before.' He pulled them down along with his underwear, past his hips. Gloriously naked, he winked and stepped out of them. 'Indeed, I seem to remember you had a good look earlier when I was showering.'

Another wink and he disappeared into the bathroom.

Furious, frustrated and who knew what else, certainly not her, Keren grabbed hold of his pillow, put it over her face and screamed into it.

Every time she thought she'd found a way to get the upper hand, Yannis trumped her.

What made it worse was being unable to deny the thrills that ravaged her every time he regained the upper hand.

She was a masochist. She must be.

What had the alternative been to sleeping in the marital bed? Hiding in one of the spare rooms and then lying on tenterhooks, waiting for him to find her? Waiting in *anticipation* because the unspoken charge that had swirled so thickly and stickily between them had let them both know that if she hid from him again, it would be an invitation.

An invitation from Keren for Yannis's seduction.

She'd dug out an old birthday present from her parents that she'd never worn—a long-sleeved, high-necked nightdress that fell to her ankles. Wearing it, she would fit right in with the prudish Victorians.

The bathroom door opened.

Even though she lay rigid and had her gaze fixed on the ceiling, she was fully aware of Yannis, magnificently naked, approaching the bed like the panther he was.

She wouldn't engage with him.

When Keren had got into bed shortly before he'd appeared in the room, she'd turned the main light off and turned his bedside light on to maximum brightness. Instead of turning it off, he climbed in beside her and dimmed it to a soft mellowness.

She clenched her jaw. She'd always loved the romance of their bedroom lighting.

Lying on his side facing her, propped up on an elbow, Yannis lifted the duvet before she had a chance to keep her half of it tightly pressed against her.

'Sexy,' he mocked.

Her jaw clenched even tighter.

'You don't think an ugly thing like that will stop me wanting you, do you, *glyko mou*?'

She would not answer. Would not engage.

'I would still want you if you were wearing an old

sack, but I made you a promise. You could lie here as naked as I am and I would still resist you.'

'Can't you put some boxers on?' she snapped before she could stop herself.

'I *could*,' he mused. 'But I won't.'

She ground her teeth back together and attempted to close her eyes. Attempted. They refused to obey, too busy trying to override her will and sneak a look at Yannis. She could feel his gaze boring into her.

'Will you *please* stop looking at me?'

'But I like looking at you.'

'Will you at least turn the light off?'

'I'm happy with it being on but if you want to turn it off, be my guest.'

And have to lean over him to do it? Not a chance.

'How many other women have you shared this bed with since I've been gone?' The question, blurted out, came from nowhere. Keren hadn't even been thinking it. Not at that precise moment anyway.

But it was a question that had weighed heavily on her in some form or another all day.

It was a question that had compressed her heart in unguarded moments since she'd left him.

'Look at me and I'll tell you.'

She kept her gaze on the ceiling.

'Keren?'

Her jaw loosened and she closed her eyes.

'Look at me.'

Opening them, her heart beating fast, she slowly turned her face to him.

What she found in his stare closed her throat.

Yannis's hand rose as if to touch her before he gave a rueful smile and rested it on his pillow. Gently, he said, 'The only woman who has shared this bed with me is you.'

A swell of unexpected tears burned the back of her eyes and she closed them before fixing her gaze back to the ceiling.

'What about men?' Her voice was too shaky for it to be the sharp quip she'd intended.

'I've managed to resist bringing a man here too,' he said drily.

She managed a short inhalation of air into her cramped lungs.

She believed him. Yannis could be manipulative and ruthless and occasionally economical with the truth but he never told a barefaced lie. If he said there hadn't been another woman in this bed then there hadn't been another woman in this bed.

That didn't mean there hadn't been other women though. The villa had eleven bedrooms. Half their own lovemaking hadn't even been in a bed.

'Has there been anyone else for you?' he asked in the silence.

'No,' she whispered.

There had only ever been Yannis.

Keren had watched a film set in Thailand when she was twelve—a film that, looking back, she'd been far too young to watch—and been transfixed by the setting. The beauty of the beach featured in it. The colours. To a young suburban girl on the cusp of adolescent who'd hardly left her home town never mind her country, it had been a gateway into a world she hadn't known existed. That film had changed her life.

From that moment, she'd watched every film and television series set in foreign locales, made frequent visits to the library to stock up on reading material set in foreign climes. The books could be fiction or factual, she hadn't cared, so long as they were set anywhere or were about anything but the UK. She had *itched* to get out there and explore the world and tread the exotic beaches with her own feet and inhale different scents and immerse herself in different cultures, and to do that required money. So she had worked: a paper round at thirteen, a Saturday job in a local barber sweeping hair at fourteen, a Saturday and Sunday job in a shoe shop at sixteen. She'd also babysat at every opportunity, averaging three evenings a week. All the money she'd made, she'd saved. Her sole focus had been to save enough money to buy herself a ticket to Thailand the day she left school. As a result, boys hadn't really been on her radar, and when she'd boarded her first flight she'd been an eighteen-year-old virgin.

Once abroad, she'd made lots of friends in lots of different countries and occasionally buddied up with them but on the whole had been content following her own path. She'd liked having the freedom of waking up in one country and spontaneously deciding to move on to another. How could you be spontaneous as part of a couple when you had to consider their feelings and opinions? Safer to avoid romance in any of its forms, and so a virgin she had remained. Until she met Yannis.

He was like no one she'd ever met before, and it wasn't just because he was rich—to make her money stretch, she'd always stayed in the safest cheap accommodation she could find which no rich person would be seen dead in, so had never mixed with rich people before—and gorgeous and sexy. His humour had tickled her. His intelligence had awed her. He'd seen so much of the world. He was a man of the world. A *real* man. And she'd fallen head over heels for him.

What they'd shared had been special. She hadn't needed experience to know that. It had been wonderful. Heady. Heavenly.

And then it had all fallen apart.

Her man of the world had wanted to lock her in a cage.

He moved his face close enough for her to feel his breath against her cheek as he seductively said, 'Did you miss me too much to want anyone else?'

Gripping the duvet tightly, she gave a dismissive *pfft* in answer. Her throat wasn't capable of working with her mouth to form speech.

If she ever reached the stage where she was ready for a relationship with someone new, deep down she knew there would be no point as what she and Yannis had shared before things had imploded had been too magical for her to replicate with anyone else. There was no one in the world who compared with him.

The warmth of his breath left her face as he twisted to turn the light off, plunging the room into darkness.

Her awareness of the man lying naked beside heightened. Her heart beat even faster. Suddenly she was aware of the cotton of her nightdress pressed lightly against her increasingly sensitive skin, and she tightened her grip on the duvet to stop herself yanking it off.

'You are having trouble breathing, *glyko mou*?'

She swallowed her parched, constricted throat. 'I'm fine,' she lied. Her lungs didn't seem to want to open. 'Go to sleep.'

'How can I sleep if I can't hear you breathe? I worry you might need the kiss of life.'

'Touch me, and I'll kick you where it hurts.'

'I love it when you talk dirty.'

She clamped her lips together. She must not indulge him. That was what he wanted. To provoke her.

He pushed his half of the duvet off and stretched. 'Is it me, or is it hot in here?'

'It's you.' The discarded half of duvet had bunched between them but the extra barrier made not the slightest bit of difference to her, not when on the other side of the barrier Yannis lay with his nakedness exposed.

'I shall turn the air conditioning up,' he decided, twisting again to do just that from the control box beside his bedside light.

'Do what you like, just go to *sleep*.'

Frustrated, both with him and herself, Keren turned her back to him.

A moment later cool air brushed her forehead and tip of her nose, the only parts of her body not cocooned in the duvet.

And then Yannis stretched back out again, except this time he rolled onto his side and inched his way behind her, positioning himself close enough that now his breath tickled then warmed the top of her head.

Trying, again, to drag air into her lungs she edged away from him. He closed the gap in an instant.

'Will you move over to your own side?' she tried to snap. It came out more like a wail.

'But your side is warmer than mine.'

'You just said you were too hot!'

'And now I am cold.'

'Then turn the air conditioning off or get back under the duvet.'

He sighed as if she were asking something that was a

major imposition. 'Okay. I will go back to my side and get cold if you insist.'

'I do.'

He sighed again and shuffled away from her.

Her body screamed at her to invite him straight back.

When he'd finally settled himself, Keren knew perfectly well that, this time, he'd positioned himself so he lay right at the edge of his half.

God help her, she *ached* to inch her way back to him.

'Keren?'

'What?' she croaked.

'I'm right here if you want me.'

'Yannis?'

'Yes, *glyko mou*?'

'Shut up and go to sleep.'

His low chuckle seeped through her fevered skin and she squeezed her eyes tightly shut.

It took a good few minutes of silence before her lungs could take in anything like vaguely normal breaths and the danger of self-asphyxiation passed. But her heartbeats didn't settle. Her racing pulses didn't settle. The heat inside her continued to blaze painfully. The throbbing ache between her legs grew.

This was torture.

Slowly, Yannis's breathing deepened.

He'd fallen asleep.

She could scream.

Yannis had always been able to fall asleep at will but for him to fall asleep now while she lay there ablaze with desire was cruelty personified.

She didn't know what she wanted to do most. Roll over and kick him for putting her in this frustrated state. Or roll over and crush herself against him and seek the relief of his mouth and...

She squeezed her eyes even tighter to drive the image out but it was no use.

If Yannis were to so much as press the tip of his finger to her, she would melt for him. She'd already melted. Lava flowed through her veins, not blood.

Without thinking, she rolled onto her back.

She turned her face to him. The thin stream of moonlight through the darkness allowed her to see his strong, masculinely beautiful features. Moisture replaced the dryness of her mouth and throat.

Her hand inched its way to his sleeping face. She snatched it back before her finger could press against his lips.

She *couldn't* make the first move. It would give him everything he wanted. Yannis had engineered everything for this moment and she couldn't just give in and put herself on a plate for him. Not after everything. What little pride she had left would be smashed to smithereens.

Before her body could take back control of her brain, Keren pushed the duvet off and climbed out of bed. Fixing her gaze on the bedroom door, she padded quietly to it then slipped out, too scared that she'd find his eyes open to look back. She took not a single breath until she'd softly closed the door behind her.

Then she climbed the stairs to the second floor and raced to the other side of the villa, as far from him as she could get.

She hurried to the high window of the guest room she'd chosen as her sanctuary, and flung it open, then settled on the wide windowsill praying for her fevered skin to cool.

Had her escape woken him? Was he, at this very moment, seeking her out?

The thought had barely formed in her brain when the handle turned and the door opened and Yannis's silhouette appeared in the doorway.

Keren jumped off the ledge.

He stepped towards her.

She tried to step back. The ledge stopped her.

He didn't say a word until he was stood before her, eyes piercing wickedly straight through her. 'Hiding from me, *glyko mou*?'

Her legs were trembling. Her heart was swollen and pounding hard. She couldn't breathe. She couldn't speak.

And then she saw that, for all the nonchalance of his husky words, Yannis, too, was struggling for breath and her heart broke free from its confines and soared.

Understanding flowed between them.

His throat moved a number of times before he speared his hand into her hair and cupped the back of her head. He gazed into her eyes for a long, breathless moment and then his lips vanquished hers with an intensity that scorched her into a burst of flames.

CHAPTER NINE

KEREN HAD FLED to this room knowing deep down that Yannis would follow her. Knowing he would recognise her hiding in the room as Keren making the first move. Knowing he would make the next one.

The firmness of his smooth lips moved against hers and then she felt the flicker of his velvet tongue against hers and the last of her consciousness vanished.

Crushing herself against his steel-hard frame, she rose onto her toes and wound her arms around his neck, fisting his hair as their kiss deepened into a fierce, hungry duel. The lava in her veins surged through her, deafening her ears, melting her core. Greedy fingers dragged over her back and down to her bottom clasping a buttock to pull her even closer.

Scratching his neck, she gasped into his mouth as she felt the hard ridge of his erection press into her stomach. Knowing that it wouldn't be long until that part of him was inside her turned her gasp into a moan.

Oh, but she wanted this so badly. Needed it. Yannis. His touch. Him. And how badly she wanted rid of her nightdress to feel his flesh against hers without any barrier.

He must have sensed her need for a breeze whipped

around her calves and then her thighs as he bunched her nightdress up to her buttocks, the fusion of his mouth finally breaking when he stepped back just enough to raise her arms and whip the offending item off her and drop it without pause.

His breathing was heavy and ragged as he dipped his gaze over her, now as naked as he.

'*Theos*, Keren,' he groaned, cupping her face in his hands. 'You are so beautiful.' And then his mouth claimed her again, almost furious in its intensity, and their arms wrapped around each other tightly, naked flesh finally meeting naked flesh, her sensitised breasts finally getting their wish, flattened against his burning skin.

Giant hands gripped her hips. Her belly dipped then her feet left the ground. A moment later and they were on the bed, Yannis on top of her, his mouth continuing its heady assault. The need in her pelvis was so tightly coiled that she automatically wrapped her legs around his waist and raised her buttocks, but his mouth wrenched from her lips to trail down her neck. His hands swept down her waist to her hips and then back up over her stomach and ribs to cup her breasts at the same moment he flicked his tongue over a puckered nipple. When he took the peak into his hot mouth and sucked with a savagery that made her hips jerk, the cry that flew from her mouth echoed around the walls.

Writhing frantically beneath him, her fingers pulled at his hair and she arched her back, desperate for his possession, but the assault of his mouth continued, lips scorching their trail down her stomach until his face was buried between her legs and his tongue snaked between her folds to settle on the nub of her pleasure.

Her head flopped back and she closed her eyes, submitting entirely to the rapture of his mouth and tongue, the coil of need winding tighter and tighter, her fingers no longer pulling at his hair but buried in it, urging him on. For the first time in so, so long, the swell of an orgasm was rising inside her but, just as she reached the pinnacle, Yannis broke away.

In moments he was on top of her, his face hovering over hers. Immediately she wound her legs around his waist and arched into the tip of his erection, but he held back, snatching at her hands and pressing them either side of her head.

The tendons on his neck were strained, his jaw taut as his liquid gaze burned into her.

'Tell me you want this,' he demanded hoarsely.

'Yannis...*please*...' she wailed.

'*Tell* me.'

In answer, she raised her head and nipped his bottom lip with her teeth. 'You know I want this.'

The words had hardly left her mouth before he thrust. Keren was so wet and ready for him that in one long, exhilarating motion he was deep inside her.

Yannis groaned, then stilled. Deep blue eyes still locked on hers momentarily lost their focus before he blinked sharply and kissed her. Tongues entwined in a hot, ferocious duel, he began to move. In and out he thrust, deeper and deeper, harder and harder, each stroke and each grind tightening the coiled tension in her core.

Sensing that he was fighting back release, Keren urged him on, nails scraping over his back, mouth fusing to his cheek, his taut neck, his shoulder. The slickness of their skin melded together as the pinnacle grew closer and closer until the coil deep inside her unwound in a bullet of spiralling ecstasy that had her clinging to him, crying out his name and begging him to never let her go, never let her go, never let her go...

Yannis grabbed hold of her hips, threw his head back and, with a low, guttural sound reverberating out of his throat, gave one last violent thrust and then his sweat-slicked body collapsed on her.

The thuds of Keren's heart reverberated loudly in her ears. The thuds of Yannis's heart thumped through their crushed chests. The heat of his ragged breath burned into her neck.

The blissful thrills of their coupling were lessening inside her but a cauldron of emotions was bubbling in their place. Hot tears stabbed the back of her eyes, and she squeezed them tightly shut to stop them spilling out. In her head she repeated the mantra, *Don't cry, don't cry, don't cry.*

The last time they'd made love was over two years ago. Keren had been heavily pregnant. The further into the pregnancy she'd gone, the slower and gentler their lovemaking had become, a far cry from the heady rampancy that had consumed them in their early days but every bit as fulfilling. That last time had been tender and loving. She'd fallen asleep with Yannis's hand pressed to her swollen belly.

His possessiveness had first properly made itself known in the pregnancy but she had liked it, she remembered. Yannis had looked out for her with a solicitude that had made her feel cherished as well as loved.

A deep wrench tore through her heart and she clenched her jaw as tightly as she could to counter it, her fingers reflexively tightening their grip on his hair, which she had been absently running through.

How had they got it all so horribly wrong?

Would things be different if she went back to him? Could they return to how they'd been before...?

Frightened at the turn of her thoughts, Keren gave herself a mental slap. One orgasm and it wasn't just her body that had melted for him but her brain too. It had softened her completely. She needed to harden herself back up and quickly.

But when Yannis shifted his weight from her, she only just stopped herself rolling with his movement and cuddling up with her head on his chest and draping her legs over him like she always used to do after making love.

Swallowing hard, she turned her back to him. He spooned into her and hugged an arm around her, pulling her to him. She couldn't stop herself from taking his hand and holding it close.

The beats of her heart ramped up again.

Usually after making love, Yannis liked to talk. Light, playful nonsense mostly, making her grin as she fell into sleep. So far, he hadn't uttered a word and the longer his silence went on, the more unnerved she grew.

'This doesn't mean I'm coming back to you,' she said as evenly as she could manage.

He hugged her even closer and kissed the top of her head. 'Let's not talk about that any more. You are here and I am here—let's just enjoy it without any pressure, okay?'

Scared her swelling heart was going to choke her, she brought his hand to her mouth and kissed it.

Closing her eyes, she listened as Yannis's breaths made their familiar deepening into sleep. A long time later, she finally drifted off too, her last conscious thought that this was the most right she'd felt in two years.

A mouth brushed gently to hers pulled Keren from the fog of sleep. Her lips parted in welcome.

Caught in a dreamlike state, she didn't open her eyes until she lay replete, Yannis still inside her breathing heavily against her ear.

Smiling, she closed her eyes and drifted away again.

When Keren next opened her eyes, Yannis's side of the bed was empty. She looked at her watch then sat bolt upright. Ten a.m.! She hadn't slept so late in what felt like for ever.

Stretching first, she retrieved the Victorian nightgown from the floor, pulled it over her head and padded back to their bedroom. Her limbs felt all liquid. Her skin buzzed. Tiny throbs of deliciousness pulsed between her legs.

After a long shower, she had a quick root through her wardrobe and selected a floaty, sunshine orange summer dress with thin straps and which fell above her knees. She couldn't for the life of her think why she hadn't taken this dress with her when she left.

And then she remembered that Yannis had bought it for her on their honeymoon. He'd awoken early and, not wanting to wake her, left her sleeping while he went to explore the surrounding area. He'd spotted the dress and known immediately that she would love it. He'd been right.

Pressing a hand to her suddenly ragged heart, she took a long, deep breath then, face unadorned and her hair damp around her shoulders, left their room.

The languidness of her mood gone, she paused at Sophia's door and pressed her hand to her heart again.

How did Yannis cope walking past this empty room every day?

Keren hadn't coped. She saw that now. Some days, she would reach the nursery door and find her legs incapable of moving another inch and her lungs too tight to take in air. Palpitations and the agony of the banshee's screams locked in her head had come close to crippling her.

She covered the door handle, closed her eyes, counted to three then opened it. She made another count to three before she forced her eyes open.

For a moment she was too dazed to do anything but blink frantically.

She'd been so certain she would find the nursery stripped bare and repainted but it was all there, exactly as it had been when she'd last stepped foot in it. A beautiful haven waiting to be brought to life with a baby's gurgle.

But the baby had gone to heaven instead.

Brushing a tear away, she fought the swell of emotions fighting to break free and walked back into the corridor, softly closing the door behind her.

Keren found Yannis where she'd guessed he would be—working off his chocolate mousse consumption via laps of the swimming pool.

Taking a seat on the poolside terrace, she helped herself to a coffee from the *briki* and leaned back, watching his powerful body strike through the water like lightning.

A long sigh escaped her lips.

How familiar and yet how alien this all was. But how right.

That's what she'd always felt with Yannis. A completeness. That he was hers and she was his. Her heart thrummed to imagine it could be like that for them again.

Could it really? Could they fall in love again, but this time do it right?

Was she already in love with him? Had her love for him ever really died?

She didn't know the answers. She was too scared to probe her feelings too deeply. What if it was just sex making her feel like this?

And what of Yannis's feelings for her? Was it just his pride that wanted her back or something more fundamental?

If it was just his pride then she would get back on her boat Monday morning and sail away.

She couldn't put her heart back on a plate for him only to watch him slip away from her again. She would not watch his love for her fade away and his hate spring back to life. She would not let the hate that had formed for him in her broken heart contaminate her again.

To go through that again would break her into pieces with no hope of repair.

But if there was a chance for them...

She watched as he heaved himself out of the pool without bothering to use the steps. Her heart turned from a thrum into a thud.

Snatching his towel off the tiled pool surround, he strode to her, a wide grin on his gorgeous face, drying himself as he went.

He leaned over and kissed her mouth, then, eyes gleaming, poured himself a coffee and took the seat next to her.

'You, *glyko mou*, look good enough to eat.'

'Maybe later.'

The devil appeared in his blue eyes before he kissed her again, harder, fingers gripping her waist. 'No *maybe.*' Then he nipped the lobe of her ear and leaned back in his seat, his gaze telling her clearly the lasciviousness of his thoughts.

Keren crossed her legs and pressed her thighs tightly together in a futile effort to dampen her flourishing desire.

'Hungry?' he asked, raising a sinful brow.

'Starving,' she replied, and not just as a double entendre. She couldn't remember the last time she'd had such an appetite and she wasn't so delusional that she didn't know where it had come from. Yannis's lovemaking. It had melted her bones, turned her brain to mush and awoken long-suppressed appetites.

His lips quirked seductively. 'I thought so. Breakfast should be served... Now.'

As if by magic, the same young man who'd served their dinner appeared with their breakfast and a fresh *briki* of coffee.

'What would you like to do today?' Yannis asked after she'd eaten every scrap of her omelette and was busy devouring a bowl of yogurt and honey. 'Go back to bed and stay there?'

She sighed and resisted the urge to lean into him and kiss him. As right as this all felt and as deeply as her veins burned for his touch, she had to keep her feet grounded. It would be too easy to succumb and allow her heart to spring free.

His phone rang from the other side of the table.

He rolled his eyes and stretched an arm to reach it. Then he frowned. 'It's Andreas. I'd better answer it.'

Leaning back into his seat, he dived straight into conversation with his brother. From the darkening of his eyes and tone, Keren guessed it was more bad news.

'What's happened?' she asked when he'd ended the call.

He rubbed his jaw. 'A potential client we were at the contract stage with has decided to go with Hoults instead of us.'

Her heart sank for him. Two clients in two days was, as far as she knew, unprecedented. 'I'm sorry.'

He nodded grimly and raised his head back to breathe deeply.

'Did they say why?'

'I missed an appointment with them.'

Her eyes widened. That was not like Yannis. He despised tardiness, was punctual to a fault.

'When was the appointment?'

He shook his head. 'It doesn't matter,' he muttered. Then he took another deep breath and fixed his attention back to her. As their eyes locked together, the sensual gleam returned. Twisting in his chair so their knees touched, he gripped her thighs. His strength and speed were such that she only realised he'd pulled her onto his lap when she was actually on it, straddling him. Through the lace of her knickers, she felt his excitement grow at warp speed and her breaths quickened at the same rate.

'I need to be inside you. Let's go back to bed,' he urged.

Heat already bubbling, she wrapped her arms around his neck and razed her teeth into his cheek.

Holding her securely, he stood, lifting her with him. He carried her like that all the way to their bedroom.

Keren laid her head back against the bath's roll-top. A swell of contentment rolled through her.

Contentment was an emotion she hadn't felt in a long, long time.

'What are you thinking?' Yannis asked casually.

They'd adopted the position they'd long ago discovered worked best for them when sharing a bath: facing each other, Yannis's legs bent, his calves resting against her waist, Keren's much smaller legs stretched out against his sides, her feet resting on his chest.

Keeping her eyes closed, she serenely answered, 'That silence is golden.'

'Not thinking about how much you want to come over here?'

'I'm good, thanks.'

'Not even for this?'

She opened one eye.

His shameless erection poked through the bubbles.

Eyes smouldering, he said, 'Want to play?'

'Didn't your mother ever tell you that if you play with something too much, it eventually breaks?'

His grin was wicked. 'Since when do I listen to my mother?'

'Speaking of your mother…'

'Do we have to?'

'Is that Legarde woman still going to the fund-raiser tonight?'

'As far as I know. Why?'

'I think you should go.'

His eyebrow rose in bemusement. 'Are you joking with me?'

'You need to be there.'

'Andreas can handle it,' he dismissed, but not before she caught the flicker in his eye.

'Not as well as you can. Your mind is more forensic than his.'

'I'm not leaving you,' he stated flatly.

'Then take me with you.'

'Now I *know* you are joking.'

'I'm not.'

'You would come?'

She shrugged. 'It's important. If you weren't holding me captive, you'd already be in Athens.'

The gleam came back in his eyes and the torpedo rose back up. 'Holding you captive, am I?'

'Bar the handcuffs.'

'Our old pair are still around somewhere. I can—'

She poked his chest with her toe. 'Stop changing the subject. Are we going or what?'

'I'd much rather cuff you to the bed. *That* will stop you leaving on Monday.'

'Maybe by Monday I won't want to leave.'

His features tightened in an instant. All amusement and sensuality evaporated from his eyes, replaced with an intensity that burned through her.

Impulse had Keren spring forward. Water sloshed everywhere as she clambered on top of him and cupped his cheeks.

Not for the first time she imagined herself drowning in the blue of his eyes.

'Yannis, I don't know how I feel, okay?' she said softly. 'This time yesterday I wanted nothing to do with you, but you touch me and I turn to goo, and now my head is all over the place. I don't know if it's sex making me feel differently about you, so I'm not going to make any promises. We can't go back to the way things were. I can't be trapped in a cage.'

And she didn't know if she could forgive him for finding emotional solace with someone else or forget his maliciousness after she left.

'I know,' he whispered, knotting a fist into her hair. 'Losing Sophia—'

Keren quickly put a finger to his lips and shook her head. *No. Not now. Not like this.*

His jaw clenched. His gaze held hers as if searching for something, but then his features softened and his lips curved into a rueful smile, and he nodded his understanding.

She hadn't realised her shoulders had tightened until they loosened, and she pressed her lips to his.

No one understood her like Yannis did.

She deepened the fusion of their mouths. How she loved the dark taste of his kisses. The way he kissed her told her how much he loved the taste of her kisses too. Their first kiss had been her first real kiss. She'd thought she would combust from the sensory explosion of that first kiss, had had no idea of all the other, even headier sensations he would elicit in her, that she would become a walking, talking tinderbox of lust.

Palming her cheeks, Yannis gently pushed her face away and stared into her eyes. 'I will never try to cage you again, I swear.'

She sighed. She yearned to believe him but promises made in the steam of lust evaporated quickly. They'd had this before and they'd lost it all.

And yet, gazing into eyes brimming with emotion that contained more than mere desire, her heart softened then expanded and another emotion she hadn't felt in so, so long slipped in.

Hope.

Maybe she was losing her mind in this steam of lust. She no longer cared. The one thing—the only thing—she was certain about was this thick, consuming desire that had drugged them both, and she threaded her fingers through his hair, closed her eyes and moulded her lips back to his, crushing herself as tightly to him as she could.

The passion of his response only stoked the furnace burning in her core. His mouth plundered hers as if her kisses were the air he needed to breathe, his hands roaming everywhere, sweeping her back, her sides, grasping her bottom, leaving a trail of sensation in their wake.

Breathing heavily, Keren pulled away from his mouth and danced her fingers down his throat to rest on his chest, moving her thighs to straddle him. She raised herself a little higher. His erection jutted against her folds.

She'd always adored making love by daylight because it meant she could soak in and revel in Yannis. And she'd loved to see the evidence of his desire for her etched on his face.

It was etched there now.

One hand now holding her waist tightly, he trailed a finger all the way down from the base of her throat to the top of her pubis, then he slipped it lower still, liquid eyes becoming hooded when he found her swollen and ready for him. But he gave her no relief, snaking the finger back up over her belly to lightly skim the underside of her breast before taking its weight in his hand. When he flickered a thumb over a puckered nipple, she cried out at the painful pleasure of it, and sank desperately onto his length.

Eyes wide on his, Keren held his shoulders tightly, raised herself up then sank back down. Sensations infused every last inch of her. The coil in her core tensed to a point.

Yannis cupped her whole breast and squeezed with just the right amount of pressure to make her cry out again.

'That's it, you beautiful creature.' His voice was ragged. Husky. 'Let go.'

The moan that came from her mouth sounded wild amongst the roaring of blood in her ears as she lost all control of herself, riding him with wanton abandon, nails digging into his flesh, his groans of pleasure feeding her until ecstasy burst through and all she could see was Yannis's face flickering in the white light.

CHAPTER TEN

'I'D FORGOTTEN HOW good you look in a tux,' Keren said, feasting her eyes over Yannis as she stepped from her dressing room into the bedroom. Sexy whatever he did—or didn't—wear, there was something about him dressed formally that always made her insides clench with pleasure. That late afternoon, he'd donned a navy tuxedo and black bow tie and it fitted his tall, rock-hard frame like a glove. Which was just as well as it had been handstitched. Freshly shaven, hair quiffed, he looked swarthy enough to be the star in his own spy thriller.

'Me?' Yannis shook his head, eyes roaming over her. '*Theos*, you look stunning, *glyko mou*.'

Feeling suddenly anxious, she only just stopped herself from biting into her bottom lip and ruining her freshly applied red lipstick. 'You're sure?'

And now she remembered that this is how it had always been before. She would select an item of clothing to wear to a function like this, get dressed and then ask Yannis's opinion. And then get hurt when he gave an honest answer, especially in those last few months when she'd deliberately chosen more and more provocatively inappropriate outfits.

It had been deliberate, she realised painfully. Deliberate but not conscious. She'd been trying to provoke him into showing her emotion. Any emotion. She'd been desperate for him to show he still felt something, *anything*, for her as a woman.

The dress she'd chosen was far removed from the haute couture the other ladies were bound to be wearing that night, but it was a dress she loved. With off-the-shoulder sleeves that tied in puffed bows just below the elbow, it was white with blood-red roses patterned on it. Floating to mid-calf in bohemian fashion, the skirt had a split in one side that ran to mid-thigh. She'd paired it with four-inch blood-red sandals whose straps crisscrossed over her feet.

Having not worn anything but flip-flops and flat sandals in eighteen months, she'd spent ten minutes practising walking in them in her dressing room while at the same time trying to remember how she'd used to sweep her hair back into an informal but reasonably elegant chignon.

Once she was ready, she'd held her wedding and engagement rings in the palm of her hand. She'd come so close to sliding them on her finger. She'd wanted to. Desperately. But she wasn't ready. Not yet. Instead, she'd placed them on the dressing table and then opened her jewellery box and finally allowed the memories contained within it to soak into her. She'd selected the pair of chunky gold hooped earrings Yannis had bought her to celebrate their first month together and three solid gold bracelets that glittered under the light.

His chest rose sharply and his throat moved. His nostrils flared before he said, simply, 'You're beautiful. You're always beautiful. And that dress is beautiful too.'

The anxiety breathed away from her and she smiled. 'And that, my love, is the correct answer.'

He didn't return the smile. 'I should never have criticised you. I think...' He sighed and ran his fingers through his hair. 'I went too far. I wanted to protect you from the cattiness of my world. I forgot you didn't need my protection. Not in that respect.' His shoulders rose and he grimaced. 'I fell in love with *you* and I will regret making you feel that you weren't good enough exactly as you are for the rest of my life. Because you were. Good enough. You were perfect exactly as you were. You still are.'

Her heart almost breaking and choking in one confused wrench, Keren walked carefully to him in her four-inch heels and placed a hand on a shoulder she knew was marked afresh from her nails.

'You've messed your hair up,' she said softly. 'Lean forward.'

He bowed his head.

Working with the tips of her fingers, she carefully put it back into place, letting the scent of his freshly applied cologne infuse her senses. No one in the world smelled as good as Yannis.

'There,' she said when she was done.

He took a hand and brought it to his lips. 'Thank you.' Then he smiled, the old devilish look returning to his eyes. 'We should leave now before I give in to temptation and rip that dress from you to devour what's underneath. But the car is waiting for us.'

Threading her fingers through his, she rubbed her nose to his neck. 'You'll just have to wait until we get back.'

'If I can...'

'You can,' she assured him.

Hands clasped together, they left their room.

Keren's stomach made its usual plunge when they passed the nursery. Some unbidden impulse had her blurt out the question that had woven in and out of her mind throughout the day. 'Why did you keep it all?'

She didn't have to explain any further.

'I didn't have the right. It was a decision for both of us when the time was right,' he explained simply. 'What do you think we should do with it? We can—'

'We can talk about it another time,' she interrupted hastily. 'Let's just concentrate on you dealing with cow-face Legarde and me dealing with your parents.'

She felt his scrutiny but kept her gaze fixed on the approaching staircase.

'You are nervous about seeing them?'

'A bit. Your mother's nails are very long and sharp.'

'Her tongue's sharper.'

'Thanks for the reminder. Do they hate me?'

'No.'

They'd reached the bottom of the staircase. She stopped walking and looked at his face to see if he was telling the truth.

'*No,*' he repeated with more force. 'They don't hate you. They will be glad to see you.'

'Have you told them I'm coming?'

'I told Andreas. He's passed the message on... And I forgot to tell you he'll be meeting us at the airfield.'

'Good.' Keren had always got on brilliantly with Yannis's older brother and especially brilliantly with his husband. Then a thought smacked into her. 'My passport!'

Private jet or not, Agon was a sovereign country and

entering mainland Greece required a passport. Her passport was in her grab-bag on her boat.

Yannis's responding wide grin immediately filled her with suspicion.

'What?'

He reached into the inside pocket of his dinner jacket and removed two passports.

Keren plucked them from his hand. The first one she flipped open had her unsmiling face in it.

'You've had this all the time?' she asked, confused.

He shrugged. 'It wasn't safe to keep it on the boat.'

'But how did you know where to find it?'

'You're a woman who thinks of safety first. It made sense you would keep it where you could easily get hold of if needed.'

'It was in a waterproof bag.'

'The bag is in my safe.'

Putting her hands on her hips, she stared at him with disbelief. 'So you've had my passport, phone and money here all this time? And you let me believe it was still on the boat?'

He didn't look the slightest bit abashed. 'I did offer for you to put the divorce papers in the safe. If you'd trusted me with them, you would have seen your bag was in there.'

She shook her head. 'You're unbelievable.'

'I think the word you mean is *incredible*. And yes, I am.'

'No, I definitely mean unbelievable.'

'All is fair in love and war, *glyko mou*.'

'You think?'

'I *know*.'

'I'll make sure to remember that.'

But, no matter how indignantly prim she held her chin aloft as she followed him out to the waiting car, Keren couldn't deny the thrills of joy racing through her veins.

All's fair in love and war.

Love…

Yannis's parents' home in Athens was an imposing neo-classical building set in the old quarter of Plaka, known locally as the neighbourhood of the gods, close to the Acropolis museum. Keren had loved the bustling area that effortlessly combined ancient archaeology and vibrant culture so much that they'd spoken about buying a home there for themselves.

She'd also loved Nina and Aristidis's sprawling terracotta courtyard garden. Filled with delights that included ancient statues and potted olive trees older than her grandparents, it was like stepping into ancient Greece, but with a modern twist, a garden far different to what she'd expected from a couple who thrived on stuffy formality.

The courtyard was already filled with people and noise when they arrived with Andreas and Pavlos, and the knotting of her stomach betrayed to Keren how nervous she was about this evening. She doubted there would be many people there she hadn't met before or who didn't know that she and Yannis were divorcing, and she braced herself for amazed looks and whispers behind hands.

She couldn't see through the crowd to find the two people she was most nervous about seeing. Yannis's parents. For all that he insisted they didn't hate her, she didn't imagine they would be as welcoming as his brother had been. Andreas had greeted her with a tight hug and a whispered, 'It is so good to see you.' Pavlos's embrace had practically choked the life out of her.

The knot in her belly tightened when she caught sight of the tall, swarthy man approaching them. The top of the head of his coiffured wife bobbed beside him.

And then they were standing before them.

They embraced their two sons and Pavlos, Andreas's husband, without even looking at her. But then they fixed their attention on her.

Every eye in the courtyard was watching them.

Keren held her breath and tried not to wilt under the weight of their scrutiny. There was something almost symbiotic about Nina and Aristidis's body language, something she thought must come from the long, enduring strength of their marriage. Her parents were the same.

She was still holding her breath when a smile, tentative to begin with, broke out on Nina's face and then Keren found herself pulled into a tight, perfumed embrace that squeezed the air she'd been holding out of her lungs.

'It is wonderful to have you home, *kopelia mou*,' Nina said. 'We have missed you very much.'

There was no time to take this in for Aristidis wanted in on the act and, with Nina keeping hold of Keren's hand, planted a dozen kisses to her face.

Utterly thrown at such heartfelt greetings, Keren responded in kind. If she thought this was an act for their audience, the tears shining in Nina's eyes told her otherwise and she found herself blinking back tears of her own.

Not in a million years had she expected that.

So much for them throwing parties to celebrate her departure.

As the crowd had drawn in around them, there were

too many other people wanting to embrace her for Keren to properly think about this startling turn of events but by the time things had settled and she'd been handed a Santorini Sunrise cocktail, the knot in her belly had loosened and she could breathe properly.

As the function was a fund-raiser for Nina and Aristidis's latest pet project, socialising was soon put to one side. Tonight, they were hosting an auction, one that was very different from the auctions the Filipidises specialised in. Rows of chairs had been set out in a horseshoe at the far end of the courtyard and everyone was invited to take their seats.

Aristidis took the auctioneer mantle and soon the most ridiculous array of lots were being furiously fought over for the most ridiculous sums. When Yannis got in a bidding war for a set of children's Japanese cartoon trading cards, Keren found herself laughing harder than she'd laughed in the longest time.

She'd forgotten that even high society could poke fun at itself.

She'd forgotten a lot of things. Like Nina's tenderness when they'd lost Sophia.

When Keren had eventually been discharged from hospital, she'd returned home to find Nina had moved in. For two weeks, her mother-in-law had cared for her with the same kind of love her own mother would have given her. Later, Keren had learned that the only reason her mother hadn't flown out to be with her—and that would have been a huge thing for her as both her parents had found flying to Agon for their wedding the most terrifying experience of their lives—had been because Nina had promised she would look after Keren for her.

How could she have forgotten that?

And how could she have forgotten the words Aristidis had whispered after the funeral? *'Don't fight the grief, kopelia mou. If it gets too much, Nina and I are always here for you. You're our daughter and we love you.'*

She blinked frantically, suddenly terrified, both from the tears that were burning to be set free and from the tempest of emotions the memories were evoking.

The next lot was for a pair of tatty plastic sunflowers and Keren fought hard to keep up with the spirit of the auction and applaud when a financier paid twenty thousand euros for them.

'Are you okay?' Yannis asked, leaning in to whisper in her ear.

She pasted a smile to her face and nodded with as much enthusiasm as she could feign.

'Sure?'

She squeezed his hand then released it to clap enthusiastically along with everyone else over the sale of something she'd missed.

'Which one's Jeanie Legarde?' she asked, groping desperately for conversation to distract her.

'Don't make it obvious that you're looking, but two rows behind us to your left—the silver-haired woman wearing horn-rimmed glasses.'

She waited until her curiosity got too much and turned her head as discreetly as she could. She clocked who he meant immediately, and as her eyes landed on the woman's face, she was taken by the strong urge to leap over the seated people between them and slap her.

The violence of her reaction to a woman she hadn't even spoken to frightened her.

'Stop staring,' Yannis chided quietly, taking her hand again.

Breathing deeply, Keren tore her stare away and dragged her attention to the final lot of the auction.

What had caused that reaction? The fact that Jeanie Legarde was threatening to use a rival auction house? That was business. It wasn't personal. Yannis and Andreas would talk to her that evening and they would change her mind with the effortless charm, expertise and nous that had served the Filipidises so well for centuries.

Blood whooshed in her head, dizzying her as she realised why she felt so hateful towards the French lady. It was because she was messing Yannis around and, for Keren, that had always felt personal even when it had been business. He used to tell her tales of difficult clients and she'd secretly longed to get revenge on them for him. Once, he'd brought a particularly obnoxious client who'd driven him to distraction to their home for dinner and she'd had to resist spitting in his food.

That had been when they'd been a team, because once, they *had* been a team. It hadn't been perfect but it had been heavenly all the same, their imperfections nothing more than the rough that needed to be taken with the smooth.

Then the smooth had disappeared and Yannis had turned away from her and the love they'd shared had turned into hate...

Except that a tiny grain of her love for him had lodged itself tight in that hate, and that tiny grain had burst out at the sight of him. Being back with him, making love, just *being* with him, had overloaded her senses with Yannis's essence, giving the grain the nourishment it needed to bloom back into spring.

Didn't that grain deserve the chance to see summer again? Didn't *they* deserve that chance? Wasn't the truth that though she'd been as free as a macaw without him, she'd never once felt a jot of the happiness she'd experienced with him when things had been good?

But wasn't the truth, too, that her misery in those last months with him had been the hardest she'd ever had to endure? Could she really risk opening herself to that again?

She watched him rise from his seat with her heart pounding and a sick feeling in her stomach that she wasn't sure was a good sick or a bad sick.

Could she do it? Give her heart back to him? Trust that he wouldn't neglect it and then turn his back on it? Trust that he wouldn't try and suffocate her again?

Trust that he wanted her back for *her*?

'We're going to have a chat with a certain Ms Legarde,' Yannis murmured.

Keren blinked herself back to the present and saw Andreas and Pavlos had joined them. She swallowed. 'Good luck.'

He winked. 'No luck needed.' Then he swiped a kiss over her mouth and strode off, his brother at his side.

'Drink?' Pavlos asked.

Expelling a breath, she nodded, glad that he was with her. Pavlos was one of her favourite people in the world. They'd always tried to rig the seating at functions they'd both attended, be it business or personal, to ensure they were seated next to each other.

Swiping the pair of them a Santorini Sunrise from a passing waitress, Pavlos lead her to a circular table which was a little more secluded than the others and which gave them a good view of Yannis and Andreas chatting to Jeanie Legarde. Nothing in their body language hinted at tension.

No sooner had they sat than Nina and her sister, Ariadne, joined them. Keren had missed Ariadne earlier and was overcome with gratitude to be swept up in another bear hug.

Nina sat beside her and inched her chair as close as she could get, holding Keren's hand tightly as if afraid to let her go.

'It really is good to have you here again,' she said in a low voice once Ariadne and Pavlos were deep in conversation. 'I have prayed every day for you to come home.'

Her throat closing, Keren could only stare into the blue eyes Nina's youngest son had inherited.

Nina covered the hand she was holding and squeezed. 'Today is the first time I've seen Yannis smile since you left.'

'Nina!'

They all turned their heads to see Aristidis, holding court with a group of self-important men, beckoning his wife.

Nina gave Keren the faintest of winks, kissed her cheek and left to join her husband.

Keren moved her chair closer to Pavlos and joined in the conversation until Ariadne went off to mingle, leaving them alone with a pair of fresh cocktails.

'How do you think it's going?' Keren asked, nodding at Yannis and Andreas, who were still in deep conversation with Jeanie Legarde.

His eyes narrowed slightly in contemplation. 'They all seem relaxed.'

As he said this, Jeanie suddenly threw her head back and laughed.

Keren met Pavlos's eye and they both laughed.

The easy conversation they'd always found together

resumed as if they'd never parted and soon Pavlos was filling her in on all the gossip she'd missed. Keren had never cared for gossip but Pavlos was so funny in the way he told his stories that, for him, she was happy to make an exception.

While he regaled her, she kept looking over at Yannis at the other side of the courtyard. The conversation between the three of them showed no sign of letting up and yet every time she looked over, it was as if he sensed her gaze on him for his eyes would flicker over to her. Even with the distance between them, the flicker of his gaze heated her veins with a frisson of arousal and she found herself having to really concentrate on Pavlos's chatter and not succumb to fantasies about what would happen when she and Yannis got back to the villa...

'How did you find living on water?'

Pavlos's swerve from gossip to personal was entirely expected. She was only surprised it had taken him so long.

She had a drink of her cocktail. 'I love it.'

He nudged her with his elbow. 'That's a *terrible* answer.'

She laughed. 'Be more specific, then!'

'Where did you sail to? What were your favourite places?'

'I mostly sailed the Caribbean then I moved on to Europe before the hurricane season started. I was thinking of doing the South Pacific next.'

'*Was* thinking? You're planning to stay? For good?'

She bit into her lip. The truth was, she was torn. How could she trust herself to make the right decision? She'd followed her heart with Yannis before and all it had brought her was pain. But the thought of leaving him again…

That *hurt*.

Whatever she decided to do, she couldn't have this conversation with Pavlos before she had it with Yannis.

Even in his inebriated state—Pavlos was now on his fourth cocktail since they'd sat at the table—he must have read something in her expression for he smiled widely. 'Thank God for that!'

'Pav, please, I can't talk about this.'

He rolled his eyes huffily. 'Okay, but before we change the subject, and as I have you to myself, can I just say that if you *are* staying…' He winked. 'Then I thank the Lord, because your husband has been a nightmare.'

Curiosity got the better of her. 'Has he? In what way?'

He pretended to shudder. 'Like Nina when she was going through the worst of the menopause.'

Biting her cheek to stop the burst of laughter that wanted to spring free, she gave him her best unamused look.

'Did I say something sexist?' he asked innocently.

'Lots of women would say so, but you were saying about Yannis being a nightmare,' she prompted.

'Just ugly behaviour,' he evaded.

'What kind of ugly behaviour?'

'You know the kind.' Then his eyes gleamed and he leaned in closer. 'Also, you coming back takes the pressure off us.'

'What pressure?'

'Aristidis and Nina are desperate for the patter of little Filipidis feet. Aristidis keeps going on about the future and the need for an heir to carry on the business and the Filipidis name. Nina keeps dropping hints about adoption even though she knows we don't want children. I'm surprised she didn't greet you with a crown of orchids to promote your fertility and—' He cut himself off mid-flow and, clearly horrified, covered his mouth. 'Oh, Keren, I am so sorry. I got carried away. I...' He grabbed her hands and pulled them to him. 'Please, forgive me, it's just so great you being back here, and I've missed you so much, and I got carried away, and for a moment I forgot.'

'It's okay,' she assured him with no idea how she was able to keep her voice even. Pavlos hadn't meant any harm and she could tell how close he was to being drunk. His words were beginning to slur. A drunk Pavlos was an indiscreet Pavlos.

'It isn't. I should never have loaded that all on you, not after everything—'

'I said it's okay,' she interrupted sharply before he could build up another head of steam.

She couldn't bear to discuss Sophia in such a crowded place. She found it virtually impossible to talk about her as it was, but if she could, it should be with Yannis.

Yannis wanted to talk about her. She knew it. He'd tried but she'd steered him away. She just couldn't do it, could only stop the banshee screams that grew too loudly in her head at the mention of Sophia with questions that required monosyllabic answers.

'I'm sorry they've been pressurising you,' she said in a softer tone. It wasn't Pavlos's fault that talking about her lost daughter felt like having iced needles plunged into her heart. 'Has Yannis been getting it in the neck from them too?'

He grimaced and downed his cocktail. 'What do you think?'

Across the courtyard, she could see the conflab with

Jeanie Legarde was over. The three of them were heading into the house. Yannis had brought the contract with him. She guessed Jeanie was going to sign it.

Pavlos indicated for another drink. 'They don't mean to put the pressure on—you know what they're like. It's what we signed up for when we agreed to marry their sons, isn't it? We agreed to become Filipidises. Andreas and I hadn't realised how much the pressure had been building on us until Yannis made his promise.'

'What promise?'

His fresh cocktail was delivered to him. He had a large drink of it and hiccupped.

She patted his back. 'Tell me about Yannis's promise,' she urged.

Taking another drink first, he explained, 'Aristidis called a family summit a few weeks ago. It turned into a big argument and ended with Andreas and Aristidis giving Yannis the ultimatum.'

Somehow, she managed to refrain from shaking his shoulders. 'Which was?'

'That he gets you back or gets kicked out of the business.'

CHAPTER ELEVEN

KEREN FORCED HERSELF to remain calm while she tried her best to take in everything Pavlos had just told her. Pavlos was drunk. She needed to be careful not to misinterpret him.

She leaned her face into his and, once his eyes were focused on her, quietly but precisely said, 'Have I got this right? Aristidis and Andreas told Yannis they were going to kick him out of the business if I didn't come back?'

He covered his mouth again.

She gritted her teeth. 'Yes or no?'

'Yes. But it's not like that. Not that bad. You know?'

'No, I don't know. I need you to tell me. You said Yannis's behaviour had been ugly. Is that the reason? Or is it the Filipidis heir thing? An ultimatum to produce the next generation?'

He shook his head. 'I can't. I'm sorry. I said too much. Andreas will kill me.'

'*I'll* kill you if you don't tell me!'

Expression pained, he finished his cocktail. 'It's not just the need for a Filipidis heir but—'

'Not *just*,' she pounced. Her heart pounced too, a painful pouncing kick against her ribs. 'But it did play a part in it. Yes or no?'

'Keren…'

Yannis, Andreas and Jeanie had emerged from the house and were now heading towards them.

How she stopped herself screaming in Pavlos's face she would never know. 'Yes or no?'

He closed his eyes.

'Yes or no?'

His eyes snapped open. *'Yes.'*

Three seconds later, Yannis and the others reached their table. Those three seconds were just long enough for Keren to slip a mask on her face and smile in greeting.

Yannis bowed his head, kissed her mouth then introduced her to Jeanie Legarde.

Seats were taken, more cocktails were brought to their table and soon they were joined by others, tables being pushed together, a happy summer evening filled with the filthy rich who'd collectively raised a huge sum of money for a very worthy cause and were now all intent on letting their hair down and enjoying the excellent Filipidis hospitality.

All except for Keren.

If her passport wasn't in Yannis's inside dinner jacket pocket, she would have slipped out of the house and made a run for it.

Nausea churned in her stomach making even the delicious-looking canapés revolt her. But she kept smiling. Kept up with conversation. Kept her expression animated. Pretended not to see the concern in Yannis's eyes every time she dared look at him. Pretended not to flinch at his touch.

Ants had been let loose on her skin and were crawling all over her. She wanted to crawl away and hide under a rock with them as escape and punishment at her stupidity.

She even managed to relate the tale, at Yannis's prompting, of how she came to be called Keren and not Karen. It was a tale he'd always found hilarious.

She left out the part about there being complications with her birth. She'd suffered from the same pregnancy high blood pressure issues her own mother had but the difference had been the outcome. Keren and her mother were both still here to tell the tale. But she had no wish to discuss that with anyone, let alone strangers.

'Mum had to stay in hospital for quite a while after having me,' she told them.

Ten days her mother spent there, two of them fighting for her life. Keren had gone through the same thing a generation later.

'So she sent my dad to register my birth. He dropped in at his workplace on the way there to share the good news and his workmates dragged him down the pub to celebrate—my dad's not a drinker so I'm pretty sure it's the only time he's ever said yes to that. By the time he got to the registry office he was drunk and slurring so much that the registrar misheard what he said my name was to be. When Dad realised the mistake, he was too embarrassed to correct it. It took him two months to confess to my mum,' she added with a grin to hide the unexpected wistfulness that clenched at her heart.

Her mum had been cross with her dad when he finally confessed but had grown to like it, had often told Keren what a pretty name it was and how well it suited her. Keren had always lived in hope her parents would accidentally try something else new and grow to like that too and now she felt another clench in her heart. For the first time in her life she wished she'd grown up to be a zebra finch like the rest of the Burridges.

If she had, she would have a nice stable job, probably in her home town, be dating a nice young man, probably also from her home town, be making plans to buy a home together or for their wedding, probably both. She would be comfortable and settled. The only danger of hurt would come from what her insurance policy called Acts of God.

She would get her boat back and then she would set sail for England, Keren decided. She hadn't seen her family since Christmas. They might not understand her in the slightest, but they had always *tried* to understand, and they had always supported her. They had always loved her.

The only person who had ever understood her was Yannis, but his support was a lie and she'd been a fool to hope that he might still love her.

He understood her so well he'd known exactly what to say and do to win her back. If not for a drunken Pavlos, she would have fallen for it.

It was late when they left Athens. Andreas and Pavlos changed their plans and shared their flight back on Yannis's jet, giving Yannis and Andreas the opportunity to fill Keren—Pavlos zonked out before they were in the air—on what happened with Jeanie Legarde and how they'd coaxed her into changing her mind and auctioning her late brother's masterpieces with Filipidis Fine Art & Antiquities *and* without a drop in the commission. From the admiring looks Andreas kept shining on Yannis, the younger Filipidis brother had been the force behind the change of mind. From the relief in both brothers' faces compared to when they'd arrived, neither had had high hopes that they could change it.

Keren had never had any doubt that Yannis would talk Jeanie Legarde round. The man could talk a sea-wanderer into buying salt water. Once he fixed those striking blue eyes on someone and gave them his full attention, they were eating out of his hands in minutes. Even she, who'd built a fortress around her heart to protect herself from him, had seen the fortress bulldozed to ash in the space of a day.

Once they landed, Andreas and Pavlos jumped into Yannis's waiting car with them for a lift back to their apartment in Agon's main town. As Yannis's villa was closer to the airfield, his driver dropped him and Keren back first. Even so, it was almost two o'clock in the morning when they finally arrived back.

Keren got out of the car and virtually sagged with the relief of being able to lose the bonhomie she'd maintained since Pavlos had dropped his bomb on her lap.

The relief was short-lived, a mere breath before she steeled herself for what must come next.

They hadn't even closed the villa door behind them when Yannis pulled her into his arms and crushed his mouth to hers.

Keren fisted her hands by her sides and fought the automatic sensory explosion that even the numbing of her mind was unable to prevent.

He pulled away and put his hands on her shoulders. 'What's wrong?'

She shrugged his hands off and summoned all her courage to look him in the eye.

She never wanted to gaze into those beautiful eyes again.

'I've decided I won't be staying. I'd be grateful if you

could arrange for whoever stole my boat to return it to me. Now.'

Shock flared in his eyes and tics played out around his lips before they tugged into a smile. 'That is a good joke.'

'Not a joke,' she refuted evenly. Turning on her heel, she headed straight to Yannis's study. 'I'm leaving and I'm not coming back.'

The knots in her belly were coiled too tightly and her energy too drained from spending hours pretending everything was hunky-dory for her to cope with a confrontation or navel-gaze at her foolishness in falling for his cruel games. Yannis's maliciousness since she'd left him meant she should have known better.

He didn't hesitate to follow her. 'What's happened?'

'Why do you assume something's happened?'

'Because I'm not an idiot.'

'No,' she agreed. 'You're not. And neither am I.' She couldn't stop herself from bitterly adding, 'I know everything, Yannis.'

He snatched hold of her wrist before she could push open the study door. 'What do you think you know?'

Hating that her skin still burned joyously at his touch, Keren prised his fingers off and stared at him with all the contempt she could muster. 'That your father and brother gave you an ultimatum. Get me back so we can produce an heir or be kicked out of the business.'

His face turned ashen. His lips parted and his throat moved but no sound came out.

'Thank you for not denying it.' She gave a tight smile and stepped into the study.

'It was not like that,' he said hoarsely.

'Oh, so they didn't tell you to get me back?'

'Not like you think they said it.' He pulled at his hair. 'Let me fix you a drink. I will explain everything.'

Feeling that she really could be sick, she went to the safe. 'I don't want anything from you but my boat, now get your phone out and make that call and get my boat back to me.'

A tiny tear cut through her heart to find the code was the same as it had been when she'd lived there. Their wedding date.

She refused to let it halt her focus. Her grab-bag was in the safe, just as Yannis had said. Probably the only thing he hadn't lied about. She pulled it out and quickly checked the contents. Her phone and money were still in it. She dropped the red clutch bag she'd taken out with her that night and which she'd put her passport in on the return journey from Athens into it, and then checked her phone. Damn it, it had run out of charge.

She closed her eyes briefly and took a deep breath before turning back to face him.

He was standing like a statue, staring at her. His features had tightened so much his cheekbones looked like they were about to poke through the skin.

'Make the call, Yannis.'

He cleared his throat. 'Keren…'

The pain from the tear that cut through her heart this time would have doubled her over if it hadn't released a bolt of the fury she'd been trying her best to contain. 'Make that call and give me back my boat!' she screamed. 'Make it now or I'm out of here and I don't care if it's the middle of the night. I'll walk to the police station barefoot if I have to and report it stolen, just give me back my boat!'

The pulse on his jaw was throbbing as strongly as

she'd ever seen it, but she must have got through to him for, his eyes not leaving her face, he reached slowly into his inside jacket pocket and removed his phone. He held it up as if to prove it really was his phone before dropping his gaze and flicking through it.

'Make the call on loudspeaker,' she ordered. 'And just so you know, if it's not here by the time the sun comes up, I will update my blog and tell the world every nasty, vindictive thing you've done to me, you cruel, selfish *bastard*.'

Even though they both knew she could understand little of what was said, he did as she commanded, speaking in clipped tones to the voice groggy from sleep on the other end of the call. She felt not the slightest ounce of guilt. They'd stolen her boat. Stuff their sleep deprivation.

By the time the call was over, she'd managed to swallow her fury back into something that resembled calm. Giving another tight smile, she nodded. 'Thank you. Now, I'm going upstairs to get changed. Don't follow me.'

Keeping a tight hold of her grab-bag, she practically flew up the stairs and locked herself in her dressing room. She quickly changed into a non-constricting summer dress, wrenched the comb holding her chignon in place out of her hair, dumped her jewellery on her dresser and replaced the earrings with the studs from her parents, and put her old, flat sandals on.

The only falter in her movements came when she left the bedroom and reached the nursery. She reached for the door handle but then backed away before she could open it.

She wouldn't put herself through the pain of entering the room still waiting for the child who would never live in it. Not again.

But she would sit with Sophia under the peach tree until the sun came up. Tell her everything would be okay. Tell her Mummy would be back to see her soon.

The front door was locked.

Keren punched in the code to override it. Nothing happened. Yannis must have changed it.

Fury filling her, she kicked it.

'Every door and window in the villa is locked. I'll deactivate the system after we've spoken.'

She whipped round and found Yannis at the threshold of the main living room. He'd removed his jacket and bow tie and undone the top couple of buttons of his shirt. His hair was sticking up in all directions. He carried a glass of what looked like bourbon.

Using all her might to harden her heart, she gazed at him coldly. 'I have nothing to say to you.'

'That's your prerogative but there's much I have to say to you.'

'I don't want to hear it.'

He shrugged. 'Again, your prerogative, but I *will* have my say. Sunrise isn't for another three hours. Block your ears until then if you must.'

The steel glimmering in his eyes told her clearly that he meant every word.

Fine. If he wanted to *have his say*, then fine. The sooner he'd said it, the sooner she could escape from this hellhole and its lying gaoler.

At the far end of the main living room was the bar. Keeping a tight hold of her grab-bag, Keren followed Yannis to it.

He clapped the lights on. 'What do you want to drink?'

'Nothing. I'll be sailing my boat in a few hours.'

His gaze clashed briefly with hers before he slipped

behind the bar and pulled out a fresh bottle of bourbon and a bottle of cola. He pushed the cola and a glass to her.

The bar had sunken seats set around a range of tables. They were wonderfully cosy and just to look at them and remember just how cosy they'd got on them had Keren hoisting herself onto a bar stool. She hugged the grab-bag to her belly as if it were an amulet that could protect her.

Too late for protection.

She'd known when she sailed into Agon's waters that there was pain ahead, but she'd never dreamed she'd be ripping open a wound that had barely healed. And it was all her own fault. Yannis had shown his true colours in the eighteen months since she'd left him, and she'd swept all that aside and for what? Because he'd made love to her with the same passion that had first cemented their hearts together? Because she hadn't been strong enough to stop the grain of love from blooming back to life?

Because being with Yannis made her feel complete?

She'd swept aside, too, the simple fact that he'd fallen out of love with her. There had been no grain of love for her left in his heart.

He'd played her like a violin and her broken strings had fused back together and let him.

And now she must keep calm, hold firm and let him speak his lies. She would watch his mouth but not let his words penetrate. If, after he'd spoken his lies, he still refused to let her go, she would smash a window. She'd smash all the villa's windows if she had to.

He strode back to her side of the bar. Rather than take a seat, he stood close to her with his back against the bar and folded the arm not holding his drink around his waist.

He stared at her. Keren stared back stonily but refused to allow her eyes to focus. She couldn't. Gazing too deeply into his beautiful, masculine face made her weak. She needed to be strong.

'It is true,' he said quietly. 'My father and brother did give me an ultimatum. There were many factors behind it.'

Startled that he'd started with a truth, Keren felt her stony features crumple and strove valiantly to pull them back into position. 'I'm sure. Must get the Filipidis production line going again.'

He flinched but didn't drop his stare. 'That was never a factor.'

She shrugged.

'It wasn't.'

'It really doesn't matter what the factors were. I should have known better. Why would the man who'd spent eighteen months acting so vindictively suddenly change his tune? As if you wanted me back.' She gave a small, sour laugh. 'At first I thought it was just more vindictiveness, then I assumed it was your pride talking—you not wanting to be the first Filipidis to divorce. About the only thing I didn't think of was pressure from your family and an ultimatum.'

'Their ultimatum wasn't the reason...' He took a deep breath and rubbed at his hair. It hurt her heart to see it stick up even more. 'Keren, I never wanted you to go in the first place.'

She dragged her gaze away from him. 'Well, we both know that's a lie.'

'You leaving... *Theos*, that was the last thing I wanted.'

'Could have fooled me from the way you threw my suitcases in the back of the taxi—'

'We've already been through this, and for someone

who said they had nothing to say, you're not doing a very good job of letting me speak.'

'I just struggle listening to lies.'

'Or are you afraid of what I want to talk about?' he challenged.

The crawling ants returned to her skin with a vengeance.

'You researched divorce on your laptop,' she blurted out. At the naked shock on his face, she swallowed before adding, 'I looked in your laptop's search history.'

Silence surrounded them as if a vacuum had sucked out all the sound.

Something dark flashed over Yannis's face before he bowed his head and sighed heavily. 'You saw that?'

'Yes.'

'Why didn't you tell me?'

'I shouldn't have been looking, should I? You'd got all possessive about your laptop and kept closing the lid when I walked in on you with it. It was obvious you were hiding something.'

'That is not an answer.' His chest rose slowly. 'You should have confronted me. I would have confronted you if the roles had been reversed. And why didn't you mention it yesterday?'

Because she *couldn't*.

Because she'd been too scared, even when Yannis had locked her in the dressing room and she'd still believed she hated him, scared of hearing in his own words all the reasons he hated her enough to wish for a divorce. Knowing he wanted her out of his life…

That had been soul destroying.

'What would have been the point?' she asked bitterly. 'We both knew we were over and then a few days later you took Marla to that thing at the palace to spite me and humiliate me.'

His eyes closed and his chest rose again. 'It was to make you jealous.'

'What?'

'Taking Marla to the palace function. I was trying to get a reaction out of you.' He kneaded his fingers into his skull and shook his head. 'An idea that backfired spectacularly.' His eyes landed back on her. 'God forgive me. I wasn't thinking straight. I knew I was losing you.'

Keren felt suddenly winded. Her next, 'What?' was barely audible.

'I was losing you. I could feel it. It was my last roll of the dice to bring you back to me.'

She hugged her grab-bag even tighter to her bruised chest. The ants were biting into her skin, ravenous in their destruction. 'That's not true,' she whispered. 'You're the one who pulled away from me. You stopped loving me—'

'Never—'

'You turned your back on me every single night!' She could do nothing to stop the rise in her voice. 'You never touched me. I went from your lover to your possession. You wanted to control me—you admitted that only the other day!—and yet you hated me doing anything without you or without your permission!'

'For God's sake, Keren, why the hell do you think I behaved like that?' His own voice had risen in volume too. 'I was terrified.'

'Of *what*?'

'*Everything!*' he bellowed. Then he stilled, closed his eyes and exhaled slowly before focusing his stare back on her. 'I see it all so clearly now but when we were living it, it felt like this unstoppable force, a tsunami crashing on us and sweeping you away from me. I didn't know how to reach you any more. You were slipping away from me and the harder I tried to pull you back, the harder you fought me. I didn't handle it well, I see that now, but I would not wish to live that time again so I could do things differently because I never want to live those days again and I would rather die than make you live a second of it. We both went to hell…'

The iced needles primed themselves against her heart. She could see where this was heading.

'Don't go there.' Her warning came out as a whimper.

He drank some of his bourbon and breathed in deeply. 'I *will* go there, *glyko mou*, because we have tiptoed around it too many times and destroyed our marriage because of it. Don't you remember how things were between us? How much we loved each other? Our marriage was working. *We* were working. From the day we met we fit together. You and me. But then we lost…'

She covered her ears and shook her head violently. 'Please. Yannis. Don't.'

But he removed her trembling hands and clasped them tightly in his.

His gaze bore into her, compassion mingled with the determination.

'We lost Sophia,' he continued. 'We lost her. Our baby died. And you broke.'

She shook her head. The back of her eyes were burning.

'You broke, Keren. And, God forgive me, I didn't know how to fix you.'

CHAPTER TWELVE

KEREN COULD FEEL the bruise of her rapid, icy heartbeats against her ribs and hear its staccato in her ear. Could feel the blood pumping through her body and gushing through the wail of the banshee locked in her head screaming its agony. A waterfall of hot, stinging tears poured down her face.

Yannis released her hands and palmed her sodden, trembling cheeks, catching and brushing the tears away with his thumb.

'I'm sorry for failing you,' he said hoarsely. 'All my life, the world has fallen on a plate for me. Bad things happen to other people. I wasn't equipped to deal with it, and I wasn't equipped to deal with a broken wife. You turned in on yourself. You hardly ate, you hardly spoke… Everyone said I had to give you time and space, and God knows I tried…'

'I never wanted space from *you*.' Her words choked their way out of her.

'But I didn't *know* that.'

She grabbed his shirt, making a fist of the cotton, and swallowed the worst of the tears away. 'You pushed me away.'

Sorrow etched his face. 'I'm sorry, *glyko mou.*'

'You stopped wanting me.'

'Yes.'

The brutality of his answer made her flinch.

She let go of his shirt, would have pushed him away if he hadn't moved his hands from her face into the tresses of her hair. 'I never stopped loving you,' he said. 'Never. But I couldn't make love to you. Those functions stopped working in me. All I could see was your face when you came round from the anaesthetic and I had to tell you we'd lost her.'

Nausea rolled violently and the iced needles plunged even deeper into Keren's heart as the most traumatic moment of her life echoed back through her, but she didn't pull her gaze from him because now all *she* could see for was the agony on Yannis's face when he'd broken the news to her.

'You broke too,' she whispered, voicing the realisation as it hit her.

'No.'

'You *did*.' She made another fist with his shirt, remembering the giant sobs that had wracked his body when the nurse had brought Sophia to them and he'd cradled her lifeless but perfect form in his arms.

She'd been swaddled in a pink blanket, Keren remembered. She'd been so tiny and precious. Like a little doll.

Keren had stayed in her hospital bed for a week. Yannis had returned to an empty home.

The silence must have been deafening for him. Torturous.

And then she'd come home the day before the funeral and it had been like she'd been submerged in dark, murky water, too blinded by the darkness to see that Yannis was drowning too.

'Everything was put on your shoulders,' she remembered, her voice cracking. 'My care, the funeral...' She shook her head against the grief swelling back up. She needed to fight her way through it before it consumed her and doused the trail of her thoughts. 'You even chose the outfit we buried her in.'

Even the peach tree had been his idea. When they'd left the villa to choose it, it was the first time she'd left their home since the funeral.

'You were dealing with your own grief and carrying the burden of a wife who was practically catatonic. That would have broken anyone.'

Yannis's jaw tightened before his beautiful face twisted and he shuddered. An animalistic howl ripped from his throat and he pulled her to him, crushing her tightly.

Keren held him just as tightly.

Her heart breaking at his pain, she clasped the back of his cradled head, wishing with all her heart that they'd done this two years ago.

Eventually, the tremors subsided and Yannis gently pulled out of the embrace. Cupping her cheeks in his hands, he gazed at her with damp eyes.

'Losing Sophia...' He swallowed. 'That was a pain I didn't know existed.' The pulses in his jaw throbbed. 'Not until they told me to prepare myself for losing you too. Keren...that would have killed me.'

The ice in her heart raced through to her veins at the starkness in his stare.

'But somehow you pulled through, and I was able to bring you home and you began to heal, but the healing was only physical. When you looked at me...' He swallowed again. 'Keren, there was nothing there. Nothing at all. And *Theos*, you were so fragile. It was like you were made of porcelain and all it needed was one little knock for you to shatter to pieces. I was terrified of being the one to inflict that knock on you. That's why I couldn't make love to you, even once you had healed, and I think it's why those functions stopped working in me—how could I make love to a woman made of porcelain without breaking her?'

Her stomach cramped violently to imagine his suffering.

Yannis had been locked in hell as much as she had.

She gently tugged his hands off her before asking in a small voice, 'Is that why you ended up turning to Marla?'

His face twisted again. 'I never turned to Marla or anyone. You have to believe that.'

'But you were with her all the time.'

He tipped his head back and sighed deeply. 'After we lost Sophia, Andreas ran the business single-handed for months. He worked himself into the ground. I owed him time off but by then I knew our marriage was in serious trouble. I didn't dare leave you for the time the business needed. Marla knows virtually everything about the business and was willing to step up to ease the workload for me until Andreas came back and we could put things back on a normal footing. It was just work. I swear.'

'But you took her to the palace function. How did you think making me jealous was going to repair things between us?'

'But that's just it—I wasn't thinking. By that stage, I was desperate and, God forgive me for this, I was starting to hate you. You'd pulled yourself out of your shell and everyone agreed you were better, but you *weren't* better.' His face tightened into a grimace. 'Not better with me.

I'd always thought your father's error with your name had been a form of divine inspiration because the meaning of your name was the most apt of anyone I'd ever met. You were a ray of light that made my world a brighter, happier place from the day we met. You'd pulled yourself out of the darkness but the light that had always shone in you had gone and I couldn't read you any more, and that frightened me more than when you were lost in the darkness. That's why I got so angry when you announced you were going off to Morocco—it wasn't anger, it was fear.'

'What were you scared of?'

The distortion of his features at this question frightened her.

'Don't you understand?' he rasped. 'You almost *died*. I thought I was going to have to bury you with our daughter. I have never known terror like it...' He clasped at his head. 'I developed this deep-rooted fear that if I let you out of my sight then something bad would happen to you. I couldn't bear to be parted from you and I *hated* the thought of you working and travelling anywhere without me there to keep you safe, but I didn't know how to reach you or talk to you and so I became more possessive and controlling. Every time I left the villa I was afraid I'd come home and find you gone. I even suggested having another baby, which is the most crass thing I could have asked of you. *Theos*, we hadn't made love in months and months. I could have made love to you, my desire had retuned, but I didn't know how to speak to you about it. To just try and make love...' He shook his head again. 'A wall had built between us and I didn't know how to break it. We hadn't really spoken either, had we, not properly, not unless you count shouting at each other as speaking. But I got it in my head that a baby would fix things, and you just looked at me like I was something dirty you'd trodden in and I knew…'

'Knew what?' she whispered when his words faltered.

His throat moved a number of times. He grabbed at his hair. 'That you were going to leave me. That's why I was looking on divorce sites. It wasn't for me. I was looking at how I could stop *you* from divorcing *me*.'

Her limbs weak, her heart ragged, Keren took his half-filled glass of bourbon off the bar and drank it in one swallow. Closing her eyes, she welcomed the burn of the liquid down her throat and the numbing of the pain engulfing her. 'I'm sorry for my part in everything too,' she whispered.

'You have nothing to be sorry for.'

'Yes, I do. I…' She swallowed. 'I…'

'What?' he asked gently.

Unable to get the words out, she brushed a tear away and swallowed as hard as she could. 'We didn't just lose our baby, did we? We lost *us*.'

'But you've found yourself again and now we can find us again. Look at how good things were for us these last few days. We're almost there. We can repair it. I know we can.'

Oh, his words hurt so much. Too much. 'It's too late.'

'No.'

'Yes. It's all gone too far. If you wanted me back because you still have feelings for me then I might have been able to forgive your despicable behaviour to me since I left and given us one more chance but not now. You've lied to me, over and over…'

'I have not.'

'You've used me, and dragging me down memory lane doesn't change that because for all that you said you were looking for divorce sites to stop me leaving you, that doesn't change the fact that the day I left, you *hated* me.' Her voice was rising again. She could do nothing to stop it. 'You threw my cases in the back of that taxi and called me a selfish cow and then you spent eighteen months systematically doing your best to impoverish me and I always knew why—you wanted me destitute so I would come crawling back, just as you predicted, and then you could have the satisfaction of being the one to kick me out and end our marriage and your pathetic pride would—'

'Yes! I hated you!'

Yannis's fury stopped her in her tracks.

'I hated that you were giving up on us without a fight, just like you're doing now, and I hated that there was nothing I could do or say to stop you, but I have never stopped loving you and God knows you've given me enough ammunition to kill my love.'

'What, wanting to start my blog up again?'

'Forget that damned blog! I'm talking about how you abandoned me and then cut me out of your life as if I'd never meant anything to you.'

'I didn't abandon you!' she cried. 'I left you.'

'It's the same thing!' he roared. 'Do you have *any* idea what it was like knowing the woman I loved was out there somewhere but not knowing where? I was going out of my mind! The first I knew you were even alive was when I received the divorce papers! I messed you around with the settlement, not because I wanted to impoverish you but because I was so damn desperate to see you. I wanted to make you angry enough to come home and confront me because I knew that if I could get you alone, we could sort things out, but you just went along with it and continued to ignore me.'

'I never cared about the settlement,' she whispered. 'I just wanted us over with.'

'You think I didn't know that? You wanted to forget I'd ever existed and that destroyed me, but I couldn't give up. And then I got an alert that your blog was active again.'

She blinked in shock.

'Does the username WannabeWanderer mean anything to you?'

All the air left her lungs.

WannabeWanderer was one of her regular blog followers, someone who commented on every post and asked a ton of questions about her life at sea.

'That was *you*?'

'Yes. *Theos*, the blog I'd grown to hate became my lifeline. I could read your words and know you were alive and safe. I could ask you questions and you would answer them—your words, your real words, directed to me. I would study the pictures and videos you posted, and I began to see you emerge. The real you. The Keren I first fell in love with. But you were too safety-conscious to post your exact location and I could never find you.'

'You tried to track me down?'

'I have spent more time on *The Amphitrite* than anywhere else this last year. But I never found you.' He shook his head with a grim smile. 'I had it all planned. How I would act when I found you. Pretend that it was coincidence. Resist from abducting you and locking you in a cabin until you agreed to come home.'

The snigger flew from her lips before she even knew it had formed.

Their eyes met. Locked.

Keren sighed. And Yannis sighed too.

When he opened his mouth to speak again, there was no more anger in his voice. Just sadness. 'I don't think I slept properly in all the time you were gone. I had nightmares about you getting into trouble on the open sea and no one being close enough to save you. I would charge to your rescue but my dreams were like my life—I could never find you.

'I neglected the business. I neglected my family. I neglected my duties. I hated the world. I picked fault in everyone and everything. Most of my household staff quit—that's why there are so many unfamiliar faces here. If not for Andreas working in the background soothing egos, we would have lost half the staff who work for the business. The Legarde contract…that's not the only mess I made. It was much worse than me just taking my eye off the ball. I lost all interest in the ball. That's what the meeting with Andreas and my father was about. They didn't really have a choice. I was screwing up too much. The only ultimatum was that I needed to pull myself together or they would force me off the board. You were mentioned only because they knew that your leaving was the root cause of it all. They gave me some home truths too, about the man I was turning into and asked me to consider why the hell you would want to come back to that man. They made me see I was screwing everything up for everyone, and they were right. I look back at the person I became and I feel shame.'

'Pavlos said they were pressurising you about producing an heir.'

His laughter was cynical. 'They were pressuring Andreas and Pavlos, sure. Lots of hints. Some subtle. Most not. The only time they ever spoke about heirs to me was when they'd had too much to drink, patronising rubbish about how you and I could try again when I got you back. It was meant to be comforting. Supportive. You know what they're like.'

Keren closed her eyes.

Yes. She did. They never meant to be cruel. Like when Nina had given her the business card of her personal shopper—she'd thought she was doing a kind deed to her future daughter-in-law. Image was important to the Filipidises, but not as important as the business itself, and that came second in the pecking order to family.

'I knew that this weekend had to be it for me.'

She opened her eyes.

'I knew you would come and see Sophia for her birthday.' A sad smile played on his lips. 'All the time I've been searching for you... Keeping my promise to let you visit her undisturbed is the hardest promise I've ever had to keep. My staff always notified me when you were here, but I kept the promise and always waited until you sailed away before setting off after you.' His smile widened. 'You always disappeared. I thought your boat must be painted chameleon colours.'

She smiled back. 'I told you—small boats can access coves and things that bigger boats can't.'

'I'm still not selling *The Amphitrite* for something smaller than my dressing room.' The brief flare of amusement died. His throat moved again, and he bowed his head before meeting her stare. 'I knew that, this weekend, I had to break that promise. It's the only promise in my life I've broken. I knew this had to be my last attempt to win you back and that if I failed, it was time for me to let you go. And now that I have failed, I will keep my word.'

Unsure what he meant, she watched him swipe his phone.

His features tightened briefly before his shoulders rose. 'As I thought. Your boat has been returned.' He poured himself a large measure of the bourbon, drank it in one, wiped his mouth with the back of his hand then visibly braced himself. 'It is time for you to leave.'

She just stared at him, hardly able to breathe.

He bowed his head over his phone again. 'Give me one minute.'

'Yannis?'

He didn't look up. 'Please, *glyko mou*. One minute...'

Her throat stayed closed until he lifted his head and said, 'Done.'

The expression in his eyes was one she hadn't seen before. It frightened her.

'I have deactivated the locks,' he explained evenly. 'You are free to leave. I give you my word I will not follow you or try to find you. I have also transferred ten million euros into your account as part of the original settlement. I will transfer the remainder on Monday...'

Panic scratched at her throat. 'I don't want your money.'

He shrugged. 'I know you don't but it's yours. Buy another boat. Give it to charity. Do what you like with it. Give the divorce papers to your lawyer on Monday. It takes ten days for a judge here to stamp it and make it official, and then we will both be free.'

'Free?' she repeated dumbly. 'So that's it? You're letting me go?'

His lips curved in a smile so sad her heart heaved. 'What else can I do? You are mine and I am yours and I would never give up on you or give up on us, but I see now that it isn't about giving up. It's about what's best for you and best for me, and that means letting you go. There were times since you came back that I thought I was winning—that *we* were winning—but I have to accept that I'm beaten. You accepted what Pavlos told you without question because you want to go—'

'That's not how it was.'

'It is,' he stated firmly. 'You never wanted to come back. I forced this time on you. I knew from the day I met you that holding onto you would be an impossible task. I have to accept that your trust in me is destroyed and learn to live my life without you. It's not fair on either of us for me to try to fix something that's beyond repair. I will always love you, *glyko mou*, but it's time for us both to move on and put the past behind us.'

Still dumbfounded at the turn of events, Keren could only stare as Yannis headed off through to the entertainment room and pressed the button that opened the bifold wall-length door. Holding her grab-bag tightly, she followed him through it to the outdoor entertainment space.

On the horizon, the first peak of the sun cut through the darkness.

The outside lights in the distance came on. A figure emerged, walking towards them.

'That will be Niki with your boat keys,' Yannis said quietly.

The keys were handed to her in silence. She slipped them in her pocket. They were weightier than she remembered.

Then Niki disappeared.

'This is where I bid you farewell,' Yannis said in a lighter voice. 'I will leave you to say goodbye to Sophia. I wish you safe travels.'

'Thank you,' she croaked. Everything had turned on its head so rapidly she was struggling to make her voice work as much as she was struggling to make her brain work. 'Keep yourself safe too.'

'Always.'

They stared at each other for a long, drawn-out moment before Yannis brushed a gentle thumb over her cheek. 'Goodbye, *glyko mou*.'

'Goodbye, Yannis.'

He bowed his head one last time and turned, his long legs taking him steadily back to the villa.

He didn't look back.

CHAPTER THIRTEEN

THE ENGINE TURNED at the first attempt.

Keren clasped hold of the tiller. She had to hold it firmly. Her hand was shaking.

The birds were out in force that early morning, flying above her, squawking and singing, drowning out the sound of her heartbeat which had been banging like a drum in her ear since Yannis had walked away.

She set sail through the still, clear waters.

Where should she go first? Crete? Sicily? She would make it out of Agon waters and then decide. The whole world was her oyster.

A small breeze whipped her hair into her face. She pulled it back and wound it into a practised knot.

It was natural that she should feel battered and bruised, she told herself. It had been an emotional night. And she hadn't had any sleep. That probably explained why she felt so sick too. Bad sick. Not good sick.

She would sail for Crete, she decided. It wouldn't take her long to get there. When she'd anchored or found a marina, she would go and find somewhere to have some breakfast. Food should quell the growing nausea.

An image of Yannis eating an omelette alone on the

pool terrace and drinking gallons of coffee from his *briki* came into her mind. She banished it.

Yannis was her past. She was free of him.

He'd finally let her go.

She spotted a ferry, guessed that it, too, was headed to Crete. No doubt it was full of holiday makers. Couples. Families.

That was what she would do. Sail to England like she'd thought of doing earlier and visit her family. Tell them she loved them. She wished she could apologise for never being physically present with them but they wouldn't understand what she was apologising for. They'd always accepted their little cuckoo. If not for their love and support, Keren would never have been able to set out on her adventures when she'd been only eighteen. They'd known since she was twelve that she would flee their nest the moment that she could and had prepared accordingly. Their leaving present to her had been a laptop and five hundred pounds. Weekly emails and the occasional visit from her was enough for them. They only wanted her to be happy, however bemused they were by how she found that happiness.

She would stay for a few days with them and…

The Filipidises had accepted her as she was too. They'd had reservations about her being an outsider, but they'd done their best to accept her into their family. Despite their differences, they'd grown to love her and she'd grown to love them. They'd embraced the cuckoo in their nest just as her own family had done.

And Yannis…

Yannis had never needed to accept her because he'd always understood her. Always. Even in their darkest days when their world had been ripped apart, he'd understood her.

A rip tore through her heart, doubling her over at the pain it unleashed.

What was she *doing*?

Turning her back and sailing away from the one person in the world she'd found her home with? The man who loved her, truly loved her, with all his possessive need for her? The one man she'd found true happiness with?

Yannis had been nothing but constant and what had she given him in return? She'd thrown his love back at him. Fear had caused that. Terror of loving him again and watching his love for her die all over again. The loss of his love on the heels of losing their daughter had been too much and she'd shut down, and she'd shut down her love and all other feelings with it.

But his love had never died. Never. She'd just been too heartsick with grief to recognise it, too blinded by her own pain to see his fear and suffering.

Her love had never died either. Yannis had awoken it again and now it blazed in her heart as brightly as the sun shining above her. He'd done many things wrong—they both had—but he'd been right about so many other things. He'd always known that if he could get her back in their home and keep her there long enough, then her love for him would bloom back to summer, because their love was everything and always had been.

And she'd known it too.

She could have left at any time. Yannis had signed the divorce papers. He'd let her keep them. If she'd been really, truly determined to leave, she would have walked out with them all the way to her lawyer and then the British Embassy. He wouldn't have stopped her.

But she hadn't. She hadn't because deep in her heart, she'd wanted to stay. She'd just been too frightened to admit it. Too frightened of opening herself to more pain.

Dear heavens, what had she *done*?

Grasping tightly to the tiller and grasping tightly to her emotions, she turned the boat around.

Agon appeared in the distance. The first tears broke through. There was nothing she could do about them or the acute pain punching through her with every beat of her heart.

Ignoring the jetty, she sailed as close to the beach as she could before the boat grounded and she jumped into the water and swam harder than she'd ever swum before. Salt water dripping off her from head to toe, uncaring that she'd lost her sandals, she ran over the sand and then up the steps. Not pausing when she reached the top, she raced to the olive grove and pulled apart the mound of rocks she'd hidden the plastic food bag under.

And then she ran to the villa, skidding to a stop when she reached the pool area.

Where was Yannis?

He must know she was here. His security team would have told him the second she sailed into his waters.

And as she realised that, realised that he must know she was there and that his absence could only mean that he'd finally given up on her, another, even bigger wrench ripped through her heart, dropping Keren to her knees with a keening wail.

It was too late. *She* was too late.

The child she'd carried with such love for eight months, celebrating each and every movement that had rippled through her belly, had died. It was too late to save her. She was gone.

And it was too late to save her marriage. That was gone too.

The banshee that had lived in her head for so long finally found its way free and Keren's wail became a scream that ripped out from deep inside her as the loss of those she'd loved with every fibre of her being finally smashed into her and through her in one huge tsunami of grief.

Burying her face in her knees and pounding at the ground beneath her, Keren screamed until she was hoarse. And then she wept. She wept for her child. She wept for her husband. She wept for the destruction of the dreams they'd held so dear and a love that had been so strong.

All gone. All gone.

A pair of hands touched her shoulders and then she was being hauled onto the lap of the man she loved and rocked and held so tightly that her tears soaked into his shirt.

Only when she had a degree of control over the tears did she lift her head and put her hands to his cheeks to face him. Seeing the rawness of his eyes sliced her with fresh pain.

She had caused that.

'Oh, Yannis,' she choked. 'I thought I was too late.'

'Never. I was running.'

'Running?'

'I thought I'd lost you for good. I needed to do…*something*. The staff spotted you and sent out the search for me. I got to you as fast as I could.'

'I'm so, so sorry. I did abandon you. I *did*. I truly thought you didn't love me any more and I just couldn't bear it.'

'Hush,' he whispered, pulling her back to him and pressing his mouth into her hair. 'It's okay, *glyko mou*. It's okay.'

'No. It isn't. I need to explain… You know what you said about an unstoppable force crashing in on us and sweeping me away from you? Well, that's how it felt for me too, but it was like you were fading away from me and no matter how hard I stretched my arms, I couldn't reach you to touch you.'

He tightened his hold around her. 'It's okay, *glyko mou*. I understand.'

'You've always understood me.' She squeezed her eyes shut against more tears. 'I can't tell you how sorry I am that I stopped trying to understand you and that I pushed you away. The whole world…everything was so *dark*, but when I found my way out everything had changed, like the sparkle had gone out of the world. And I found that I hated you.'

She felt him flinch.

Lifting her face to look at his, she stroked her fingers across his cheeks. 'I did. I hated you for not wanting to make love to me. I hated you for having to work. I hated that you didn't want me to work. I hated you for suffocating me but then I hated you for giving anyone else any kind of attention. I was so *angry*, and so wrapped up in my fears and pain, that I never appreciated how scared you were too.'

'My fears were all wrapped up in us and I know now that I made things worse for both of us.'

'We both did.'

'Yes. And that is why I now think that you leaving was for the best.'

'How?' She disentangled herself so she could

straighten and look at him properly, utterly bewildered that he would say such a thing.

'You couldn't heal here,' he answered simply. 'That's all you needed. To heal. And you couldn't heal here with me... You cried in your sleep nearly every single night.'

That bewildered her even more. 'I did?'

His face spasmed and he said hoarsely, 'I would stroke your hair to calm you—it's the only time I dared touch you. Then in the morning you would wake, and I knew you didn't remember but I couldn't talk to you about it. I didn't dare. But if I hadn't made you hate me by acting like such a possessive fool, you would have confided your feelings and fears in me.'

'And if I hadn't got lost in the darkness I would have reached harder for you before you were frightened into acting like such a possessive fool.'

The whisper of a smile played on his lips but his eyes were full of sorrow. 'Keren, you were suffering from depression.'

'And you weren't?'

'I didn't carry our baby inside me for eight months.'

'But you loved her the same as I did. You had the same hopes and dreams as I did.'

He cupped her cheeks tightly and stared at her as if he were trying to burrow into her head and imprint his thoughts into it. 'It wasn't the same for me. I always knew that. And it tears my soul to know I couldn't be the rock you needed to lean on to get you through it, but I swear on our daughter's soul that I will never turn away from you again.'

'I will never turn from you either,' she swore. 'Never.'

'If you stay, I swear that I will love and cherish you

until my dying day. If bad days come for us again then we will face them together.'

Her chest filled with an emotion so sweet she could almost taste it.

She pressed her nose to his. 'There has not been a minute of my life since I left you when I haven't felt you with me. You are everything to me. My whole world. I love you, Yannis.'

A spasm of emotions flittered over his face before his features relaxed and the darkness in his eyes lifted. 'And I love you. More than anything.'

Yannis's kiss contained such love and tenderness that if she'd had any lingering doubts they would have been expelled. But she didn't. The feeling of rightness was too strong.

Palming his cheek, she gazed into his eyes again and whispered, 'What do you think about us going to her nursery and deciding what we're going to do with it?'

He breathed in deeply. 'You are ready?'

'If you're with me.'

'I will always be with you.'

'I know.' She smiled. 'But before we do anything else, I have something for you.'

His brow furrowed in question.

She pulled the plastic food bag out of her pocket and handed it to him.

He stared at it blankly before understanding had him drop it as if it were laced with poison.

'Shred it,' she told him.

'Shred it then burn it?'

'Then throw the ashes into the sea.'

Laughing, he kissed her again.

Wrapping her arms tightly around him, melting into

the heat of his mouth, the feeling of rightness grew even stronger.

The cuckoo had found her way home. Her home was wherever Yannis was.

EPILOGUE

THE PHOTOGRAPHER'S SMILE was starting to look a bit forced, Keren noted. His entreaties for everyone to hold a pose and smile for him were starting to sound a bit clipped, and she tried not to laugh when she caught Yannis's eye and saw that he'd noticed too.

'Phoebe, get back here!' she called when their youngest daughter once again escaped her grandfather's clutches, this time to chase a butterfly.

Keren let go of Yannis's hand and, laughing, hair streaming behind her, ran after their wilful three-year-old and scooped her up.

As she marched a frantically wriggling Phoebe back to Aristidis, she noticed six-year-old Ioanna, her hand clasped in Andreas's, shake her head at her uncle over her little sister's antics. Just as Keren had always baffled her family, Phoebe baffled Ioanna. Her daughters came from opposite ends of the personality spectrum. Ioanna was bookish and already developing a love for art and history. Phoebe was away with the fairies. Keren loved them both so much her heart hurt.

Realising that Phoebe was building up a head of steam for a full-blown temper tantrum, which would no doubt cause the harassed photographer to have his own full-blown temper tantrum, Keren whispered, 'How would you like to go fishing with me tomorrow?'

What she called fishing actually meant taking small fishing nets to the rock pools at the cove on the opposite side of the jetty, scooping up the crabs and tiny fish caught in them, putting them into seawater-filled buckets and then carefully putting them back out to sea. Phoebe was fascinated with sea life and, having recently watched a cartoon film about a mermaid, declared that she was one too.

Phoebe stopped wriggling and considered the question. Then she cupped her plump hand to Keren's ear and whispered back, 'Nanny Nina come too?'

Keren sniggered. Nina had recently accompanied them on one of their fishing expeditions. Phoebe had held a crab in her hand and proudly lifted it up to Nina's horrified face.

'We can ask,' she told her, 'but only if you behave yourself.'

She was rewarded with a mischievous giggle.

Handing a now-docile Phoebe back to Aristidis, Keren hurried back to Yannis's side. Grinning at each other, their hands clasped together and their fingers interlinked.

With the troublemaker now on her best behaviour, the photographer quickly barked fresh orders and the entire Filipidis clan retook their original positions in front of the peach tree and, on his order, smiled widely.

Click, click, click.

Keren and Yannis's tenth wedding anniversary portrait was immortalised.

Within an hour, just as the sun was starting to set, the best photos of this day of celebration landed in Yannis's in-box. He called everyone over and opened his laptop at the table by the pool and connected it to the projector he'd had set up in anticipation.

Keren sat herself on his left lap to watch, Ioanna on his right, cuddling in to Keren, her soft dark curls tickling Keren's neck and chin. Yannis held them both tightly. He always held them tightly.

Phoebe had fallen asleep under a table.

One by one, the photos flashed before them. The photographer had captured all the best moments of the day, from her supposedly gluten-free mother-in-law stuffing her face with a piece of anniversary cake, to Pavlos being pushed into the pool by the kids, to Keren and Yannis stealing one of a hundred kisses stolen that day. But it was the family portrait beneath the peach tree that Keren and, she knew, Yannis were most looking forward to seeing. These were the photos that included Sophia, their eldest child. Her peach tree had grown so huge and sprawling that her branches made a canopy over the entire family.

Their daughter was lost to them from life but not from their memories or their hearts. Her tree made her at one with them, something that brought them both great comfort.

There were a dozen pictures of the whole family under Sophia's tree, and as the images on the projector changed, Keren reflected on what a lucky cuckoo she was. She had a husband who worshipped and cherished her, who took pride in everything she did and whom she was as madly in love with as she'd been the day she married him. She had two clever, inquisitive, beautiful daughters, a loving family at home in England and a loving set of in-laws here at home in Agon.

Her heart swollen with happiness and love, she lifted

Yannis's hand to her mouth and kissed it. He dropped a kiss into the top of her head.

Just as she was thinking, again, that she was a very lucky cuckoo indeed, the sniggers started.

The very last picture on the digital album being projected before them had the entire Filipidis clan: Keren and Yannis, their children, Yannis's brother and brother-in-law, parents, grandparents, aunts, uncles, cousins and cousins' children, all smiling in perfect harmony. All except for Phoebe, who had her tongue out and was making devil horns above her oblivious grandfather's head.

'That one is going to be trouble,' Nina observed in an undertone from behind them.

Yannis caught Keren's eye, grinned and winked. 'I know,' he said. 'She's just like her mother.'

* * * * *

If you got lost in the drama of
Stranded with Her Greek Husband
you're sure to love these other stories
by Michelle Smart!

The Billionaire's Cinderella Contract
The Cost of Claiming His Heir
The Forbidden Innocent's Bodyguard
The Secret Behind the Greek's Return
Unwrapped by Her Italian Boss

Available now!

ONE
SNOWBOUND
NEW YEAR'S
NIGHT

DANI COLLINS

MILLS & BOON

To my delightful editor, Megan Haslam,
who suggested I write about a couple snowbound
for twenty-four hours in Canada on New Year's Eve.

Writing this romance became its own jigsaw puzzle,
as I tried to fit all the expected glamour
and emotion and heat into that tight frame,
but I had so much fun with it.

Thank you!

CHAPTER ONE

THE SOUND OF harp strings increased in volume, dragging Rebecca Matthews from a sound sleep to disorientation. It was daylight, the window blinds open to a view of falling snow on cedar trees. How—?

Oh, right. She was back in Canada.

She closed her eyes again and groggily reached to the night table to turn off the alarm. She didn't even recall setting it.

Her hand couldn't find the phone, but the sound abruptly cut off.

"Don't scream," a male voice said quietly.

She screamed, scrambling into a huddle against the headboard, snatching up one of the giant pillows to clutch it across her slamming heart, all while her brain processed that it was Van's voice. She was perfectly safe. He wasn't supposed to be here, but this *was* his house. Or would be, as soon as she signed it over to him.

Donovan Scott, her soon-to-be ex-husband, stood in the doorway holding his phone in a loose, dangling grip. He wore jeans and a cable-knit sweater and had an even darker, more imposing level of sex appeal than she remembered. That quiet force reached out and wrapped around her like an invisible hand, squeezing the air from her lungs.

She hadn't seen him in four years, not even stalking him online except for a handful of photos her sister had shoved under her nose. In appearance, he had changed only in small ways. He wore a fade on the sides of his hair and had shortened it on top so it no longer flopped rakishly toward one brow. His closely trimmed beard was now shaped with precision to accentuate his jaw and made his golden-brown eyes seem even more eagle-sharp. His mouth held the stern tension of gearing up for a race. All of him radiated that familiar bunched energy he'd always contained. He wasn't competing any longer, so he wasn't lean to the point of wiry, but his body was still pure muscle, all wide shoulders and long legs and power.

There was something vastly different in his demeanor, though. He had no easygoing smile for her. Rather, he exuded suspicion and hostility and harsh judgment as he held up his phone and drawled, "I didn't want you to hear me downstairs and think I was an intruder."

"Well done," she said facetiously. "I told the lawyer to tell you I was coming in to pick up a few things. Did you not get that message?"

"I did. That's why I'm here." His cool, pithy tone made her heart *thunk* in her chest.

She closed her fist into the pillow. She wanted to bury her face in it. Could he tell she'd been crying? She was a train wreck. She'd had a few hours of sleep and a shower after she landed in Vancouver yesterday, but she wasn't wearing makeup and her hair was falling out of its topknot. Oh, gawd. She inwardly cringed as she noticed the green-and-cream plaid on her arm. She'd pulled one of his flannels over her thin sweater and *smelled* it before falling on what used to be their bed for a hard, ugly cry. Jet lag had taken over and she'd pulled the corner of the duvet across her, escaping anguish and loss by falling asleep.

"I was cold," she mumbled, straightening the collar of his shirt against her shoulder. Definitely not cold any longer. A hot, mortified blush rose from the pit of her stomach at being caught in his bed like Goldilocks. "I thought you were in Calgary?"

"Where's Courtney?" he asked at the same time.

They both fell silent.

When the quiet dragged out and she realized he was waiting for her to speak first, she said, "Her, um, flight was delayed. She was going to miss her connection and I didn't want her to spend New Year's Eve stranded in Winnipeg, so I told her to stay home."

Becca's first and best Canadian friend had offered to meet her in Vancouver and hold her hand while Becca closed out what remained of her life here in Whistler. It had felt like a horrific imposition to let Courtney fly all the way from Halifax for a handful of rough emotional days and a glass of champagne at midnight, but Becca really wished she had a wingwoman right now.

"I thought you were spending Christmas in Calgary with Paisley?" she asked, mentioning his sister.

"I did."

"Her kids must be getting big." She smiled faintly, wishing she'd had a closer relationship with his niece and nephew, but she and Paisley hadn't gotten on.

"They are."

"I only meant to be here a few minutes, but jet lag…" She trailed off, feeling as gauche as ever around him.

This was so stilted and awful. Latent adrenaline was burning through her veins, leaving her entire body stinging. This was why she'd wanted to come into the house while he was away, so she wouldn't have to face him and the mire of memories between them.

"The lawyer initially told me February. I was surprised when he said you wanted access over New Year's Eve."

"This was when Courtney had time off work. She thought it would be fun to celebrate New Year's Eve here like old times…" Becca's voice faded as her throat constricted. Nothing about this was fun. "It was all organized at the last second."

"You didn't have to work through the holidays?"

"I—" A hard jab of inadequacy struck. Why did it make her feel like a poser to admit this? "I'm not tending bar anymore. I'm, um…" She cleared her throat. "I'm starting school soon. I worked until Christmas Eve, spent a few days with Dad and Ollie—he remarried— then I have a prep course I want to take before the actual classes start."

"Oh? What are you studying?" His brows went up with interest that had to be good manners and little else.

"Lab tech?" She didn't mean it to sound like a question, as though she wanted his approval. Maybe she did. She'd finally found something she felt remotely passionate about. It wasn't particularly sexy, but it meant a lot to her.

"I told the lawyer I could send everything down to you. You didn't have to come all this way." His gaze flickered toward the empty suitcase she'd opened and left on the floor. So far there was only a cotton sundress inside it.

"I need to close out an old bank account and…sign the papers." Finalize their divorce. Release the title on this house to him. Everything could have been done electronically, but… "I don't actually want many of the clothes." What was she going to do with designer gowns and high-end skiwear working as a lab tech in Sydney? "And I was…"

As she remembered why she was here, she pushed the pillow off her lap and hooked her heels on the far side of the bed. Her jeans rose up her calves as she dragged herself off the bed. She shook her legs and brushed her bottom as she got to her feet, then folded his flannel across herself, more from defensiveness than chill.

She didn't want to admit she'd paid high-season airfare and come all this way to find a cheap gold locket her mother had given her. Wanda had started wearing hers after Mum passed and Becca was angry with herself that she'd left hers here.

It was Van's fault. He'd started buying her earrings with precious stones and a tennis bracelet and art deco pendants on links of white gold. A modest gold locket didn't go with the sort of upscale designer names his family wore. She would have told him to send the locket to her if she had known where she had left it, but she couldn't recall the last time she'd worn it.

"I'm surprised you haven't moved all of this into storage." She glanced from the door of the closet, where her clothes had been zipped into garment bags to keep the dust off, but were otherwise exactly as she'd left them.

"I'm at the condo in Vancouver most of the time."

Condo made it sound so modest. It was a penthouse with views of Stanley Park, Coal Harbour and the North Shore.

Van moved to the night table and tilted the bottle of wine she had spitefully opened and poured into a glass, bringing both up here with the intention of drinking it all herself.

"Are you mad?" she asked dolefully.

We can drink it on our fifth anniversary, she had said when he purchased the bottle. They'd been touring Okanagan wineries on their honeymoon. It had been one of the vineyard's select vintages, meant to be cellared at least five years, and had cost two hundred dollars when it was released.

"Depends," he said drily. "Is it corked?" He picked up her glass as if they had been sharing dishes all this time, sipped. Considered. His brows went up. "Worth the wait."

The look he leveled at her put tension in her belly and a cavernous feeling in her chest.

"It dropped me like a tranquilizer dart," she mumbled, and went into the closet where her drawer of accessories had already been mined without success. "Do you mind reaching that shoebox for me? I have a vague memory of putting my old glasses in there with some of my travel paperwork. I want to see what else is in there."

"You kept your glasses?" He'd paid to have her vision fixed shortly after they married.

Her frames were cheap and outdated, the prescription completely useless. She should have donated her glasses after the procedure, but, "Growing up, I was threatened with slow and painful death if I ever lost or broke my glasses."

Her family had been poor. She still was, compared to him. Her sister had told her to let Van ship everything to her so she could sell what she didn't want on consignment, but his family had thought her a money-grubbing gold digger as it was.

No, she had decided. She would let him dispose of the jewelry and clothes however he saw fit. She would divorce him and sign over the house with only a nominal settlement. Irreconcilable differences had never seemed so literal, but they had always been far too unequal to find any middle ground—especially once Becca had learned she couldn't give him the children he wanted.

After privately coming to terms with that hard news, she was working on envisioning a future where she was happy with herself and by herself, not thinking happiness could only be achieved by being a wife and mother.

She was here to draw a line at midnight. New year, new life, new Becca.

Because reinventing herself had worked out so well in the past.

The closet was as big as her bedroom in her new, tiny leased studio in Sydney, but it felt like a broom closet when he entered and stood close, emanating his spicy, woolly, snow-fresh aroma all over her.

He brought the shoebox down and angled it away from them, blew the dust off and tilted the lid open. He looked at her expectantly.

There were her glasses in their cloth case along with a charger cord for a redundant phone, a handful of receipts and some purple, green, and gold beads from a Mardi Gras party they had attended shortly after they married.

Flash me, he'd invited when they'd arrived home afterward, slightly drunk and very horny. She'd whisked off her shirt and bra, then sat across his lap on the edge of that bed while he twined the long necklaces around her breasts before cupping her butt and lifting her onto her knees so he could suck her nipples.

Did he remember...?

One tentative glance upward and she nearly melted under the flare of heat in his gaze. He remembered *everything*. Carnality hardened the sharp angles in his face and sent a golden spear lodging itself behind her navel.

Her skin tightened and she grew so hot she felt scorched. It was mortifying to have desire rise up like an apparition between them, but yearning pinned her exactly where she was. She couldn't escape the way she had completely let him have his way with her that night. Many, many nights, but that one in particular. When he'd urged her to take him in her mouth, she had knelt at his feet and caressed him, listening while he petted her hair and told her in intimate detail what he wanted to do to her.

Then, before he lost control, he made good on his promise. He stripped her down to only those beads and gave her what he'd denied himself, going to his knees on the floor as he buried his head between her thighs and made her scream.

She'd still been panting in reaction when he had thrust into her. He'd been rough, but in a good way, making her climax again before rolling onto his back and bringing her astride him where she did everything she could to take him over the edge.

Van was ruthlessly self-disciplined, though. He was a world-class athlete with ridiculous endurance. In a gravelly voice he had told her how hot she was, how much pleasure she was giving him as he thrust up into her. How much he loved watching her succumb to pleasure.

She had shattered and he sat up, gathering his knees beneath himself while holding her with her legs twined around his waist. She had arched back so the beads sat as a collar-like weight across her neck while he bent to feast on her breasts, drawing forth a fresh, pulsating desire that completely overwhelmed her.

No one had ever made her feel like that—like a goddess. Irresistible. Pure and unashamed in the way she gave herself up to him.

As she grew wild and ready to explode, he brought her up into his lap, so she clung around his neck and kissed him with utter abandon. The beads had dangled down her back and her damp nipples had rubbed deliciously against his hot, hard chest as he rocked up into her.

She'd been mindless. Uninhibited and insatiable. Smothered by his kisses and writhing with him in a way that melded them as close to becoming one as it was possible to feel. Words were gone. In those throbbing, exquisite moments, they were completely attuned, speaking a primitive language all their own.

Culmination arrived, striking both of them at exactly the same time, propelling them into another world where reality didn't exist, only heat and white light and exquisite pleasure. The kind that should have kept them sealed for all eternity.

But it hadn't.

Her awareness came crashing back from that iniquitous memory to see his pupils had expanded so his irises were mere golden halos around black, depthless orbs.

With sensuality weakening her bones, and craving for lost passion snarling like a demon inside her, Becca absently licked her lips.

His mouth had finally softened from its unyielding line. There was a distant pair of small thumps, one barely heard, the other louder and accompanied by the spill of beads.

All she really felt or saw or perceived was the force that pulled them together. Magnets finding their opposite and snapping together in a way that resisted separation. Van's mouth descended on hers as his hard arms drew her body into a firmer fit with his.

Longing and loss and sensory starvation acted like sparks on the kindling that was always there. Always. His mouth slanted and swept and *stole*. She loved it. She gave herself up to him with a roping of her arms around his neck and a mash of her breasts to his chest, dragging herself into him even as his arms closed so tightly around her they hurt.

She was glad for that ache. For those implacable bands that nearly cut off her breath. It was like being caught close after a near-death stumble at the edge of a cliff. *Hold me tighter. Keep me safe.*

His mouth was equally hard as he raked it across hers, plundering as though he'd been starving for years, exactly as she had been. His hands went down to her backside and angled her hips into his groin while his mouth consumed hers, tongue thrusting exactly as it had that night when he'd been buried inside her.

This was the sort of instant lust that had brought them together in the first place. It was wild and glorious—a crashing storm that roared and excited and blew down any obstacle in its path.

It was a storm that had left devastation in its wake.

With a gasp of alarm, Becca jerked back her head and fought free of his hold, shoving her arms between them and stumbling as she stepped on her glasses. They snapped in their case beneath her socked heel.

Van caught her arm long enough to steady her, then ran his hand down his face.

"I didn't mean to do that." He swore sharply and turned away. She saw him make an adjustment at his fly as he left the closet. He kept walking, disappearing out the bedroom door into the hall.

Shaking, Becca knelt to scoop everything back into the box. She closed the lid and set the box aside, moving in frantic shock, returning everything to the way it had been so she could pretend nothing had happened.

That was why she hadn't wanted to do this while he was here. Her skin was tight and hot and prickling. Her heart knocked clumsily around the hollow space in her chest. A lump rose to her throat. Feelings were meant to be felt, she reminded herself, but why did they have to *hurt* so much?

Van had never deliberately inflicted pain upon her, but being with him had been one hurt after another and still was. It hurt to look at him, to feel herself come alive as though leaning on atrophied muscles. It hurt to feel the sharp pleasure of his touch and it hurt to kiss him with such intensity and watch him walk away.

It hurt to be apart from him while still wearing his name.

That's why they were divorcing, she reminded herself. That's why she had planned to slip in, find the locket and leave him a note that wished him well. She had spent an hour picking out the right card to do exactly that.

She wanted bygones to be bygones. She would quit nursing what-ifs and disappointments and blame. She would *not* take fresh recriminations home with her.

Still shaken, she moved out of the closet to the night table and lifted her wineglass in a hand that trembled. She set her lips where his mouth had been.

Don't think of it.

But it was too late. Her mind and body were already alight with the memory of all of the places his mouth had been. All the places she had nearly let him go within minutes of seeing him again.

Hot tears pressed against the backs of her eyes.

Damn you, Van!

Damn you, Becca.

Van stepped into the bracing cold of the veranda off the kitchen, trying to slow his racing blood so he could think about something besides the way Becca had just dismantled his self-control as effortlessly as she always had.

He'd forgotten how easily she took him from zero to sixty and kept him there.

Maybe he'd deliberately blacked it out because it was so lowering to lose a fight so quickly and resoundingly. Against *himself*.

He pinched the bridge of his nose, thinking it felt like a weakness that he'd come here at all. Their divorce was long overdue, and he was ready to finalize it, but he had gotten February into his head and had been blindsided by the email from his lawyer that she was slipping in while he was away.

As he'd packed and climbed into his SUV, he'd told himself he was protecting what was his, ensuring she was only taking what genuinely belonged to her. He was no longer the gullible fool who believed people who were close to you wouldn't screw you over.

He and Becca weren't even close any longer. It had been four years, but unlike his father, Becca didn't come from a long line of people who took things that didn't belong to them. She had never capitalized on his wealth, always seeming uncomfortable with it.

That's what she wants you to think, he could hear his father saying about her.

How ironic that Van had vehemently defended Becca to a man who had ultimately betrayed him far worse than she had.

Actually, it was still a toss-up which knee to the stomach had been harder to get up from. When Becca had told Van their marriage was a mistake and stayed in Sydney, he'd walked away thinking no one could have sucker punched him quite so devastatingly.

Within the hour, however, he'd learned his father had cleaned out the family vault. Van had rushed home to deal with that, allowing his marriage to finish dying of neglect while he raced to save hundreds of jobs, multi-million-dollar housing projects and the corporate dividends his mother and sister relied on.

He had managed to keep a lid on the scandal for a week until he could control the narrative, but the fact that Becca hadn't reached out when it was announced that his finances had taken a tumble spoke volumes about why she had married him in the first place.

The entire thing had been a scathing reminder of something he'd always known, but had begun to think was pure cynicism on his part—that anyone could betray you. In fact, trusting people was an open invitation to be deceived.

Since then, Van had been waiting for Becca to show her true colors, expecting another knife in the back at any moment.

There'd been a whole lot of crickets. Years of silence when he regularly considered starting the divorce proceedings himself, but why shake that can?

A few months ago, the request had finally arrived. She wanted him to buy her out of this house. That's all. She wasn't staking any claim to his various family or personal business interests. She wasn't asking him to ship all her belongings down to her. She would come and take what she wanted before the paperwork was finalized.

It had all sounded too easy and, sure enough, she'd tried to get in here while his back was turned.

To take what, though? The jewelry he'd given her? The art that was valuable, but not priceless? The sexy convertible that was in her name and would cost twice as much to ship to Australia as he'd paid for it in the first place?

He'd ruminated on all of that while driving through ever-worsening conditions, foot heavy on the gas in his urgency to get here.

When he arrived, he'd been sure he had missed her. There hadn't been any tire tracks in the long, steep driveway, only a trail of footsteps that were so filled by the steadily falling snow it was impossible to tell which direction they were headed. He had fishtailed his way down to the house and slid the SUV into a drift of snow that would have to be shoveled away from the garage door before he could put the vehicle away.

Entering the house, he'd seen the envelope on the dining room table and crossed to read…nothing. The card was completely blank. It didn't even have a lame, preprinted platitude about everything having a reason or some other greeting card BS.

He didn't understand how a lack of words had scratched hard enough to leave a mark on the granite where his heart was supposed to be, but as he'd stood there feeling as empty as this card, his gaze had caught on the jacket and shoes in the alcove by the door.

She was still there.

He had removed his snow-covered boots to look for her, calling her name. The door had chimed when he had come in, but she hadn't heard any of it. She'd been dead asleep when he got to the bedroom.

The sight of her struck like a kick in the chest. Lower. Hell, if he was honest, his libido had started revving before he'd left Calgary.

It wasn't like she was naked and lying there all enticing, either. She was wearing one of his flannel shirts, but aside from a socked foot and the ash tips in her hair, he couldn't see much more than the tan across her freckled cheeks. Summer Girl, he'd called her sometimes, when she burrowed into him complaining she was cold. She'd playfully called him Jack Frost and squealed at cold hands sliding under her shirt.

We're too different. It was a mistake.

It had been. He'd come to see that they'd been children when they eloped five years ago, too naive to know better. *He* should have known better. His family's failed marriages had taught him that marriage needed a lot more than an impulsive "I do" in order to go the distance.

Van could live with making mistakes. They happened. He caught an edge or misjudged a turn. The important thing was to learn and recover and do better next time. Making a mistake didn't mean it was time to quit. As long as you were trying, you weren't failing. Maybe he hadn't won every single race he entered, but he didn't fail. He always kept at something until he mastered it and won.

Looking at Becca sleeping for the last time in his bed, however, he'd tasted the bitterness of failure.

Turn it around, he had chided himself. *End this on a good note and call it a successful divorce.*

Maybe it could have been if they hadn't sucked onto each other like a couple of lampreys. His erection was still stubbornly pressing against the fly of his jeans despite the fact that he stood on the porch with a biting wind gusting icy snowflakes straight into his face.

That was how he'd wound up marrying on a whim and earning an F for failure. Becca pulled him off keel with a single, smoky look. It was time to put that firmly behind him.

Except... He swore under his breath as he took in the fact that he could hardly see the lake through the blowing snow.

A sixth sense had him glancing back through the windows as Becca appeared at the bottom of the stairs. She'd removed his flannel and now wore a belted cardigan over her jeans and snug pullover. The soft cashmere in raspberry pink followed every curve of her knockout figure.

He swallowed and pulled his collar away from his neck, releasing a fresh rush of randy heat.

Inside, Becca glanced around. Her shoulders heaved with an annoyed sigh as she spotted the grocery bag on the floor by the door. She moved to snatch it up.

The more things changed, the more they stayed the same. Milk wouldn't spoil sitting out for five minutes, but she couldn't stand it when he forgot to put it away.

Van slid the door open and stepped inside only to have her squeak and dance her feet, nearly dropping the groceries.

"You knew I was here," he insisted. "That's why I woke you, so you would know I was here and you wouldn't do that. I *live* here," he said for the millionth time, because she'd always been leaping and screaming when he came around a corner.

"Did you? I never noticed," she grumbled, setting the bag on the island and taking out the milk to put it in the fridge. "I was alone here so often, I forgot I was married."

"*I* noticed that," he shot back with equal sarcasm.

They glared at each other. The civility they'd conjured in those first minutes upstairs was completely abandoned—probably because the sexual awareness they'd reawakened was still hissing and weaving like a basket of cobras between them, threatening to strike again.

Becca looked away first, thrusting the eggs into the fridge along with the pair of rib eye steaks and the package of bacon.

She hated to be called cute and hated to be ogled, so Van tried not to do either, but *come on*. She was curvy and sleepy and wearing that cashmere like a second skin. She was shorter than average and had always exercised in a very haphazard fashion, but nature had gifted her with a delightfully feminine figure-eight symmetry. Her ample breasts were high and firm over a narrow waist, then her hips flared into a gorgeous, equally firm and round ass. Her fine hair was a warm brown with sun-kissed tints, her mouth wide, and her dark brown eyes positively soulful.

When she smiled, she had a pair of dimples that he suddenly realized he hadn't seen in far too long.

"I don't have to be here right now," she said, slipping the coffee into the cupboard. "If you're going skiing tomorrow, I can come back while you're out."

"I want to make some of that." He reached for the coffee before she closed the cupboard.

She snatched her hand back and staggered away a few steps, glowering an accusation.

You kissed me back, Becca.

Their gazes clashed before he turned away to dig into a drawer for the coffee scoop.

"Would you like a cup? You're not coming back because you're not going anywhere. We're ringing in the new year right here." He chucked his chin at the windows that climbed all the way to the peak of the vaulted ceiling. Beyond the glass, the frozen lake was impossible to see through the thick and steady flakes. A gray-blue dusk was closing in.

"You have four-wheel drive, don't you?" Her hair bobbled in its knot, starting to fall as she snapped her head around. She fixed her hair as she looked back at him, arms moving with the mysterious grace of a spider spinning her web. "How did you get here?"

He made himself keep his eyes off her chest, but he deserved a medal of honor for managing it.

"Weather reports don't apply to me," he replied with self-deprecation. Otherwise, he would have turned away from many a race before getting up the mountain to compete. "Gravity got me down the driveway and I won't get back up until I can start the quad and attach the plow blade. Even then, I'll have to throw down some gravel for traction. I don't know if I have any." He scratched beneath his chin, noted her betrayed glare at the windows.

Believe me, sweetheart. I'm not any happier than you are.

He thought it, but immediately wondered if he was being completely honest with himself.

"How was the road?" She fetched her phone from her purse, distracting him as she sashayed back from where it hung under her coat. "I caught a rideshare to the top of the driveway and walked down. I can meet one at the top to get back to my hotel."

"Plows will be busy doing the main roads. And it's New Year's Eve," he reminded. "Drivers will be making surge rates moving drunks between hotels in the village. They won't risk ditching their car by coming all the way out here."

"So what am I supposed to do? Stay here? All night? With *you*?"

What was he? A serial killer?

"Happy New Year," he said with a mocking smile.

CHAPTER TWO

BLOODY TYPICAL. NOTHING ever went her way. *Nothing.*
Her best friend had canceled, her almost ex-husband
had turned up and now she was snowed in here with
him? Who wrote this script? Someone with a taste for
the absurd, that's who.

"Please do *not* make me watch you do that wrong,"
Becca blurted as Van started to tear the sack of coffee
beans rather than cut it neatly.

Van set it down and lifted his hands into the air.

"Is this what we're doing? Bickering until the snow
stops? You could stay in the carriage house if you're so
offended by my presence. The heat and water haven't
been turned on out there since... Actually, is the water
turned on in here?" His lofty arrogance dried up as he
tried the tap.

Nothing.

"I'll be back." He detoured to the front door for his
boots and jacket and disappeared.

Heaving a sigh, Becca ground the beans. She was
desperate for a coffee after her nap. Her head felt stuffed
with cotton. When water began dripping from the open
tap, she filled the reservoir on the coffee maker and

set the first shots of espresso to brewing, then started milk to steam.

As she scouted through the cupboard for chocolate flakes, she took a quick inventory of the freezer and pantry. There was a bag of stir-fry veggies and she could use that jar of pesto to make the noodles Van liked. That would go well with the steak. There were crackers and caviar, olives and gherkins for an appetizer. The cake mix was only a few weeks past its due date, so dessert was sorted... And she was *doing it again.*

Her mother had catered endlessly to her father. Despite swearing she wouldn't become just like her, Becca had slipped on a 1950s apron with her wedding ring and had fallen into the same pattern with Van.

Is this shirt ready for the wash?

Of course I'll pick up something for your mom's birthday.

You bring home the bacon, darling. I'll fry it up in the pan.

The sound of stomping feet approached the side door.

"Only you could walk sarcastically," she said as Van entered and bent to unlace boots that wore traces of snow.

"I went out to start the sauna."

"Why?"

"So we can have a sauna if we want one."

They used to do that naked. Was that what he was imagining would happen again? Probably, seeing as she had practically jumped him in the closet.

She turned away, embarrassed, but it had always been that way when he returned after an absence. He would disappear to train for a couple of weeks and they would barely say hello when he walked in the door, preferring to crash into each other naked on the sheets. Only then were they ready to talk.

She missed that. She had missed him, she acknowledged with a searing ache in her throat. She had missed this house and feeling snug while snow fell and the excitement of being alive because this one particular human was close enough for her to touch.

"You have that," he said as she finished making his coffee and reached for the sprinkles. "I'll make my own."

A jumble of emotions instantly clogged her throat. Rejection, because he didn't want the coffee she'd made, and a wash of vulnerability because he was being considerate and she had never known how to take it when he did that.

Like her mother, Becca's whole life had been orchestrated around service of some kind. If she wasn't cooking a meal for family, she was pouring drinks for strangers. Becca had gone back to Sydney to help get her mum to doctor appointments and had arranged her sister's wedding because Wanda had been in the middle of finals. She had done the very hard, painful work of ending her marriage both initially and legally so Van wouldn't have to.

One cup of coffee hardly made up for that and it wasn't as if Van had even made it. She had, but she said a humble, "Thank you," and sat down on the far side of the island, thumbing her phone to hide how affected she was by such a small gesture.

A text from her sister Wanda wished her a happy new year and asked,

Did you find it?

Becca texted back.

Not yet.

She could have told Wanda she was staring at Van's extremely nice butt and long legs, but she set the phone aside, never able to ignore him. She should continue sorting through her clothes upstairs and search out the locket, maybe ask him if it was in the safe. Instead, she asked, "How is your family? Is your Mom still with Werner?"

"She is," he said with a note of marvel at the achievement. "They stayed here this summer with his kids." He set the fresh grounds with a firm twist of his wrist.

"Stella and Morgan," she recalled. "How are they?"

"Stella was caught shoplifting in the village."

"Oh." Now she couldn't even mention the locket because that could implicate his adolescent stepsister. Becca had only met Stella twice. The girl had struck her as starved for attention, but sweet. She had a soft spot for kittens and secretly wrote poetry. Honestly, if Stella had taken Becca's locket, Becca was inclined to let her keep it. She knew all about feeling un-special and more of a bother to one's parents than a gift.

As she studied the tension in Van's spine, she tried to make herself ask about his father. She only knew what had been reported online, that Jackson Scott had skipped off to an island in the Caribbean with the company's chief financial officer, taking pension funds and other liquid assets, nearly bankrupting the family real estate corporation in the process.

The story had broken shortly after Van left Sydney. Becca had wanted to reach out to him, but she'd been in a very dark headspace at the time.

Looking back, Becca could see she had probably been suffering depression brought on by all she had been going through. She hadn't been the most secure person in the first place and had become very down on herself during her marriage, feeling like a fish out of water as Van's wife. When she learned about her mother's failing health, guilt had smothered her over being away from home for so long. Learning that she couldn't get pregnant had filled her with anger and self-blame and living with her parents had had its own challenges. Anyone who had moved back home after living away understood how hard that was.

Maybe it hadn't been fair to Van to only give him half the story when he came to see her, but it had all felt too heavy and humiliating to unpack, especially when she'd been convinced their marriage was doomed anyway. She had honestly believed she was doing what was best for both of them. What was inevitable.

Of course, she had second-guessed herself by the following morning, but he'd been on his way to the airport by then. They'd both been caught up in family stuff after that. Time had marched on and now here they were, forced to make awkward small talk while pretending they hadn't locked lips a few minutes ago.

She blew across her coffee, lungs burning.

Van finished making his and sprinkled it with chocolate. He turned to lean against the sink. He eyed her as he said gravely, "I was sorry to hear about your mom."

She looked down, unable to bear his seeing how raw

she still was a year later or how affected she had been by his small act of condolence.

"I got the flowers and the card about the donation. Thank you." It had been the last thing she expected. Not so much the generosity of his donation to cancer prevention, but the fact that he'd gone to the trouble when they'd been officially separated and firmly estranged.

"I would have come to the funeral if you'd told me."

"It was family only."

Did that make him flinch? His expression shuttered so it was hard to tell.

"There were all those travel restrictions," she reminded him. And funerals were expensive even when they were small. Honestly, she had feared he would see her reaching out as some kind of effort to get him back. If he hadn't responded, she would have been devastated, so she had thought it best to let him find out through social feeds. "To be honest, we were kind of done with accepting sympathy by then. That sounds terrible, I know."

"No, I get it. It's exhausting when people keep asking how you're doing and the truth is you're terrible, but you have to say, 'fine.'"

"Yes." She lifted her lashes, surprised he understood so well, but she supposed he did. His father wasn't dead, but he was gone. She couldn't imagine people had been as charitable in expressing their feelings about Jackson Scott as they had been about her mum.

Becca started to ask if he'd tried to find his father, but he said, "And your family? You said your father remarried. How is your sister?"

"Also married. Wanda and Cliff had their wedding in Mum's hospice room so it was very small, but it was a bright spot. They're in Bali now as an anniversary celebration. Dad married Ollie back in July. Ollie was their neighbor, always coming over with meals while Mum was in treatment. She and Dad got closer once she was gone. They're a good fit." Ollie nagged Dad to take his blood pressure meds and Dad drove her to her hair appointments, exactly as things had been with Becca's mother.

"And you? Are you seeing someone?"

"What? No." Did he remember that kiss in the closet? "Why would you think that?"

Something flickered across his expression, but he only said facetiously, "We've covered weather and family. 'Are you seeing anyone?' comes next, doesn't it? I thought that might be why you asked for the divorce." He looked aside to find the sprinkles.

"No. I thought it was time. Don't you?" She held her breath.

"Yes."

A cavern opened in her chest. She dropped her gaze back to her coffee, refusing to ask if he was involved with anyone. It would hurt too much to hear, especially on the heels of that kiss they'd shared upstairs.

Becca's lashes went down and she firmed her mouth as though to hide a tremble in her lips.

Van had forgotten how sensitive she was. He was only speaking the truth and had learned the hard way that secrets and lies were far more harmful than honesty, but Becca felt everything twice as much as anyone else.

"I've been busy with other things and haven't made a priority of starting the proceedings," he said by way of softening his blunt agreement. In fact, when he'd sent the card after her mother's death, he'd half expected it would at least start them talking again, but he had only received a thank-you card signed by "the Matthews family." "But you're right. It's overdue. Thank you for getting that ball rolling."

Her nod of acknowledgment was solemn, her mouth still holding that injured pout. "I thought I should do it since I kind of cornered you into our marriage. You were trying to help me stay in Canada and I left anyway."

An unexpected pang hit his chest. He had thought they had more between them than some inconvenient immigration paperwork, but okay.

"I wanted to believe that eloping with someone I barely knew was romantic, but we were foolish babies who married in secret, like we were committing a crime. We kind of were," she said with a wry smile. "That's how we should have known we were doing something wrong."

It hadn't felt wrong. Maybe his libido had been the one doing all his thinking at the time, but Becca had seemed different from everyone else around him. Refreshingly honest without any hidden agendas.

Perhaps that had been wishful thinking. He'd become far more cynical since, able to see she had used him even if he'd willingly allowed it. At the time, he'd only seen what he wanted to see and she'd kept *a lot* from him.

His mind leaped to what he'd learned shortly before he had hugged his niece and nephew goodbye two days ago.

"Paisley told me she was the one who dented your convertible."

"What? Why on earth would she bring that up?"

Becca picked up her coffee mug and shoved her nose into it, earnest brown eyes sliding away from his.

His ire dug in with deeper talons.

"I told her you were here, that the divorce was going to be final. She asked if you were selling the car and asked if she could buy it. She couldn't believe you had never told me. Neither can I."

"Tsk." Becca sat up straighter, shifting in a way that denoted guilt while asking dismissively, "When would I have?"

"When it happened?" he suggested with pointed sarcasm.

"Did she tell you *why* she left the kids with me that day and took my car?"

"Yes." And he was outraged that Paisley had involved Becca in her infidelity, if completely unsurprised. Everyone in his family seemed to think promises and integrity were really more of a guideline than values to live by. "She also told me she tried to *pay* you not to tell me she was having an affair." He'd been about to tear a strip off Paisley for that one, but her son had come in the room. "What the hell, Becca? You don't even like Paisley. Why would you lie to me to protect her?"

"It wasn't my place to start a family row and put her children through a divorce, was it?" She wrapped both hands around her cup, as if they were dishing at a tea party, when she asked with gently raised brows, "Is she happy with John?"

"No. They're separated. That's why she wanted me there for Christmas." His family had more divorces than gold medals and that was saying something considering his mother's career and his own. "Tell me what happened, Becca."

Her mouth tightened and she sent him a glower that was impossible to take seriously because she looked like a kitten pulled off a curtain, indignant and injured at being scolded even though she was clearly in the wrong.

"It's not even interesting." She balanced her cup between two hands and let the steam rise to warm her nose. "Paisley asked me to watch the kids and took my car so I'd have the car seats if I needed to go out. I didn't ask her where she was going, but she came back and said the car had been dented while it was parked. She didn't want you to start asking her questions about it so she asked me to report it and say it happened while I was running errands. I said, 'Why? Were you at a hotel with someone?' It was a tasteless joke, but she got very stroppy and said she'd pay me to keep my mouth shut. I got stroppy and told her what she could do with her money. So it's not that we don't like each other, it's that I had something on her and kept it in my back pocket so she wouldn't be such a cow to me."

"What do you mean?" He folded his arms, having a feeling he already knew.

"Come on, Van. Your whole family thought I married you for your money and they made sure I knew it. That's why Paisley thought she could offer me money to stay quiet."

"Who else treated you like that?"

"Everyone. Your mom loved to remark on the way I dressed and how that reflected on you. Paisley said it was nice that you didn't mind my not working, but...*ew*, no. I couldn't go back to being a bartender or a liftie at the ski hill. That wasn't a real job. Your dad was constantly giving me career suggestions, but what were my options? Tuition here is obscene, especially for an international student. How could I train for a 'real' job without asking you to pay for it? If I did, that would only prove I'd married you for your money. There was no winning." Her profile was stark as she looked toward the windows where snow and dusk were growing thicker.

"They knew I didn't like the idea of you working late in bars, coming home to an empty house, when I could easily support you." Guilt sat thornily in the pit of his gut. He'd shot down any of those sorts of digs when he'd heard them, but it hadn't been enough, obviously. "You could have told me they were being rude."

"No, Van, I couldn't," she said tiredly. "Any time I brought up any sort of problem, you said I needed to hang on until after the games. Then you would say you had to train and walk away."

"I thought you understood—"

"Oh my God," she cried at the ceiling. "Yes, of course I understood. I saw how hard you were working. Even if I hadn't, it was drilled into me by every single member of your family that you had to be supported and protected. Do you want the real reason I didn't tell you that Paisley was having an affair? Because I wasn't allowed to tell you anything that might cause you the slightest distraction. Paisley laid a guilt trip on me. She said I had to keep quiet because *we* didn't want to be the reason you failed to win gold. Did we?"

Nothing could have lit the fire of his temper faster. At a distance, he heard the layer of support beneath her actions, but he still grew raw with contempt.

"You're no better than the rest of them," he accused. "For years, everyone else decided what information I had a right to know. Paisley knew Dad was sleeping with his CFO. Mom knew something was funky with the numbers. No one told me." He jabbed at his chest. "*I* wasn't fit to be informed until the coffers were empty and a payroll needed to be met."

Then, yes, it had been *expected* that he would hurry home to sort that out.

His anger wasn't all directed at Becca. From the time he had started to show promise as an athlete, his mother had begun putting up shields around him until his whole family had been keeping him in the dark for months and years at a time. The fact that Becca had played right into that game was galling.

"Secrets matter, Becca. They blow up lives." He clapped his cup into the sink so hard, it cracked. He braced his hands on the far side of the island as he confronted her. "So tell me. What else have you kept from me all this time?"

There must be something, given the way she'd sneaked in here when she'd thought he would be away.

She held his gaze for so long, the air in his lungs began to incinerate and turn to ash. Her eyes dampened and his heart lurched.

He thought, *Wait. I don't want to know.*

"Nothing that matters," she finally said in a voice that was frayed thin.

"Liar," he accused, but there wasn't any heat in it. He dropped back on his heels and crossed his arms, feeling as though he was courting the sort of tailspin that left him tangled in a snow fence, worried he'd snapped a tendon.

"It's true," she said in that awful, emotionless voice. "Our marriage is over so nothing that happened back then matters anymore."

CHAPTER THREE

Untrue, Van thought, but Becca walked away and he told himself it was far more important to get his vehicle into the garage than press her to tell him things he may or may not wish to hear.

Which proved her point?

He bundled up, but still shuddered against the wind and blowing snow as he found the shovel and put his back into moving the drift from where it blocked the garage door.

It didn't escape him that he'd been grasping on to this coping strategy for as long as he could remember. He had a distinct memory of going outside in his pajamas, winter boots and down jacket to shovel the driveway, just to get away from the shouting inside the house. The sooner the driveway was clear, the sooner his mother would get in the car and take him and Paisley to the slopes.

Of course, once there his mother would meet other men. Van would see her having coffee with someone or she would disappear for an hour. Van had tried to ignore it, but his father would press him when they got home. *Don't protect her. You know who she was talking to. Tell me.*

Sometimes his father was drunk and would grow very needy and sentimental beneath his belligerence. He would accuse Van of letting his mother "take" him and Paisley from him. He would pressure Van and Paisley to side with him. *You missed me today, didn't you? Make sure you tell her that.*

If they were lucky, his father would have gone out and peace would reign for an evening, but even Paisley became a source of drama over time. She hadn't had Van's competitive spirit on the slopes, preferring to make conquests of his fellow athletes. Van had soon learned that his ability to make and keep friends depended largely on whether Paisley was courting or breaking a particular heart.

Those dynamics had been bloody exhausting, ratcheting up as his profile and success grew until he was convinced everyone who was the least bit pleasant to him had an ulterior motive.

Becca had given him a place to land that had nothing to do with any of it. She maintained an arm's length from his family, was only interested in the racing circuit for his sake and didn't care about social climbing or using his money for her own purposes. She hated drawing attention to herself, so the only drama in her world was the occasional drunk stranger who'd been ejected from her workplace.

He'd just started to trust she would always be his island of peace when she had pulled the rug out from under him in Sydney, proving herself as fickle as everyone else around him. Why? What had he done? What had he failed to do that caused her to turn her back like that?

He hit a layer of frozen snow and jabbed the shovel

in with aggressive might, throwing the scoop blindly into the growing shadows, working out his anger because, damn it, he *was* angry. He'd been angry with Becca for a long time.

Shock and denial had still consumed him as he had boarded the plane to come home. He'd still been trying to make sense of Paisley's call about his father taking all the money. The brutal plummet from the height of a personal best to financial disaster was impossible to process and Becca's decision to end their marriage had been equally bewildering.

But anger had crept in over the ensuing days, tangling with his anger toward his father, one fueling the other. If his father had set a better example on how to keep a marriage together, maybe Van would still be with his wife. If his marriage hadn't come between him and his father, maybe his father wouldn't have done something so heinous.

Van had told himself again and again that he understood why Becca had had to stay in Sydney with her mom, but ending their marriage hadn't been necessary. He resented her for that. He resented that she had turned him into a failure.

As time had worn on and they remained in a cold war, he had decided his family was right. Even the closest people in his life could treat him as temporary and throwaway, so why allow anyone to *get* close?

He no longer did.

Becca had walked away too scorned and bereft to tell Van what she hadn't had the courage to say when he had come to see her in Sydney. If he hadn't agreed so quickly and bluntly that it was time they divorced, she might have opened up and explained about her inability to make babies, but what was the point now? The last thing she wanted was for him to turn around and say, *You're right. It doesn't matter.*

Because it did matter. Very much. And there were many reasons their marriage had been doomed. Dredging up the most painful one wouldn't make any of the rest easier to bear.

She heard him go outside, and the garage door sounded a short time later. She peered out a guest room window to see he was only brushing the snow from his caked vehicle and pulling it in.

She was still poking through the drawers in that room when he said from the door, "What are you doing in here?"

Flattening a hand on her chest, she said ruefully, "I thought you were still outside."

The house was extremely well-built, that was the problem. Its walls were thick, its floors never creaking. Sound traveled from the great room to the loft and down the stairs to the game room, but the bedrooms were well-insulated and Van moved with athletic grace. Becca tended to get caught up in whatever she was doing and it all made for constant jump scares.

Van hovered in the door, glancing at the nightstand where a stack of fashion magazines had been shoved into its drawer. Melting snowflakes glistened on his hair and a trickle of water made a trail down his temple and the side of his cheek.

He swiped at it, sharp gaze still flickering around as though searching for clues.

"I was looking for something to do later." She elbowed toward the jigsaw puzzles in the closet and drew a romance novel off the bookshelf. It was one she'd read, but she remembered liking it. She would read it again.

"Hmph. I'm going to shower." He carried on to the master bedroom.

Don't think of it, she scolded herself. But how could she not? Donovan Scott was a name-brand athlete for more than his talent and achievements. He was six foot one of finely toned abs, pecs, biceps and glutes. His jaw-line was chiseled granite, his eyes a smoldering fire of muted gold. Showering with him had always been a lot of working up lather and scrubbing dirty bits until they were both too weak to move.

Intensive heat flared up from her chest, making her whole face burn. Becca escaped memories that were quickly becoming fantasies by going all the way down both flights of stairs to the basement rec room.

It was always a few degrees cooler here. The back of the house was built into the slope of the mountain. There was a walk-out patio with a path to the beach that was covered by the terrace above. The terrace extended far enough out that the patio mostly stayed clear, but the accumulation of snow on the lawn was high enough to block the view of the lake, not that it was light enough to see it anyway. Dark was closing in.

Becca turned on the gas fireplace and started searching through drawers.

Van arrived at the bottom of the stairs a few minutes later. He wore fresh jeans and a waffle-weave pullover that clung to his muscled shoulders, accentuating his physical power.

Her mouth went dry and she dragged her gaze back to the drawer of old remotes and computer cables she was pawing through, coming across a mini Polaroid photo that jolted her.

"Do you feel like a margarita?" he asked.

"Do I look like one?" She closed the drawer and quirked her mouth at her lame joke. She came across to set the photo on the polished slab of reclaimed wood that formed the top of the bar. "How's that for a blast from the past?"

She scooted around him into the small, well-stocked space behind the bar. As she looked for ingredients, she surreptitiously watched his reaction to the photo of her in a black turtleneck tucked under his arm. She was beaming at the camera while he was caught in profile, gazing on her with a wolfish expression.

Courtney had taken it and quietly singsonged, "He *liiikes* you," as she handed off the photo.

Lust. That's all it had been, but boy had it felt nice to be wanted that much. Becca was experiencing a hint of that old breathlessness, probably because that same lust was still alive, if their kiss and her involuntary fantasies were anything to go by.

"You haven't changed," Van said.

"No?" Becca hid how deeply that stung by turning to see what was in the fridge. When she straightened and glanced at him, Van was hitching onto one of the stools, dragging his gaze up from her backside.

"Déjà vu," she mumbled under her breath.

"I can't help it if you have a great ass, Bec. That is your cross to bear."

She snorted, trying to be annoyed because *men*, but she'd privately ogled him several times since waking to find him standing in the doorway of their old bedroom. Maybe lust was all they'd had, but they'd had buckets of it.

It was still a mystery to Becca that she'd met Van at all. Or that he'd pursued her when she'd so clearly been not of his world.

"You *have* to come," Courtney insisted. She was dating someone on the ski patrol who invited them to a party hosted by one of his old hockey teammates.

"It's my one night off," Becca groaned.

"Exactly why you should come with us. There's a hot tub," Courtney coaxed.

Becca did like hot tubs. As much as she liked Canada and skiing and spiders you could cover with a cup rather than a mixing bowl, it was bloody cold here sometimes. Sitting in a bubbling, steaming tub while snow fell made her feel very posh and decadent.

"I'll come for a little while," she relented, collecting her togs.

Becca had been in Whistler for four years, but still didn't have a strong grasp on the national sport or the big names on any of the teams. Nearly every Canadian she knew took to the ice in a beer league so *hockey player* didn't compute in her head as someone who played professionally in the NHL.

As they approached the "ski-in, ski-out" mansion, Becca realized this was less a party and more a who-do-you-know? flex. Any celeb who was in town had been invited. The sparkling lounge was full of people dressed way nicer than her plain turtleneck and jeans.

She quickly hid her cheap tote under the coat she'd bought at the ski swap and wished she'd made more of an effort with her makeup. Her hair was nothing but static and flyaway once she'd removed her alpaca wool hat. She self-consciously smoothed her dark brown waves into the indent of her neck as they worked their way into the party.

"Where's your bathing suit?" Courtney asked as she noted her empty hands.

Becca was *not* putting on her faded togs here.

"I'll meet you out there," she said weakly. "I want to get a drink first." Maybe she knew the bartender. It was a small world and an even smaller town.

She didn't know the bartender, but ordered a gin and tonic. While she waited, a silky-voiced Grammy winner came to stand beside her and said a pleasant, "Hello."

Becca was so intimidated, she flashed a smile and hurried away. She wound up beside a man telling animated stories that made her laugh until he glanced at her, giving her a top-to-toe look while asking, "Who is your agent again?"

He was a Hollywood director and, after she stammered out that she was not an actor looking for a part, she slipped away from that circle, too.

How do I not belong here? Let me count the ways.

She glanced outside, but feared Courtney would pressure her to join the half-naked bodies carousing in the hot tub if she went out to say she was leaving.

Still clutching her drink, she wandered the palatial house, pretending she was looking for someone while skimming her gaze away from any men who tried to make eye contact. It wasn't that she struggled to meet people. Men always wanted to talk to her, but they never really wanted to talk.

A number of framed photos and accolades on the walls of a staircase had her edging down them as she studied them. When she arrived at the bottom, easy-going laughter drew her to peek through a door into a den where a big-screen television was predictably showing a hockey game. A handful of men, all tall and fit, were chucking darts at a board, trash-talking each other as they did.

No women, Becca noted. She started to turn away before they noticed her, but her feet were rooted to the floor.

Goodness. Who *was* that? He wasn't any taller than the rest. They were all six-foot-something, all ripped and in prime health, full of swagger and athletic power. They were all dressed in casually upscale clothes.

One man in chinos and a snug green pullover with the sleeves pushed up shouldn't have stood out so starkly, but he did. He had a star power that made the rest part of a colorless herd. He had an economical way of moving that didn't allow her gaze to leave him and the way he glanced over and pinned her with a bright golden stare curled sensual claws into her.

"Do you want to play?" he asked, practically drawing her into the room via tractor beam.

The other men said things she didn't hear. She shrugged in the most deplorably unsophisticated way while he walked toward her with a handful of darts and offered them.

Her throat went so dry she could only croak, "Sure."

Becca's usual comfort zone was to stand on the side-lines listening to other people share snippets of their lives. If men wanted to flirt with her, they could do so from the other side of a bar and buy drinks for the privilege. Being in the spotlight of this man's attention was painful, but she felt drawn along as though caught in a rip current.

"I'm Donovan Scott. Call me Van. These are some of my friends." He introduced the other men. "And you're...?"

"Rebecca. Becca, not Becky."

"Do you know how to play darts, Becca not Becky?"

"Mm-hmm." She nodded, but maybe the fact that she was so overwhelmed by him made her come across as unsure because the four of them started telling her the rules and coaching her on where to stand and how to aim and throw.

It was a little too reminiscent of her tween years when the boys in after-school club had been mercilessly patronizing, snapping her bra and turning everything into a sexual innuendo. She forgot to be nervous and fell back on the cheeky retaliations she had used to survive that.

She took her stance and deliberately held the dart with its flight forward.

"No, that's backward—" Van started to say.

She threw it so it flipped in the air and stuck into the left of the bull's-eye.

Into the dumbfounded silence, she asked, "Do you know what mansplaining is, gentlemen?" She threw the other two conventionally and hit dead center with two hard, dull thuds.

"Do now," Van had said, scratching the tip of his nose. Then he quickly said, "We're playing teams. You're on mine." He caught her elbow and pulled her next to him.

Her heart swerved to catch up and she laughed over the other men's protests.

The evening became fun. The men accused Van of sneaking in a ringer because they won every game. Becca was in heaven, brushing hands with Van as they transferred darts to each other, standing close and murmuring jokes about strategy and technique. He made her feel incredible. Lighthearted and extraordinary.

Don't let it go to your head, she warned herself.

She dated, but cautiously. A seasonal town like Whistler had people her age coming and going all the time. The culture was very breezy about hooking up and moving on. She'd been stung a couple of times right after she'd arrived. Young men she had thought genuinely liked her had dropped her cold after a few weeks. She wasn't anxious to relive how naive and insignificant it made her feel.

Van, she learned, was an alpine racer who would represent Canada at the next winter games. His mother was a renowned gold medalist and his father's family had started buying up land in this area before a ski hill had even been proposed. His father now developed properties across Canada, making their family one of the richest in the country.

Between that, and the yoga studio and boutique owned by his sister and Van's constant presence on the slopes, he knew everyone.

Van Scott could *have* anyone.

Becca was confident he had approached her because she was literally the only woman in the room. Everything about him was so far beyond her reach it was laughable, but she still basked in the glow of his attention. She couldn't help it. She'd never had a man with this much charisma act as if she fascinated him.

When he said, "I have six hours of training first

thing tomorrow so I need to get home and get to bed. Do you need a lift home?" she knew exactly what he was asking.

He probably picked up women all the time. She would only be a fresh notch on his bedpost, but the way his gaze sparked with embers that arced to land in the pit of her belly mesmerized her. She was having fun here, but only because she was with him. Once he left, she would be back to feeling out of place and awkward.

She wasn't ready to say goodbye to him. Not yet.

"I should tell my friend I'm leaving," she said with a rasp of anticipation in her throat.

"Sure. Let's go find her."

Courtney had been out of the tub and catching up with a friend Becca didn't know. She was quick to flash her camera at them. As she handed over the snapshot, she whispered that she wanted a full report in the morning.

Becca was blushing as they walked outside, feeling as though everyone knew she was going home with him when, in reality, she doubted anyone but Courtney had noticed or cared.

Van's SUV was already running, snow melting off the windows.

"Remote start," he said, showing her the fob in his hand. "Are you driving?"

"What? Oh." She was so nervous she'd absently started around to what was the passenger side back home. Also, she wasn't used to a man opening a door for her. It felt pretentious to go along with it.

She came to where he stood and climbed in past him, setting her homely bag on her boots, feeling too gauche for words.

He stayed in the open door where the glow of the interior light lit only half his face. "I can take you home. I absolutely will if that's what you prefer, but..." He watched her closely. "Would you rather spend the night at mine?"

"This is my bathing suit," she was compelled to explain, pointing at her bag. "I wasn't planning to go home with anyone."

"I know." He choked a laugh. "I wasn't either. I never do this."

She doubted that, but confessed, "Neither do I."

"I mean I *have*," he joked. "This isn't my first time. Don't worry."

"Just me then."

His face fell with shock. "Are you serious?"

"No." She chuckled at the way he clamped his lips flat and tilted his face up to the flakes drifting from the sky, as though he couldn't believe she'd gotten him again. "I mean it would be my *second* time so maybe you should worry a lit—"

His cool hand cupped her cheek and his head ducked in. His mouth covered her grin, stilling her lips before drawing her into a slow, hot kiss that was *him*. She instantly understood this was the essence of the man. He knew how to hold back and wait for the right moment. When he finally took action, he went all in.

That was the last sensible thought she had because he took her with him on a blazing, wild journey. His hand shifted to the side of her neck and their noses bumped and their tongues brushed. Her pulse throbbed in her throat and her breasts felt heavy and her hand rose to the back of his head to encourage him.

The snow could have stopped and spring arrived for

all she knew of time and space, because her world was only heat and his tantalizing taste and an earthy invitation to pleasure. So much pleasure beckoned it was irresistible. She instinctively recognized him and this as one of those things in life that others were allowed to experience and indulge in that she wasn't entitled to have. Not material possessions, but luck and joy and those wonderful blessings that certain people fell into without trying. Such things always seemed to evade her best efforts to grasp them, but she bet he got all the best parts of life without even trying.

"Scott!" someone shouted. "Get a room."

With a sharp inhale, he broke away, but stayed close enough to balance his brow against hers. He breathed a laughing curse against her chin.

"Bad form on my part, doing that here, but I've been dying to kiss you all night. It's these dimples." He brushed a fingertip against one, then pressed his lips to it. "Too cute to resist."

"No," she groaned, losing her smile. "Koala bears are cute. I want to be admired for my character, like my conscientious recycling and my reliable punctuality."

"Mmm." He nodded with amusement. "Those are also qualities I find completely irresistible." He chuckled and kissed her once more before he drew back. "What I was trying to say before you emptied my brain was that I don't know if I have any condoms at home. I'll have to stop on the way."

Her senses were still spinning, but beneath it was the knowledge that a hard crash would follow whatever soaring heights she achieved with him. If she had any sense of self-preservation, this was a good moment to exercise it and ask him to take her home after all. She didn't want him to break her heart and she knew without a doubt that he could and would.

"Okay," she said.

"What are you doing later tonight?"

Becca's ears rang as Van's voice dragged her from her ruminations. Her heart swerved at the jarring sensation of leaping from the beginning of their relationship to the end.

"Pardon?"

"You said 'déjà vu.' Never mind," he dismissed with a self-deprecating wave.

She finished cracking ice into the blender, scattered thoughts coming together in a realization that he was replaying the way he'd surprised her the next day, after their hookup.

She'd gone to work that next afternoon feeling blue. She had fallen rather hard for him in the course of one passionate night. They'd made love three times, including at five thirty before they'd risen and he'd dropped her home on his way to the slopes. As he kissed her goodbye, he'd said with a wince of apology, *I don't have a lot of time for a private life.*

It's okay. I understand.

She'd been painfully aware he hadn't even gone through the charade of asking for her number. She would be forgotten before he rounded the corner at the end of her block, but she would remember him forever.

Maybe she should have felt more chagrin for letting him treat her as a hit-and-quit, but he'd been a gentleman the whole time, ensuring she was enjoying every second as much as he was. It had been incredible.

Wait. *Had* he enjoyed it? That had been the question

that struck like a slap hours later. As her self-confidence had tipped into a nosedive, she had turned from refilling the pub's beer fridge and there he was, hitching onto the stool while asking what she was doing with her evening. She'd been stunned into babbling exactly what she said right now.

"You're looking at it, mate. Here 'til closing." She quirked her brow because it still applied.

"Guess I am, too." He repeated his line with equal irony.

On that long-ago night, he'd added, *Give me a menu and whatever is on tap. Don't let me have more than two.*

When she'd served his beer, she'd said, *You're not staying until my shift ends? I'm here until closing.*

Would you rather I didn't?

It's a free country.

She'd been trying to play it cool. She didn't regret their night beyond the fact that she had thought it would only *be* one night, but there he had been. It was confusing, especially since Courtney had teased her about pulling him.

Van Scott doesn't take anyone home, especially not ski bunnies like us. Do you know who his family is?

"Why—?" Becca was still feeling splintered between then and now. Her heart was sheared on all sides, eroded by the time they'd been apart, jagged and as susceptible to breakage as it had been that evening.

His turning up to see her again had been a betrayal of her expectations, one that had filled her with more hope than had been good for her. If he had ghosted her, she would have recovered from a dented ego. Instead she was...this. A ghost of a woman still trying to figure out how she had even been married to him, let alone in the middle of divorcing him. It didn't feel real.

She couldn't look at him as she tossed in measures of tequila, pineapple juice and tamarind nectar.

"Why what?" he prompted.

"Why *me*?" She jammed the lid on the blender and warily lifted her gaze.

He made an impatient noise and his hands opened to turn his palms up on the bar. "Why *not* you, Becca? I have never understood why you have such a low opinion of yourself."

Seriously?

"Look around, Van." She hit the button, making it churn ice with the decibels of a cement mixer. When she released it, she blurted into the abrupt silence, "Look at where I am. Look at where you are. You said I hadn't changed. It's too bloody true."

"I would apologize for the money I was born into, but my dad took all of it," he said with gritty disdain.

She pushed her own hurt aside and asked, "Do you want to talk about that?"

"No," he said firmly, accepting the glass she poured him. "But I did wonder if that's why you left." His gaze flashed up, sharp and hard. Watchful.

"I— We had already agreed it was over before you left Sydney."

"Did we?"

Best to sidestep that one. She poured the drinks.

"I didn't know anything about your dad until it started making headlines after you were home. I got a few things in my social feed and followed up."

"Really?" His narrowed gaze picked apart her ex-

pression like a surgeon with a knife. "Mom and Paisley never talked to you about it before it happened?"

She tucked her chin, taken aback. "Why would
they?" She'd barely been speaking to either of them.

"I don't know, but it seemed suspicious that you
ended our marriage right before Dad's crimes came
to light."

"I went to Sydney because Mum was sick, full stop.
Once I got there, it was very obvious how little you and
I had in common." Becca wasn't embarrassed of her
roots, but coming from this house to move back into
her childhood home had shoved their differences into
her face. Her dad had still been complaining about ba-
sics, not begrudging Mum a fan in the sweltering heat,
but having choice words about the electric company
over the bills. She'd been back to sleeping in the bunk
beds she had once shared with Wanda. Her Dad kept
up the modest bungalow, but not all the neighbors were
as diligent. Some were very dodgy, getting police visits
in the middle of the night.

By the same token, even though she wasn't embarrassed of her husband, Becca had played down Van's
wealth. When Wanda teased her about her designer sunglasses, asking if they were knockoffs, Becca had said,
"Van gets things like this for free," which was true, but
it saved her boasting that he would buy her a dozen pair
without batting an eyelash if she asked him to.

She simply hadn't known how to bridge that without her parents thinking she was putting on airs or Van
thinking she was using him to better herself. Given his
remark a second ago, she was probably right.

"I've never cared about your money, but it's starting to sound as though I'm not the only one with a low opinion of me." *Jerk*.

She sipped her tangy drink. She had sugared the rim rather than salting it and licked the grains from her lips. Beyond the darkened window, the snow was reflecting the colored Christmas lights that Van must have turned on when he'd been outside earlier.

"You do, though," he muttered with a flinty look. "Care about my money. You're getting salty about it right now. *I* never cared about the difference in our advantages. I thought you were smart and funny and hot as hell. Same as me," he said with a fresh dose of self-deprecating irony. "I only asked why you've never seen how great you are."

"Because I didn't grow up surrounded by people telling me that I *was* great, day in and day out," she said scathingly.

His head snapped back and she realized she was salty.

"I'm not saying you didn't deserve to hear it." She wiped up a small spill. "Only that I didn't have a natural talent and even if I did, my parents didn't have money for lessons and coaches and time to stand around watching me race or sing or whatever. I was reminded that I was noisy and messy and expensive and needed to pull my weight. So I did and I do."

She also kept her head down and her needs simple. Simple enough that she could meet them herself. She tried very hard not to dwell on how good it had felt when this man had built her up, making her feel special and interesting and desired.

"I know you worked hard in your own way," she allowed. "I'm not saying you didn't."

"Was he hurtful?" he asked through his teeth. "Abusive?"

"Who? My father? *No*." She scowled. "He said it as a joke like, 'you costly little blighters better make yourselves useful and fetch my slippers.'" She was compelled to defend her father even though his teasing words had held enough brutal honesty to leave a mark. "He's a bit of a sexist and was always more inclined to chase me around pretending to be a monster than say anything sentimental, but I knew he would kill anyone who hurt me. There were hard times and we knew it, that's all."

"How hard?"

"Not so hard I ever went hungry," she made sure to clarify. "But there weren't any frills or extras. Dad worked any sort of labor job rather than miss a day's pay, but he didn't have a trade and never had anything that could be counted on long term. Mum hurt her back when she was pregnant with Wanda, so it took a long time before she was able to return to the grocery store. She would get stroppy if I put Dad on the spot by asking for things we couldn't afford and tell me not to get above myself. Or Dad would tell me to get a job and buy it myself."

That was another reason she hadn't told them how rich Van was. She hadn't wanted her family to think she was skipping over the hard work of earning things for herself and living off Van—which she pretty much had been.

"It's totally normal to want what the other kids have, Becca."

"I know." She shrugged. "I also know it doesn't matter that I didn't have those material things."

"Is that what he told you?" he asked with sharp insight. "I forgot that he's really your stepdad."

"*That* doesn't matter," she insisted. "He wasn't trying to be cruel, Van. He just never saw any point in mollycoddling. Whinging doesn't solve anything so he'd tell me to get on with it."

When he had called about Mum, he hadn't couched his words. *Doctor says your mum has cancer. Best get back here to help out.*

"You always said Wanda was spoiled because she was the baby. That's what you really meant, isn't it? He favored her because he made her. You felt second best."

He hit the nail straight on the head and seemed to pound it home so firmly he nearly cleaved her in half. Her eyes grew hot.

"My father loves me." She looked him straight in the eye, refusing to let him see how badly she was squirming inside. "It's not his fault he struggles to express it. Or that he has a closer bond with Wanda because he was there when she was born. I was five years old when Mum married him. We had to learn how to be a father and daughter."

Be good, Possum. We don't want your new dad regretting that he asked us to live here with him.

"You're being very generous to the person who was the adult."

"Because it serves no purpose to be critical of him," she said with an impatient fling of her hand. "I wish Dad had been different. There. I said it. Does it change anything? No? Shocking."

"You still could have told me."

"As if you had time to hear it! You needed to train, Van. You always needed to train." Her voice died to a murmur. She gulped her drink and the hot-cold mixture of frozen alcohol worked its way down her tight throat to sit like a glacier behind her heart. Like an ice cream headache that encompassed her whole body and made her ears ring.

His own features froze except for a tic that pulled at his cheek.

"I'm not trying to make you feel guilty," Becca mumbled. "You asked why I don't puff myself up. I told you." She set her drink on the bar as she moved out from behind it. "I will, however, be happy to hand you your backside at pool or darts. See? I'm very confident when I have a reason to be," she said over her shoulder. "Let's play pool. I feel like we've thrown enough darts already. I guess you're right. I am funny."

CHAPTER FOUR

VAN TURNED ON the stool, watching Becca pull balls from the pockets and roll them toward the foot of the table while he pondered the contradictions in her.

In certain ways, she was poised and self-possessed. The night they met, she had trounced a handful of men who were used to winning. It had been entertaining as hell, and when he had brought her home, she'd been so abandoned and passionate he'd thought she had a lot more experience with relationships than she really did.

It took some time before he realized that Becca had the opposite of an Achilles' heel. She had one or two spots where she was completely sure of herself and the rest of her was head-to-toe vulnerability that felt the tiniest arrow.

She hid her insecurities well, employing snappy comebacks and deflecting any compliments she did earn. That had puzzled him until he realized that she got way too much of the wrong sort of attention from men.

Van had often earned stares because of his visibility on the racing circuit, but he hadn't appreciated what it was like for a woman to get stared at constantly until he'd begun dating Becca. He'd gone out with pretty women before her, but they'd been sophisticated types who knew how to put off a serious don't-touch-me vibe.

Becca was this incredible combination of sensual and approachable, often smiling and flashing her dimples, all big brown eyes and freckles like chocolate sprinkles across her nose and cheeks. Then she was curvaceous as hell. No hiding that sex appeal. Even when she wore a loose hoodie and a slouched beanie, she couldn't walk through a pub without every male pair of eyes touching her ass. Van had often been hard-pressed not to knock some teeth in. It was damned tiresome and he wasn't even the target.

So he understood why she took compliments as false flattery and dismissed them, but he hadn't realized that she had rarely received sincere praise in the first place. He tried thinking back, wondering if he'd ever properly expressed his appreciation for the small things she'd done—picking up protein powder or returning an email—when he'd been consumed by his goals.

Probably the most sincere compliment he could have paid her was listening when she was hurting, and she was right that he hadn't.

"You're wrong about one thing." He rose from the stool.

"What?" she prompted.

"I wasn't told how great I was." He moved to turn on the sound system, rolling through the satellite channels past the last of the Christmas carols to find acoustic covers of pop songs. "I was told how great I *could be*, if I met all the necessary expectations."

Everything about her softened—her shoulders, her mouth, her gaze. He didn't want her pity any more than she wanted his.

"Training was a double-edged sword." He brought their drinks to where she stood near the cue rack. "You're right to accuse me of using it as an avoidance tactic. A-type personalities like mine are the result of two people exactly like me fighting over who should control the star power they had manufactured. When I was young, I got into a bad habit. If I didn't like what was going on around me, I said I had to train and walked away."

"Get out of jail free?"

"Something like that." He was embarrassed to realize how often he'd done that to her, but even small discord with her had felt too big to manage in the narrow slivers of time he'd had available. He hadn't been looking to date or get involved at all, but he'd glanced up to see her watching him through an open door and— Hell, he couldn't explain it. It had been like those times when he was skiing and operated solely on instinct and muscle memory, completely in tune with his surroundings and following an invisible line in the snow.

That night, the line had led directly to her and he'd been swept along it without questioning where it was headed.

He'd rationalized that it had been his competitive nature coming to the fore, wanting to claim her before anyone else had the chance, but it was more than that. From the first glance, Becca had been more than he knew how to handle. He had never wanted to deconstruct why so he'd used what was available to avoid deeper thoughts.

"Training was a blocking drug," he acknowledged. "You can't worry about anything but keeping yourself alive when you're hurtling down a hill at ninety miles an hour. As far as altering one's mood goes, it's highly addictive." He still missed it, but he also knew that he'd missed important things by succumbing to its lure. "That excuse is gone now. For both of us."

Her gaze flashed up to his with alarm.

He didn't like it either. A restless itch in his chest warned him he was more vulnerable than he had ever been.

"Anything we put off saying in the past because I had one foot out the door can be said tonight. We've got…" He glanced at the clock. "Seven hours and fourteen minutes to say it."

She swung her gaze to the clock and her profile flexed with…he wasn't sure what that was. Anguish? Desperation? Something that made him want to grab her arm as though she were falling off a cliff.

In the next second, she slipped on the blasé expression he recognized as her easygoing bartender guise, the shield she used to deflect whatever made her uncomfortable.

"Then one of us runs into the snow without their shoe?" she asked.

"Then if one of us runs away, that is exactly what we're doing."

"I didn't run away. I went home to help Mum." A guilty sting constricted her throat because Becca had been running *from* as much as *to*, but she didn't want to talk about it.

Hypocrite, she chided herself.

She set aside her drink. "Lag for break?"

The long pause as he ran his tongue behind his lip

before he said, "Sure," told her he knew she was dodging the challenge he'd just thrown down.

They chalked the tips of their cues before they both bent and tapped a ball down to the far cushion. Becca's two ball came back to halt a mere finger-width from the cushion in front of them while his was at least two hand-widths away.

"You're such a show-off," he accused.

"I can't help that my after-school club had a table." Plus darts and foosball. She was excellent at all three. She moved to finish racking the balls and rolled the triangle to snug them, then lifted the triangle away.

"Call me old-fashioned, but I don't think children should be taught to hustle."

"It's a life skill, same as bartending. Care to make it interesting?" She came back to set the cue ball left of center and eyed him with a deliberately cheeky up-and-down. "Too chilly-willy for strip, I think. I don't want to embarrass you."

"I will if you will," he dared.

Her brain flashed an image of him with his layer of fine hair across his muscled chest tapering down to flat hips and bare, thick thighs. The tip of her cue wavered.

She straightened and took a sip of her icy drink. "Do you really want to stand there naked while I clean the table?"

"Did it ever occur to you that I used to let you win so I'd have a head start when we moved on to other things?"

She chortled. "Van Scott has never, in the history of an undecided contest, allowed someone to get the better of him on purpose. You go ahead and say whatever you need to say to soothe your ego while you watch me break some balls."

She moved back into position and glanced at him to see if he had a comeback.

"I'm letting you have that one to prove my point."

"Which proves mine."

He sipped his drink, but he was hiding a smirk.

The way he was looking at her was so sweetly familiar, it sent flutters across her heart.

Foreplay. That's what this had always been, because if they weren't fighting, they were flirting. Banter or bicker. It had always been a fine line and they'd always gone to bed rather than get to the root of an issue.

Until they hadn't.

What else have you kept from me?

Becca blocked that out and lined herself up. She didn't have advantages like reach and strength, but she was accurate and had great follow-through. As she thrust her cue and sent the white ball cracking into the one, the bunched balls scattered in all directions, clacking against one another. The four, seven and two all rolled into pockets as cleanly as if she'd planned it that way.

"There goes your socks and belt." She swaggered around the table, pondering her strategy. "I don't want your clothes, though. Or your money. What else have you got?"

"Let's keep to the spirit of telling each other things we should have already said," he suggested. "You want three of those?"

Since she planned to win and wouldn't be backed into saying anything she didn't want to give up, she accepted those terms. She tapped the six into the side pocket and said, "Four."

"Let's see." He scratched under his chin. "I suggested margaritas because cocktails make you chatty and I want to know why you're really here."

"Mate. If you think I don't know men try to use alcohol to get things from me, you seriously underestimate all women. Mine's mostly ice and I plan to let it melt. Try again."

"All right." He waited until she was about to shoot. "I'm planning to sell this house as soon as... What?"

She bobbled her shot and straightened to glare at him. "That's cheating."

"How is it cheating? It's something you didn't know." Such a smug tone. He came around to nudge her aside and bent to smack three stripes into pockets. "Now we both have to cough up three confessions."

"I thought you loved this house."

"I thought you did."

"I thought you could afford to buy me out. If you're still bouncing back from what your Dad did, we can make a different arrangement."

"Are you serious?" He was looking at her as though *she* was underestimating *him*. "Is that why you only asked for half the house? You thought I was still broke?"

"I didn't want to ask for anything. My lawyer insisted. This seemed like the only thing I was remotely entitled to since we chose it together and I lived here more than you did."

"I'm fine, Becca," he said shortly. Indignant. "I had to invest a pile of my own money and things were touch-and-go the first year, but we're back on top. I wondered why you only wanted half the house. My lawyer said not to look a gift horse in the mouth. You can have more if you need it. I can support you while you go to school."

"I don't want your money," she said again, slow and firm and with plenty of tested patience. "I never did."

"That one sounds familiar." He bent to continue his turn. "Dig deeper."

She didn't bother counting or reviewing or arguing that if he refused to believe her about not wanting his money, then he didn't really know it, did he?

"I know you only married me to tick off your mom," she blurted as he shot.

"What?" He swore as the eleven went in, but the white plonked in behind it. He moved to the pocket to retrieve it. "*You're* cheating."

"I thought that's how we were playing." She carried her stick around the table and set the retrieved cue ball.

"We're throwing out unfounded accusations? Because if that was my reason for marrying you, I would already know it."

"Maybe I should say that you liked the fact that marrying me annoyed your mother."

"Good God, Becca. I was twenty-five, not five. I didn't *care* that our marriage annoyed her. That's different."

"Not from this side," she muttered, sending the cue ball to tap the five into the corner before it rolled across and dropped another ball in the side. "She resented me, full stop."

"Mom didn't want me to have any distractions. Between her and my coaches, my days were regimented down to the last minute. She didn't resent *you*. It was the fact that I was married at all."

"Oh, yes. That's true. She made sure I knew it

wasn't personal." She dampened her tongue with a sip of margarita, then adopted her snippiest Canadian accent. "Van is asserting his independence, Rebecca. It's a symptom of the pressure he's under. As long as you don't impact what he's worked his entire life to achieve, you and I will get along."

"And that's why you fell in line and never told me about Paisley or any of the other things they said or did?" His voice was filled with smoldering disgust.

"You *had* worked your whole life toward winning gold. I respected that. I wanted to be part of the team that got you there. Falling in line, as you call it, was the best way I could support you."

"Then why weren't you?" he ground out, voice so bitter she straightened before taking her shot. "If you were part of the team, Becca, why weren't you there when I *won*?"

Becca could have touched down in any country when she arrived to watch Van compete. People from around the world were converging here, so the local sights and sounds were diluted by a buzzing multicultural stew. Plus, her brain was in such a fog from racing back from Sydney, preparing to help her mother through her treatments and dealing with what she'd learned about her own health, she wasn't taking in details like architecture or food.

Van's family had been planning this trip for years. Long before Van married Becca, his mother, Cheryl, had booked a house. She had promised to "find room" for Becca since Van would stay in the athlete village, avoiding distractions and preparing for his races, but Becca couldn't face them. Through a friend of an old roommate in Whistler, she secured an air bed in a jumbled flat of excited fans who were coming and going and didn't take any notice of who she was or where she went. It was exactly the anonymity she needed right then.

She arrived the day before Van's first, most important race—which was actually two runs. She picked up her ticket for the venue, but when it came time to take a seat beside his mother and her husband, his father and the woman he'd brought, Paisley and their assorted children, Becca couldn't do it.

She hung back at the top of the stairs and might have seen his family leap to their feet as his perfect form flashed by at lightning speed, but the crowd went wild and her eyes were blurred with joy. He arrived at the finish line in record time. The second race a couple of hours later put him on the top of the podium.

As she absorbed that he had achieved what he'd been working so hard for, Becca felt tremendous hope. Maybe this was all that was wrong between them. Skiing had been a mistress in their marriage from the beginning. Now that he would retire from competing, they could move forward as a couple and plan a future that would fulfill them both.

As she wove through the crowd to where Van was talking to television commentators from around the world, however, she could see he was still as popular as ever. He had stripped off his helmet and was surrounded by avid fans. A heavyset man lifted his tablet, blocking her from seeing anything but Van's image as he scanned the crowd.

When she moved to where she could see him again, Paisley had joined him. Van was holding his four-year-old niece, looking into her eyes with such a happy, tender expression, Becca's heart stretched itself out of shape. Van kissed little Flora's forehead and Flora hugged his neck. Becca crashed into the agonizing reality that he would make a wonderful father, but she could never carry their children.

She had hurried back to the flat and changed her flight despite the rebooking cost. When Van showed up in Sydney a week later, she told him it was over.

CHAPTER FIVE

"Bec? You keep zoning out on me." Van wanted to wave his hand in front of her blank stare, but she looked so damned *sad* his heart turned over.

Her lashes lifted and her gaze focused on him, but her eyes were welling with tears.

His heart lurched. He swore.

"That wasn't fair of me." He set his stick on the table and took her by the shoulders, drawing her into him. "You were going through a lot with your mom, I know. It's okay that you missed it."

That old sting of disappointment and dismissal had been wrenched out of him by her talk of wanting to be part of the team. Not having her there to share in his victory had made his gold medal a hollow chunk of worthless ore that hung heavy around his neck. It had taken everything in him to keep a smile on his face as he accepted it.

A week after the closing ceremony, his medals were merely symbols of how much *he* had missed and all the things he had failed to see. By then, he'd retired from the sport that had consumed him, his wife had left him, he'd been betrayed by his father, and he was facing financial ruin. Van had tried to accept that Becca had been going through her own turmoil, but it had been a bitter, frustrating time.

"You were right to be with your mom while you had the chance." He pressed his lips to her hair while he used the other hand to take her cue stick and set it next to his.

As he closed his arms around her, she took a shaken breath and gave a shudder, so rigid as she tried to hang on to her self-control, she was trembling.

Had she cried at all over her loss? If he knew her as well as he believed he did, she had been the one to hug and cater and soothe everyone else, soldiering on through her grief so others could indulge their own.

"It's okay," he assured her, rubbing her back. "I've got you."

A choking sob broke through. Her arms slid around his waist and her fists clenched into the back of his shirt. She began to quake, starting to weep her great big heart out, damn near breaking his in the process.

"Babe." He closed his eyes, wrapped his arms around her and one word rang in his head. *Finally.*

It hurt to hear her cry this hard, but she quit feeling like sand slipping through his fingers. He had all of her in his arms again, clinging and real. He drew her around to the middle of the sectional and cuddled her into his lap. She tucked her face into the crook of his neck and he held her close while she completely fell apart.

He hated like hell that she was hurting, but God, it felt good to hold her again. This was why he couldn't so much as buy another woman coffee. No one fit exactly like this against him, soft and round and warm and firm. No one smelled like this or leaned so trustingly into him.

It made him sick with himself that he hadn't insisted on staying in Sydney so he could have held her like this every time her sorrow rose up to swallow her. Why had she sent him away when she had needed him? *Why?*

Despite Becca's abrupt return to Sydney, Van had been convinced she would turn up to watch him race. He had told her he would understand if she couldn't, but he had wanted her there. Deep down, he had believed she would move heaven and earth to be there.

When he had looked around after winning the most coveted prize in his field and didn't see her, he'd felt slighted. Forgotten.

He hadn't known yet that worse was to come. He'd wrapped up with two more medals and a bronze in a team event, then flew into Sydney. He'd been coming off his adrenaline high and was still in the headspace of self-involvement that competing required. It had all combined to make him defensive and remote, but she had been just as obdurate.

He texted from the airport.

I'll rent a car at the airport and arrive at your parents' house around four.

She texted back, responding lot quicker than she had to any other text lately.

I'll meet you at your hotel.

Bring your family. We'll have dinner. I want to meet them.

He'd checked into his suite, shaved and showered,

put on his suit pants and a new shirt, his good watch and his wedding ring—which he only wore for dress because it would have caught on equipment otherwise. His pants were so loose from his intensive training, he had to use the tightest hole in his belt. He was pared down to his leanest form, cheekbones standing out so his mouth was a wide, severe line, his nose hawkish, his muscles confused because he was amped with tension and not burning it off with exercise.

Nervous? That wasn't like him. He had met Becca's family via the tablet several times. He had no reason to think they disliked him, but he *had* married her to keep her in Canada. She spoke about them with affection, but rarely shared much about them. It was past time he got to know them better.

He waited in the lobby and saw her come through the revolving doors before she saw him. He was dying to hold her, but something held him back.

She was alone. Strangely, he was unsurprised. It acted as a type of forewarning, if that was possible. He instinctively grew more guarded, sensing an impending blow of some kind. He wasn't sure why. Becca was the furthest thing from a threat. She was small in stature, had those big, vulnerable eyes, wore an off-the-rack sundress and rubber flip-flops. Her hair was in a ponytail, but fraying out of it as though blown by an open car window.

She was always thinking of other people before herself.

Even before they spoke, however, he started to question why and how he'd drawn her so quickly into his inner circle. He'd learned years ago to protect himself from mind games and heart fractures. As this scent of danger arrived in his nostrils, he suddenly realized how unguarded he was with her. Why had he married her so impulsively? How well did he really know her?

Her mouth firmed with dismay as she took in the marble floor and the live pianist, the fountain and the crystal chandelier.

It doesn't matter, he wanted to growl as he walked toward her, latching onto superficial frustrations so he had somewhere to place the deeper aggravation that was starting to eat at him.

She spotted him and flinched as though the mere sight of him hurt her in some way. He started to draw her into an embrace and kiss her, but she barely let their lips touch before she dropped her gaze to the floor between them. Her hands on his arms held him off drawing her closer.

"I was in such a hurry, I forgot to put on my proper sandals," she noted, lifting the toes of one foot.

Not, *I missed you.* Not, *Congratulations.*

When she looked up at him, her cheekbones wore a streak of stark pink that could have been sunburn or hectic heat or the heightened emotion of an impending conversation he suddenly realized they were both dreading. His gut filled with cement.

"How's your mom?" he asked.

"Sick," she said with a twist of her lips. "Dad's home with her right now. Wanda's picking up takeaway after she finishes her classes at uni."

All good excuses for her to be here alone, but the ball of concrete in him hardened.

"Do you want to talk about it?" he asked.

"Not really." She released him to hug herself tighter. "The prognosis isn't very good. Mum had some health problems when she was younger and the doctors weren't very helpful. It made her reluctant to see anyone so she left it too long…" Her expression flexed with pain and sadness. "She's accepting some treatment, but she reckons when it's your time, it's your time, so she won't allow anything too aggressive."

"Bec, I'm sorry." He tried again to draw her into a hug. "Do you want to go upstairs where it's quiet?"

"No," she said with a firm shake of her head, holding herself off from him. "The restaurant is fine."

Her rejection was a resounding kick in the chin. He dropped his hands to his sides and nodded. He began to shore himself up by thinking of all the things he needed to do in the next hours and days and realized… There was nothing. Nowhere he had to be.

Slightly dizzy, he walked with her down the hall to the restaurant. He told the hostess they were only two, not five. She showed them to a table that overlooked the harbor.

They were seated on the corner of the table so they both faced the window. Their elbows and knees might have brushed, but Becca shifted her chair away to make that less likely.

If things had been the way they should have been, he would have ordered champagne and dragged her chair so close he could have looped his arm around her shoulders.

Hell, if things were normal, they would already be naked upstairs, earning noise complaints.

He offered her the wine list. "Would you like to choose something?"

"I'm driving," she said with a tightening of her lips that was neither smile nor apology.

"You're not staying." A trapdoor inside his chest fell open. "Becca—"

"Let me say it."

"No. *You* let *me* say it."

He saw her mouth tighten and he knew he was blowing it by asserting his will, but Becca usually came around to whatever he wanted. He wasn't used to this woman who had flown back to Sydney while he was in Tahoe, not waiting a few days to talk things out with him. Since she'd been here, she'd become less and less communicative, taking longer and longer to get back to him. He'd blamed the time change and his own schedule, but now she didn't even want to be alone with him. Didn't want to touch him.

He had to grapple things back under control. Now.

"I'm done. With skiing," he added quickly when she seemed to pale. "I'm prepared to stay here in Sydney as long as you need to be here."

"Why?" She was looking at her hands in her lap. "I have to live at home and be with Mum so Dad can work and Wanda can go to school."

"I can help with their bills. Your dad doesn't have to work."

"Don't." Her eyes widened, appalled. "Dad's work ethic is important to *me*. And he needs to stay busy. Don't make him feel as though he's not able to provide for Mum."

"That's not what I'm trying to do. I want to help." He wasn't used to feeling useless any more than her father was.

She brushed away his offer and sipped her water. "Why even retire? You just turned twenty-six. You could easily keep at it for another four years and win more medals."

"Easily?" he scoffed. "I'd like to be able to use my knees when I'm forty, thanks." And there was something very irritating in her "go outside and play" attitude.

"Your mother doesn't want you to retire," she noted.

"No one does." Certainly not his sponsors. Between his mother's legacy and his own success, Van had become one of those breakout athletes who couldn't be spotted buying chewing gum without the item going viral.

"What will you do, then?" she asked. "Work for your father?"

"No." God, no. Their relationship had been contentious for a while now, mostly because his father was trying to merge their businesses. Van didn't want to give up his autonomy. They'd had a proper blowout right before Van left Vancouver. He'd told his father he might need to stay with Becca in Sydney. The word *ingrate* had been thrown at him along with some other choice insults.

Becca was still looking at him and he rubbed his thighs. This question on his next steps had plagued him for years. He had never had a good answer, always putting off making plans until skiing was no longer the dominant weight on his time. The mountain that had been in front of him his whole life was gone now. It was time to consider what would come next. He didn't need anything that would get him more fame or fortune.

"I thought I—*we*—could start our family?"

Becca didn't move, didn't say a word. Her cheekbones seemed to stand out like tent poles under stiff canvas. Her lips went white.

"My timing is terrible. We don't have to, Bec. We haven't talked about it and you have a lot on your plate." He sighed with frustration and dampened his own dry throat. "It's true that I don't know what I'll do, but I have some ideas. I've been thinking about a fitness app." It was very nascent and not something he was ready to talk about. "It's something I could develop here as easily as I could at home. I can buy us a flat near your parents so we always have a place of our own here— Quit shaking your head. *Why not?*"

"I'm not going back to Canada."

"I just said I'll stay here as long as you need."

"Ever," she corrected, still with that tight-skinned expression.

"Ever?"

The anguish around her eyes was that of someone being persecuted beyond what they could bear. "I think you should go home and…get on with things."

"What the hell does that mean?" His heart stalled.

"We're too different, Van. Getting married was a mistake. You know it was."

"No, I don't."

"Then you've been too busy to see it," she said with a frustrated break in her voice. "Once you've had time to reflect the way I have, it will become glaringly obvious." She sent a hounded look to the piano man, who was playing both too loud and not loud enough.

The notes were jangling in Van's head, but he suspected people could overhear them.

"Where is this coming from? We were perfectly fine when—"

"We were not," she said.

"No? Well, that's news to me. Tell me what's wrong. Let's work it out," he said through gritted teeth, growing defensive as this started to feel like the sort of scene his sister staged.

"There's no point." She shook her head, part refusal, part disbelief. "I can't deal with Mum *and* this. I can't." She genuinely looked at the end of her rope. "Just *go.*"

This was going to be a bad fall. That was the one clear thought that flashed in his mind. He would dissect later exactly where he had erred and how to do better next time, but in the moment he had to make the split-second decision as to whether he would fight the fall and risk the sort of injury that could destroy his life, or go with it and control how badly he got banged up.

Either way it would hurt like hell, but protecting himself for the long haul was always best practice. He braced himself and let the fall happen.

"Is that really the only way I can help you? By *leaving*?" His chest was so tight, he could hardly speak. "Getting on with things?" he mocked.

She flinched. "Yes."

The server showed up to ask if they were ready to order.

"I can't stay." Becca rose abruptly, looking like she was going to cry.

"Bec." He caught her arm but guilt over his neglect of their marriage and empathy at her situation collided into a desire to cushion her, too. He sure as hell couldn't push her when she was this fragile. "I'll stay a few days. If you decide you want to talk…"

She gave a jerky, noncommittal nod and hurried away.

His brain was so rattled, he might as well have been concussed. He ordered room service and went upstairs where he picked up a text from his sister telling him to call.

It's about Dad. There's something you need to know.

CHAPTER SIX

SOMEHOW BECCA HAD a box of tissues in her lap and a handful of crumpled ones in her fist. At some point, she had stopped crying and was now resting in Van's lap, shoulder tucked under his arm, forehead against his throat, hearts beating in unified rhythm. He was playing with the pieces of her hair that had fallen from its knot. She was warm and safe and her mind was empty.

And, because she wanted this sense of closeness and accord, not the harsh words that caused tissues to be yanked from boxes and old anguish that got crumpled into fists, she angled her body into his. She tilted her face so her lips touched the edge of his beard under his jaw and slid her hand from where it rested on his chest to twine behind his neck.

"Becca," he breathed, body going still while his Adam's apple bobbed in a swallow. "Don't do that."

"You don't want—?" *Me?* Her voice died before she could say it. A chasm opened behind her breastbone and she started to pull away.

His arms hardened, dragging her deeper into his lap so she could feel his erection against her bottom. "Always," he growled. "But I'm not going to take advantage of you when you're hurting."

They both were, weren't they?

She searched his conflicted gaze.

"When, then?" she asked with a humorless catch of laughter. The clock was ticking.

He released a jagged noise and there was a flash of hot desperation in his expression, one she'd only seen once before, when she rose and walked away from him in Sydney. It had been the hardest thing she'd ever done and he didn't let her do it now.

He closed his arms more firmly around her and crushed her into his chest as his mouth landed on hers.

Here it was, the whooshing sense of being picked up and thrown into a bonfire of passion. Heat and hunger and elation swallowed her. Craving closeness with him after too long and a ferocious, greedy need to fill herself up for the future. She shaped his shoulder and cupped the bristles of his beard and their tongues dueled for possession of each other's mouths.

It became a battle of sorts. He had always been the one to lead, but if this was all she would have, then she would have it all. She shifted to come up on her knees and straddled his thighs, caught handfuls of his hair and dragged his head back so she could crush his lips with her own. She feasted on him as if he were still hers and would be forever.

He let her think she was in charge. It had always been his habit to indulge her before he slaked his own desires. It made her feel extraordinary. Strong and skilled at making love to him. As if she were capable of conquering him in some way when he held so many advantages over her.

His wide hands shaped her hips and massaged the backs of her thighs and cupped her backside, urging her to rock against the thickness behind the wrinkled fly of his jeans.

She did, undulating while she ravished his mouth until his hand streaked under her top. He dislodged her bra and took possession of her breast in his hot palm, two fingers trapping her nipple in a pinch that sent electricity shooting straight into that place where his fly rubbed.

The hand against her tailbone kept her there as he slouched and lifted into her spread thighs, increasing the pressure. It was sexy and primitive and sent her straight into the sun. She was suddenly trying not to bite his bottom lip clean through because climax had her in its grip as surely as he did.

Her cries went into his mouth and he moaned as if they were the best sounds he'd ever tasted.

She could have wept, she felt so good under those ripples of joy, yet so utterly bereft. It had also always been this way between them. They weren't even undressed and he had destroyed her. She had been aching with emptiness for years and even as the latent pulses were quivering through her, her need for him grew a thousand times worse.

She was both terrified and hopeful that he might end this encounter here. She didn't know if she could withstand whatever else might happen if they let this go further.

But as she picked her heavy head off his shoulder and he began tugging at her clothing, she helped him. Cashmere stretched as he brushed the fine knit off her shoulders.

She pulled her arms free, then lifted them so he could sweep her sweater over her head. She tried to pull at his shirt, but he was scraping his beard across the upper swell of her breasts and muttering, "Mine," before taking possession of her nipple with his hot mouth.

A hiss left her as he pulled her to the border between pleasure and pain and held her there. Her heart thudded because she knew this place so well. Here she ached and yearned and exalted and believed in happily-ever-after. Here, she was just like him, entitled to all the joy there was in this world.

It was a lie, but she threw herself into believing it. She pushed her hands down his back and caught handfuls of his shirt, trying to scrape it up so she could pull it off.

He twisted, tipping her sideways so she landed on her back on the cool, overstuffed cushions. He followed to press his glorious weight over her, squashing her. She forgot what she was trying to do because his clever mouth made her gasp as he kissed her neck and bit her earlobe and sucked her nipples until she lifted her knee and writhed in abandon.

"You make me so hard. Hot," he muttered, lifting his head to send her a look of amused lust as he finished pulling his shirt off one arm and over his head, throwing it away. His hand went to the button on her jeans. "Do we need a condom?"

"I'm still on the pill. There hasn't been anyone unless—" Her organs twisted into knots, but she refused to ask. *She* had left *him*.

"I haven't been with anyone." For a long, potent moment, he stared at her, gaze blazing with outrage. "Damn you, Becca. Why did you do that to us?"

His hand jerked at the waistband of her jeans, wrenching her zip open before he pushed his hand inside the seat and dragged them off her bottom, taking her underwear so the cool suede of the cushions caressed her cheeks.

There was no "us." Not anymore. There never should have been, but exactly like the first night she'd made love with him, her brain refused to stop something that was too alluring to resist. He stripped her jeans until she wore only one sock, then he ran a reverent hand over her thigh and hip, caressing and reacquainting. His touch slowly made its way to her inner thigh and stroked from her knee up, opening her legs while he slid to his knees on the floor.

"Van." She didn't know if it was protest or invitation, fear or anticipation. Then it didn't matter because white-hot need engulfed her.

He was her *husband*, he seemed to say, claiming her with such blatant intimacy, scorching her with flagrant licks and a touch that caressed and incited and stole deep.

"Van," she gasped again, because this almost felt like a punishment. She wasn't certain she could bear to give herself up to pleasure again, without him and at his mercy. She *was* losing herself because there was no hiding anything as he made love to her like this. He knew she was his, only his, always his. She had to be, since she was incapable of doing anything but melting under his thorough, intimate touch.

When she was at the brink, panting and unable to form his name, he rose over her and jerked open his jeans, pushed them down to his feet without removing them. He used his hard thighs to nudge hers farther apart, and the broad head of his sex slid against her slick folds.

Then he was thrusting in. Claiming.

It didn't hurt, but it was so powerful and impactful she made a helpless, agonized noise. All her carefully constructed defenses against him became cobwebs and insubstantial mist because he was *in* her. Profoundly. He always would be.

He cupped her cheek and the full weight of his hips crushed hers into the sofa, the hardness of him thick and hot and indelible inside her.

"Look at me," he growled.

She dragged her eyes open. His were pure gold.

"Tell me you missed this," he demanded in a voice she'd never heard. She'd never seen him look like this—like a predator who had landed his prey and was catching his breath before he finished her off.

"I did." It was a small confession. She could give him that much, couldn't she?

It hurt, though. She felt walls inside her crumbling, leaving her without protection. She would fall for him again and it would be far more devastating than their first time.

"So did I." That was more of an accusation. He raked the pad of his thumb across her lips, shifted and carefully withdrew before he returned in a heavy, hard thrust that was so thrilling, it was nearly too much to bear.

She groaned sharply.

"That's what we get for waiting so long," he growled. His mouth went to her neck and she felt him sucking a mark onto her skin. The sting only made her body tingle more.

She scrabbled her hands across his naked shoulders and back, trying to ground herself. There was nothing

but satin skin and heat and weight and blinding pleasure as he began to move with steady purpose, unleash-
ing his power.

This was sex and lovemaking and that other base
thing that was ancient and primordial. It was reunion
and goodbye. Celebration and loss. It was all the turmoil
between them imbued into one act. Every caress was
needed and welcome, but their cries held ragged edges
of anger and despair. When she set her teeth against
his shoulder, it was an attempt to keep him. When he
hooked his arm behind her knee, it was so he could
claim her even more thoroughly.

And they fought—not each other, but together they
fought the foe of culmination. Of ending. They clung
to each other, clung to the climb and the journey, and
when they reached the wide ledge that promised ecstasy,
they held themselves on the edge of it. They pulled hair
and clashed in hard kisses while he surged into her
again and again.

But the ending was always the goal and here it was.
An abyss opened before them and Becca felt as though
they were suspended. Breathless. Eternal.

They held on to each other, held on tight.

And fell, bursting into flames on the way.

CHAPTER SEVEN

VAN DIDN'T LET her up when she touched his shoulder. He couldn't. He had poured his entire soul into her and was wrung out, coated in sweat, trying to reel his brain back into his head while his heart was still rolling like a loose coin.

He managed to shift the weight of his chest so he wasn't crushing her, but he pressed his hips more tightly against hers, sealing his relaxing erection inside her.

Becca made a huffing noise as if she wasn't satisfied with that and tried to reach for the box of tissues. "I don't want to stain the couch."

"It doesn't matter." He wanted to shout it loud enough to cause avalanches up the valley. They had just elevated the act of procreation to performance art. Surely reality could wait until he could keep his eyelids open.

"It matters to me." Her voice was small and stiff with offended dignity that seemed incongruous to the way they were lying here without any claims to pride or grace. His jeans were around his ankles. He was pretty sure they would both be wearing hickeys like teenagers. She would definitely have fingerprint bruises where he had gripped the back of her thigh as he came.

Her fluttering fingertips managed to draw the box close enough she could pick it up.

Van reluctantly pulled a few tissues and eased from her heat, rolling onto his elbow so she could untangle from beneath him. She rose and gathered her clothes, slipping into the powder room and firmly closing the door.

He sighed with defeat and rose to pull up his jeans. He still had his hands on his fly tab when she came out wearing only her cardigan. She clutched it closed like a housecoat and held the rest of her clothes in a ball against her stomach.

She barely looked at him as she headed toward the stairs, mumbling, "I need fresh underwear."

He went into the bathroom she'd vacated and washed his face, then braced his hands on either side of the sink, wondering if he had made things better or worse. He had tried to tell her now wasn't the time for sex, but he hadn't exactly put up a fight.

Because he had really needed that. *Her.*

For long minutes, he closed his eyes, reliving her taste, the scent in her neck, the texture of her nipples in his mouth, the press of her breasts against his chest, the twine of her leg around his and the abandoned noises she had made in his ear. The way she had bucked and shuddered beneath him had been exquisite. Her body had squeezed every last drop of ecstasy from his and he would never again feel that good.

He slammed back to earth.

At least one nagging question had been answered, he thought with a dour look at the lusty color still on his cheeks. He hadn't imagined how good the sex was.

Being inside Becca, making her his, was the definition of paradise.

Van didn't look at women as possessions or objects. The women in his life were too strong for him to even tolerate throwback sentiments from other men, but when he and Becca were at their earthiest, she belonged to him. No one else. Ever. Like wolves mating for life.

He stopped on the way back to the pool room, clutching at the door frame as he breathed through that jarring thought. He hadn't found anyone since their separation who even turned his head. There'd been a whistling howl inside him the whole time they'd been apart.

Disturbed, he tried to ignore what that might mean and moved to tug on his shirt. When he picked up the crumpled tissues she'd used to dry her tears and took them to the bin beneath the sink in the bar, his gaze snagged on the photo from the night they had met.

He winced at the naked hunger in his profile, recognizing that for all the upheavals he'd been through since, he hadn't changed either. He was still that man who hadn't been able to lift his eyes off her long enough to smile at a camera.

It had never been his habit to pick up women. While he'd been competing, he hadn't been able to afford the distraction, and the demands on his time had made him a poorly attentive partner. *Clearly.* But he'd brought Becca home that night and it had been as incredible as what had just happened between them today.

So incredible that, even though he hadn't intended to see her again, he'd spent the following day trying to recall which pub she had said she worked at. Hours later, when he was exhausted and was supposed to be at home making travel arrangements, he had sat down across the bar from her and waited for her to finish her shift.

Over the next weeks and months, she had been willing to put up with his demanding schedule so they'd kept seeing each other until she had said one day that her visa was running out. *I don't want to go back to Australia. I love you.*

That was the other reason he didn't pursue relationships. Eventually those words came up and, even though Becca had probably meant them on some level, he had heard what she was really saying with that declaration. He knew what she wanted in response.

I guess we should get married so you can stay, he had replied.

Until then, marriage had been something Van had put off thinking about. Asking her had been as impulsive an act as the rest of their relationship. She wasn't wrong in saying they'd done the deed like a pair of thieves in the night. He had known his mother wouldn't be happy, but what he hadn't realized was how happy it would make him.

Van had *liked* taking control of his own life. There had been relentless pressure on him from the day his mother had strapped a pair of skis on his toddler feet. By the time he'd been old enough to question whether he wanted the gold medals she had promised him, he'd been too deeply committed to the sport, and winning too frequently, to turn his back on it.

He had loved competing and was proud of all he had achieved, but those rewards hadn't come without constant sacrifice in other areas of his life. Keeping Becca in his life had been his one selfish indulgence. She'd been an easygoing respite from the pressure, an escape

valve, and maybe his marriage had even become something he had wielded the same way he had his training.

Becca's waiting, Mom. You and I can talk later.

It was a childish reason to marry and he would have
been ashamed if that's all it had been, but he'd been
enthralled by Becca. He'd liked being married and the
sex had been incredible. It didn't surprise him a bit that
they had locked lips within minutes of seeing each other
and had already surrendered to passion. If anything, he
was shocked it had taken this long.

Where did they go from here, though? One tussle on
a sofa didn't reconcile a marriage and that wasn't what
he'd been trying to do by making love with her. In the
years since she'd told him their marriage was a mistake, he'd come around to seeing it that way himself.

Plus, he still didn't know why she was here. He
couldn't—*wouldn't*—share his life with someone who
refused to be honest with him. Not again.

But that man in the photo was still inside him, still
obsessed with having more time with her. And they
only had tonight.

Becca turned from the pantry and gasped when she saw
Van at the top of the stairs from the basement.

"Really?"

"I didn't hear you," she grumbled defensively.

She'd been lost in thought, not regretting their lovemaking, but not sure how to react to it. It had been as
powerful and deeply affecting as always, leaving her
trying to shore up her inner defenses in a way she hadn't
had to in the past because she'd loved him and trusted
him and believed in his promises of "later."

They didn't *have* later. Which left her unsure whether

she wanted to cry or rage or curl into a ball or pretend it was no big deal.

All of this was his fault! When he had dropped her off after their first night together, that should have been the end of it. She had known she would never forget him, but she'd been determined to try.

Until he'd shown up at the pub that evening.

From then on, she'd been in this state of defenselessness and uncertainty. He had disappeared every few weeks to train and she had held her breath, waiting for the blade to fall. Or rather, she had waited for the silence that would tell her it was over. A day or two would go by without a word and she would resign herself to never seeing him again. Then he would text out of the blue.

I'm trying to sleep on a plane and a baby just spit up all over my sleeve.

In some cultures that's lucky. What color was it?

Gross. But thanks. I knew you'd keep me from yelling at a child. I'll call when I land. Gonna try to sleep more.

Or he would text that he was exhausted and having an early night, so he wasn't coming by the pub. She would interpret it as him pulling away, but then he would text again.

Come sleep here if you want.

He gave her a key that she used when he invited her. Sometimes they would make love when she slipped into bed beside him, other times he would simply pull her close for a kiss and a murmured, "Hey." Then he would leave her sleeping when he left a few hours later to train.

He had never said he loved her, but all of those small things had added up to her believing he did. Or could. Someday. When he had more time.

"I'll cook," Van said, dragging her back to the kitchen.

"Pardon?"

"Is it jet lag? Where do you keep going?"

"Nowhere. This is just weird." She was so acutely aware of him, she felt as though she walked on a bed of nails. She set down the things she'd retrieved from the pantry and turned to find a wall of a man beside her, watching her with his eagle eyes.

"Should we talk about it?" he asked in a low voice.

She longed to play dumb. Her heart already felt peeled down to its pulsating core.

"And say what?" She tried very hard to sound dispassionate. "That you haven't lost your knack?"

"Neither have you."

She could have wallowed in the heady joy of making love with him for the rest of the night. She had wanted to, but she'd slipped away from him as fast as she could out of self-preservation. Their intimacy had stirred up all the embers of passion and hope she'd harbored through those tense times of feeling ancillary and unaccepted by his family and simply not good enough. Not *enough*.

She couldn't let herself start dreaming again. It would make their parting tomorrow all the more heartbreaking.

"It was nostalgia, Van. You think we're the first couple to have one for the road?" She couldn't hold his penetrating stare, but as she dropped her gaze to his wide chest, she only felt despair.

In her periphery, she thought she saw his hand come up, but she was already turning away to fiddle with the jars and boxes she'd set out.

"What's all this? Did you work up an appetite?"

She flicked him a look of rebuke. He had his arms folded across his powerful chest and his expression had become inscrutable.

"My stomach is still in Australia. It's asking why it's lunchtime and I still haven't eaten breakfast." She opened crackers and Parmesan-encrusted *croustilles*, a tapenade of artichoke and olives, pickles and nuts, caviar and shrimp with cocktail sauce.

"All you've had today is wine and a margarita?" He frowned at the clock that would chime seven soon.

"There were muffins at my hotel this morning, but I wasn't hungry." It had been a bargain hotel, the food uninspiring, and her belly had been knotted up with anxiety. It still was.

"I'll start some eggs." He opened the jar of gherkins she handed him and turned to the fridge.

"No, I'll cook pasta and vegetables with the steak in a little while. I just need a bite while I put the cake in the oven."

"I'll make the cake. Sit down and eat." He picked up the mix and frowned at it. "Why do you want cake?" He had always been careful about empty calories.

"It's New Year's Eve." And she loved angel food. "I'll do it." She spooned some caviar onto a cracker and shoved it into her mouth, then reached for the box.

"I can do it," he insisted, avoiding her attempt to take

it while continuing to read it. He pointed at the back of the box. "Do I own a pan that looks like that?"

She *tsked* and moved to the cupboard where the mixer and baking pans had resided. The moment she set them out, he commandeered them.

"Maybe the reason you're always on this side of the bar is because you never sit down on the other side. Eat."

Look at where I am. Look at where you are.

"My limitations are all in my head? Gosh, you really missed your calling with the pop psych advice. Thanks." A hot sting arrived behind her eyes and she moved to take a seat, but she wasn't sure if she could swallow anything.

She bit her lips, afraid they were trembling. She wasn't even sure why she was so hurt, just that it felt as though he was saying it was her fault that she felt like everything was her fault. It was circular logic, but it rang true as it churned inside her.

"You do limit yourself," he accused, eyes still on the baking instructions. "You want to argue over something stupid like a cake when you're really mad we had sex. Spit the dummy, as you like to say."

"I'm not mad."

"You're not happy."

"Are *you*?"

"I'm making you a cake, aren't I?" His gaze flashed up, no mockery or laughter there, only molten gold.

He turned his back to plug in the mixer so he didn't see her biting back a smile, rolling eyes that grew damp.

This was why he'd snared her heart so quickly and easily. He was funny and thoughtful and took charge while making her feel special.

Oh, get over it, Becca. It's a freaking add-water cake.

And she wasn't special. Van was a thoughtful man who did nice things for everyone. For all his hyper-focus on his training, he'd never been curt to anyone no matter what had been damaged on a flight or who had been slow to get back to him. He had taken time to speak with any young athlete who had a case of hero worship and spoiled his niece and nephew relentlessly. Even his family, who drove him around the bend much of the time, were people he would do nearly anything for.

Deep down, Becca had always wondered if he had married her as a favor more than anything. Now was the time to ask, but if it was true, she didn't think she could stand to hear it. It would finish her off, it really would.

"I don't think we should put much stock into it," she said when he turned off the mixer. "We both have lives on separate continents. I don't have any expectations as a result." Longings, maybe. Wistfulness. But she knew better. "It was nice. Thank you."

"Nice," he chided. "We both broke a four-year dry spell and doing it on that couch always left me needing a chiropractor, but okay. Yeah. It *was* nice. Thanks."

She smirked at his back while he got the cake into the oven.

After he'd set the timer, Van sat down next to her and helped himself to what she'd left. "Why lab tech?"

"Why not lab tech? Are you going to say I'm limiting myself? I don't have the stamina or the grades to become a doctor. I'd be thirty-five before I could practice. This is a two-year program and most of the second year is practical." Getting the prerequisites had required extra tutoring on her part. She'd worked really hard and was proud she'd been accepted.

"Don't be so defensive. I only thought you'd be put

off by anything to do with medical care after going through everything with your mom."

"Oh. Yes. A little," she said sheepishly. "But that's also how I know it means a lot when you find someone who is willing to give you that extra minute to roll up your sleeve or ask a question. I don't blame the doctors and nurses who are trying to help as many people as possible. Burnout is chronic because they're so over-worked, but they're also people we need, so health care is a good career sector. I looked at a lot of different fields and thought taking blood would be like serving drinks. People sit down for a few minutes, you listen to them talk about their day or tell a joke to brighten their mood." She gave a self-deprecating shrug. "I'm good at that."

He didn't laugh, only nodded agreement. "You are."

His gaze was narrowed, as if he was putting together what she'd said earlier about pulling her weight with wanting a job that made her feel useful and necessary—which was pretty much right on the nose.

"At least I'll *be* something." She ate one more olive, leaving the last few for him.

"What does that mean? 'Be something.'"

"You know, when you meet someone and they ask what you do. I'll be able to say, 'I'm a lab tech.' They'll nod and that will be the end of it. When I say I'm a bar-tender, I get a look that implies it's not a real job. Peo-ple think it's a great job for someone in their twenties on a working holiday visa, but it's not seen as a serious career. Which isn't to say I'm embarrassed I did it for so long or would never make it my career. I'm glad I'll always have it to fall back on, but I'm ready to work daylight hours and deal with people in a different way."

"I never once introduced myself as Donovan Scott, alpine champion, but that's what I was for the longest time. Now I'm CEO of Scott B&D and you should see the looks I get." His mouth twisted with dismay.

She knew the B&D stood for builders and developers, but his expression was so grim at taking over from his father, she had to tease, "Because of the bondage and discipline jokes? Yeah, that has to wear thin."

He closed his eyes in an exaggerated reach for patience. "No one ever makes that joke. Only you."

"How does anyone resist? It's right there." She opened her hands to point at the invisible bowling pin that begged to be knocked down.

"They like to live?" he suggested as he crunched a tapenade-laden cracker and gave her a look of mock warning, but there was reluctant humor beneath it.

She propped her chin in her hand, pondering. "I want to say something about how you should have had a safe word for all the pain your father caused you, but maybe it's too soon?"

"Way too soon," he assured her as murderous rage replaced the lazy humor in his eyes.

Her insides caved in and old fault rose like a ghoul inside her. She had had a lot to deal with when she'd walked away from him in Sydney. Her world had been collapsing on all sides as she gave up her marriage, accepted her inability to get pregnant and faced the loss of her mum.

Even so, she could have reached out to Van when his troubles had started making headlines. She had been tempted to. She had nearly gone back to the hotel to see him the very next morning after leaving him there, still unaware of his father's troubles, but wondering if they could figure something out after all.

She had gotten a text first thing that he was headed to the airport because of a family issue. She had texted back that she hoped everyone was okay and that had pretty much been their last direct communication.

"There was nothing I could do when I realized what was going on," she said, heart heavy as she swiveled to face him. "I couldn't leave Mum and I thought I would just be a distraction if I came back. I honestly thought it was simpler for you if I was out of the picture and you could focus on whatever you had to do. It must have been awful."

"It was." His expression remained shuttered.

"It's okay if you don't want to talk about it."

He ate in silence a minute before saying flatly, "There's not much to say beyond what was in the headlines anyway. Dad colluded with his CFO in a smash-and-grab. They took mortgages on properties that were already leveraged to the gills, scraped everything into liquidation accounts, shifted it all offshore, bought a yacht and *hasta la vista*, baby." He flicked his hand in a careless salute.

"There's no way to catch him and get any of it back? Is he still moving around?"

"Hell, no. He bought a house on an island that has an electrified gate and a couple of dogs that don't like strangers. I buzzed and he refused to see me. I would have settled for an explanation, but he wouldn't even give me that. So I left. Screw him."

"He wouldn't see you? Van." She touched his arm.

He was like iron, barely controlling his fury. He

stiffly removed his arm from beneath the weight of her hand.

"He'd been bleeding red ink for years and kept it from the board. I always let Mom or Paisley vote my share, trusting them to be up-front if something was wrong. Mom had suspicions, but she and Dad were always so hostile toward each other any of her criticism was dismissed by the rest of the board as bad blood. Even Paisley didn't take her seriously. She thought Mom knew Dad was sleeping with the CFO and that's why Mom was raising all these red flags. Neither of them brought it up with me because…" He made a noise of frustration.

"Training," she murmured.

"Exactly." He rose and went to the fridge, taking out two bottles from the multipack selection of microbrew beer he'd bought with his groceries.

"We have open alcohol all over this house," she reminded him.

"Not on this floor." He put one back when she flicked her wrist in refusal. He opened his bottle and tilted a squat beer mug to pour. "Everyone expected me to work for Dad once I retired from skiing. Mom and Paisley saw no harm in letting their suspicions slide until the games were over. They had every expectation that I would deal with things soon enough. Maybe Dad thought I would finally merge my business with his and save his ass."

"He was serious about that? I thought it was a joke whenever he said it. I mean, real estate and sports equipment? It doesn't even make sense."

"No, but I knew he wasn't joking. That's what makes me angriest. I didn't ask myself *why* he wanted my money. Yes, Mom and Paisley could have been more forthcoming, but I trusted him to tell me that something was wrong. I pushed aside the suspicions *I* had."

"You can't blame yourself, Van. Who would think their own father was capable of something like that? I'm still shocked. It doesn't seem like the man I met at all. He was always very proud of you. He was there when you won gold." She quickly bit her lip, afraid Van would ask how she knew that, but he was deep into his own introspections.

"When my achievements reflected well on him, yes, he was proud." He retook his seat next to her. His profile was angular and his voice crisp. "But he had a petty, superficial side. I saw it when my equipment line started doing well. Growing up, Mom took credit for my genes and the quality of my training, but Dad paid for my coaching and travel. It all went through the company as a marketing expense, but he liked to say I wouldn't have been able to develop as an athlete without him which…" He wobbled his head as he debated that. "It's not *un*true, but it's not the whole truth." He took a deep drink of his beer.

Van's father had been an arrogant sort, but Becca had always taken his little asides about all that he had done for Van as a knock against herself and whatever contribution she thought *she* was making to Van's success.

"I would have had a much harder time rising to such an elite level if I hadn't had his backing in my early years," Van admitted. "But Mom had a lot of connections that were arguably more valuable. Once I got enough sponsorship to pay for my own training, Dad had fewer bragging rights to my accomplishments. Things got really contentious between us a year or so before I met you. We kept it quiet, but there was a claim from a local band over a swath of land my great-grandparents had bought when they first moved up here from Vancouver. It was a gray area as to whether their purchase was legal in the first place. I mean, if we're talking about treaties and lack thereof, it wasn't legal at *all*, but it was on the company books as an asset. The band called it out as improper seizure. Dad wanted to fight it all the way to the Supreme Court to keep it. He was trying to gather investors so he could develop the property to pay the legal fees. I voted with Mom and Paisley to give it back and eat the loss. It was the right thing to do, but Dad took it very personally that I didn't side with him."

"Is that why the company was struggling? Because you gave up that land?"

"Yes, but we had a plan to recover and it seemed to be working. All the right things were being said at the board meetings, anyway. Dad and I seemed to move past the worst of his resentment, but that's why I should have paid attention when he kept assuming I would bring my capital with me when I joined the company."

"Maybe you would have, if he'd been honest about why he needed it."

"Not likely," he said flatly. "I didn't want to work with him. I already knew we would be at odds. I wanted to build affordable housing and he was all about maximizing profit, driving down wages, cutting corners. Once we clashed over the land claim, I knew we would never be able to work together. I told him that, but he figured I would come around. He finally started to believe me when you and I bought this house and it wasn't one of his."

Becca bit her lip. She had found this house kind of by accident. She had heard through the grapevine that the builder was running out of money. It had been very whirlwind. She and Van had come out for a look and happened on the owner as he was installing a gutter. They made an offer on the spot, he accepted it. A few weeks later, they were finishing the house to their own tastes.

Van had given Becca free rein to turn it into their dream home. She had made the bulk of decisions and paid for incidentals as it was completed. Since she hadn't been working, this had been her full-time job, chasing contractors and looking at swatches and shopping for furniture, but she still felt wrong laying any claim to it. Now another layer of remorse was upon her. She hadn't realized this house had caused such a big rift between Van and his father, one that had led to Jackson doing something truly atrocious.

"You didn't have to buy it, Van. Not if it was such a bone of contention between you and your father."

"I wanted to. It's a great house, a perfect location. Frankly, I loved that Dad didn't have a single fingerprint on it. Maybe I'm as petty as he is," he muttered into his mug. "But I was tired of my parents using me as a weapon against each other. Or being the trophy they fought over. Marrying you, buying this house… It wasn't rebellion. It was growing up. I was becoming my own person. That felt good. I refuse to apologize for it."

"But he felt threatened by that? By your buying a house without his input?" By *her*? How laughable, but it did explain why his father had been so disinclined to like her.

"Was he peeved that I bought a house in which he

made no money on the transaction? Absolutely. And it's not as if I made any effort to reassure him." His thumb moved restlessly on the handle of his mug. "When you flew home to Sydney, I pulled the pin. I told him I'd be staying with you there after the games, if that's where you needed to be. He was furious. He said he wanted to retire and I was a selfish ingrate who went back on his promises."

She swallowed a sickly lump from her throat. "I didn't know you told him that before you left."

"Don't," he dismissed gruffly. "You don't bear any responsibility for his actions, Becca. I wish I could blame someone else, but if anyone else is to blame, it's me. I told him those were assumptions on his part, not promises on mine. B&D has always had succession plans in place, things the board can do if something happens to the CEO. I said if he wanted to retire without my taking over, there were options and he should exercise them. I never imagined he would watch me win, look me straight in the eye when he shook my hand, then fly home early to take the money and run."

It was a breath-catching shock to hear it stated so flatly. "I can't fathom what a blow it was when you heard. I'm so sorry."

"Not your fault," he assured her. "And it was hard for a while, getting past the shock, taking on so much responsibility. I knew how to run a company, but Van Scott Equipment started very small and I handpicked all my leadership. Designing a pair of skis and approving a marketing strategy did not prepare me to plan and execute a housing project. We had dozens in different stages of completion across the country. Investors wanted to cash out. If only Mom and Paisley had been affected, I would have dusted off my hands and found a way to get them back on their feet. That wasn't an option, so I threw my own money in to cool tempers and got down to work."

"*And* you made the fitness app. I've seen it."

"I actually put Paisley on the team and it's done surprisingly well. It boosts equipment sales, too. And I don't mind working at B&D because I'm in charge. I can steer us toward the projects I think are valuable in ways beyond financial—passive design, minimal environmental impact, a mix of affordable and upscale housing. Our teams are winning awards. We're getting tons of contracts."

"That's great."

"It is. That's why it's so strange that you've chosen *now* to turn up again."

"What do you mean?" Her blood seemed to still in her veins.

"This whole thing left deep scars, Becca. I'm not nearly so trusting as I used to be. People you're supposed to be able to believe in—your father, your wife— can turn on you." He swiveled his head to send her a look that slammed hard into her own. "I mean it this time. I want to know why you're here."

The antagonism in his voice was such a baffling shift, she took a moment to absorb it.

"You think I want to *turn* on you? How? Steal from you the way your father did?"

"I don't know. You tell me."

Every time she had a glimmer of thinking maybe they had something worth saving, she came smack up against what a lost cause they really were.

"I want my locket." She touched her empty throat

where the small pendant had sat in the early days of their relationship. "I used to wear it before we married. It's a small gold heart—"

"I know which one you're talking about, but do you really expect me to believe that? It's worth less than a bus ticket from Vancouver, nowhere near a plane ticket from Sydney."

So disparaging. She understood why he was embittered, she did, but she wasn't his father. Did he realize that? Tears came into her eyes.

"No. I don't expect you to believe me," she said with a pang of despair. "I completely understand that things like sentimentality for a parent would be foreign to you, especially now." She gave a couple of rapid blinks to clear her vision. "But my mother gave it to me and Wanda has hers. I'm not leaving until I find mine."

She shoved herself off her stool and hurried up the stairs.

CHAPTER EIGHT

"BECCA."

The timer on the oven sounded as Van tried to call her back. *Damn it.*

He rose to check the cake, then had to find and wash an empty wine bottle to set the thing to cool upside down on the neck. What a ridiculous procedure, but he'd be damned if he would burn or ruin it.

I'm making you a cake, aren't I?

It was nostalgia, Van. You think we're the first couple to have one for the road?

He'd been stung by that, still awash in postorgasmic chemicals and wanting to keep that train rolling. But she didn't think they should put much stock into it.

Any leftover tenderness from their passionate clash had completely faded as he revisited his father's treachery. He'd almost forgotten the part Becca had played in all of that. Not that she'd done it on purpose, but his father had seen Van's decision to stay in Sydney as choosing Becca over plans that had been in place for at least a decade.

That final altercation had been a lot worse than Van had revealed to Becca. Even though he had been determined to do his own thing and genuinely didn't want to work with his father, his father's accusations had landed hard. Van had wondered if he was more like the rest of his family than he wanted to be, using people when they were convenient, walking away from a commitment when it no longer suited him.

In his mind, he'd been sticking by the vows he'd made to Becca—only to have her tell him their marriage was over. That had been enough for him to pigeonhole her under "people who screwed me over" and expect her to do it again.

She'd been injured by his accusation, though. He'd watched her big brown eyes dim with startled hurt. The fact was, Becca was exactly sentimental enough to come all this way for a modest locket. That earnest softness in her was the reason he'd been drawn to marry her. She wasn't like most of the people who surrounded him, all pushing and shoving for higher returns and status symbols and whatever else they thought he could give them.

Was the locket her only reason for being here? He just didn't know. As he'd been thrust back into the swamp on the heels of his father's departure, he'd resented Becca for leaving him to navigate that alone. For not having her calm warmth to come home to. It wasn't like her. He'd grown used to her being there for him.

He closed his eyes in a wince, recognizing his father's selfishness in that thought. Worse, Van had been busy when he returned. So freaking buried under work, traveling, taking calls at all hours… He would have fallen into the pattern they had already established. Instead of telling her he had to train, he would have said he had to work. Despite his best claims in Sydney, nothing would have changed for her.

I was alone here so often, I forgot I was married.

She was divorcing him because she hadn't had a husband in the first place. That was the undeniable truth. If she had wanted his money, she could have been spending it all this time, but she hadn't.

No, she had booked her trip back here around her friend's schedule—which was exactly like her to accommodate someone else. It made perfect sense that she would retrieve something that held deep meaning for her while she was here.

Ah, hell. He had some explaining to do about that locket himself.

Silently cussing himself out, Van left the kitchen and detoured into the den where his laptop lived on his desk. His gold medals were locked in the safe behind an enlarged glossy photo of him catching air during a long-ago race in Switzerland.

As he retrieved the small envelope, he winced again at how creased and dingy it had become. He almost reached into a drawer for a new one, but Becca wouldn't care about the envelope. She wanted the contents and… Damn, damn, damn.

He made his way up to the bedroom where Becca was in the closet, going through all the pockets on an assortment of handbags. A half dozen of them were scattered on the floor.

"Here," he said, offering the envelope.

"You found it?" She hurried out of the closet. "Where was it?"

"In the safe."

"Why? It's not worth much, as you so bluntly pointed out."

The sharpness of her tone cut almost as deeply as her

small whimper when she poured the necklace into her hand and realized the front of the heart was no longer attached to the back.

"It's broken." Her voice cracked as she sank onto the foot of the bed, shoulders sloping, corners of her mouth curving down.

He closed his eyes in remorse. When he pushed his hands into his pockets, a full year after he'd realized the front had broken off, his fingertips still searched for the tangled chain and the small nugget of the heart, as if he would still find it in the bottom corner, tangled with lint.

Becca pinched the chain and gave it a delicate shake, plucking in an attempt to loosen the knots. "Why is it so tangled and beat up? Did it go through the washing machine?"

"No. I…" He scratched the back of his head. "I actually had it on me in Sydney. I forgot or I would have given it to you." That was true. His mind had been firmly shattered by her desire to end their marriage, then the news about his dad.

"Why did you bring it to Sydney?" She blinked her surprise at him.

"I grabbed it as I was leaving for the airport. It was on the hook by the bathroom window. I took it because…" He shrugged, trying to make light of what had actually become an important talisman during his two weeks of competing, especially when he realized she wasn't coming. "It was a mind game. I told myself I already had gold."

"Mmm. Manifest what you want by believing you already have it?" She smiled faintly. "I think it's only nine karats, but whatever works." She was putting a brave face on it, but he could see she was blue at having it returned to her in such bad shape.

He opened his mouth to explain that she was the gold he'd had, that he'd wanted her with him for every nanosecond of his races, but he didn't want to lay another guilt trip on her for not being there. The first one had sent her into hysterics.

It was also too revealing to admit how important it had been to him. He was as superstitious as the next athlete and had worn his share of playoff beards or whatever else might have kept him on a winning streak, but that didn't explain why he'd put the damned thing in his pocket every morning for months after their marriage was over, when he'd been so angry with her he should have been happy it snapped in half. Instead, he'd carried a crushing guilt, carefully tucking the pieces into that envelope until the creases had started to wear at the corners. He'd been seriously worried he would lose some part of it, so he'd put it in the safe.

"I've been meaning to take it to a jeweler to get it fixed." He hadn't wanted to give it up. Not even for a few days. At least while it was in his safe, he knew it *was* safe.

"This is why I limit my expectations," she said with a tone that was supposed to be ironic but held an underlying despair. She tried to line up the front of the heart with the back. "All I wanted was to put it on and even that's beyond my reach."

Self-reproach nearly buried him. The locket would have been fine if he'd left it alone, and he had to wonder if it was a metaphor for them. *They* might have been better off if he'd left her alone. He couldn't blame her if she thought that.

She carefully poured it back into the envelope, then stood to tuck it in the front pocket of her jeans. "Thanks. I feel better now that I know where it is. Sorry about the mess. I'll clean it up."

She moved into the closet and started gathering handbags off the floor, putting them on the shelves, not throwing anything into the suitcase. The box with her glasses and the beads had made its way into the case along with some of Paisley's branded yoga wear and a Van Scott hoodie, but little else.

"I should have brought the rest of the jewelry from the safe. I'll get it." He turned.

"Don't bother. Give it to Paisley or your mom." She was rehanging a quilted parka, fixing the pockets she'd turned inside out. "Save it for Flora."

"I bought it for *you*, Becca. Don't you like any of it?"

"I love every single piece." She looked up with surprise. "But it seems rude to keep it. I brought my rings to give back to you, too. They're in my purse. I'll get them as soon as I finish cleaning up."

"What the hell am I supposed to do with your wedding rings?" His voice grew loud enough that she fell back a step.

"What am *I* supposed to do with them?" she asked quietly, crossing her arms. "I'm not going to walk around wearing wedding rings when I'm divorced."

"Sell them and use the money for school. Put a down payment on a place to live." He flung a hand in different directions, not caring how she spent it so long as he knew she was building some security for herself. "I want you to have what you need, Becca."

"Van." She blew a breath out to the ceiling. "If I take the jewelry and sell it, I might as well have asked you for the cash four years ago. I don't go anywhere that requires me to dress up in evening gowns and diamond earrings, so I don't need any of this." She waved at the garment bags hanging next to his suits. "When I say you and I were always too different, this is what I mean. You do this. I don't."

"You don't expect any hospital fundraisers in your future, once you're working in that industry?" A searing blaze of jealousy with a flame of green burning in its center swept up, nearly burning him alive. "Doctors are even more devoted to their jobs than I was to skiing, you know."

"That's kind of a mixed message. Should I plan for a gala or not? How about I'll take one just in case?" She peeked into an open garment bag and plucked out purple silk. "I've always been sad that I never got to wear this one." She came out to drop a pair of silver shoes into the suitcase and shook out the gown, trying to work out how to fold it. "Happy?"

"Is that the dress you were going to wear to the reception Mom was planning if I won?"

"*When* you won," Becca corrected mockingly because his mother had trained all of them to play those mind games of assuming a wanted outcome had already happened. Cheryl had booked a hotel ballroom, had the invitations printed and pressed Becca to have something suitable to wear long before they'd known Becca would be in Sydney and unable to attend. "What happened with that party? Did you have it?"

"No," he said flatly. "Mom canceled—" very begrudgingly "—when I told her I wouldn't come back for it regardless of whether I won or not." She had tried to resurrect it when he did return, not seeing that the issues with Van's father would have made such a party tasteless in the extreme.

Becca turned to the mirror and held the dress against herself, cocking her head to admire it. "Maybe I'll call up Mum's oncologist, see if he has any events coming up."

"Don't wear it for someone else. *That's* rude."

"He's sixty and his husband organizes casino nights for charities," she said in a pithy tone. "Plus, women wear clothes to please themselves, not the male gaze." She looked back at her reflection. "And to feel superior to other women. Obviously."

"Obviously," he agreed drily.

"But that's part of pleasing ourselves." She hugged it to her waist. "Are you really not going to let me take it? I'm genuinely sad I never got to wear it."

He was feeling cheated he would never see her in it. "Wear it now." *Wear it for me.*

"Don't be silly. Swan around the house for an hour trying not to spill wine on it?"

"Why not? I won. We never celebrated that. And it's New Year's Eve. I'll put on a suit. One last date." His heart pinched as he said it.

"Last meal, more like," she said out of the side of her mouth.

He snorted so he wouldn't give in to other more conflicted emotions. It bothered him that the heart was going home with her and little else.

When I say you and I were always too different, this is what I mean.

"I can't cook in this." She frowned.

"I said I'll cook. I've already showered. I only need to change. You, on the other hand, will need at least an hour to go through whatever makeup Paisley left in the spare bedroom before you even start getting ready."

Becca made a noise of offense. "*That's* rude. I can be ready in ten minutes when necessary." She wrinkled her nose with indecision. "But I was feeling sooky that I wouldn't get my New Year's Eve with Courtney. Should we? It would end things on a good note."

A heavy weight settled inside his chest. He didn't think there was such a thing as ending a marriage on a "good" note, but this would beat the hell out of that death walk he'd made back to his hotel room in Sydney.

"Might as well go out with a bang."

"Oh, I'm pretty sure we already did that." She winked and sashayed down the hall.

Becca hadn't been on a date since she'd returned to Australia. She hadn't had time and hadn't been interested in more than catching up over coffee with a few girlfriends. Dating men had felt like something that should wait until she was divorced anyway.

Even back when she'd lived here with Van, proper dates had been few and far between. They would have dinner out sometimes, but she had often preferred to cook so she could have him to herself, otherwise they invariably ran into someone he knew and any sense of intimacy would be lost. Between his parents and Paisley and his own company, they'd attended family gatherings and charity dinners and product launches that weren't about spending time together as a couple, more like showing up and showing off as one.

Much as those events had made her feel out of her depth, she had liked how popular she felt when she was out with him. It had been an incredible confidence booster that people sought them out. They wanted to talk to Van because he was Van. They liked to talk to her because people at a party were no different from people at a bar. They wanted to talk about themselves and Becca always encouraged them. She was often told that she was charming and "a great listener" when really, she just preferred not to talk about herself and made self-deprecating jokes when she did.

Van had always been very attentive when they were out, which had added to the pleasure of an evening. He stayed near enough to touch her back or hold her hand, fetched a drink and exchanged little asides.

That guy was married to my mom for nine days.

That woman plays bass in the band on that singing show you like. Maybe she can introduce you to that singer you have a crush on.

She smiled to herself as she recalled those fun times, teasing each other and doing good work here and there, raising money for different causes like climate change and Lyme disease. She had actually enjoyed those sorts of functions, feeling like she was making an important contribution when she sat on a phone bank or sold raffle tickets.

She had deliberately blocked out the fact that when things had been good, they'd been really good. If she had allowed herself to remember that, she would have stayed blind to all that was wrong because it had only been as she got back to Sydney, and all the underpinnings of her hope and happiness in her marriage had begun snapping, that she'd lost faith in him and them.

She grew introspective as she showered and worked with a few items from Paisley's collection, adding them to the mascara and lip balm in her own bag.

It occurred to her that this was exactly how she had behaved back then, allowing her hurts to be glossed over by the bright life Van offered, never confronting them. In one way she was touched that he'd carried her necklace with him when he raced, but she hadn't let herself be angry that he'd trashed it. Her first thought had been that it was her fault for leaving it here. Rather than say, "You should have taken better care of it," she had tucked it away to fix it herself and was letting herself be distracted by playing dress-up.

The truth was, she had leaped at the chance to relive a time when he had admired and wanted her. She was trying to impress him and maybe she wanted him to feel at least a little of this loss that was sitting inside her for a marriage that never should have happened in the first place.

"Hey, Bec?" his voice called through the bathroom door. "You almost ready? I'm putting the steaks on."

Becca had never worn a lot of makeup even when Van's credit card meant she could afford the fancy stuff. Once she was married, however, she had had a woman at a salon give her some tips on applying everything properly. She had her cheekbones accentuated and her eyes wide and long-lashed as a baby fawn. Her hair had always liked the water here and had come out like the sassy end of a shampoo ad. She had already glossed her lips and was wearing a pair of earrings with colorful, dangling crystals and an armband with similar beads hanging off it.

"Yes, go ahead," she called back. "I'll be down in a sec." She was out of time. He liked his steak rare.

She didn't bother searching out an adhesive bra. Van had seen what she had a couple of hours ago and this halter bodice would be ruined if she had bra straps showing. When she had had this gown made, she had fallen in love with its wide satin waistline and skirt that fell in a graceful drape. It swept back from a thigh-high slit as she walked. Once she stepped into the sinfully sexy shoes, she almost looked tall and lithe.

Nerves attacked as she gripped the stair rail with a damp palm and descended to the living room.

Van had everything under control. He'd switched the music so it played a lulling melody beneath the sizzle of the steak. The table was set with a pair of embroidered linen place mats. He'd found the good silver and cloth napkins and even lit a candle. He must have grabbed the wine from the bedroom while she was in the shower because it was on the table with fresh glasses.

He had changed into his tuxedo, the impossibly handsome wretch. He knew she couldn't resist a pleated shirt and a bow tie. He wore only the vest, no jacket, and she would have teased him about dressing like a maître d', but they both knew he only had to shoot his cuffs and said, "Scott. Van Scott," and he could have her right there on the dining room table.

He flipped the steak with a pair of tongs, cut the gas and fan, yelling over his shoulder, "Becca! I'm plating—"

"I'm right here."

He swore and swung around. His head went back as if he'd been struck. He raked his gaze down and up, swore again and let his gaze take another long sip, this time more slowly.

She pressed her lips and planted her hand on her hip, hitched her weight to one side so her thigh poked from the slit. With a preening flick, her hair went behind her shoulder.

"Really?" she asked to the ceiling. "You knew I was here."

"I forgot exactly how superior you are to other women."

She sputtered a laugh. "Oh, please. I'm easy, but I'm not that easy." She walked toward the island, blushing with pleasure at his silly compliment and trying to dispel it. "Do you need help?"

"I got it." He plated the food and prepared to carry it to the table, nodding for her to walk ahead of him.

She didn't need to glance over her shoulder to know his gaze was sliding all over her backless gown and swaying hips. She felt it as a delicious shiver down her naked spine.

She glanced back anyway, and his brows went up, unapologetic, as she dipped her chin in a scolding *caught you.*

It was a cheeky exchange that warmed her through, but also pushed her onto the seesaw of wishing and wanting and fearing a hard bump was coming.

He set the plates, saying ruefully, "You're not easy. I thought you were, but you're not."

"We're ignoring what happened downstairs?" It was supposed to be a throwaway joke at her own expense. She was certainly trying to ignore it, but when she met his gaze her shell of self-deprecation fell away and she was all raw nerve and exposed emotions. Her throat stung all the way down to between her breasts.

The heat and humor in his gaze banked. "In that way, we're both pretty damned easy," he said solemnly and held her chair, then poured their glasses before seating himself.

It struck her that they were trying to be silly and fun and make the most of a situation the way they would have while they were married, but those tactics of falling back on lust and playful avoidance no longer worked. They had grown up too much.

"This looks very nice," she noted. He had added the last of the shrimp to the pasta along with sun-dried tomatoes and artichoke hearts. Broccoli and carrots and red bell pepper burst with color beside the well-peppered steak. "Thank you."

"Go big or—" He stopped himself.

"And then go home?" she suggested. She gave a chagrined sigh as they began to eat. "I didn't find you easy, either. Maybe it was this." She waved at the house and the meal and what she wore. "I was always waiting for you to realize I didn't belong here. I was waiting for you to get tired of me. Waiting for you to *be* here," she acknowledged with a twist of her lips.

"I thought you wanted to be here." His brows came together in an absent frown. "You came to Canada and married me so you could stay. You found the house and made it ours. I thought this *was* our home, Becca. Where did I go wrong that you didn't see it that way?"

"It wasn't you." She twirled noodles onto her fork, but didn't eat them.

Her temptation was to make some remark, deflect, steer the conversation away from herself. Who even cared what she had to say anyway? That's why she didn't talk about herself. She didn't feel interesting and griping never changed anything.

But he was waiting so patiently to hear where *he* had gone wrong.

Chest aching, she tried to explain.

"You're right that I limit myself. That I don't have a lot of self-confidence. Part of it was growing up in a rough area and having—not a bad reputation, but not a good one." She had never wanted him to know this. That's why she hadn't told him. "School was not a happy time for me. I developed early so that made girls jealous and boys a nuisance. I was teased because I scrubbed toilets at the petrol station and had caught lice once. I wanted to train for a 'real job.'" She air quoted. "But even my teachers didn't think I had much potential. One said it was a lucky thing I was built to sell cars since I didn't get good grades."

"A *teacher* said that? Give me his name," he said in a voice so deadly it raised the hairs on her arms. "He and I need to have a conversation."

"It was a woman," she said with a curl of her lip. "I've since heard she's no longer allowed to teach, but her comment stuck with me. It made the fact that I would even think about coming here a bold move. You've always traveled for races and training and vacation. It's no big deal to you to hop on a plane, but as a family, we hardly went down to the beach. I didn't tell them what I was planning. I saved up in secret and applied for the visa thinking I wouldn't even be selected, even though I knew heaps of people who got them. I've always had this constant sense that *I* don't get things that others do. Maybe that's why I don't," she said with a small shrug of realization. "I mean, if you can't imagine yourself winning a gold medal, you don't even bother trying, right?"

She had never been so honest and he was listening intently, not saying anything. Somehow that made it harder to continue than if he'd told her not to feel this way. It made her listen to herself and hear how she had let her own insecurities weigh her down and hold her back.

"Mum was like this, too. Maybe she taught me to be this way by example. She really struggled after my birth father died. Her family hadn't approved of her living with him outside of marriage and refused to help her. They were teaching her a lesson, you know? That's what you get when you go against the grain."

Keep your head down, possum.

"Dad is kind of the same," she continued. "He likes a simple life and they lived in what they viewed as the natural order of things. They both worked, but he watched footie while she cooked his dinner. My grades weren't the best so when I said I wanted to try a year at uni, Dad said I didn't need to go there to find a husband. He thought I should take hairstyling or something that I could do between having kids." Her heart twisted as she repeated that.

"It's a real mystery why you didn't tell them you were planning to come to Canada."

"Right?" She cleared her throat, recalling with another pang, "Mum was so upset. 'What do you want to go there for?'" she repeated in her Mum's broad accent. "She knew I was trying to reinvent myself away from the life she'd given me. She took it as a criticism and rejection. For her, getting us settled with Dad was so much better than the life she had been able to give me that my wanting more than that was just me being greedy."

"You were doing exactly what young adults are supposed to do. You struck out on your own and tried to figure out who you were." He sat back, sipping his wine.

"I know, but I thought I would *show her*. I would become this amazing, successful person and she would realize I was right to come here, but four years in I hadn't achieved anything. I was still screamingly ordinary and had new mistakes dragging behind me like a broken tailpipe." She had bumbled between a half dozen service jobs and gotten herself dumped by a couple of second-rate men. She had made some new friends, but had still been sharing a bedroom and eating too many packets of instant ramen noodles. "I started to realize it wasn't the place. It was the person. That was demoralizing."

"Don't say that, Becca. No one has their act together at that age."

"You did," she said on a scoffing laugh. "You were winning your hundred-bazillionth race. You had always known exactly what you wanted and you were doing the work to get it. So when you looked at me…" She gulped, but the shards in her throat only sank into the space behind her breastbone. "It didn't make sense. You could have had anyone."

"I wanted *you*."

"I didn't see why you should, though." She opened her hands, pleading for him to understand. "I let us happen because I thought some of your drive and success would rub off on me. At the very least, I could tell Mum I had this famous boyfriend. *Husband*."

"*That's* why you married me?" He set down his cutlery and sat back, expression frosting over.

"I married you because I loved you." Her voice shook as she said it, feeling as though she had inched out on a thin plank over a chasm. "But I knew you would never love me. How could you? I was boring and small and ordinary." Her eyes welled so she couldn't see him properly. She could feel his gaze drilling holes through her, though. She used her napkin to dab beneath them. "I didn't have grand ambitions or any hope of achieving them." That wasn't quite true. She had known exactly what she wanted. It hadn't seemed all that grand, either. In this modern age, it was almost regressive to aspire to make a baby, but even that very ordinary dream was beyond her reach. "Your family saw what a fraud I was. They knew I wasn't like the rest of you. I knew it was only a matter of time before you saw it, too."

She didn't have much appetite, but swirled a fresh bite of noodles onto her fork and ate it, tentatively glancing at him as she chewed, not sure what to make of his silence.

He wore a thunderous expression that turned her mouthful into sawdust. She quickly washed it down with a swallow of wine.

"Two people *like* me got married and would have killed each other if they hadn't divorced. One of them was so full of ambition and entitlement he destroyed the life he had supposedly built for me and my sister and his *grandchildren*. Adjust your vision of what great people look like, Becca." He shoved to his feet and walked away.

She swung her head to watch him cross into the living room. Beyond him, she caught her indistinct reflection in the blackened windows.

"I didn't ask you to be anything but who you are." He pivoted to confront her, voice booming up to the rafters of the loft. "If you had ended our marriage because you thought you deserved better, I could accept that. Instead, you thought you knew what I wanted." He jabbed at his chest. "And decided you weren't it. You don't know what I want, Becca."

"I did so!" She rose so quickly her chair skittered and almost tipped. She took a few agitated steps toward him, skirt brushing her legs, and waved her arm at the kitchen and the stairs and herself. "You wanted a Cinderella mouse who would cook and keep your bed warm, but also throw on a dress like this and talk nonsense to CEOs and their wives."

"Sure," he agreed, nodding. "And you were damned good at all of that. I also wanted someone who wanted the man, not the name on a pair of skis. I didn't even believe in love, let alone the kind that comes without conditions attached, but I almost believed that's what you offered me. I *wanted* to believe it."

A flaming arrow seemed to shoot across and land in her chest, stopping her breath.

"Then you cut me off the minute I retired." His hand sliced through the air. "I came home to my father's disaster and you... What? What did you tell your mom about me then? I guess I wasn't such a catch at that point. She probably congratulated you on having the sense to leave me behind."

"That wasn't what I said. I told her our marriage had just been for immigration." Becca hadn't been able to tell her mum why she'd defaulted on her marriage any more than she was able to admit it to Van. "I didn't want her to think badly of you."

"That's okay then, I guess?" He ran his hand down his face.

He was hurt. She could hear it. She stared at the floor with stinging eyes, hands folded before her, contrite and

filled with sorrow and despair while all sorts of words
gathered in her mouth like hard, oversize marbles.

I did love you, she wanted to insist. *You should have
believed me.*

She had wanted the same thing, to be loved without
condition. It had never seemed possible and it wasn't.
Not if he thought love was an illusion. A manipulation
tactic. How could she ever convince him otherwise,
given his experience? She couldn't.

The clock in the corner, the one he called "my grandfather's clock" because the long case had belonged to his
father's father, chimed eight times. They both stared at
it until it silenced. Then there was only the sound of the
guitar notes picked out beneath a ballad that bemoaned
a time "when we were young."

"I don't want to fight," she murmured. "Can we…?"
She motioned to the table.

They weren't fighting. They were doing what they should
have done four years ago. Talking. *Really* talking.

It was uncomfortable as hell, which was why they
had skirted it then.

Van needed a minute to gather his thoughts so he
nodded jerkily and came to hold her chair. They both
sat, but only picked at their food.

Had she loved him? He still didn't understand what
that emotion was, only having received a version of it
that had been loaded with obligation and guilt. His parents had said it to him when he had been very young,
but he hadn't really heard it much after their divorce.
When he had, love had seemed to be a quantifiable
feeling, something they expected to receive from him
in measures of greater amount than he gave the other.

Paisley hadn't been much better, sneaking around with a lot of, "Thanks for covering for me. Love you, bro."

Love had never been the soft, reassuring, healing emotion the pop songs and rom-coms promised.

He supposed he felt something like that toward his niece and nephew. They showered him with affection for the small trade of his giving them his attention. He easily imagined risking his own life to save theirs, but that was the same primitive emotion any man felt for his tribe. He felt the same thing toward his mother and sister and yes, toward Becca. She'd been his mate, so he wanted to protect her and provide for her even now.

There'd been other layers between them, too. Passion and sexual possessiveness and friendship, but he'd kept a wall up. They both had.

For all his bravado tonight, saying that they ought to get out whatever they'd held back in the past, he wasn't sure there was value in tearing down that wall. They would part again in a few hours, this time for good. Did they want to do that with their souls intact? Or in tatters?

He definitely didn't want to crack the subtle self-assurance Becca had gained. She still had a certain vulnerability in her shadowed expression, but she was more mature and confident than four years ago. She had a sense of purpose. An aspiration that put a spark of excitement in her voice and face.

It put a fiery streak of knowledge behind his sternum that she wanted things beyond their marriage and him. She always had and he'd refused to see it.

"You must have felt like this, a bottle in a cellar." He picked up his glass and tilted the ruby liquid in its bowl. "I stuck you in this house and expected you to be here whenever I returned." He hated coming into an empty house. That was the real reason he was selling it.

"Sometimes," she murmured, lashes flickering.

"In my defense, I dreamed of having empty days with no one clamoring for my time or attention, no one correcting my form or counting my reps. If I couldn't have that myself, it seemed like the next best thing to give it to you. I shouldn't have assumed you'd want that. I should have asked you what you wanted and supported you while you achieved it."

Her mouth wobbled. She set down her fork and pressed her hands into her lap. Her eyes were misting up again and he couldn't take it. It made his lungs burn.

"If you're not going to eat, let's dance." He needed to hold her, just hold her and stem what felt like a deadly bleed in his chest.

Helpless bewilderment flitted across her expression and she nodded-shrugged, allowing him to help her stand.

They moved to the area rug that sat beneath the two sofas, the very space he'd stood when he had railed at her a few minutes ago. He kneed the coffee table out of the way and they shuffled close in the small space. It wasn't dancing. It was an excuse to hold each other because they'd always been better at physical communication than verbal.

He wrapped one arm around her waist and drew her in. Her arm went under his and her hand flattened against his shoulder blade. He held her free hand against his chest and after a few offbeat steps, she sighed and let her head rest in the hollow of his shoulder.

His thumb traced the spot where her backless gown exposed her spine and that's all it was for two whole songs, them swaying in place while they held each other. Everything within him settled for the first time in eons.

Then she tilted her face up and pressed her lips to his throat. Her breath warmed his neck as she asked, "Do you want to go upstairs?"

Which was when he realized he was hard. She must have felt it against her stomach and his brain was too fogged with arousal to notice anything beyond how good he felt holding her again.

"Yes," he rasped, distantly thinking he ought to be more rational. Think this through.

She stepped back and her nipples were peaked against the front of her dress. Hell, yes, he'd known she was braless, but it was an erotic sight all the same. Her eyelids were heavy, her bottom lip caught in her teeth. She picked up her skirt, turning to walk away in that seductive swagger that extremely high heels gave a woman.

His heart thudded in time with every step. He had enough awareness to detour across and blow out the candle before he followed her up the stairs. A voice in his head warned him that making love again would fix absolutely nothing, but who the hell cared? They'd already crossed this line. There was no making it worse.

Was there?

She was removing the armband from above her elbow when he entered the bedroom. He didn't let her take off anything else, stepping close behind her to sweep her hair to the front of one shoulder so he could press a kiss to the side of her neck.

Her small shudder and gasp were music. Heavenly. Earlier, he'd fallen on her like a man finding a mirage in a desert. He had plunged into the relief of being with her.

Not this time. This was an all-you-can-eat banquet and he intended to sample and taste every delectable inch of her. He brought her hand up to kiss the back of her knuckles and nuzzled along her forearm, dabbing his tongue into the crook of her elbow, smiling when her breath hitched again.

As her arm bonelessly sagged backward to drape behind his neck and she arched her breast beneath his lowered gaze, he smiled against the point of her shoulder and said, "Slowly this time. We have all night."

Only tonight. The knowledge weighted each touch with deep significance. This had to be sweet and perfect. Memorable. It would have to sustain him for the rest of his life.

"Becca." He breathed against her ear and swirled his tongue against the whorls, closing his eyes when she pressed her ass into his groin and released a helpless whimper.

How had he survived without the pliant globe of her breast in his hand? The taste of her skin when he scraped his teeth against the tendon down the side and kissed the love bite he'd left there earlier? Or the thrill it gave him to feel her head loll and her body sway into his as she grew weak?

It seemed impossible that she had bottled all this passion, not sharing it with anyone else. He was almost angry at her for denying herself. If she hadn't wanted anyone else, why hadn't she come to him?

He hadn't gone to her, either. A thousand tangled assumptions and threads of pride had been in his way.

Now he wanted nothing between them. He used one

hand to open the button on the collar of her dress while kissing her flexing spine. The front fell forward over his hand where he still massaged her breasts. He moved his hand and now he cupped warm, bare skin. Her nipple poked into his palm and he groaned against her back, kissing his way down.

She was writhing, trying to turn, but he didn't let her. He sank to his knees and released the zip at the base of her spine, setting a kiss on her tailbone. The dress fell away and a midnight-blue thong framed the tops of her round cheeks. He groaned again and lightly bit each one.

"Van. I can't stand." Her hand was scrabbling backward for his shoulder, her legs wobbling.

He steadied her, then let her turn, staying on his knees while he shed his vest and left it on the floor. Heels. He was as helpless as any man to their sex appeal. He ate up the sight of her round hips and juicy thighs. Her stomach pulled in with tension and her breasts were lush and round and topped by those pretty nipples that made his mouth water with wanting the feel of them against his tongue.

"What's wrong?" Her voice was hazed with lust, her smile witchy as she tugged his bow tie loose. "You can't stand, either?"

"Hell of a view from here," he managed to say, caressing her ankles and calves and knees and thighs. When he got to the slash of midnight blue, he drew it off one hip, rose on his knees and kissed the soft spot beneath her iliac crest.

"Take off your clothes," she urged, fingers running along his collar, searching for buttons.

"In a minute," he murmured, wrapping his arm around her hips as he drew her thong down. He kissed across her stomach and blew softly against the fine hairs that covered her mound.

She shook in his hold, hands spearing into his hair.

"Step," he coaxed as he reached her shoe and drew the silk off and away.

This, now. His hand wasn't quite steady as he caressed back up her leg, finding the inside of her thigh and urging her to open her legs a little more.

"The shoes make you just the right height." He'd been too wild with need earlier, aching to be inside her. This time he indulged himself, losing himself in the taste of her, the way she quaked and moaned and clutched at him. The way she sobbed his name and finally shattered, crumpling in the aftermath so he had to pick her up and carry her to the bed.

He took off her shoes, liking that she was too weak to do anything but watch him, stomach still quivering as she tried to catch her breath.

He threw off his clothes, then started to pick up her leg, intent on throwing it over his shoulder as he said, "Let's do that again."

"No." She stopped him with that low, lust-soaked voice. "Me first." She sat up and motioned him to stand before her.

By the time Van said a guttural, "Turn around," they were both mindless, stripped down to pure sensation.

Becca had caressed him with her mouth until he insisted she stop. He had pressed her back onto the mattress again and slid his arms beneath her thighs and did it to her until she was arching and pulsating and calling his name.

It was only the beginning. His hands and mouth went

everywhere. His body surged into hers and he drove her over the edge, then he pulled her atop him where she relaxed with him hard and throbbing deep inside her.

She luxuriated in his petting and kisses and lazy thrusts until need drove her to sit up on her knees and ride him. Perspiration broke out on her body and the excited flush of orgasm followed. She was sure there was nothing left in her, but now he was pulling pillows under her stomach and covering her. He slipped into her with exquisite ownership and tangled his hand in her hair while he whispered filthy, sexy, wicked things.

"I can't get enough of you when you're like this. You're so hot, so incredible. Tell me how hard you can take it." He started out slow, teasing her senses awake again until she was completely his, all inhibitions gone.

She groaned her encouragement and held herself still for his powerful thrusts. Each one sent cataclysmic sensations through her. "Van. Van!"

"Come with me." His fingers bit into her hips and her whole body was one live nerve. "I need you with me, Becca. Come now. *Now*."

Ecstasy struck like a meteor, demolishing her hold on reality. They exploded and dissolved.

CHAPTER NINE

"ARE YOU OKAY?"

Van's question pulled Becca from her coma-like doze.

No. She was devastated that this was the last time she would feel this way. The last time his naked body would be half sprawled on hers, his thigh threatening to give her a dead leg, his voice a quiet rumble against her temple, his hand loosely cupping on her breast.

"I should have limbered up. I'll be sore tomorrow," she prevaricated, blinking her eyes open long enough to note they hadn't even turned the lights off. How debauched of them.

"Sauna's on," he reminded.

His breath was causing her hair to tickle her brow, but she was too weak to lift her arm and rub away the itch.

"Will you carry me out there?"

"I was going to ask you that."

She didn't want to move, but the sauna was a great place for making like a lizard. Somehow, they gathered their strength, put on robes and made the short trek through the falling snow.

Becca left her robe in the change room and walked

naked into the sauna, where she spread two towels on the cedar benches. She took the lower one and released a luxurious exhale as the hard warmth of the wood radiated into her back.

Van came in a moment later with a bucket of snowballs. He threw two onto the hot rocks, releasing sizzles and puffs of steam. He left the bucket by her feet and stepped over her to take the top bench, setting his head on the end by her feet so he could reach the bucket and throw more snow on the fire.

Becca sniffed. "Sage?"

"Whatever was out there," he said of the essential oils that were kept on a shelf in the changing area. "I set the timer so we don't fall asleep and cook to death."

"Worse ways to go."

"S'pose." He dropped his hand off the edge of his bench. His fingertips tapped her shin.

She obeyed his silent request and crooked her knee so he could rest his hand there and trace circles against her skin, the way he always had.

It was easy and familiar and perfect. She could have wept.

She was going to have to tell him. She knew she was, but they'd come all this way to such lovely accord. Her brain was going so far as to wonder if she could take a similar course in lab technology here in Canada even though Van had made no mention whatsoever of wanting anything but the divorce they'd agreed to.

"It matters, Bec. It shouldn't, but it does."

"What?" She blinked her eyes open to the orange glow of soft recessed lights that lined the ceiling.

"Mom and Dad cheated on each other. On anyone they ever made commitments to. If Mom has been faithful to Werner, that's a first. And Paisley…" He squeezed her knee. "I get why you kept her affair a secret. It would have been more drama than I was up for at the time, but I never wanted to be like them. I thought I'd lose my mind with sexual frustration sometimes, but we were still married and I couldn't cross that line. I didn't expect you to go without, though. I wouldn't have thought less of you if you had, but it means a lot to me that you didn't."

"You're taking my word for it that I haven't been with anyone?"

"Shouldn't I?"

"Yes. But you did accuse me of coming here to steal from you."

A pause, then, "Yeah, I did."

He didn't say anything after that, but he hadn't fallen asleep. His thumb was rubbing her kneecap as though he would wear a groove into it.

After a long time, he admitted quietly, "I wanted to see you. I wouldn't have cared about anything you took, not really. It would have reaffirmed some of my most cynical beliefs about human nature, but the settlement you asked for is a joke. You should get more. Take the jewelry. Take whatever you want. But if you had refused to see me, I would have felt robbed."

He still expected them to divorce, then. She blamed the burn in her lungs on the hot air of the sauna.

"I don't want anything else," she assured him, voice husky as she lied, "This is enough."

Van was still pensive after the timer woke them. They showered together in the change room and he teased Becca, calling her "raccoon eyes" as he helped her wash the last of the makeup off her face. They kissed and lazily washed each other, and it was all as good as life could get, but a one-night, two-person sex orgy was *not* enough. Not for him.

That was the reality he was confronting as they went back inside and Becca went upstairs to dry her hair. He warmed his plate, which she had shoved in the fridge on the way to the sauna.

He was wolfing down what remained of his dinner, chasing it with wine, when she reappeared. She wore her robe, and her hair was still damp on the ends, but swept back in waves off her face. Her skin was glowing, her eyes sleepy and her mouth soft.

She was the most beautiful woman he'd ever seen, especially when she lifted a smug brow at him. "Worked up an appetite, did you?"

An old, familiar sensation hit him. He wasn't one to soul-search and identify his feelings and examine them and *sit* with them. He lived his life and dealt with whatever hit him in the face, but he hadn't felt this sweet, soft, elusive feeling since she had left so he chased it, trying to figure out what it was.

Amusement? It was a desire to laugh, yes. Nostalgia? Maybe that's all this bizarre night was, but this was a shade of both without being either... Hell, was it happiness? He usually associated that with the triumph of winning or the base contentment of being physically comfortable. His male ego was damned satisfied right now so yeah, he was happy in that regard. Maybe it was just the feedback chemicals of great sex and a full stomach?

"Yours is still in the fridge. I'm trying to be a gentleman and leave it for you," he said as she took out an empty plate.

"Help yourself." She flipped the cake onto the plate.

"Becca, no," he said firmly. "You haven't eaten your vegetables." She had the worst eating habits, she really did. "I'll warm your dinner if you don't have the strength. *Then* you can have dessert." He rose to put her plate in the microwave.

She ignored him and cut a generous wedge of cake, dropped it into a bowl. She opened the freezer to take out the mint chocolate chip ice cream.

"No. That is all sorts of sacrilege. I forbid it."

She threw a scoop onto her cake, sat down, dug her spoon into the concoction, and looked him straight in the eye as she closed her mouth over the first bite.

The feeling hit him again. Harder. He wanted to grab her and laugh with her, kiss her and roll his eyes and argue that she really ought to eat something decent all at the same time.

He usually only felt this light when he was flying down ten kilometers of empty slope on a spring day, powder spraying around him. The kind of day he loved best.

He wanted to stay in this moment forever. He wanted her to stay here. With him. Forever.

The sassy light in her eyes faded into something that caught in his heart and tugged him to move closer. He shuffled to stand beside her and cupped the back of her head, memorized the open, defenseless look on her face. He felt the yearning he read in her expression because it was expanding within him.

He started to lower his head, wanting to kiss those cold lips and taste mint and sugar and something intangible that he needed more than food or air or a spring day on...

His phone began to burble with an incoming video chat. He brought his head up, breaking their eye contact as he glanced at it.

"Mom," he noted with a prickle of dismay as he recognized her photo. He dropped his hand from Becca's hair and stepped away. "She probably wants to say happy new year. They're in Mexico." He nodded at the clock, which showed it was ten past ten here. That meant it was after midnight there. "Do you mind?"

"No, of course. She'll wonder why you're not answering if you don't. Should I leave?"

"No." He unplugged his phone from the charger and accepted the call. "Hi, Mom."

Cheryl Brimley, still using her maiden name after more marriages than Van could count, wore a hotel robe and full makeup. She was removing her earrings.

"Happy new year," she said briskly.

"Happy new year. I thought you and Werner were going to a party. You left right after 'Auld Lang Syne'?"

"We had a fight." She looked to her left as she settled onto a chair with a painting of a seascape behind it. "He's about to become an old acquaintance I've forgotten."

"Mom." Van winced at how cold she was after six years of a relationship that had seemed to be good for her. "Don't talk like people are disposable."

"We want different things. It happens to the best of us. *You*, according to your sister." She adjusted a cushion behind her back. "I called Paisley expecting to speak to both of you. She told me you drove back to Whistler because Rebecca was in town. She wants to take some things from the house before the divorce is finalized?"

"Becca is here," he said with a note of warning. *Say one thing, Mom. One. Thing.*

Becca was not here. She rose and went downstairs, leaving her bowl melting on the island.

Van watched her go while his mother's "Oh?" hung like a soap bubble on the air.

Maybe she was taking in the fact that he didn't flip the camera to allow the pair to greet each other. Maybe she was noting he also wore a robe.

"I suppose the hotels were booked," she said, dragging his attention back to her image on the screen.

"This is still Becca's house as much as mine. We got snowed in, had dinner and a sauna. It's all very civilized." She should take some notes.

His mother made a noncommittal noise and smoothed a brow. "I was concerned when Paisley said you had rushed off to meet her. Rebecca always seemed to distract you from more important things."

"Like what?" He was genuinely taken aback. "My *wife* was important to me. Maybe you enjoy failing at marriage. You must or you wouldn't keep doing it, but I hate it."

"Donovan," she scolded.

"No, Mom." He was glad Becca was out of earshot. "If you had put one fraction of support behind my marriage that you did behind my career as an athlete, I would still be married."

"Do *not* lay that at my door." Her back shot iron-straight. "*Or* lecture me on support. She didn't even show up to watch you compete in the most important—"

"Her mother was sick," he cut in starkly. "You

didn't even call her to ask *why* she hadn't shown up. You had a thousand opportunities to make her feel like she was a part of this family and you squandered every single one. When I came home without her, you were glad. Why? Did you feel that threatened by her?" He hadn't meant to let all of this erupt out of him, but the tap was open and wouldn't close. "Did you feel like I was choosing her over you? Was that it?"

"Because you were planning to stay in Australia? For God's sake, Donovan, I didn't say one peep about that, did I? My focus was on getting you through the games without anything impacting your ability to perform. I did. *You're welcome.* You could have stayed in Sydney after that, and stayed married with my blessing. Your father was the one who took issue with your life choices and made off with the petty cash, if you recall. You came home to deal with that and I bear no responsibility for the fact your marriage didn't survive the distance. That is on you."

He bit back pointing out that his mother's not sharing her concerns with regards to said business had allowed his father to make off with the "petty cash" as she called it, but the harsh truth was Becca had already ended their marriage when that happened.

"As for whether I felt threatened by Rebecca, of course I did. Every mother feels her son's wife is taking him away from her. I didn't *dis*like her. I simply saw no point in growing attached if your marriage wasn't likely to last. I surmised correctly, didn't I? If you had had children, and I had foreseen a lifelong relationship with her, I would have made more of an effort, the way I have with Gavin." She referred to Paisley's first husband, a man she still invited to barbecues and other events for the sake of her grandchildren.

"It's the part where you didn't expect my marriage to last that bothers me, Mom. Manifest the things you want, right? You know what's ironic. I thought you and Werner would stick. I wanted that for you. Happy new year."

"Donovan!" Her sharp use of his name made him hesitate in ending the call. "What are you saying?"

"I'm saying you should make an effort to work things out with Werner. Quit acting like marriage doesn't require give as well as take."

She touched her throat. "Is that what you're doing with Becca? Working things out?"

"I don't know, Mom. Not if I'm talking to you instead of her. I'll talk to you later." He ended the call.

If you had had children with her...

Becca heard most of Van's conversation. His voice and Cheryl's had drifted clearly down the stairs as Becca shakily poured out their watery drinks, set the glasses and blender to go upstairs into the dishwasher and ensured the bar was as pristine as it had been when she arrived. She also shamelessly pocketed their photo, deciding she wouldn't even ask him if she could have it. Somewhere there was a printed book of their honeymoon photos. She might steal that, too.

Van came downstairs looking shuttered and shut down the way his family always made him look.

Becca tensed, too aware of his, *I don't know, Mom. Not if I'm talking to you instead of her.*

"Too bad about her and Werner," she said, putting away the cue sticks.

"Yeah." He came to the other side of the table where

he rolled a loose ball toward the far cushion and caught it when it came back to him. "I actually really like him, but that's Mom. She doesn't expect marriage to last so it doesn't bother her when it doesn't." Another dull thump as the ball silently rolled across the felt, bumped and came back. "And fine. I don't think anyone should stay married simply to say they did. Life is too short to be miserable, but it was drilled into me that you only fail if you give up. As long as you're trying, you still have a chance to get whatever it is you want."

He lifted his whiskey-gold eyes and pinned her in place with the mesmerizing fire that burned there.

She shoved her hands into the pockets of her robe where she curled them into tense fists, unconsciously bracing herself.

"I want *you*, Becca," he said simply.

Her heart skewed offside. She swallowed, both elated and devastated at once. She shook her head in refusal. It was hard. Harder even than when she'd done it in Sydney.

"Why not?" he asked grimly. "Look how good we are together."

"For a night," she said in a strangled voice. "This isn't real life, Van. I don't know if it ever was." She stared at the ghostly reflection of herself in the blackened window, exactly as she had always been here. Not solid, but translucent. More of a blurry version of herself than Becca, fully formed.

She longed to try again with him, she realized with a jolt that wasn't nearly as shocking as she wished it was. She could already see herself moving right back into that bedroom upstairs. Sharing their bed, cooking for them in the kitchen, walking down to the water in the summer and watching the snow fall in the winter.

It would be as simple as slipping into a warm bath because—and this truth exploded with the force of a sonic boom within her—she still loved him. God knows she had tried to stop, but it wasn't something that was dispelled by a good cry and a walk down memory lane. It was the enduring kind that would never lift off her heart because that's what her heart was made of, now—love. For Van.

It shouldn't surprise her that he had taken complete possession of that pulsing organ, not when she had come all this way to retrieve a damned necklace without asking him once if he'd seen it. He could have mailed it to her if she had asked. Instead, as the clock had ticked down on their marriage, she had bought herself a plane ticket and come here for exactly this. One last hit of the drug called Van Scott. One last chance to see…him.

One last chance for him to convince her to stay and try again.

Why shouldn't she? Why go home and go to school and build a fulfilling career in a city where family who loved her resided, when she could give up her own aspirations and live in the shadow of a god again? Van always got what he wanted. If he wanted *her*, who was she to deny him?

Maybe you enjoy failing at marriage. You must or you wouldn't keep doing it.

With a small throb in her voice, she said, "No, Van. I won't stay here so you can tell yourself you didn't fail."

"I'm not asking you to stay. I'm telling you I'm coming with you to Australia."

"What? Why? How? *Why?*"

"I just told you why. To try again." Van sent the ball rolling into the far pocket and pushed his hands into his pockets. "We'll do what I wanted to do four years ago. We'll get a flat and live together and work things out from there. I'll have to come back at least once a quarter, but I already do a lot of work from home or wherever I happen to be traveling." He shrugged that off.

"Van." She rubbed between her brows. "Once I get my certification, it will be for working in Australia. I can't go to school there and come back here to work." She flicked her hand in vague directions.

"Well, you could. You would need to jump through some sort of bureaucracy hoops, but we'll cross that bridge if we decide to live here. Right now, the goal would be to pick up where we left off and see what sort of future we might have. Decide where we want our home to be."

"Why are you saying this? We agreed that our marriage was a mistake." She threw that at him like an accusation. Like he was being unreasonable. "Why put off the inevitable? Let's make a clean break now while we can."

"Our marriage wasn't a mistake." He'd never been so sure of anything. "We made some, sure. Plenty. Both of us did. But we were learning how to be married, Bec. The good news is, we made all our mistakes up front. Now we know what not to do. It puts us in a stronger position moving forward."

"Yech." She folded her arms and hunched her shoulders, glaring at him. "That sounds like something you say to the board of directors at the strategy meeting."

He had lifted a few pat phrases, but, "It's still true. I didn't make our marriage a priority. I own that. I allowed my family to think you weren't important to me.

You can bet they'll know in the future that nothing is more important to me than making our marriage work."

"Oh, like it's an engine that needs constant maintenance? That's very romantic, thanks." She was wearing her stubborn look, putting him on his back foot.

"I'm being honest with you, Becca. More honest than we were in the past. That's another area where I refuse to keep making mistakes." He gave her a stern look. "As for you, I get why you struggle to feel you deserve this kind of life. I'll try not to throw my money around if it makes you uncomfortable."

"And how will you do that?" she scoffed, still hugging herself. "By saying you'll move around to the other side of the world and buy a flat in Sydney as if it's not some of the most expensive real estate on the planet?"

"Okay, yes." He was losing patience. "I will throw my money around if it means we can be together and comfortable. For God's sake, Becca. If we can afford nice stuff then I want to give it to you. That doesn't make me a bad person."

She was shaking her head again.

Frustration pushed him around the pool table toward her.

She stiffened and he halted. Sighed.

"Look at us. Neither of us has been with anyone else. We fell straight back into bed. *Twice.* Everything else between us clicks exactly the way it always has. We belong together. Why are you fighting that? *Be honest.*"

"You're just trying to prove to your mother that you don't fail the way she does! Yes, I heard you say that!" she threw at him as he jerked his head back.

He flattened his lips. "You listened to all of it?"

"I couldn't help overhearing, could I? You were right

there." She waved at the stairs where he'd stood near the top. He should have realized their voices were drifting down. "You want to stay married because it galls you to be like the rest of your family. Gosh, I can't wait to be that thing you work really hard on so you can be *right*."

"That's what you took from everything I said? Because I also let her know that I expected better of her while we were married. I sure as hell will in future."

"Oh, you mean when you told her it was okay that I didn't show up to watch you compete and it was her job to phone and ask me why? I was there, Van. Okay? *I was there*."

"Where?" His mind went completely blank, white as a bowl of blowing powder.

While her expression crumpled and she buried her face in her trembling hands.

She couldn't mean... He took a few steps toward her, touched her elbow. "Becca."

She dropped her hands and lifted her face. Her eyes were inky pools, so big and filled with pleading for understanding, they were almost cartoonish. His heart lurched, while the cogs in his brain clicked over like the ones in the clock chiming upstairs. Because he knew what she was saying. He knew where she had been. He'd felt her. Looked for her, certain she was there.

"When I raced? You were there when I won?"

"The first gold, yes." She gave a tiny nod, lips clamped together to stop their trembling, chin crinkling.

The important one. The one he'd wanted with every cell in his body.

"Mom said you told her you didn't need a room at the house. You didn't call me or text to say you were there."

"I stayed somewhere else."

"Where?"

"With people I knew through… It doesn't matter. It was an air bed in a flat full of strangers. That's how I wanted it." She looked down to her hands, knotting them together between them.

"Because of the way Mom and Paisley had been treating you?" He swore under his breath and ran his hand into his hair. "Dad was at a hotel. You could have—" He cut himself off. Everything had been booked years in advance. At best she might have had a pullout sofa in his father's suite and, given what had happened after the games, that was the last place Van would have wanted her to be.

Still.

"Why didn't you tell me? Why didn't you come see me after that race?" He was as dumbfounded and gutted as he'd been when she had failed to emerge from the crowd. He'd pushed through his next races and the team event because he'd trained his whole life to shut out emotional turmoil and focus on the run before him.

And because he'd felt the small lump of her gold heart each time he rubbed the spot above his own.

"I wanted you there, Becca. I understood that your mom needed you and I accepted that's why you stayed away." He had made himself accept it, but to now learn she had been there and hadn't told him? Not even when he came to Sydney? "If you were there, why…" Why had she ended their marriage immediately after? "Did something happen?"

It was starting to compute that something must have, something terrible. There was no other reason she would turn on a dime like that. His stomach filled with concrete.

"What was it?"

She lowered her lashes. "I need to explain a little more about Mum." She rolled her lips in and bit them. "And why she was so sick."

His lungs seized. He had really been hoping she would tell him he was wrong, that nothing had happened.

He waved at the sectional where they had made love hours ago. Where they had made love dozens of times years ago. It now felt like an electric chair as Becca curled defensively into one corner and he took the far end. She faced him, but he looked forward at the blank screen of the TV.

"The reason it took Mum so long to get diagnosed was because she had a rough time with doctors in the past. It had to do with her periods being really painful." She linked her fingers in her lap and tick-ticked her thumbnails against each other. "She was embarrassed to talk about it and when she did, the doctors just, you know, told her to take paracetamol and cuddle a hot water bottle. Long after she had Wanda, she had a hysterectomy and felt good for the first time since puberty. When she started having pains in her abdomen again, she put off having it looked at, thinking they would treat her like she was still making a fuss over nothing."

"You have painful periods," he recollected. A cold specter seemed to invade his being. "That's why you take your pill without taking a break and try not to have periods at all."

Not if I can help it, she had said the first time he'd realized she hadn't had one. He'd been convinced she was pregnant, but then she had missed a pill while they'd been away for a weekend. When she got her period a week later, she had been doubled over, pale and nauseated, alarming him with how ill she was.

She nodded. "I thought it was kind of normal for it to be so painful. Not *normal*, but every woman complains about it to a different degree. I wasn't suffering every single month the way Mum had so I wasn't abnormal, if that makes sense. Just unlucky. As long as I was on the pill, it was manageable so I did what Mum did and put up with it. But Mum started going for tests while I was still here and that's when she told me, 'It's probably just my endometriosis acting up.' It made me wonder if I had that."

His heart swerved. "Do you?"

"Yes."

A barbed hook caught into him and yanked his soul, tearing a hole in it. "It causes cancer?"

"No! And it's not infectious, either," she hurried to assure him. "You're completely safe."

He shrugged that off, knowing she would have warned him if there were risks to his health. "I'm more concerned about the fact that you were seeing specialists while we were married and you didn't tell me. Have I got that right?"

"Yes." Her profile stiffened.

"No, Becca." He shoved off the sofa and walked away. "Screw training. I had a right to know that you were going for medical tests."

"What was the point in worrying you when I didn't even know what to worry about?"

"Quit saying there was no point to anything. You were the point, Becca. Our marriage was the point."

"Do you want me to tell you what I learned?" Her

chin set belligerently. "Or do you want to stand there and yell at me?"

"Talk," he commanded, folding his arms and staying on his feet because he was too agitated to sit again.

She picked at a hangnail. "I was waiting on some results when Dad called and said I had to come home to help Mum. You were in Tahoe and I was homesick."

He flung up a hand.

"Yes, I should have told you that," she said in a beleaguered voice. She drew up her knees and hugged them, letting out a frustrated breath. "It was hard being here alone, Van. I was used to loud bars and chatting with mates at work. Nothing about being here felt right unless you were here, and you never were. The whole time I'd been in Canada, I took for granted that Mum and Dad and Wanda would be there when I was ready to go home, but I suddenly had to face that maybe Mum wouldn't be." She chewed at the corner of her mouth, trying to steady her lips. "So I went home. I had to. That wasn't up for negotiation."

"I know," he said, because he had, but it had still stung that she hadn't waited to see him. That she had kept her medical tests from him.

"I was in Sydney when the ob-gyn finally got back to me."

His fists closed defensively and he wasn't sure why. He moved so he could see her face even though she was balled up like a pill bug, eyes lowered.

"Endometriosis causes scar tissue. Lots of women can still get pregnant when they have it, but the specialist could already tell that it was unlikely I would ever be able to conceive or carry a pregnancy to term. In fact…" She swallowed. "She recommended a partial hysterectomy. I'm putting that off as long as I can because I'm managing for now, but probably before I'm thirty I'll have that done."

Van blinked as if it would clear the dull buzz in his ears. His head felt as though it floated off his body. "Are you saying you can't get pregnant?"

He had heard wrong. She had gotten it wrong. The doctors had. Surely.

She was biting her lips again, brow tense as she nodded.

As he started putting all the pieces together in his head, his chest grew so tight, he could hardly draw a breath. When he swallowed, it felt as though he forced razor blades down his throat. His voice was frayed when he managed to speak.

"You knew this in Sydney when I came to see you? That's why you told me this was all a mistake, that you didn't want to stay married?"

She nodded again.

No.

"I was finished with competing, Becca. I told you I was ready to retire. I wasn't training." His whole body had become pinched in a cage of spikes. "You had no reason to keep that from me. Not then."

"I didn't *want* to tell you." Her eyes flashed up. "I had a lot to deal with, Van. I had just learned my mum was terminal and that I couldn't have kids. I didn't want to believe either of those things." She blinked her matting lashes. "I got that news and had to get on a plane to go watch you race. I could *not* face your family, but I saw you set a record and I was so proud and happy for you. I made my way to the winner's circle to see you and you were with Paisley and the kids and you were holding Flora and looked so…" Her face crumpled.

Van swore and rubbed the place where his breast-bone felt fractured.

"I couldn't talk to you," she choked. "I couldn't make it fit in my head that we would never have a baby of our own."

"Becca—"

"No." She shot to her feet and quickly tightened the belt on her robe. "Don't say there are other ways to make a family. *I know that*. It doesn't mean I wasn't devastated. All I could see was what I couldn't have. Everything was wrong between us, Van. *Everything*. Not just that one thing." She held up a finger.

He couldn't get past the fact that she hadn't told him, though. He was gritting his teeth, chest aching with the hurt of betrayal. "I still deserved to know."

"Oh my God, Van! You came to Sydney and said you were ready to start a family. That's what you said to my *face*." She pointed where the tears brimming her eyes began to roll down her cheeks. "How was I supposed to tell you that was impossible?"

He had said that. He rubbed his hand across his face, feeling as though it was melting off his skull.

"I couldn't, Van. I couldn't say it." All the wind went out of her sails. "And I couldn't keep pretending I was the wife you expected. You brought everything to our marriage—the house and the money and I brought…" She waved at herself. "At least when I thought I could give you kids I had something to offer, but—"

She turned away and swiped at her cheeks, sniffing back tears.

She was killing him. "Becca." He reached for her.

She shrugged him off. "Don't. Don't say we could have worked it out or found a way." She hugged herself. "This isn't about finding a workaround. It's about me thinking I was being realistic in wanting this one thing. A thing that is supposed to be the reason I exist at all. Getting pregnant is so easy and natural for some women, it happens to them without them even trying. But not me. I don't get that. Do you finally see why I keep my expectations low and refuse to believe in brass rings and fairy tale endings? It's too painful when they don't work out."

Becca didn't wait for his reaction. She moved in a fog to the stairs. *Finish packing*, she thought, distantly aware she was operating on shock-induced autopilot again.

She hadn't wanted to relive the anguish of learning she couldn't get pregnant. Yes, there were long-shot treatments that might allow her to conceive. She had read up on them and understood that she could put herself through all sorts of agonies, emotional and physical, and may or may not carry to term. She didn't want to put herself or Van through any of that.

So, for those first painful months, she'd held the knowledge inside her like an abscess, letting it eat at her. Eventually she had confided in Wanda, and later the grief counselor who was helping them work through their loss as they cared for Mum. One time, Becca had completely fallen apart at a bus stop and an elderly woman had missed her bus while she sat and listened, then patted her knee.

Living life means feeling the pain of it, the old woman

had said. *That's why you have to enjoy what little plea-sures there are when they're handed to you.*

She had given Becca a butterscotch candy. Becca still found the taste too bittersweet to bear.

In the bedroom, the bed was wrecked from their antics earlier. Clothes were scattered on the floor...the hair dryer was on the table by the mirror. It looked like she still lived here.

Ignoring the slicing pain that sent through her, she made herself dress in a pair of yoga pants and a T-shirt with a snuggly pullover that did nothing to comfort her. Then she lingered in the closet, staring at the dregs of her life with Van.

Nothing made sense. Nothing. Not meeting him a million years ago, or marrying him, or buying this house and calling it their home and filling it with all these clothes that were too posh or heavy for the life she led in Sydney.

It didn't make sense that she had come here now and he was here and they were saying things that lanced inner boils and left her so drained she felt as though she were bleeding out.

It didn't make sense that she was crying because she had done all her crying. She was sure she had. She had cried when she pushed him away in Sydney and when she had filed the divorce papers. She had cried this morning when she arrived here and smelled him in this closet. She had cried downstairs before they'd made love on the couch.

Her chest was hollow, sobs ringing inside it, throat scorched, eyes swollen. All of her hurt, scalp to toe-nails. Hurting and hurting and hurting.

She should be finished with it. With all of this. She

was divorcing him. Starting fresh. So why was she still hanging on to a white eyelet lace sundress and hugging it to her broken womb as she sank to her knees and fell against the laundry hamper? Why was she aching with loss because she was no longer the woman who had put on this dress with such delusional hopes? She was smarter than that now. Wasn't she?

"Becca."

Weirdly, it made perfect sense that he came in without her hearing him over her storm of heaving sobs, and she wasn't startled at all by his sudden appearance. He gathered up her shuddering body in his strong arms and carried her to the bed and it felt *so right*. Exactly what Van would do because he was perfect and she was not.

"I'm just so sad," she choked. "And I'm so tired of pretending I'm not. When Wanda has kids, she'll have Mum with her again. I never will. And I'll never have your baby and see your eyes or your smile or…"

"Ah, babe. It's not right. It's not." He came with her onto the sheets and aligned her along his strong frame, dragging the covers over them and sheltering her with his whole body.

"I'm sorry," she sobbed into the fuzzy lapel of the robe he still wore, cold fingers petting the line of fine hair against his sternum.

"It's not your fault."

"I mean for all of this. I didn't know how to do any of it. I thought I could fake being your wife and I left when it got hard. That's not love. I know it's not."

"Stop. You're enough, Becca. Okay? Quit thinking you have to be something else. Be you. That's all I ever wanted. Just you."

She didn't even know how to be that. Her. But she was wrecked and exhausted and her eyes were burning with the salt of her tears. She swore these would be the last ones.

CHAPTER TEN

VAN CAREFULLY PUSHED his leg out from beneath the covers, too hot under the comforter with his thick robe and Becca's weight burrowed into his side, but she'd fallen asleep and he wouldn't move more than that, afraid he would disturb her.

He didn't want her to start crying again. Or roll away. He needed to hold her. His chest was a giant ache, as though cleaved open.

Kids. Bloody hell. He'd experienced a certain ambivalence suggesting it to her after the games, but he'd thought that starting a family was something she wanted so he'd been willing. Becca had always been turning her head to smile at babies and toddlers. Kids loved her for the same reason adults did—she gave them her whole attention and made them laugh and feel important.

Van's own feelings toward having a family had been more complicated. He rubbed a tendril of her hair between his thumb and finger as he acknowledged that.

He'd been confident that Becca would ensure he was a decent parent, but he hadn't felt any natural affinity for it, not given the upbringing he'd had. His mother had never once thought, *Maybe I shouldn't do this because it will break my kids.* She had simply kept her churn of marriages and affairs with his coaches and the occasional death threat from an unhappy wife to herself. Until they leaped out and bit him.

His mother would say she'd been trying to protect Van, but it had been a hell of a lot more traumatic to find out his parents were divorcing through change room chatter than from her or his father. That's how it had happened, though.

As for his father... Van blew out a suppressed sigh toward the ceiling.

Van didn't blame his mother for divorcing Jackson Scott. His father had had wealth and social standing and an ability to charm when he wanted something, but he was selfish and jealous and as a father he'd been...absent. When Van looked for a cherished father-son moment, or times when his father had demonstrated what sort of man Van should become, he drew a blank. All his role models had been coaches and teachers and the athletes ahead of him.

What scared Van was that he shared his father's single-mindedness. His drive. Yes, his mother had possessed a similar focus and stubborn refusal to quit, but Van's father had been cutthroat and very self-involved. When Van looked back, he saw some of that in his own actions, especially when he had married and bought a house and installed Becca inside it, all to please himself.

Van's worst nightmare was that his own kid would wind up feeling about him as he did about his own father—contemptuous. Wanting him out of his life and glad when he was.

He hadn't even considered whether he wanted kids since he'd suggested it to Becca. Given what his own father had done shortly after, Van had shoved parenthood well onto the back burner. It was one of the reasons he hadn't pursued divorce. Yeah, he missed sex, but dating led to marriage and that presumed family, so he'd put off the entire topic.

At least, he had imagined Becca presumed that was their next step. He had wanted to give her what she wanted and he could see now there had been a part of him trying to tie her closer to him, sensing she was pulling away. Besides, why *not* have kids with her? He couldn't think of anything sweeter than a round little face with her dimples and freckles. Her accent spoken in a child's high voice…

Ah, hell. He closed his eyes, trapping the sharp sting that rose behind his lids while he fought to hold back the choke of emotion pressing up from his chest.

After she'd dropped her bomb downstairs and walked away, he'd stood there trying to read his phone, as if that held the miracle information that would alleviate her suffering.

And his.

Because this was a blow. He breathed through the pain as if it were a physical injury. It was exactly as bad as any broken bone or torn ligament that had ever sidelined him from whatever he had been planning. It hurt like hell to know Becca couldn't get pregnant. And yeah, he knew this wasn't the end for either of them to have a family, but it was the end of something. A dream he hadn't realized he'd harbored close and quiet, barely acknowledging it because it was already so fragile.

Now it was gone. Losing that possibility left a hollow inside him that would be empty and tender all his life.

Becca had been walking around with this ache for years. He'd come up here knowing she would be breaking her heart over it and there she'd been, hiding her grief in the closet like it was something to be ashamed of. Like she wasn't entitled to be angry and hurt by the injustice of it.

He tightened his arms around her, noticing anew how small and soft she was. Becca had such a bright, spicy personality, she always seemed taller and tougher than she really was. Resilient. But she was vulnerable and generous and deserving of every good thing.

I'm just so sad. And I'm so tired of pretending I'm not.

"Me, too," he whispered, nose filling with the tears he was fighting. He rubbed his lips against her satin-smooth forehead. "Me, too."

A loud bang snapped Becca awake. She sat up on a shocked gasp, disoriented by the dark, unfamiliar surroundings, the tangle of blankets and the weight of heavy limbs on hers.

"Fireworks," Van said in a rumble. His hand rubbed her back. "It's midnight."

"Poor dogs," she murmured as there was a *pop-pop-pop* and long hiss. She had once seen a mate's kelpie cower under a sofa and had felt for animals ever since.

She liked watching fireworks herself, though. With a superhuman effort, she dragged herself free of the blankets and walked to the balcony doors, scraping back the drapes to see.

Someone farther down the lakeshore was setting them off. She opened the door and stepped onto the icy, covered balcony, moving to the end where she could lean out to see the bursts of orange and yellow and violet through the falling snow.

Van came out behind her and pulled her back against his chest, wrapping both of them in the comforter he'd brought from the bed.

For ten minutes, they stood there listening to the whistles and bangs echo across the frozen lake, watching the spirals and explosions flash sparks and color onto the monochrome landscape.

This is it, she thought as another bloomed into feathers of orange fire. It was midnight. There was still paperwork to finish, but in her mind this was the end point. Their marriage was over.

But she stood in the circle of his arms for an extra few minutes, leaning into his chest, heels on his slippers and toes curled against the bite of cold beneath her feet.

She waited until the last spark winked out before she turned to go back inside. She rubbed her feet on the small rug inside the door to dry the damp and work some feeling back into her soles.

Van came in behind her and closed the door. He wafted the comforter back over the bed, then retied his robe.

She didn't know what to say or do. Crawling back into bed so he could put his arms around her sounded appealing, but it would only put off the unavoidable.

She knelt and straightened the few items she'd thrown into the suitcase, making sure the Polaroid photo was in the envelope with the locket before she secured it into a zipped pocket. The rest of the contents were useful, but meaningless.

Van sat on the corner of the bed, elbows on his knees, watching her close the suitcase and stand it up.

"I did fail you," he said with quiet gravity. "The fact

that you felt you couldn't tell me something so important is pure failure on my part."

"Let's be done with pointing fingers and throwing blame. I told you now," she said simply. The tension in her shoulders had dissipated as though a weight had been lifted. "It feels good that you know. I've been carrying it around like it was this great big letdown on my part— No, listen." She held up a hand when he made a noise of protest. "That was how it felt. Like it was my fault our marriage fell apart because my body didn't work the way I wanted it to. I wanted to believe I would have stayed if that hadn't happened, but it was only the final straw."

"It is absolutely not your fault, Becca," he said firmly.

"I know that up here." She tapped her head. "It took a long time to accept it in here." There was still a deep, hollow ache in her chest. Her voice wavered as she added, "Telling you was hard. It makes it real, but hearing you say it's not my fault and not trying to offer to fix me…" She wobbled a smile at him. "That means a lot. Thank you."

He stared at her with incredible intensity, jaw working as though he wanted to say something.

"Yes, I know you would pay for any treatment that would help," she said, biting back an even more tender smile.

"I would," he burst out, shooting to his feet. "That's not about fixing you. You're perfect. I want you to be happy, that's all. Anything that would make you happy, you only have to tell me and I'll do whatever I can."

He was going to make her cry again and she was

done with tears, she really was, but oh, he was a very sweet, good man.

"I know, Van. Thank you." She swallowed down her emotion and stood.

She moved to hug him. *Last one*, she promised herself as his arms folded tight around her. His heart thudded heavily against her ear. They made the tiny adjustments so they fit just so. She closed her eyes and hung on to him for a long time, long enough she forgot they were standing until he rubbed her back.

"Let's get to bed," he said gruffly. "You're falling asleep on your feet."

Pulling away caused a visceral tearing sensation down her front. She made herself breathe through the pain and concentrate on pressing back the hot tears behind her eyes.

With a nod of agreement, she moved the suitcase into the hall.

"Where are you going?" He frowned.

"The spare room."

"Stay here." He waved at the bed.

"It's your house now, Van. Your bed." Her emotions were all over the place, heart feeling flattened and smeared.

"I mean *stay* here," he said more forcefully. "The fact that you can't get pregnant changes nothing. I don't know if *I* can make babies. Did you think of that? We'll figure out how to have a family if and when the time is right. I'm still coming to Australia, Becca. We're staying married."

"Your presumption that you can have anything you want is astounding." She swiped the heel of her hand beneath her eyes. She kind of loved him all the more for it. It was inspiring. She definitely ought to become more like him if she wanted to be happy. "I want this to be easy, Van. Can you at least give me that?"

"You want me to give you up without a fight? That's really what you want from me?"

His voice was jagged with offense, the line of his shoulders iron straight and rock hard. "I don't know how to give up, Becca."

The irony didn't escape her. She was asking a man who never surrendered to do just that. She wanted him to give her what she wanted, and it was a loss so deep she didn't expect she would ever fully recover from it. In fact, she knew she wouldn't. She hadn't gotten over him in four years so she doubted she would feel any better tomorrow or the next day or the next.

Nevertheless, she made herself say, "Yes."

"You won't give us one more chance," he scoffed with disbelief. *"One."*

"Van." Her voice was gentle. She couldn't even be angry with him anymore. All the fuel for hurt and resentment had been burned away by the fire of brutal honesty that had roared between them over the last hours. There was only one last hot, painful lick of truth. "We *never* had a chance. We had great sex and good laughs, but you didn't love me. When I told you I loved you, you got that look right there."

His entire demeanor hardened as if warding off this final, troubling fact.

"You didn't believe me when I said it. You thought after all this time I was coming back to steal from you. If you want me to say things I should have said four years ago…" Her throat tried to close. She clung to her elbows, too adrift to feel anything but loss. "After I learned I couldn't give you a baby, love was all I had to offer you. But you didn't *want* my love. How the hell could you expect me to stay married to that?"

CHAPTER ELEVEN

BECCA WOKE TO the sort of morning she had always loved in Canada. The sky was so blue as to pierce the eyes, the sun opening like an eye in the notch of the mountains, casting beams and sparks and glittering promise in every direction.

Overnight, the wind had quit churning the snow. Like her emotions, all was settled into a thick blanket of calm. The world was unmarred and quiet. A blank slate. No mistakes yet made. New day, new year.

New Becca.

She looked to the closed door of the master bedroom, but didn't walk down to knock on it for a final goodbye. They had said all that needed to be said. She touched her fingertips to her lips in a softly blown kiss and tiptoed downstairs with her nearly empty suitcase.

The kitchen was a disaster zone. She used her app to book a rideshare and quietly loaded the dishwasher while she waited, then sat down to write her card to Van.

A million things had run through her mind when she'd bought it, nothing feeling right. She had thought there would be apologies to make, but she wasn't sorry, that's what she realized as she sat there staring at the white card. She was glad she'd been married to him. Glad to have known him. Glad they had had this final night to bandage up old hurts. Now they could both move on and heal.

There was only one thing left to say.

I love you. I always will.

She glanced at the app and hurried to put on her boots and coat, and grabbed the suitcase and her purse before she rushed out into the bracing cold. The dry air made her nose sting and her eyes water. This was the kind of day she loved to look at, she thought wryly. Preferably from a hot bath or beneath the down comforter on the bed with a naked Van beside her.

He would be happy when he hit the slopes later, though. This was what he called champagne powder, so dry it didn't even melt as it coated her jeans.

It made for a heavy slog, though, reaching as high as her thighs in some places. She worked up a sweat as she hoofed through it. Her breath was fogging, lungs aching as she very ungracefully grunted her way up the hill toward the gate.

The car appeared at the top and honked. She waved and hop-stepped, trying to run, but it was no use. At least the driver saw her and sent a friendly wave.

Still, with someone waiting she had enough sense of urgency she wasn't tempted to look back.

Van woke to a profound sense of absence, one that left a resounding echo inside him. She was gone; he knew she was.

He sat up, angry with himself because he hadn't meant to fall asleep. He'd been sitting on the bed, hearing her say it again and again.

You didn't want my love. How the hell could you expect me to stay married to that?

He hadn't known what to say because it was true. Every time she'd told him she loved him, he'd felt those words as an obligation she was placing on him. All his life, love had been a transaction. His parents, coaches, even fans had only ever said they loved him because he won. Shareholders loved him because he made them money and his sister, well, theirs was a comrade-in-arms sort of love that demanded he always be at her disposal because she didn't believe in that emotion any more than he did.

Unconditional love simply didn't exist in his world. It was a unicorn, just like Becca. He had never been able to figure out what she wanted from him in exchange for this outpouring of acceptance she offered. He had given her jewelry and a dream home and the ability to stay in this country, all the while aware she really wanted his time, but when he'd finally offered her that, she'd rebuffed him.

It still turned a knife in his belly.

He'd done the same thing last night, offering his time and his money and his support. Whatever she wanted. He just wanted her in his life.

But it wasn't enough for her.

Love was all I had to offer you. You didn't believe me when I said it.

He hadn't. He had wanted to, but he hadn't. Now he was sorry. He should have seen her love for the gift it was and kept it. Protected it and hoarded it because now he'd lost it for good and that made for a very bleak future.

He rose from the bed feeling as though he'd lived a

thousand years overnight. As though he had been partying and was suffering the worst hangover of his life.

He tightened the belt on the robe and blinked his gritty eyes at the belligerently beautiful day. As he stepped out of the bedroom and glanced down to the guest room, he saw the bed didn't even look slept in. Downstairs, the kitchen was clean.

It was almost as though her presence here had been nothing more than a prurient fantasy and a tragic dream—if not for the card she'd left propped against the cold candle on the dining table.

His hesitated as he reached for it, wanting to know what she had said, but not sure he could bear it. It was probably still blank. They'd said everything they had needed to say.

Hadn't they?

As he opened it, he heard a distant honk of a car horn.

"Beccaaaa!" A door slammed in the distance.

She stopped at the gate, out of breath, jeans clammy and coated with snow to above her knees. Her fingers ached where they fumbled with the icy metal clasp. The rideshare car was running its exhaust and she gave a wave to brush the fumes from her face.

"Becca, damn you, don't leave." Van's voice was so angry, she was tempted to make a run for it in reaction.

She stood frozen in place as he appeared at the bottom of the drive.

He still wore his robe and nothing else but a pair of unlaced boots. The robe was pulling open as he ran so that—

"Van. For heaven's sake." She motioned for him to

close the robe. "You'll catch pneumonia." And start rumors that most men found unflattering, given how the brisk winter air was liable to affect him. "What's wrong? Did I forget something?"

"Yes." He was clomping up to her with way more agility than she'd had even though he was practically naked. Snow had to be falling into his unlaced boots, but he didn't seem to care. His hair was disheveled, his jaw unshaved. He looked like a grouchy, shaggy bear awakened early from hibernation.

"What?" She left her suitcase at the gate and motioned to the driver for patience as she tromped back toward Van.

His breath gusted out in big clouds as his chest heaved from the exertion of coming after her. He was twitching with shivers as he thrust out the card she'd left him.

"Van…" she trailed off helplessly. "I wanted you to know that…"

"Open it."

She did, cautiously, and saw her own words. That's all. Nothing else.

Her heart had swooped up so incredibly fast with hope. Now it fell just as swiftly, landing hard. Tears of disappointment sprang to her eyes.

"Why—?"

"I want this, Becca." He pointed at the card. "This love of yours is *mine*. I want it more than I want anything else in this world. But I have to give it back to you. Right? That's how this works? You give me yours. I give you mine?"

"But you *don't* love me, Van."

"Don't you doubt me," he said with affront. "We're

not repeating old mistakes. Remember?" He clomped a step closer and cupped her cold cheeks in his cold hands, looked deep into her eyes. "You are the only woman I want. I'm selling this house because what is the use in having it if you're not in it? I don't know how to love except by…" He shrugged and looked at their surroundings. "By giving you everything I have. I didn't think words *could* be enough." His brow flexed. "But if that's what you need, if that's *all* you need, then you have them. As much as you mean those words, so do I. *I love you. I always will.*"

She had never fainted in her life, but she almost did right then. Her heart took a hard bounce and she forgot to breathe and her vision tunneled into pinpoints so all she saw was him. His warm hands cupping her cheeks was the only thing holding her upright.

"Don't say it's too much," he warned gruffly. "I don't know how to give you enough love."

Her eyes were watering so hard she had to blink to clear her vision. "It does feels like too much. It does," she choked. "Because I'm…"

"Be careful what you say next, love." His hands gentled. His thumbs settled at the corners of her mouth and his lips touched the tip of her numb nose. "I have very high standards and I will not take kindly to hearing that my wife is anything less than utterly amazing."

She tilted a wet look up at him and the sunlight glinting through the trees turned everything into halos and sparkling light. The world was silent and the air crisp and fresh. The moment too big with possibility.

"I'm scared," she admitted in a whisper.

"Me, too. But I can't do another four years without you. I can't do four minutes."

Behind her, the driver opened his car door. "You folks hosting a polar bear swim?"

"No," Van called absently, gaze locked to hers. "But that's how I've felt since you were gone, like I was naked in a frozen lake. *Come back.*"

Hard shivers were chasing through his body, but he didn't mean she should come back in the house to warm up. He meant forever.

Be smart, Becca. You might get your heart broken again.

Or she might not. She wouldn't know if she didn't try. Maybe she could have things other people got.

Or maybe she could have this one thing that no one else had—Van's love.

She began to tremble, but it might have been shivers. She nodded jerkily.

Van grabbed her shoulders and planted a kiss on her lips, a hard, hurried one that was no less powerful for its brevity.

Then he released her and brushed past her, grabbing up her suitcase as he told the driver, "She's staying with me, but don't knock her rating. Do you ski?" Van quickly had the man grinning at the news that he could pick up a full complement of Van Scott gear from a local shop.

As the car drove away, she and Van slipped and skittered down to the house, laughing and clinging to each other.

"I swear, if you locked us out of the house…"

"I might have. I wasn't thinking of anything but catching you."

The door was open and they tumbled in, kissing and falling into each other's arms. It was exciting and sweet and so achingly good, she couldn't help pausing and sobering.

"Is this happening too fast?"

"Probably. That's how we do things." He rubbed her arms.

"That's how *you* do things," she said pointedly.

"It's okay if you need time, Becca. It is." He dipped his head to look straight into her eyes. "But *tell* me if that's what you need. Don't shut me out, okay? Not again. Promise?"

She gave a faltering nod. "You, neither."

"Open book. I swear."

They kissed with their still-cold lips, but it was sweet and hopeful and made her want to believe in this. That she could have him. That they could be like this forever.

He was still shivering, and she slithered her arms inside his robe to try to warm him. Her clothes were cold and the snow clinging to her jeans was melting and damp, making him flinch and pull away with a laugh.

"Look, I know I *just* said I wouldn't rush you." He winked one eye as though he suspected he was pushing his luck. "But I need to warm up. Any chance you want to join me in a hot shower?"

"Is the sauna still on standby?"

"Oh, yeah, let's do that."

Van changed her flight so Becca could stay a few extra days in Whistler and they could travel together to Sydney. Becca had given a private eye roll when he upgraded her ticket to first class, but also gave a private squeal of glee because she'd never had the promise of free champagne when she boarded before.

They were leaving tomorrow, and she was already

second-guessing her school plan, but Van insisted he would live his life around hers while she started her classes to see if lab work would be a good fit for her.

These few days of reconciliation were almost too ideal. They skied and made love and talked about everything and nothing, but she kept having faltering moments of worrying it couldn't last. She feared she would come crashing back to earth any second.

Each time it happened, Van seemed to notice, catching at her hand or saying a quiet, "Hey. You know I love you, right?" And when he said it, he pulled her into his arms and held her like she was the most precious thing in the universe.

He wanted to remarry in Sydney, but with a proper wedding with both families in attendance. "I'm sorry we didn't do it right the first time, so your mom could be there. Let's do better this time."

"Your family doesn't want to come all that way for a second marriage," Becca protested as they left a pub where they'd just had lunch.

"Are you kidding? Paisley is dying for an excuse to bring the kids—wait. We're not going home yet." He drew her in a different direction from his SUV. "This is why I wanted to have lunch here. I need to go across the street."

She tugged him to a halt as he led her toward a jewelry store.

"Please don't buy me new rings. I like these." She adjusted hers on her finger.

"So do I." He wore his wedding band, too, even though their arrangements with their lawyers meant a certificate of divorce would appear in roughly a month. "This is something else."

"My locket? You got it fixed?" She hadn't wanted to give it up, preferring to take it home to get it repaired so she wouldn't risk leaving it here again, but Van had sheepishly confessed how he'd broken it—turning her inside out with love for him. He had insisted on ensuring it was mended so she had tentatively entrusted it to him again.

Now he was giving her a cagey look that made her tense with apprehension as she went through the door he held.

The upscale shop was full of custom items. Van gave his name and the clerk disappeared. She came back with a small velvet box and a big smile.

"I saw the goldsmith working on this. What a lovely idea."

"Thanks. Would you give us a minute?" he asked in the most charming "shove off" in history.

As the woman walked away, Van opened the lid, still eyeing Becca as though he wasn't sure how she would react.

She looked down and saw her locket, mended and encased in a bigger heart-shaped locket with a glass front. A plethora of diamonds embedded the gold border of the larger one and it hung off a chain that looked like braided gold.

"Van," she breathed, absently touching her empty neck.

"I was worried about your little heart getting all banged up again. I want to protect it with my own."

She bit lips that began to tremble with an emotive smile.

He took the necklace from the box, holding it up as he opened the clasp. "You can see right into mine.

And you could break it," he warned somberly. "But I know you won't. Not on purpose. That's why I'm trusting you with it."

"You…" She didn't have words. She was blinking hard so she could continue to see and lifted her hair to let him put it on her. It was a cool, tickling weight accompanied by a soft kiss against her nape.

Across the room, she saw a blurry pair of women with their heads together, hands on their chests.

"You like it?" Van asked as she turned back to him.

"I love it so much I don't even know what to say." She shifted so she could see it in the mirror, but was still trying to clear her matted lashes.

"Say you'll keep it always."

"Always," she vowed, learning the shape of it with her touch, enjoying the press of it on her throat. It was a heavy, extravagant statement that was proof he understood what was most important to her. It was utterly priceless. "I'll take such good care of it. I promise."

He turned her and nudged it a millimeter to center it, then cupped her neck and swooped his mouth down to hers in one of his heady, mind-bending kisses. Her eyes burned and he sent her soaring with joy.

Maybe this was what love really was, she thought fleetingly. Sometimes it was a hard shell that kept you safe, other times it was a dangerous fishtail that thrilled and blinded and left you breathless.

Maybe that's just who they were and maybe that was perfectly fine.

EPILOGUE

Five years later

"MY TEACHER SAID there's no such thing as second birthday." Liam blinked his big brown eyes behind his thick glasses. "Only if you're two. I'm five." His free hand starfished while he kept a firm hold of Van's fingers with his other one.

"I know, son. Your teacher is right." Van's heart turned over with love for the boy. He wanted to pick him up and squeeze him, but they were working on respecting personal space at school. There was a time and place for wrestling, and a jewelry store wasn't it. "That's just what your mom calls it and it's really for her."

"Is that why we're getting her a present?"

"Yeah. Can you hold your thumb while we're in here or do you want to hold my hand?" Van held the door open.

"I can just look."

"That's what I thought. You're the best kid in the world. Did you know that?"

Liam nodded his floppy hair because, yeah, of course he was the best kid in the world. His parents had been telling him that as long as he could remember.

He'd been quite a handful in the beginning. Becca had wanted to try a foster-to-adopt situation, which Van had completely supported even though he had privately worried that Becca would get her heart broken if something went awry. Hell, he'd been worried he would, once he'd met this little rascal. They'd all fallen in love immediately.

Liam had been two, which was always a challenging age. He'd been affectionate and curious, but his lively and sometimes stubborn nature had become more than his grandparents could handle, especially after suffering the loss of his mom.

At that time, Liam had grabbed *everything*. Often, he had impulsively run to look at something that caught his eye, not paying attention to his surroundings and putting himself in danger when he did. He'd constantly been tripping and tumbling and keeping Van and Becca on guard.

One day, when Liam had stood in front of the television refusing to move, Becca had said, "Do you think he has trouble seeing?"

They'd booked him an appointment and within a couple of weeks, the boy had been wearing a pair of thick glasses. He had still grabbed for everything in his reach, but once his depth perception improved, he wasn't knocking things over as he did. When they read to him, he began pointing out animals, mimicking the sounds. Words quickly followed and being able to make himself understood had made his tantrums mostly obsolete.

It was a bittersweet victory. As his behavior improved, they were sure his grandparents would change their minds about relinquishing him to adoption. Instead, they agreed to an open situation and still took Liam for a weekend every month or two, joining Van and Becca for Liam's birthday and Christmas and any other occasion when family was gathering. Becca and his grandmother were really close, both having a hole in their life that the other filled in her own way.

Van was glancing over earrings and bracelets, conscious that Becca wouldn't expect or particularly want anything expensive, but the anniversary of Liam's adoption was important to him, too. He wanted to mark it with something special.

"Daddy, that one's a plabbidus." Liam kept hold of his thumb while he pointed at some crystal figurines. "Mummy would like it."

Van came to look at the modest little sculpture of a platypus, always getting a kick out of the way Liam mixed up his words and imbued a few with Becca's accent. Maybe they hadn't made him, but he definitely reflected bits of both of them. The boy had taken to skiing like a duck to water last winter.

"She would, wouldn't she?" Becca would love it because her son had picked it out.

They had visited Becca's family twice since Liam had joined them and both trips had included visits to the zoo with Wanda's kids. Wanda was bringing her family this Christmas, excited for her kids to see snow for the first time.

Van nodded at the clerk to wrap it, and thirty minutes later, they entered the house to the scent of angel food cake. It would only be the three of them, but all the more special for being an intimate celebration.

Becca had already changed out of the floral scrubs

she wore to the lab and waved, pointing to show him she was on the phone with the Bluetooth.

She worked at the lab on a casual basis, also running a foundation funded by Van Scott Equipment that ensured underprivileged kids could learn to ski. Van mostly worked from home and scrupulously limited his hours, keeping his schedule flexible so he could pick up Liam from school when Becca had commitments of her own.

"My husband just walked in," she said to whoever she was talking to. "Let me discuss it with him. We'll call you back in the next day or so? Yes, thank you." She hung up.

"Bec. Are you crying?" Van moved to take her arms, blood chilling in his veins as he noted the redness around her eyes. "What happened?"

"I'm fine. I promise." She beamed him a smile through her misty eyes and patted his chest, giving him a distracted kiss before quickly bending to reassure Liam. "I missed you while I was at work today. Where have you and Daddy been? How come you're late getting home from school?"

"We got you a present." He proudly offered the gold-embossed bag.

"Goodness! That wasn't necessary." She gave Van a you-shouldn't-have look and weighed it. "I wonder what it could be."

"A plabbidus."

"Oh. Does he need water?"

"Not a real one!" Liam said with a giggle.

She chuckled and hugged him again, gaze soft with love. "I can't wait to see it, but I'll open it after tea, if that's okay. Do you want a few minutes of screen time? I need to talk to Daddy."

Liam nodded and she set the timer on his tablet, sending him toward the stairs where he had a playroom in the loft.

"Who was it?" Van asked with concern as Liam started up the stairs.

"Tamara," she said in a lowered voice, mentioning the social worker who had assisted with their adoption of Liam. "There's a little girl she thinks would be a good fit for us."

"Babe." It was a heart-punch of hope.

Van took her trembling form into his arms. They had planned to wait a little longer before bringing another child into their lives, worried about risking Liam growing attached to someone who might not be able to stay. Van was trying to be patient, but he really wanted to fill out their family.

"I know what you're going to say. It's always risky," she pointed out. "This little girl only has an elderly grandfather who wants to be in the picture, but can't take custody of her. It wouldn't be a foster situation. We could adopt her right away. She's three and has a small health concern that requires injections which was one reason Tamara thought of us. That, and we already have the open situation with Liam's family so she knows we understand that dynamic. I know we said we'd wait a little longer before we made any moves, but…" She raised a pleading gaze to his. "I really want Liam to have a little sister. She could be with us by Thanksgiving."

"I want a little sister," Liam said. He had only gone midway up the stairs and sat there, tablet held in two hands before him.

Van couldn't help a guffaw at the kid refusing to be left out of a private conversation. Or not having his vote counted on something so important to all of them.

"Sounds like three out of three," Van said wryly, hugging Becca tight. "Motion carried to proceed?"

By Christmas, their daughter Sarah was with them. She was round and assertive and still getting used to her new family. When Wanda offered her a gift to unwrap, she grew overwhelmed by her new cousins and all the noise as they tore into presents with Liam.

"Sarah, come sit with Mummy, love," Becca invited, opening her arms.

Sarah quickly took refuge in her mother's lap. She absently played with the pendant at Becca's throat as they watched all the action from a safe place in the corner of the sofa. Becca accepted the gift from Wanda and they opened it together, admiring the puzzle of marsupials it contained.

"Hey." Van waited for Becca to lift her shining eyes before he snapped his photo. "You look really beautiful."

She wrinkled her nose, but didn't protest that she was in rumpled pajamas with uncombed hair. She hadn't had much sleep, either. She'd been up late with her sister, wrapping presents, then the house had been awaked early by excited children who wanted to know if Santa had come.

"I'm happy," she told him. "It's the best makeup there is."

"That's all I wanted for Christmas. Ever, really."

"And you got what you wanted? There's a surprise." She was teasing him, sifting fingers through their daughter's hair and kissing the girl's brow while wearing the most incandescent expression he'd ever seen.

He would have taken another photo to capture that look, but he saw it often enough he was just as satisfied to shift across and kiss her instead.

* * * * *

If you thought
One Snowbound New Year's Night
was magical
you're sure to love these other stories
by Dani Collins!

What the Greek's Wife Needs
Ways to Ruin a Royal Reputation
Her Impossible Baby Bombshell
Married for One Reason Only
Manhattan's Most Scandalous Reunion

Available now!

COMING SOON!

We really hope you enjoyed reading this book.
If you're looking for more romance, be sure to
head to the shops when new books are
available on

Thursday 20th
January

To see which titles are coming soon, please visit
millsandboon.co.uk/nextmonth

MILLS & BOON

THE HEART OF ROMANCE

A ROMANCE FOR EVERY READER

MODERN — Prepare to be swept off your feet by sophisticated, sexy and seductive heroes, in some of the world's most glamourous and romantic locations, where power and passion collide.

HISTORICAL — Escape with historical heroes from time gone by. Whether your passion is for wicked Regency Rakes, muscled Vikings or rugged Highlanders, awai the romance of the past.

MEDICAL — Set your pulse racing with dedicated, delectable doctors in the high-pressure world of medicine, where emotions run high and passion, comfort a love are the best medicine.

True Love — Celebrate true love with tender stories of heartfelt romance, from the rush of falling in love to the joy a new baby can bring, and a focus on the emotional heart of a relationship.

Desire — Indulge in secrets and scandal, intense drama and plenty of sizzling hot action with powerful and passionate heroes who have it all: wealth, status good looks…everything but the right woman.

HEROES — Experience all the excitement of a gripping thriller, with an intense romance at its heart. Resourceful, true-to-life women and strong, fearless m face danger and desire - a killer combination!

To see which titles are coming soon, please visit

millsandboon.co.uk/nextmonth

MILLS & BOON

Coming next month

DESERT PRINCE'S DEFIANT BRIDE
Julieanne Howells

Lily watched as Khaled came closer, all smouldering masculine intent. Seconds ago she'd been in a snit. Now she couldn't remember why. By the time he reached her she was boneless and unresisting, letting him gather her hand and lift it to his lips.

'*Habiba*, you are beautiful,' he purred.

Beautiful? Her breath fluttered out. Dear Lord, she'd sighed. She'd actually just *sighed*.

He dipped his head. He was going to kiss her. She shivered as warm lips brushed the tender skin of her ear. A delicious, scintillating caress.

But not a kiss.

He was whispering to her.

'Something has come up. Follow my lead.' Louder, for the benefit of the others, he said, 'Mother, ladies, our apologies. An urgent matter needs our attention and we must go.'

Okay. It was part of the act.

'Can I leave you to gather everything Miss Marchant will need for her stay? You have her sizes?' The assistants nodded vigorously. 'And please send a selection of everything you think appropriate.' He turned to gaze adoringly at her. 'Don't stint.'

As if they would. They were staring at him as if he were a god come down to earth, imagining all their commission.

His long fingers curled through hers, warm, strong and wonderfully comforting—drat the man. And then he set off for the private lift they'd arrived in.

Focus, Lily.

He'd said something had come up. Perhaps there was news on Nate?

The lift doors closed. 'What's so…?' Where had that husky note come from? She tried again. 'What's so urgent that we needed to leave?'

'This.' He gathered her close and pressed his mouth to hers.

She should have pushed him away—there was no audience here—but his mouth slanted over hers in a kiss so tantalisingly gentle she leant in. He began a delicate exploration of her jaw, her throat, and found a tender spot beneath her ear, teasing it with a slow swirl of his tongue.

Her fingers sank into his biceps.

When he nudged a thigh between her legs she instinctively rubbed against it, seeking contact where she needed it most.

'Come,' he said.

Yes, oh, yes…

Wait…no. What?

He was walking. He meant her to go with him. He was leaving the lift.

She teetered in her new heels and he drew her protectively against his side. Together, eyes locked, they crossed the foyer and stepped outside into the now familiar intense heat and something else—something new.

With the dazzle of sunshine came camera flashes. A cacophony of voices. Crowding figures.

'Your Highness? Sir? When's the wedding?'

'Lily? Has he bought you a ring yet? When did you know it was love?'

She blinked as the lights exploded, over and over. With a jolt she realised he'd walked them into a press pack—and he knew enough about those for it not to be an accident.

Continue reading
DESERT PRINCE'S DEFIANT BRIDE
Julieanne Howells

Available next month
www.millsandboon.co.uk

LET'S TALK

Romance

For exclusive extracts, competitions
and special offers, find us online:

MILLS & BOON

HEROES

At Your Service

Experience all the excitement of a gripping thriller, with an intense romance at its heart. Resourceful, true-to-life women and strong, fearless men face danger and desire - a killer combination!